1/13

MICHELANGELO'S LAST PAINTING

Its Chilling Revelation

A Novel By

ANDREW A. BOEMI

This is a work of fiction. Names, characters, organizations, places, events, and incidents are creations of the author's imagination or are used fictitiously and are not to be construed as real. Any resemblance to actual or other fictional organizations, places, events, or incidents or persons, living or dead, is entirely coincidental EXCEPT as discussed in the Author's Notes at the end of the book and on the website www.michelangeloslastpainting.com.

For information about this title or to order other books and/or electronic media, contact the publisher:

Dodd Merrill Press
1000 Hart Rd
Suite #210
Barrington, IL 60010

Library of Congress Control Number: 2012949249

978-0-9883229-0-5 Paperback
978-0-9883229-1-2 eBook

Publisher's Cataloging-In-Publication Data

Boemi, Andrew A.
    Michelangelo's last painting : its chilling revelation : a novel / by Andrew A. Boemi.

    p. ; cm.

    Issued also as an ebook.
    ISBN: 978-0-9883229-0-5 (pbk.)

    1. Michelangelo Buonarroti, 1475–1564. Christ on the cross—Fiction. 2. Christian art and symbolism—Fiction. 3. Art historians—Fiction. 4. Jews—Persecutions—Fiction. 5. Conspiracy—Fiction. 6. Mystery and detective stories. I. Title.

PS3602.O36 M53 2012
813/.6   2012949249

I Thank You and Praise You, O God
—DANIEL 2:23

This book is for my mother, Flora, father, A. Andrew, and three wonderful children, "Lee," Andy E, and Meg. And for Lori, my most special person; without her wisdom, common sense, and dedication, this book would have never been completed.

Prologue

**AD 29
DECAPOLIS REGION
SEA OF GALILEE**

WHEN JESUS STEPPED ASHORE, he was met by a demon-possessed man from the town. For a long time this man had not worn clothes or lived in a house, but had lived in the tombs. When he saw Jesus, he cried out and fell at his feet, shouting at the top of his voice, "What do you want with me, Jesus, Son of the Most High God?"

"I beg you, don't torture me!" For Jesus had commanded the impure spirit to come out of the man. Many times [the evil spirit] had seized him, and though he was chained hand and foot and kept under guard, he had broken his chains and had been driven by the demon into solitary places.

Jesus asked him, "What is your name?"

"Legion," he replied, because many demons had gone into the man. And [the demons] begged Jesus repeatedly not to order them to go into the Abyss. A large herd of pigs was feeding there on the hillside. The demons begged Jesus to let them go into the pigs, and he gave them permission. When the demons came out of the man, they went into the pigs, and the herd rushed down the steep bank into the lake and was drowned.

When those tending the pigs saw what had happened, they ran off and reported this in the town and countryside, and the people went out to see what had happened. When they came to Jesus, they found the man from whom the demons had gone out, sitting at Jesus' feet, dressed and in his right mind; and they were afraid. Those who had seen it told the people how the demon-possessed man had been cured. Then all the people of the region of the Gerasenes asked Jesus to leave them, because they were overcome with fear.

The man from whom the demons had gone out begged to go with him, but Jesus sent him away, saying, "Return home and tell how much God has done for you."

So the man went away and told all over the town how much Jesus had done for him.

—Luke 8:27–39 NIV

Chapter 1

1546
PALACE OF THE COLONNA CESARINI
ROME

A FASHIONABLY DRESSED WOMAN with coiffed brown hair, a delicately sculpted face, and penetrating dark eyes sat at a gold-inlaid writing desk in the elegant library of her imposing mansion, the Palace of the Colonna Cesarini in Rome. The richly paneled library, lined with rare books and fine-art masterpieces, overlooked her formal gardens and always provided an inviting sanctuary for this woman of letters. Yet this afternoon was different, as she looked with intense interest at a black chalk drawing before her. She held it in her soft, white hands, knowing the drawing was singularly valuable and would, once she gave her approval, become an oil painting—*Christ on the Cross.*

A smile danced across her lips as she thought of how much she loved the intriguing, brilliant, yet tender man who had promised her the painting as his personal gift and an expression of the faith in Jesus Christ that they both shared and treasured. She whispered, "Oh, my darling, I shall pray from now on only to this sweet Christ you have given me. I have never seen anything by your hand of our Lord that is so inspired."

The woman was Vittoria Colonna, the Marchesa di Pescara—a wealthy widow in her mid-forties and a prominent member of Renaissance Rome nobility. She had become well known to the hierarchy of the church by leading reform-minded Catholics to embrace the beliefs of Martin Luther and the fires of Reformation sweeping across Europe. On this particular day it was the fires of love, not Church politics, that occupied her mind.

Vittoria gently put down the chalk drawing, opened the desk drawer, and took out a clean sheet of fine linen paper. She took up a pen and then rested it against her chin momentarily, searching her heart for just the right words. How could she say thank you to the man who had brought light back into her life? Though several decades her senior, Michelangelo Buonarroti had unexpectedly stirred the cold ashes of her heart until they now burned and danced with passion once again. Yes, this man, this towering genius, had become to her all that his namesake, Michael the Angel, promised.

His gesture alone—drawing this work for her—overwhelmed Vittoria. She picked up the finely etched chalk study and shook her head in wonderment. "You ask if I approve of your work, Michelangelo," she thought. "How can I do anything but commend something so rich, so exquisite, and so compelling from your hand to mine? You are the first man I have felt passion for since my husband's death."

Vittoria had known seemingly endless days of loneliness as a widow. Her nobleman husband had died in a war against the French while she was still a young bride. Rather than remarry, she threw herself into a life of poetry, study, and befriending the leading nobles and thinkers of her day. Her intellectual curiosity and giftedness led her eventually to meet the great Michelangelo. He at once recognized in the marchesa a woman of exceptional character and beauty, and she appealed to his love of interacting with nobility. Rather than riches, Michelangelo had always admired lineal nobility as the distinct separation of the few from the masses.

Soon, their mutual esteem blossomed into a quiet romance as they exchanged letters and expressions of admiration. Vittoria felt alive once again, bonded to a man who had never been married except to his art. Yes, she was aware of his rumored fondness for men, but she personally knew better. Now, with his chalk study before her, she wrote in earnest, inscribing in elegant letters:

> Unique Master Michelangelo and my most particular friend, I have received your letter and the crucifix study, which has certainly crucified itself in my memory more than any other picture that I have ever seen. Certainly I could not explain how subtly and marvelously it is made. And for this reason I am resolved that I don't wish it to be in the hands of anyone else.

The marchesa knew full well that lesser artists were all too eager to get hold of anything the Master Michelangelo produced so they could copy it and then sell it as their own. Such flagrant forgery was common practice and Vittoria would have none of it with her chalk study.

Gazing back at the drawing of *Christ on the Cross,* with two mourning angels in the sky, she suddenly detected something in it—something curious. She picked up a magnifying glass to take a closer look at the background chalk sketching on either side of the crucified Christ.

She squinted through the glass, darting her eyes back and forth. She let out an audible gasp and quickly put the magnifying glass down.

"What was that?" she wondered. "I must look again." Her heart pounded as she cautiously lifted the glass up to her eye once more. She hoped that the image she had seen was gone and would prove only a product of her imagination. But it was still there. "Wait," she thought. "There are more of them!"

One by one, appearing from the dark swirls of chalk, images of *grotteschi*—the grotesque in the form of faces—came sharply into focus. The malevolent eyes of these strange figures seemed to glare out at her, daring her to continue to look.

Vittoria put down the magnifying glass, nervously got up, and walked away from her desk to look out at her beautiful gardens. This is the last thing she had expected in what was to be a gift of love from her Michelangelo. Her face drawn, she asked aloud, "Michelangelo, why have you added such horribly ugly and terrifying faces to so lovely a study?"

She paced the room for several minutes until she slowly regained her composure. She took a deep breath then slowly exhaled. She would look at those faces again, but this time she would do so without fear. Scripture told her that she should fear no evil. "God, please give me the wisdom to understand their meaning," she silently prayed.

Summoning her courage, she first walked to another table and picked up an oil lamp. She trimmed it until it reached the peak of its glow. She then returned to her writing desk and carefully raised the lamp in one hand and picked up the chalk study in the other. She brought the two together and looked again at the lower sections of the drawing, to the left and right of Christ.

The added light brought out even further *pentimenti*—images hidden beneath other images. These were distinct, malformed, animal-like faces. She also noticed, embedded among them, hideous demonic and sinister human faces. And there were still other strange faces, including a bizarre face with vampire teeth, which was glaring at Christ on the cross. "Dear God, Michelangelo, who are these horrid faces? Are they a product of a vision or a nightmare?" Vittoria wondered.

Yet as she tried to look away, an image came into view that startled her most. "It is me!" she cried out. There, in the lower right-hand corner of the study, was the faint outline of a woman's face—one that looked both frantic and terrified. "But w–why? Why have I—why have I been added to this dark gallery of the grotesque?" she stammered aloud. "Michelangelo…you have never done anything like this to me before."

At this, she could no longer bear to study the chalk drawing and blew out the lamp. She put the drawing back on the desk, face down on a clean sheet of paper. Her forehead beaded with perspiration as she slumped down in her chair.

Determined to get to the truth behind this unexpected turn of events, Vittoria picked up her stylus and wrote furiously,

> *Oh great Master Michelangelo, pray tell me! Why have you included me among such disturbing faces in what is otherwise a sublime work? What is their meaning and source? I must know!*

Tears ran down her soft cheeks as she struggled for more words.

> *What is it you are saying to me in this chalk study, Michelangelo? What is this dreadful world of hidden faces surrounding the beauty of Christ? Do they align with God's true Holy Word? Otherwise, I cannot receive it. I will not receive it!*

Vittoria, upset by her own confusion, threw the pen down and walked out on to the balcony. What she had anticipated as a lovely gift had now broken her heart. As she blinked back tears, the magnificent dome of St. Peter's Basilica in Vatican City loomed before her in the distance. It was clearly silhouetted in the city's skyline as the sun continued its afternoon descent. The man she loved so dearly—more than life itself—was in the Sistine Chapel at this very moment refining certain parts of his masterpiece *The Last Judgment*. She remembered something he had once said to her, "If people knew how hard I worked to get my mastery, it wouldn't seem so wonderful at all."

The Last Judgment. Could that have something to do with the *grotteschi* of the chalk study? Perhaps, just perhaps, Michelangelo was saying something too mysterious to say in words. Her breathing became calmer the more she thought of him. "What do I know of true genius? Oh foolish woman that I am to think that my beloved would mean me any harm by this chalk drawing. No, it cannot be. There must be another explanation. And I know he will tell me," she decided.

Vittoria now felt almost ashamed for her angry thoughts towards the master. She returned to the library and once more sat down at her desk. She drew out a fresh sheet of paper and began again. After initial words of praise, she wrote,

> *Please clarify this for me: the surface modeling and its highly wrought nature is beautiful, yet am I correct in observing numerous pentimenti? To wit, I have seen very unusual and disturbing grotteschi around the contours of Christ's blessed body. They are especially visible in the area of the left and right hip. Pray, tell me their meaning and the inclusion of my face with them. Are you going to remove them from the painting? Are these the work of another hand, or are they from yours?*

Convinced that her beloved would offer her a satisfactory answer once he read her concern, she turned to even more important matters—those of the heart.

> *My dear love, I long to know when I will see you next for I tremble at the pace you keep. Surely you are working yourself to exhaustion these days. Forgive my candor, but*

I must know this: Is there yet a place for me in your heart?
When will we again enjoy the sweet communion of a walk
together? It cannot be too soon. I await your response, my
love. And may our Lord's blessings be upon you.

Then, with a beautiful, flourishing movement of her hand, she
signed,

Vittoria, Marchesa Colonna di Pescara

Vittoria put down her stylus and smiled with intuitive female
satisfaction. He would soon come calling once he received this. She
knew it.

The soft voice of her private secretary, the Viscontessa di Muro,
interrupted her musings. "Marchesa, *pardone*," the secretary politely
asked.

"Yes, Flora? What is it?"

"Marchesa, you do remember that you are having dinner with
Cardinal Pole this evening at his residence? His carriage will be pick-
ing you up shortly."

Cardinal Reginald Pole of England served as a spiritual advisor to
Vittoria. He was also a leading Catholic advocate of Martin Luther's
controversial teaching that salvation comes by believing in Christ
alone. Like Luther, he did not believe salvation could be the result of
any human efforts or Church loyalties. He had persuaded Vittoria of
the same. She now often sought Pole's wise counsel.

"Oh, yes, of course. Thank you for the reminder, my dear. Please
wait for a moment, as I have something for you to have delivered."

"Most certainly, Marchesa," the secretary said and respectfully
nodded.

The graceful woman folded her letter and slid it into an envelope.
She then applied a wax seal bearing the Colonna coat of arms to the

envelope and, closing her eyes, kissed it. She handed the letter to her secretary with instructions to have it delivered to Michelangelo's residence at once.

After an enjoyable evening with the cardinal at his Rome residence next to the Vatican Gardens, Vittoria returned to her mansion in the cardinal's carriage. She retired to her luxurious bedroom suite, assuming that the matter of the drawing would soon be settled. Yet, in the dead of night, she found herself unable to sleep. The more she tried to relax, the more disturbing her thoughts became. The grotesque faces kept returning despite her best efforts to put them out of her mind. Not even a glass of hot spiced wine, brought upstairs by her night maid, was able to calm her troubled imaginings.

As she pulled the covers up to her neck, a passage from Paul's Letter to the Corinthians came to her: "For what fellowship hath righteousness with unrighteousness? And what communion hath light with darkness?"

"Yes," she thought, "what friendship can good have with evil? Those faces are wicked and most evil-looking and do not belong here in my home. I know it and cannot bear to encounter them daily. Even if there be some cryptic meaning to them, there is no loveliness about them. If I leave the chalk drawing as it is, it will haunt my home for the remainder of my days. I cannot allow that. Oh, dear Michelangelo, forgive me for what I am about to do!"

Vittoria Colonna got up and put on her royal blue robe of the finest silk and her hand-crafted slippers with the raised red-and-silver Colonna crest. Leaving her master bedroom suite, she steadfastly walked down the gilded hall, past the palace's numerous other bedrooms, and down the grand staircase to her library. She lit every lamp in the room until it blazed with white light. She then produced a small, delicate handkerchief from her robe and leaned over the drawing.

"Resist the devil and he will flee from you," she quietly prayed. Working slowly and deliberately, she softly rubbed out each of the grotesque faces in the *pentimenti*, leaving only dim shadows in their place.

The last erasure was the most difficult of all—that of her face. "Michelangelo, I believe you will understand. I simply cannot abide such dark company," she thought. A few swift strokes of her handkerchief and the last traces of her fearful likeness disappeared from the chalk study.

Her work completed, she experienced a wave of relief. "It is finished," she said quietly. With that, she moved methodically about the library extinguishing each of the lamps. After she turned down the last wick, Vittoria exited the room, quietly closing the door behind her.

The chalk drawing of *Christ on the Cross* by Michelangelo remained in total darkness.

Chapter 2

SEPTEMBER 10, 2001
NEW YORK CITY

There are people who have money and people who are rich.
—Gabrielle "Coco" Chanel, iconic French fashion designer

It was a clear, crisp, early fall morning in New York City. The sound of morning rush-hour traffic filled the air as street vendors sold coffee and pastries from the backs of trucks. Busy commuters scurried down the steps of the subways underneath the streets of Brooklyn on their way to work in Manhattan. Children in school uniforms pushed and laughed as they ran down the street to catch a city bus.

Richard Arenell, a tall, debonair man with a trim athletic build, stepped out of a black town car at the Brooklyn Museum of Art and immediately caught the eye of a pretty woman walking by. She smiled broadly at the "women magnet," as he was called in polite circles, and he returned the smile with an engaging, boyish grin. She took in his black hair, dark blue bedroom eyes, and handsome patrician face punctuated only by a facial scar and dimpled cleft chin. The well-dressed thirty-year-old made his way to the top of the well-worn steps of the museum. Looking around, he glanced at his watch and said in a low voice, which carried an air of his aristocratic British upbringing, "Nine-thirty and she isn't here. This isn't like Sao. Where in the world is she?"

Prior to coming to New York, Richard had spent one month cruising the Mediterranean on his parents' elegantly appointed Monte Carlo–based 173-foot Feadship motor yacht *Xanadu*. When Richard wasn't busy consulting for his clients in the world of fine art, he enjoyed spending as much time as he could on the *Xanadu* with friends— including, on this past cruise, a certain well-known, stunning female royal who had made the most of being away from the paparazzi. He particularly enjoyed the repositioning voyage from the Mediterranean in the summer to the Caribbean in the fall replete with spectacular Atlantic sunsets. During winter holidays he could be found in the Caribbean either on board the *Xanadu* or at his parents' estate on the French island of St. Barts. For everyone, being on the Arenell yacht was like staying on a luxurious floating five-star resort—with its own social and athletic director and scholar-in-residence when Richard was on board. In providing live entertainment—before an appreciative audience mostly made up of the female passengers—Richard liked launching his superb physique into expert twists, tucks, and somersaults off an adjustable ten-meter diving platform that could be aimed either into the yacht's massive swimming pool or into the sea.

There was another fascination on the yacht for first-time guests: his mother's virtually exact likeness to her seventeenth-century ancestor Margarete Theresia, Empress of the Holy Roman Empire, Queen of Bohemia, and the subject of Velazquez's famous painting *Las Meninas*. An outstanding portrait by Jan van Leperen of Empress Margarete on horseback hung in the yacht's sumptuous living room and attested to the uncanny resemblance of Richard's mother, also pictured on horseback in a nearby gold-encased photograph.

Born an only child, Richard was accustomed to the trappings of wealth and privilege, having been raised in a palatial townhome in the exclusive Belgravia section of London. His mother, Maria Berengaria—an extremely wealthy German Protestant noblewoman, the former Countess Conrad von Bohmen—and his father, David Arenell, a very successful investment banker in the City of London as well as a Reformed Jew and a descendant of Disraeli, England's only Jewish prime minister, were members of European high society. Richard's family on his father's side had been very close friends with Queen Victoria, the great-great-grandmother of Queen Elizabeth. The Arenell family maintained this friendship with the English royals over the centuries and, as a result, Richard and his parents could be seen at parties in Buckingham Palace with the Queen and in the company of other members of the royal family.

Richard's introduction to the world of fine paintings had begun years earlier, when he attended Le Rosey in Switzerland, one of the oldest and most prestigious prep schools in the world. For more than a century, Le Rosey had been educating European royalty, and it was where Richard's mother had received her schooling. Inspired by his courses in art history at Le Rosey and his family's important collection of Impressionist painters—along with the Queen's private art collection, to which he had access—Richard went on to major in art history and art forensics at Christ Church College, Oxford. His world, however, was not solely about art. A natural all-round athlete, he was an outstanding rugby player and Oxford's diving champ. After university graduation, he attended the Royal Air Force College, serving briefly in the RAF. However, he was soon selected to serve as a pilot in the elite British Special Air Services wing.

This highly secretive special-forces group was formed during World War II to conduct raids behind Rommel's lines in North Africa. Their motto still defined their mission: "Speed, Aggression, Surprise." Richard had participated in several dangerous covert SAS operations in the Middle East and had received his facial scar from shrapnel during an air operation. He kept it as a reminder of the banality of war. By the time his enlistment ran out, Richard had risen to the rank of captain and been decorated with the Distinguished Flying Cross.

Following his stint in the military, Richard returned to his love of paintings and pursued a rigorous dual master and doctoral degree program in art history and art forensics at the Sorbonne. It was there that he developed a deep interest in Renaissance art, specifically in the Old Masters from the sixteenth century. He was also a natural linguist and was fluent in French, German, Arabic, and Italian. The young Englishman was now considered an up-and-coming expert in painting diagnostics, authentication, and exposition, especially of works produced during the Renaissance.

Richard lived in a stylish flat overlooking Berkeley Square in London's Mayfair district and had come to New York City as a favor to his one-time girlfriend Sao Damrey. He was momentarily distracted by the deep blue sky and the beauty of the harbor, where the Statue of Liberty stood tall and proud with her arm extended towards the heavens. "This is still quite a city," reflected Richard. "Now if only Sao would show up."

A fire truck and ambulance wailed past him on the way towards some emergency. Richard glanced at his watch again and took out his cell phone. He knew it was silly to worry; maybe Sao had been delayed for some reason. Though they had not seen each other in two years, as much as he fought it, a part of him still belonged only to her.

Richard had first met Sao on a ski trip with friends to Gstaad, the tony, yet charming, resort town in the Swiss Alps favored by the cream of European society. There, on a small tram carrying skiers up the steep mountain to the deep-powder black diamond runs, he found himself sitting next to this breathtaking Eurasian beauty with an alluring smile.

He could not help but notice the young woman in her early twenties. In fact, he could look at no one else. Luxurious raven black hair under a white ermine ski cap, exotic long-lashed almond-shaped green eyes, a perfectly shaped nose, apple cheeks, luscious lips, and a light, dewy complexion made Sao Damrey Richard's idea of a living art masterpiece. A curvaceous body poured perfectly into a sleek blue Bogner ski outfit completed the picture.

Small talk between the two turned into a day spent skiing together. And then another. For the remainder of the week, they were inseparable as they found out—in a seeming twist of fate—that they had much in common besides an intense physical attraction. In the evenings, they sat in a cozy corner by the fireplace at Zoraida's, an elite private club next to the Gstaad Palace, or lit up the dance floor with their fashionable friends. The club played all the latest tracks but during the evening switched to classics, two of which—Madonna's "Who's That Girl" and Kim Carnes's "Bette Davis Eyes"—resonated with Richard and brought a smile to his face as he looked at Sao. Within a month, they were living together in Sao's large designer four-bedroom duplex in the chic Boulevard St. Germain area of Paris's 6th arrondissement. Both frequently traveled from the City of Light, where Sao consulted to the Louvre, and the high-end Left Bank art dealer Galerie Guy Frank & Paul Philipp Vollard.

Sao was also an only child born into a life of significant wealth and privilege. Like Richard, her introduction to the world of fine paintings began years earlier, when on a spring day in May a Citation X jet began its final descent into the small Teterboro Airport, used primarily by private jets, given its close proximity to New York City. On board the jet that day was a dashing Eurasian financier from Singapore, Marc Damrey; his wife, Adara, a stunning Venezuelan French Jewess and heiress to a sugar fortune; and their daughter, Sao. What brought the Damreys to Manhattan from Palm Beach, Florida, was the annual Spring Art Sales held at all the leading auction houses in the city. Sao's parents avidly collected art, in particular Dutch Old Master paintings, to fill their homes. Though born in Venezuela, Sao spent winters in her parents' mansion on prestigious Jungle Road in

Palm Beach and summers at their magnificent Tudor Revival in the Hamptons on the Atlantic, which was formerly the estate of Pierre Townsend of Tuxedo Park. Sao, like Richard, was also a natural athlete, and she enjoyed playing golf and tennis throughout the summer at the exclusive Maidstone Club in East Hampton, near her parents' gated compound. At the club or around the Hamptons, where celebrities and the beautiful people frolicked, Sao's spectacular beauty always caught the wandering eyes of men of all ages, envy from their female companions, and jealousy from her boyfriend of the moment, which included one young American movie star.

Her summer activities changed, however, when her parents divorced. Sao began to spend more time with her globetrotting father, traveling everywhere with him on his jet and acting as his personal assistant and meeting his business associates. It was on one of those business trips that Sao met an unusually secretive software mogul and art collector from Asia known only as the "Manchurian," at her father's permanent suite at the Peninsula Hotel in Hong Kong. Sao was fascinated by the mysterious man, who was almost the same age as her father. She, however, kept her fascination and feelings about him to herself.

In the winter, Sao lived with her mother in Palm Beach, soon graduating from the nearby private St. Andrew's School with honors. A smart, stylish, and cosmopolitan young woman, Sao's gorgeous bikini-clad body could be seen poolside relaxing with her socialite friends at the ultra private Bath and Tennis Club, appearing in the latest designer outfits in the *Shiny Sheet* and *Town & Country*, or driving her red 911 Porsche Targa to the local karate studio. As did her father before her, Sao went on to attend Georgetown University, where she pursued her love of art and art history. One of her professors told her that "to know good art one has to look at it." She therefore spent hours, usually with her posse of admiring male students, in all the top art museums in Washington, New York, and Boston studying the masterpieces in depth and developing a sharp eye for collectible art.

On a bet with a male classmate, Sao decided to take some time off from college to enter the Miss Universe beauty pageant in the Venezuelan state of her birth. Sao went on to win and almost be crowned Miss Venezuela. However, she got into a controversy with the Venezuelan government on a dual citizenship issue and was subsequently made first runner-up. Unfazed by the incident, proud of her feat, plus happy she won a big bet, Sao graduated Georgetown cum laude and went on to do graduate work for a masters in art history at Yale. Like Richard, she was not only multilingual but also experienced in marksmanship, along with being a blue belt in karate. She was known in her circles as one who truly had it all.

Together, Richard and Sao were soon recognized as a glamorous young couple, with significant art expertise and a great network, in the rarefied, highly competitive, global art market for great masterpiece paintings. As a result they became elegant, sophisticated nomads, close advisors, and friends to a small circle of mega-rich art glitterati, including members of Europe's royal families, constantly traveling the world with them by private jet. There were many reasons the two had fallen in love so quickly—and an equal number for why they couldn't seem to sustain the relationship.

The sound of jet engines caused Richard to glance overhead. A United Airlines jet was rising up from LaGuardia, heading west and passing just above the soaring glass architecture of the World Trade Center's North and South towers, which dwarfed the other buildings in lower Manhattan. As an experienced pilot himself, thanks to his time in the SAS, Richard immediately recognized the sleek contour of the Boeing 767. Looking up at the plane, he thought, "I wish I was that pilot this morning." He looked again at his watch. 9:45. Still no Sao. "This couldn't be her idea of joke, could it?" he wondered.

Since their painful break, Richard had heard from Sao only twice. Each time, she talked about getting together and feeling very sorry about the end of their relationship. Then, two months ago, she surprised him with an intriguing e-mail.

> *Richard, I will always love you and especially for a reason that I want to tell you about. Besides, I really need your expertise and help to verify the authenticity of a painting in New York in early September. My employer will pay you very well and cover all expenses to bring you to NYC on one of his jets. I will be staying alone at my father's apartment at the Pierre instead of our corporate apartment on Park. Dinner for two? Father has his own personal chef on call! I miss you blue eyes and do look forward to seeing you. I will close by saying I doubt you've met anyone more beautiful than me. LOL.*
> *Sao*

Richard's first instinct had been to say no. He had moved on with his life and loves. But the more he thought about her and their wonderful times together, the more he regretted the way they had parted in Paris. Perhaps if he had approached their relationship differently—listened to her more and given her more time—things would have been different. Maybe they could have stayed together and married. Ultimately he e-mailed her back, and the two agreed to meet in New York in September.

Richard again glanced at his watch, an IWC Mark XI Aviator, which had been through dangerous missions with him during his SAS days. It was 10:00, and still there was no Sao. He felt a surge of irritation as he stepped inside the museum and moved to a quiet corner to make a call. "If she's going to make it in the art world, she is going to have to learn…" His unhappy thoughts were suddenly interrupted by a familiar voice behind him.

"So, did the SAS tolerate your being over an hour late, Captain Arenell?"

Richard whirled around. And there was the dazzling Sao Damrey. Seeing her, his blue eyes lit up and he broke out in a broad grin. "Sao, it's you! I say, where have you been, love?" he said.

She pushed back her glossy black hair, fully revealing her beautiful, exotic green eyes and supermodel face; her lips parted into a radiant smile, and her eyes lit up as they met her former lover's. Her chic suit impeccably showcased her hourglass figure and gorgeous legs in sheer black nylon.

"Yes, it is me, Richard." The two blinked at each other for a moment, then rushed into a tight embrace. Richard put his cheek close to hers and immediately recognized her seductive signature scent—Hermes 24 Faubourg—and the magnetism of her supple sensual body. Always a perfect fit, he thought, as they warmly kissed. He felt the rising physical excitement of the moment from her soft lips, which brought back a flood of passionate memories. He then took a step back and looked into her glistening eyes.

"You're more outstanding than ever, dear Sao. Do you mind me saying that?"

For her part, Sao conveyed a charming control over her emotions as she looked closely into Richard's eyes. "I see you've kept yourself up, too, Richard, except for this…" Reaching up to lightly touch near his ear, she said, "I detect a touch of silver at the temples, old boy." But he was still as hot as ever with those bedroom eyes, she thought. "Ah, and still the Continental touch—that really good-looking rep tie with the three red swans crest."

"Why, thanks." Richard raised his hand to his tie, personally designed for his mother's royal line by Hugo Boss. "As for the silver, my sweet, that's only the aging of a fine wine." His dark blue eyes twinkled and his manly face broke into a dimpled smile.

"How self-abasing, just like always, love," she said, with a slight English accent mimicking his. "I do believe you were asking where I have been. I've been right inside the museum, where I said I would be. And by my estimation you are over an hour late for our appointment.

You did get my voice-mail last evening saying we needed to be at the curator's office at 8:45 and not 9:30?"

Richard looked down at his cell phone and shook his head in embarrassment. "No, I guess I didn't. I need to check if my new London cell service is working here. It should be. I do apologize, love."

Sao softened her expression. After all, she now had him just where she wanted him—in a place of acquiescence. She tantalizingly reached up and touched his nose and said, "I see nothing has changed, has it, my Richard? You always suffer for it when you don't pay attention to me. But we can fix that problem later, can't we?" Seeing the sly smile on her face and her long-lashed green eyes closing then opening wide and looking intently into his, he knew just what she meant.

"All right, gorgeous," Richard said, winking as he clasped her waspish waist. He pointed her towards the museum doors. "I am sure the curator is keen on seeing us. And I shall make the necessary apologies. Shall we go?"

As the two hurried towards the elevators, Richard pointed to a tall poster detailing one of the museum's current exhibitions, *About Time: 700 Years of European Painting.* "I guess I could benefit from that, couldn't I?" he said, and laughed.

"Only time will tell, Richard," she said, feigning serious-ness. "Speaking of the subject at hand"—she glanced at her slim diamond-laced watch—"the curator is on the second floor and we are indeed late."

Once the elevator doors closed, Richard turned to Sao. "Exactly what is it you want me to do for the Manchurian once we get in there?"

"I just need you to authenticate what we believe is a genuine Gustav Klimt. It's the *Portrait of Lorianda Chasanovich.* The museum is selling it as an attribution because there is doubt whether Klimt alone finished it. You need to tell me whether it is at least a solid attribu-tion and whether it is worth the asking price of ten million dollars."

"I know the painting. Ten million—is that all? Your Asian employer must be looking for something for his bathrooms."

"Richard, I've never known you to be jealous of someone else's wealth. It doesn't become you at all."

"Pardon me, mademoiselle, would I like this employer of yours if I met him?"

"No one has ever really *met* him, Richard. He is quite secretive—but let's save this conversation for later. Just confirm for me whether the painting can be given a strong attribution to Klimt and we'll be done in there."

"Did you check the provenance? You know that Klimt's work was listed among paintings stolen by the Nazis. The museum could be unloading it before someone alleges that it's theirs."

"Of course we checked thoroughly. This particular Klimt is not involved in that issue. Interestingly, though, that is how the Manchurian has been able to get some truly fine works of art. He leaves the alleged heirs high and dry when they try to get the paintings back from him—which is virtually impossible, because in many cases the paintings were not theirs to begin with."

"Sounds like a real prince, Sao."

"Oh, stop, Richard."

The doors of the elevator opened onto the second floor. Inside a plush office complex, Ann Wersching, the museum's cosmopolitan head curator, greeted Sao with news that the museum board had raised the asking price for the painting to fifteen million dollars.

"Are we in an auction?" Richard wondered. He fully expected Sao to walk out, at least as a negotiating ploy. Instead she stood there, unfazed, as she introduced Richard, as her advisor, to Wersching.

"Ann, we are much more concerned with the issue of the attribution and will agree to the price, subject to my associate examining the painting."

"But of course, Sao. Follow me," replied Wersching. They proceeded into a special viewing area where the painting was located. "Take as much time as you like, Mr. Arenell," said Wersching. She stepped aside to allow Richard full access to the Expressionist work.

He opened the weathered Louis Vuitton duffle bag he'd had sent over to the museum and went to work as the two women walked back to Wersching's office.

After closely inspecting the painting, Richard returned to the curator's office and motioned Sao to follow. "If you will, Sao," he said in his most polite English accent as he led her to the viewing area. He felt her warm, lithe body lean into him as they approached the painting.

"Observe this, Sao," said Richard, smiling at her special closeness to him. "Using this color-differentiating scope, you can see the particular hue of yellow and real gold. The brushstrokes and their placement are identical to several of Klimt's paintings. No one else in his time was ever quite able to duplicate his subtle use and intensity with gold.

"Furthermore, Klimt had a trademark sensuality in his women that was singularly his style. His trademarks are seen here and here," Richard added, pointing to parts of the painting. "Notice the subject's graceful neck; the firm, smoothly formed natural breasts; the wonderfully curved back; the perfectly formed hips and derrière. Why, she is shaped like you, love."

"Oh, please, Richard," she said, her smile blasé, as her eyes widened at the Klimt painting.

"The *Portrait of Lorianda Chasanovich* is a classic Klimt, and this particular painting I actually know reasonably well."

They stood admiring the woman in the painting with natural blond hair, green-blue eyes, and a Mona Lisa smile. As she reclines seductively on an elegant red sofa in a very sheer, revealing low-cut black dress, a strand of natural white pearls encircles her sculptured neck. A rare, flawless nine-carat natural canary yellow diamond surrounded by three carats of perfect white diamond baguettes glitters on her ring finger.

"The diamond ring was known as the Ivanovna Diamond," Richard said. "The piece had been given to Ivanovna Kovaleva, a great opera singer, by Catherine the Great of Russia. Kovaleva was a serf who was freed by an immensely rich and noble count, who became her husband."

"What a lovely piece and romantic story behind it, honey," Sao remarked.

"Yes, it really is, but there is an equally interesting story surrounding the lovely Lorianda. It turns out this Russian beauty from Kiev was a professional card-counting gambler seen frequently in the most exclusive European casinos. She mysteriously came into possession of the quite valuable Ivanovna Diamond—rumor had it through gambling. Soon after the fall of the Tsar at the start of the Russian Revolution in 1917, Chasanovich suddenly had to emigrate from Saint Petersburg to Vienna. Upon arriving, she settled in a distinguished residence near the Hofburg Palace, the Austrian imperial residence. Chasanovich was both beautiful and rich—thus having both of Klimt's desired attributes for the subjects of his paintings."

"She was quite the lady, wasn't she?" Sao said with a wink.

"Yes, she certainly was," Richard said. "And the museum is saying it's an attribution—which, at the very least it is—because the paint dating is there. At the end of his life, Klimt used much less gold, as we can see in this painting. But I agree with you. It could be real. Yet there is even more mystery surrounding Chasanovich, who was also a painter, and Klimt. Supposedly, they were romantically involved until his untimely death in 1918. The question, among others, that remains to this day is whether Klimt finished the painting by himself or if perhaps Chasanovich did. There has been extensive physical brush and paint analysis done to try to prove the point, but it has never been fully resolved.

"I know the museum has done what it thinks is a satisfactory analysis and has determined that Chasanovich most likely was involved, so it will be an uphill battle for the Manchurian to try to prove that Klimt did the entire painting himself," he concluded. "But it is a superb painting, and it is truly representative of Klimt's style."

"And the price, Richard?"

"As an attribution, it is very fully priced at fifteen million—but if it can be proven to be solely by Klimt, of course, that is another story."

"Very well, then, I need to call my assistant in Singapore."

Within five minutes, Sao had walked back into the curator's office and extended her hand, saying, "Ann, we have a deal. The funds will be wired from the Banque IOS in Bangkok to the museum account you designated at Bank of America."

Wersching and her associates broke out into smiles. In a matter of minutes the formal bill-of-sale papers and provenance documentation with museum guarantees had all been signed and notarized.

Back in the hallway, Richard turned to Sao and said, "Parting with fifteen million for an attribution appears relatively painless for the Manchurian, doesn't it?"

"Totally painless—he owns the bank the money came from and is the sole depositor."

"How did he wind up with a bank in Bangkok?"

"My father was a financial advisor to the Manchurian and arranged to have one of the Manchurian's companies buy, at a deep discount, all the secured debt of a bankrupt old line Burmese company dating back to the British Raj. My father restructured all the debt, enabling the Manchurian to eliminate all the current shareholders and take over complete ownership. I remember the Manchurian got a company with a really mixed bag of assets including casinos, a leasing company with some oil tankers, cruise ships, and yachts, along with a few 747s—all based in Southeast Asia. He also got the Banque IOS, an old private bank in Bangkok—all that remained of the long-defunct Investors Overseas Services financial empire—along with Bangkok massage parlors and opium dens thrown in as part of the deal. The bank actually owned part of the casinos, or maybe it was the other way around—I can't remember."

"I say, a bank and opium. Terribly high finance." Richard chuckled as he put his arm around Sao's waist and hugged her close.

"Something like that," she casually replied. Her eyes became enigmatic as she momentarily looked away. "Anyway, honey, I hate to admit it," she said with a smile, "but I'm glad I had you with me on this. As you know, in this business, with art prices the way they are, there is no room for mistakes. It needed to be a solid attribution."

"Do you really mean that, Sao? You were glad I was there to help? I thought I'd never live to see the day."

"Oh, stop it, Arenell. Sarcasm is far beneath you. You're good at what you do and you know it. So let's just leave it at that. Anyway, now that we officially own the Klimt, I can tell you that we have in our possession a letter from Klimt to Chasanovich. It details that Klimt did the entire painting but allowed her to make three significant brushstrokes, out of his love for her, so that she would be part of the painting—and in appreciation for her substantial payment for the portrait, of course."

"You must be jesting."

"Would I kid you, my dear?" She pushed a finger into his chest with a wry smile. "It adds significant value and an interesting twist. And now all we have to do is go through the painting analysis to find her strokes. We have already done the letter dating and it proves out. With the supporting evidence on the three brushstrokes, the appreciation could be significant."

"Where did you get the letter?"

"You will find the Manchurian has his ways, besides getting his way."

"Kudos to him." Richard then added enthusiastically, "I've got an idea. Let's make a quick stop at the fourth floor. There's a newly found Nardo di Cione altarpiece and exhibit from the fourteenth century I'd like to see. It's the talk of the city, I understand."

"Talk of the city," said Sao cynically. "Nothing will ever rival the Saatchi brothers' exhibit *Sensation* here at the BMA last year as the talk of the city. The New York masses lined up around the block for several days."

"Oh, yes." Richard walked towards the stairway, the smile gone from his face.

"Did I say something wrong?" Sao said as she caught up with him.

He scowled. "I'm sorry, Sao, but I find it hard to characterize the Saatchi exhibit of the *Virgin Mary*—showing the mother of Jesus Christ clotted with elephant dung and surrounded by pornographic cut-outs—as an 'art exhibit.' And the BMA wasn't alone. The Guggenheim with its *Stations of the Cross* depicting the scene of Christ's death, surrounded by people fornicating, was nauseating. And the Whitney: the *Piss Christ*, a crucifix supporting the body of Christ submerged in a glass of the artist's urine, was equally outrageous. But, as you say, the New York masses loved it."

Sao had rarely seen Richard so upset. She put her arm around his waist. "Oh, honey, please don't take it so seriously. Let's forget about it, and the di Cione, and just enjoy this day."

He was still frowning.

"Richard, there was no transcendent message to the Saatchi exhibit. It was simply avant-garde art. The only disappointing message was what came from Mayor Giuliani."

Richard stopped and looked Sao straight in the eye. "You and I both know Giuliani's response was no public relations stunt. When he vowed to try and stop the exhibit, he was acting from his personal and professional convictions."

"And I suppose the museum was wrong to condemn the mayor for trying to prohibit free speech and expression?" Sao replied testily.

"Free expression of obscene vulgarity that ridiculed people of faith, Sao? Why, I am sure even the Muslims in town were offended. They still consider Mary in a favorable light," he countered.

"I disagree with you about the exhibit, Richard. I bet the sanctimonious Giuliani acted the way he did because he probably thought the wrath of God was going to befall New York City someday if exhibits like that weren't stopped."

"I doubt if he thought that way at all. In any event, I happen to have nothing but admiration for him. He more than likely thought the show was exactly what it was—filth. Can you imagine what sort of bloody riot would break loose in this town if a Torah—or worse, an Islamic subject—were given the same treatment as Christ or Christ's mother? And if spiritual leaders other than Christ were displayed in urine?"

"Pardon me, Richard, but who's zoomin' who here? I still can't believe you're saying this. You—a leading art expert—can't admit the Saatchi exhibit was a resounding artistic and financial success? People from all over came in droves to see it. The museum made nearly a million dollars on ticket sales alone."

"Then we should invite them all back next time the garbage workers go on strike. They can view that type of fine art on every corner. It will be piled ten or twelve feet high. This time they won't have to pay to see it."

"I resent your calling the exhibit, which frankly I helped facilitate, 'garbage.'"

Richard was momentarily speechless. "You personally helped facilitate the Saatchi thing? I can't believe it, Sao." He stared at her in surprise.

"Well, you'd better. I work for a man who is on his way to becoming one of the wealthiest people in the world. I personally direct his art acquisitions worldwide. You don't get a position like that exhibiting 'garbage' around the globe."

"I take it your employer liked it?"

"He most certainly did."

A middle-aged couple on their way to the Egyptian galleries stopped and looked in their direction. Richard caught their glance and nodded to Sao. They let the conversation drop, and the other couple walked on. With sullen expressions, the former lovers walked together down the hallway until they were back outside, on the museum steps, in the broad sunlight.

Richard broke the silence. "Sao, I can't believe we did this again. I came to New York to apologize for the way I treated you the last time we were together, and here I am acting the same way I did in Paris."

"I guess it's my fault, too. I need to respect what you believe, even if I don't understand it," she said, a touch of sadness in her voice.

Their seemingly ideal romance had abruptly ended after Richard experienced a "spiritual awakening," as he put it. When they first met, Richard had shared both his parents' and Sao's passivity towards spirituality and religion in general. But on a trip to London for a speaking engagement at Sotheby's, everything changed when he met Messianic Jewish professor and noted philosopher Dr. Maurice Lessinger of the University of London. He challenged Richard to search for himself "and see if Jesus Christ isn't the promised Messiah foretold in our Old Testament scriptures." That singular observation by Lessinger piqued Richard's scholarly interest. In London, he undertook weeks of independent study into Messianic Judaism and its origins in England in the nineteenth century. Richard came to the inescapable conclusion that not only did Jesus Christ seem to be the true Messiah foretold by Moses, David, and the other Old Testament prophets, but also that Christ filled a certain emptiness he had always felt—an emptiness that not even Sao could fill. The clincher for him came when he read Psalm 22, a passage written nearly one thousand years before the life of Christ, which nevertheless seemed to describe Christ's crucifixion exactly:

> *Dogs have surrounded me;*
> *A band of evil men has encircled me;*
> *They have pierced my hands and my feet.*
> *They divide my garments among them*
> *And cast lots for my clothing.*

What further amazed Richard was that the psalmist had written this prophecy some five hundred years before the Romans invented crucifixion. For Richard, there were just too many coincidences, too many prophetic fulfillments, for him to see Jesus Christ as simply another ordinary teacher and prophet. Richard Arenell had found God, and Jesus Christ had become the Messiah to him.

When he returned to Paris, he sat down on the couch in Sao's living room one evening and told her that he had decided to become a Messianic Jew. He said he felt it was a true Christian theology with elements of his father's Jewish culture and ritual. In making his announcement, Richard hoped Sao, too, would embrace his newfound faith.

Though Sao was fundamentally secular and embraced no particular religion, she followed his process of spiritual rebirth with interest—until one evening, when Richard calmly told her that they should no longer just live together but should seriously consider marriage.

"Richard, I am really not ready to marry and settle down," she replied. "For one thing, the timing is bad." He knew Sao was referring to the engagement she was just beginning to become deeply involved in: building a major art collection for the Manchurian. "Darling, we love each other. Isn't that what is important? Certainly God is in favor of love," she said with a smile, her eyes sparkling.

"Yes, He is, my dear," said Richard. "But I am finding it increasingly difficult to just live together without any purpose."

"Oh, really, Richard? Without any purpose?" A flash of anger suddenly turned her beautiful face shades of red, and her green eyes flashed. Pouting, she continued, "If you're telling me you're now too good for me—excuse me, too *pure* for me—then maybe you should just take your Jesus and the rest of your things and leave. I'd hate to sully your 'purity' any further."

At this apparent rebuke of him and his newfound faith, Richard also got upset, and they argued about each other's perceived uncompromising positions for almost an hour. They, however, made up later that evening in her luxurious bed, with the intense physical pleasure they still felt for each other. Afterwards, as their moist bodies entwined in perfect contentment, her eyes closed, his lips gently on her soft breasts, and her lush black hair touching his face, she felt his warm lingering presence inside her. Within days, however, she revisited what she had said, and so did Richard. She calmly told him it was probably time for them to take a break from each other.

Richard was more than obliging. Shortly after, he found himself on the Channel Ferry on his way back to his residence in England.

Now, on the steps of the Brooklyn Museum of Art, Richard touched her on the shoulder, "Listen, I do apologize for sounding so zealous, love. It's not my intention. It's just the respect I have for God."

"Time for me to go, I guess." She shook her head, brushing her glossy black hair away from her face.

"Sao, I was hoping it wouldn't end this way, really." Richard thought he detected tears in her eyes as she reached into her bag and produced sleek, blue-tinted aviator sunglasses.

"I certainly can't tell him now what I need to," she thought. Then, seeing a sad look on Richard's face, Sao spoke quietly: "Richard, will you just concede to me that you Christians, or born-again Jews, or whatever you call yourselves, don't have the corner on all truth?"

"Yes, I will," he said. "But Christ is the most painted figure in all of human history. The Renaissance artists understood this, and their visions changed the world. We should at least treat Christ and his mother with that much respect."

"Let's just drop the subject of religion for now, can we?" Sao asked. "Religion and politics are definite relationship potholes for us—that's for sure." She touched him gently on his face and smiled softly into his blue eyes. "I have a few hours until my next appointment and I was hoping we could do lunch. I know just the place I want to take you."

"Really, where?"

She led him to her chauffeured car, a sleek new 2002 gray Mercedes-Benz Maybach 62, waiting in front of the museum. Its New York license plates simply read MI6. "The Four Seasons, old sport—to celebrate the Klimt purchase. Their fromage and scallions for lunch are simply superb."

Sensing a truce was in the offing, Richard said wryly, "I'll go, but on one condition."

"What's that?" Sao cautiously replied.

"Lunch is on me. After all, I need some place to spend my significant honorarium from your employer—what is his name again? The Mongolian?" He winked.

"Stop it, Richard! You know it's the Manchurian. He's from Outer Manchuria. Even I don't know any other name for him."

"Of course, the Manchurian." Richard's good mood was revived by this familiar banter. "Any man who's named after a major section of China and Russia must be, as they say here in the States, a thousand-pound gorilla. Or perhaps it's the other way around—they named Manchuria after him?" He laughed out loud, satisfied at his own joke.

"You're impossible. Let's go eat."

"All kidding aside, I believe he has a contingent of my former SAS colleagues working for him on his yacht. I think her name is *Voodoo* and she is quite large. I've seen her anchored in Monte Carlo."

"You mean large *yachts*, Richard. He has several anchored around the globe."

The Rolling Stones' "Shattered" wailed out of the car's radio as the gray-uniformed chauffeur turned down the volume and jumped out to open the door for Sao and Richard.

"Hashim, take us to the Four Seasons," she said as the couple slid across the spacious soft black leather backseat of the Maybach.

"Yes, of course, madam." Her Egyptian chauffeur turned off the radio and announced a call from Mercedes-Benz. Sao nodded.

"Ms. Damrey, Jim DeRosa here. I am sorry to bother you, but where would you like us to deliver the other Maybach that has arrived?"

"Jim, it goes to Mercedes in Laguna Niguel for prep and then to our office in town. Please call my assistant there and she will give you specific delivery instructions."

"Looks like the Manchurian will be first on the block with his new 2002 Maybachs," Richard remarked with a smile.

"And more are on the way to his other offices around the world. As I said, the Manchurian always gets what he wants," said Sao, laughing.

Ten minutes later, as they approached the Brooklyn Bridge, the chauffeur looked up at the World Trade Center gleaming in the distance, a wry smile on his wizened face.

Chapter 3

AFTERNOON OF THE SAME DAY
FOUR SEASONS RESTAURANT
NEW YORK CITY

Her voice is full of money.
—F. Scott Fitzgerald, *The Great Gatsby*

WHILE THE TUXEDOED WAITER topped up their glasses of sparkling mineral water, Sao stroked Richard's hand with her finger, adorned with an exquisite six-carat ring encrusted with emeralds and diamonds. The Manchurian had given her the ring, designed by Graff. It matched her green eyes, now gleaming in the sunlight that streamed into the famous aerie. Sitting next to a window in the posh Pool Room near the marble reflecting pool and beneath a canopy of seasonally changing trees, Sao captured the gaze of every well-dressed power broker seated around her. Her focus, however, was solely on Richard.

"Honey, can I ask you something?" Her hand was on her chin, her moist, sensuous lips parting into a smile, as her gaze focused directly into his dark blue eyes.

"If it has to do with recent art exhibits, perhaps you shouldn't." He laughed, his eyes twinkling.

Sao laughed, too. "No, no, I promise you, that's not it."

"Then what is it?"

She looked down and caressed his outstretched hand. "Well, it's just that we once shared something very special. A unique mental and physical love that, believe me, is still in my heart today." A shadow crossed her face. "And then suddenly it was gone. What happened to it, Richard? What happened to us?" Her eyes glistened as she grimaced and searched his face.

Richard cleared his throat. "I thought we were going to stay off controversial topics, love."

"Please, I need to talk about this." She looked at him intently.

He nodded for her to continue.

"It's just that it didn't make any sense to me. And it still doesn't. One moment we were in the middle of a wonderful love relationship, but then all of a sudden you changed and became someone I didn't recognize. And then you left me and never called—not once in two years. Why? What did I do?"

"Sao, if memory serves me right, you asked me to leave," Richard gently replied, a slight grin on his face.

"All right, maybe I did." He took her hand in his as she leaned towards him in her chair. "But tell me," she said. "You need to at least tell me this. I mean, how did a truly wonderful, intelligent, sexy guy—I really mean that with emphasis on wonderful and sexy—a man I loved so much and frankly still do—how did you become so religiously flipped out overnight?"

"I realize this all must seem a bit daft to you," he answered as the waiters deftly served lunch around them.

"You're right, Richard, it does." Frowning, she looked up at the restaurant's intricately designed ceiling.

"Look, I'm not religious." Her eyebrows arched with his statement. "Really, I'm not. It's about a relationship I discovered. One that made me feel more fulfilled and less empty."

"That doesn't do much for my ego, Richard. Is there another, like, religious, woman involved here?"

"Stop jesting," he said. "You know that you are the perfect woman," he said. "It was God. I really met God for the first time in my life."

"Darling, they put people on medication who claim to have met God," she replied through tightly pursed lips.

"Oh, come on, Sao—not in person, yet in reality, it was just the same." His voice reflected the seriousness of his conviction. "I realized that although I have really always been searching for Him and not knowing it, He was actually the one searching for me. I discovered God's perfect grace and forgiveness."

"I think I need another drink," she said. Richard motioned to the waiter.

"Yes sir."

Richard nodded to Sao.

"A Cosmo, please," she said, and then leaned towards Richard with a touch of sarcasm in her voice. "You know, Richard, I am glad that He discovered you." She lowered her voice, her eyes darkening. "Remember how many times I discovered you in such a drunken stupor that I had to take *you* home? You were born again, all right—the next morning you were usually born again with a hangover. Do you remember *that*, my dear?"

"I do and I guess I was as drunk as a lord in those days." He stared down at his hands.

"Yes, you damn well were as drunk as a lord. And it didn't make me feel particularly fulfilled spiritually or less empty. But I stuck with you." There was an air of sternness in her voice as she took a welcome sip of her second drink.

Minutes passed as they quietly ate the light lunch they had ordered.

Richard broke the silence. "Yes, you did stick with me and I guess that's the meaning of grace. Even though we're guilty in the eyes of God for our transgressions, when we repent, He offers us the gift of what we need, not the punishment we deserve. And that gift was you, Sao."

Sao sipped her drink as she looked sadly out the large windows to bustling East 52nd Street below. "Oh brother," she thought. "I just can't tell him. My whole life would be disrupted by the way he thinks." She looked back at him with softness in her eyes and a smile on her face. "I appreciate what you just said about me," she remarked. "And having said all we've said to each other, I'll be honest. I've very much enjoyed seeing you again."

"So have I, darling." He looked intently at her with a warm glow in his eyes.

"Then you'll understand why I want to do this, Richard…"

She moved closer to tenderly touch his face, and then gave him a slow, passionate, lingering kiss. Wrapping her leg sensuously around his, she let it caress his leg, sending a surge of physical emotion through him. He placed his hand on her thigh as he gently pulled her closer for a second kiss, their lips softly encircling. As she slowly moved away, she could see the passion in his eyes. She threw her head back, smiling, her green eyes sparkling.

"Uh-hmmm, excuse me. Would the gentleman or the lady like anything from our dessert tray this afternoon?" Their waiter stood before them, looking away to minimize the moment's awkwardness.

Richard quickly replied, "No, sir, we've actually just had dessert. Check, please."

When the check arrived Sao pulled out her black American Express card from her handbag and then changed her mind. "Come to think of it, put it on our house account. I believe the number is 713M."

"Sao, you do not have to do that."

"I want to, honey."

"Whatever you wish, madam," the waiter replied with a slight bow. Walking away, he added in an almost imperceptible whisper, "They had dessert, all right, and a warm one at that."

Sao and Richard said very little as they emerged into the bright September sunshine and walked, hand in hand, towards the limousines lined up in front of the Four Seasons. The noise and congestion of the city brought them quickly back to Earth from the quiet interlude above. Her chauffeur was waiting with the back door open at the curb.

Richard handed her in, then stood back. Sao rolled the window down and, smiling, reached for his hand, and then pulled him to her for a parting kiss, her eyes closing as their lips touched. "Later my darling, call me," she said as her car slowly pulled away.

He was left standing on the sidewalk following the car's progress, baffled by how easily he was hers again, and how much he missed her touch. She waved to him through the car's rear window until the Maybach became part of the midday traffic.

As he turned to walk away, his cell phone rang.

"You're still thinking about me, aren't you?" A soft seductive voice was on the other end. "Admit that you are. You desire me, don't you?"

He said nothing.

"So why don't we meet tomorrow morning around eight for an early breakfast? I have an appointment later on at Liberty Tower, so meet me at Windows on the World."

"That place at the top of One World Trade?"

"That's right. It will be lovely on the 107th overlooking the city. My appointment won't take long, and then we can spend the rest of the day together and have dinner at my place. And then…remember our Parisian nights, my Ricardo?"

The phone went dead.

"Signature Sao," Richard reflected. "I hate it when she knows what I'm thinking."

He checked his cell calendar. He needed to get back to the Lotos Club later for drinks with his Manhattan chums Nora and Glenn. Then that night he was having dinner with newlyweds Dana and Jed in the Trustee's Room at the Met at 7:30. The weather for tomorrow looked good and Sao was right—he did want to see her and he did desire her. And she had wanted to tell him something important, but they had got off track. He also wanted to learn more about this Manchurian fellow of hers. Meeting for breakfast at Windows on the World sounded perfect. "Let's see if I have anything else going on tomorrow that would conflict," he thought. He scrolled ahead a day on the calendar. September 11th. "One call to London to make late morning, otherwise nothing important I can see."

Chapter 4

DECEMBER 13, 2001
BUENOS AIRES, ARGENTINA

THE FRAIL EIGHTY-SEVEN-YEAR-OLD white-haired woman
with sunken facial features stooped forward in her wheelchair. She
fumbled with her glasses and managed to put them on to help bring
her television screen into focus. It was early evening and time for the
Sky News World Report from London. The woman usually viewed the
news in the sitting room of her spacious apartment off the exclusive
Avenida Matilda Ibarguren in Buenos Aires. A knitted beige shawl
was draped over her bony shoulders to provide warmth. She seldom
felt warm these days, even though it was early summer in Argentina.

As the Sky News reporter came on with breaking news, she
found herself nodding off. "*Ich muss schlafen*," she mumbled in her
native German. I must sleep. Her head bobbed down momentarily
and then jerked up; she was fully awake again. She picked up her cup
and saucer from a side table, and sipped her evening tea. "Cecilia!"
she called out to her maidservant. "What time is it?"

"Five o'clock, Frau Nuller." The reply came in Spanish-accented
German from the kitchen area.

A Fox World News correspondent in New York now appeared on the double screen, joining his *Sky News* colleague in London. "Today the major Arabic news channel Al Jazeera released this videotape of Osama Bin Laden discussing the recent 9/11 attack on the World Trade Towers. This new tape features Bin Laden and his chief aide, Ayman Al-Zawahiri, claiming God guided their Islamic brothers in their attack on the decadent and evil American imperialists."

Continuous images of a bearded man in a white turban lifting an AK-47 assault rifle above his head flashed across the screen.

The old woman suddenly dropped her tea in her lap. "It cannot be," she cried out in disbelief. Now the searing pain of the spilled tea burned her leg. "Cecilia, come quickly! I need you!"

"Yes, what is wrong?" the maid asked as she ran towards the sitting room.

Mariel Nuller, a blue-eyed Berliner, attractive and blond in her youth, ignored the burning pain and rolled her wheelchair as close as she could to the television set. "It cannot be, yet I am sure I have seen his face before," she said. Her weak eyes were glued to the picture of a thin, sinister-looking Osama Bin Laden. "Not after all these years…"

Cecilia arrived to find the teacup and saucer strewn about the floor. "Frau Nuller! What has happened? Are you hurt?"

The woman looked up with a mixture of fear and astonishment in her eyes and said, "Take me to my room. Immediately!"

"But we must tend to your legs. Are they burned? I will get a cold cloth."

"Never mind, damn it! There's no time for that. Just do as I say! I must go to my bedroom at once. Now! *Schnell!*"

The thoroughly confused maid relented. "Certainly, Frau Nuller, I will do whatever you wish." She turned the wheelchair around and pushed Frau Nuller down the hallway towards her bedroom. Once inside, she let go of the wheelchair and hurried over to the bed. She pulled back the covers.

"No, Cecilia. I'm not interested in going to bed! Take me into the closet!"

"The closet, Frau Nuller? You wish for me to perhaps get you a different robe?"

"Don't ask questions. Just do as I say!"

"*Sí, señora,*" replied the flustered maid in her native language. She pushed her employer into the large walk-in closet that held rows of designer dresses, shoes, and hats, old enough to be considered vintage, which had not been worn in years. They were all that remained of a very social period of Frau Nuller's life in Berlin.

"Turn on the light at once!"

"*Sí, señora,*" she replied automatically.

Once the closet was illuminated, Frau Nuller pointed with her gnarled finger. "Over there, against the far wall."

By now the young maid was considering whether she should call an ambulance. Perhaps her mistress was suffering a seizure or stroke. Nonetheless, she obeyed the order and pushed the matron to the far end of the closet. "You may leave me now," said the old woman in Spanish.

"But, Frau Nuller, how will you get out?"

"Get out, I said! This very minute, damn you!"

"Yes, Frau Nuller. I will wait in the hallway for you to call for me."

The woman simply grunted and waited for her maid to leave. Once she was alone, she removed the dry, yellow calendar from 1969 that hung on the wall. Behind it was the rectangular door of her safe. No one knew of its existence except her and her daughter Katrina, both of whom were émigrés from Germany after World War II.

Adjusting her glasses, she mumbled the code quietly, "*Achtzehn, fünf, neunzehn, fünfundvierzig.*" That was the day her Albert, the only man she ever loved, was killed. She reached up and struggled to read the small numbers on the safe's dial. She repeated the numbers—eighteen, five, nineteen, forty-five—twice more, and the safe door swung open.

"I never thought I would look at this again as long as I lived," she thought. "I hoped I could die in peace. This cannot be. It just cannot be."

Struggling to stand up from her wheelchair, Nuller reached back into the vault. Her arthritic hand retrieved an ancient, weathered book bound in black leather. The cracked and worn leather had a musty, vaguely unpleasant scent, but the woman held it close to her as she sat down again.

Fear showing in her eyes, Nuller opened the book. Several yellow pages almost ripped as she carefully turned one after another. Finally she came to the page she was looking for. There he was again: the sketch of a face, shown from two angles, that she had never forgotten and that the world would never forget. This was the man who had taken everything of value in the world from her and millions of others, and who had left her life and her glorious homeland in ashes. The hate she once felt for him suddenly welled up again, and she cursed his name out loud.

But this man was not the reason she had opened the safe after all these years. No, it was the face she had just seen on television—the angular face of a man wearing a turban and beard. For she remembered she had seen him in the book, as well.

She scanned the sketches of faces until her heart suddenly jumped up into her throat. "It is him! It is him!" she said. She broke down and sobbed uncontrollably. "What am I going to do now?" she cried out. "It is all happening again. Again! I am cursed!"

"Frau Nuller, are you all right?" came Cecilia's voice from the hallway. "I hear you crying."

"I never imagined I would live to see another murderous face alongside the first," she thought, as she peered into the centuries-old book. She knew she should have contacted the authorities long ago, but she was so afraid something would happen to her daughter and to herself, just like it did to her Albert. They would want to destroy her and Katrina with the knowledge of these faces in this book. "Dear God, please help me!" she wailed in German.

"Frau Nuller, will you please allow me to call you a doctor?" Cecilia called anxiously, contemplating whether or not to override her orders to stay out.

The old woman covered her face with her hands, muttering, "This book, with the sketches of the faces and his letter, has haunted me for more than sixty years. Why cannot I escape its curse? I simply cannot bear it any longer."

"Frau Nuller, I have made my decision. I am going to call the doctor. I must get you some help." The young maid turned and rushed down the hallway to the telephone in the kitchen.

"Oh, Albert, what should I do?" cried the woman, her shoulders convulsing. "I should have destroyed this cursed book years ago, when you first gave it to me. Is now the time, Albert? Is now the time to destroy it?"

"Yes, doctor, we need you to come quickly," the breathless young maid shouted into the phone. "Something is terribly wrong with Frau Nuller. She is hysterical—she is screaming in the other room. Yes, yes, I understand. I will meet you at the gate and open it for you. Thank you. Please, come quickly."

Meanwhile, the elderly woman's face was buried in the cloth of an old dress. "They know I have the book," she thought. "They know I have the book, Albert. They know."

When the local physician arrived, he found his patient sitting perfectly still in her wheelchair. The closet was undisturbed and the old calendar was hanging in place on the wall. He put his stethoscope up to Frau Nuller's chest and listened for a moment. He then slowly removed it and put it back in his bag.

"I'm afraid I'm too late for Mariel Nuller."

Chapter 5

He is the highest exemplar in life...being rather divine than human.
—GIORGIO VASARI, *LIFE OF MICHELANGELO*

MICHELANGELO BUONARROTI'S dark, tired eyes, framed by bushy eyebrows, peered out from his deeply etched and drawn face on this gray winter day. His stooped shoulders, although covered by a heavy wool coat, shivered from the cold wind and freezing rain, which followed his large, black-and-gold carriage through the narrow streets of Rome. His two drivers carefully guided the sturdy black horses from the great master's villa at Piazza di Macel de' Corvi through the slippery side streets until they reached the wide avenues leading across Rome to the Palace of the Colonna Cesarini.

The carriage finally came to the walled courtyard of the regal residence. Two footmen in red-and-silver livery quickly opened the massive iron front gate. The Colonna coat of arms embedded in the iron gleamed: a column of silver crowned with gold on a background of red. The footmen saluted Michelangelo as his carriage entered the large courtyard.

With the assistance of one of his drivers and a footman, Michelangelo carefully disembarked from the carriage, a folded canvas in a sheath under his arm. He slowly climbed the finely etched granite steps leading up to the imposing entrance hall. Tuscan columns of pink Sepulveda limestone framed the high ceiling of the gilded marble foyer. The foyer drew visitors' eyes to a grand marble staircase and large masterpiece paintings overlooking the second-floor landing high above.

Michelangelo had arrived at the home of his beloved Vittoria Colonna. As a maid took his coat, she pointed him towards one of the sitting rooms, where a warm fire blazed in a large fireplace with a carved mantel. The elegantly attired Grand Principessa Giulia Colonna—a kinswoman by marriage to Vittoria and a leading member of Rome's nobility—along with Vittoria's secretary, Viscontessa di Muro, sat waiting for him in the room. A servant girl stood silently at a discreet distance.

The aged principessa slowly rose and extended her hand when Michelangelo entered the room. "It is indeed always a great honor to see you, most esteemed Master Michelangelo."

"The honor is all mine, Principessa," he replied as he bowed and kissed her hand. "I came as quickly as I could. Why would she not tell me of her malady?" He set the sheath down on a nearby table.

There was a moment of silence, and then the principessa spoke carefully, her face creased with pain. "It is unfortunately not a simple malady, Michelangelo."

"Then what is it, Giulia? I implore you to tell me everything." His lined face reflected growing consternation.

The noblewoman pointed Michelangelo to a sofa where they could both sit.

"Great Master, I tremble to tell you this, but our Vittoria is seriously ill and I am not sure that she will recover." Sadness showed in the principessa's tired blue eyes and quivering lips.

The words hit Michelangelo with the force of a sculpting hammer. For several moments he sat speechless, his eyes closed, his face turned away. His gaze rose to the ceiling, and he clasped his well-worn hands to his chest. "No, Giulia, you must be mistaken. She cannot die, she simply cannot. Almighty God will not allow this to happen to me. It cannot be His will."

The principessa said nothing, but nodded for the servant girl and the viscontessa to leave the room. She reached over and gently put her hand on his rounded shoulder. "It is not for us to decide the hour of departing, dear Michelangelo," she said.

"She cannot leave me, Principessa. Do you hear me? She cannot! What is wrong with her?" He looked up. "I will tell the great God to save her, and I am sure He will listen to my plea."

The principessa, her eyes moist with tears, whispered, "We have all loved her, Michelangelo. Yet it is well known that none have loved her more than you."

"Then why would my merciful God take her from me?" he cried out.

The principessa realized that she could offer no answers to any of his questions. A moment of silence passed, and she stood up. "I shall see that the servant girls and her very close friend Sister Alicia Antonia will prepare her for your visit," she said. "I'll send for you when she is ready."

Michelangelo nodded in appreciation. As he looked out at the regal grand staircase and the frescoed ceilings through teary eyes, he felt the sudden emptiness of the palace and, in spite of the roaring blaze in the fireplace, the fading life within it.

Awaiting his summons, he remembered the letter he had brought with him. He retrieved it from his right pocket and pressed it to his lips with a kiss, then opened it. It was from Vittoria, and her fragrance lingered on it. She had sent it to him just days after learning that he had finished her painting, *Christ on the Cross*. He lifted the letter close to his face so that he could clearly read each line.

> *To my darling Michelangelo—the effects you produce have a power to dazzle the mind. And 'tis proof of this that I should have mentioned the possibility of enhancing what was already perfect.*

A faint smile crossed his face as he remembered her delicate suggestion for him to add one detail to his painting. "Oh, Vittoria, you are the only person alive who could tell me how to change my work and I would oblige without a moment's objection. You were correct—the painting did benefit from adding the skull at the feet of Christ. Yes, Golgotha, the place of the skull, where our Lord was crucified," Michelangelo reflected to himself.

As he read more of her letter, she seemed close to him once again. "I had always the greatest faith that God would grant you supernatural grace in the making of this *Christ on the Cross*," Vittoria had written.

"Oh, Vittoria! I put my feeble hand to the brush for cardinals and emperors, but always at their command or for a price," he thought. "But this painting was born of love and love alone for you."

The Viscontessa di Muro reappeared in the room and with a sad look told Michelangelo, "Master Buonarotti, the principessa has sent me. The marchesa will see you now."

"Thank you, Viscontessa," Michelangelo replied. He struggled to his feet, retrieved the canvas he had brought with him, and followed the viscontessa up the grand staircase of elaborately carved Carrara marble to the second floor landing and then down the long hallway to Vittoria's bedroom suite. Portraits of the scions of the noble Colonna family lined the walls, and majestic ceiling frescos of angels and saints greeted Michelangelo, but he paid them no notice.

He only glanced down again at the letter and the sheathed canvas he carried in his hands.

"If you please, most esteemed master," the viscontessa said, bowing and pointing towards a large door inlaid with gold and silver. "The principessa and Sister Alicia Antonia are with her, and are waiting for you."

Michelangelo, now suddenly filled with trepidation, hesitated before pushing open the heavy door. An inviting glow from the marble fireplace in the foyer of the suite greeted him. The regal principessa, standing next to Vittoria's canopied mahogany bed in the adjoining room, motioned for him to approach.

Elegant furniture, paintings, sculptures, and tapestries tastefully adorned the sitting rooms off the large bedroom. Textured wallpaper in royal blue, red, and silver—the colors of the Colonna coat of arms—covered the high walls. Michelangelo saw none of this. Reverently laying the sheath on a side table, he walked to the side of the bed. His first thought was that the person before him was not his beloved Vittoria. Her lovely round face and penetrating dark eyes—the fond subject of more than one adoring painter's brush, including his own—were now pale and ashen. Michelangelo, struck with grief at the sight, concealed his feelings as best he could as he leaned over and kissed her forehead.

"We shall leave you two to your privacy," said the principessa. With those words, the kindly noblewoman and nun left the room, quietly closing the door behind them.

Michelangelo, his face tired and his eyes revealing the wrenching sorrow he could no longer conceal, sat down next to Vittoria and gently clasped her right hand. He was still captivated by her when she looked directly into his eyes with the look and smile, though weak, that he adored. The hands that once fashioned the Pietà out of pure marble now trembled with age and emotion. He struggled to find words, but they failed him, and he began to cry. Though Vittoria's skin was now yellowish and translucent, there was the familiar warmth in her eyes. She was the first to speak.

"Oh my darling Michelangelo, you must not do this. You must not grieve for me like this. Heaven could summon and I dare not resist its sovereign call."

"No, no, Vittoria, please say heaven does not call you yet." Michelangelo wiped away his tears with his handkerchief. "You shall revive. You shall revive this day to finish the work the Lord has given you to do."

The ailing friend to poets, kings, and cardinals smiled up at him and shook her head. With effort she reached up and stroked the cheeks of her beloved, begging him, "Please, my darling…it breaks my heart to see you cry."

Michelangelo kissed her hand. In a soft voice, he said, "I have often implored heaven that we should marry, Vittoria. You know I have always physically desired you and you alone."

"Yes, I most surely know, my Michelangelo," Vittoria replied, smiling warmly. Her eyes glowed with the memory of their passionate times together. "Our love was there, yet our marriage was not meant to be. You became wedded to your work, as I did to mine. We both knew it was not meant to be, darling, yet I never forgot your passion for me." She smiled again, looking tenderly into his reddened eyes.

Michelangelo pressed his swollen face closer to hers, whispering, "I cannot live without you. I am lost. I am utterly lost, my love."

"Hush, my dearest," replied Vittoria. "Let us talk of sweeter days. Please, do me this favor. Show me what you have brought." With a faint smile, she pushed herself up in bed, resting upon soft feather pillows, while Michelangelo retrieved the canvas. "What have you brought me, my Michelangelo? Is it my painting?"

Michelangelo removed the painting from its protective covering. "Yes, my darling Vittoria. It is your painting."

He slowly unfolded the magnificent oil painting of *Christ on the Cross*. Against a background of dark swirling hues, Christ—astonishingly real looking, in perfect flesh tones—triumphantly gazed towards heaven.

"Bring it over here, my dearest," Vittoria said softly. "We shall gaze upon the countenance of our Savior and let Him refresh our souls together. Set the canvas on the empty stretcher over there and then bring it closer, where we may behold its beauty."

He did as she instructed. As she focused on the figure of Christ, her countenance brightened almost immediately. "You have my eternal gratitude for this sweet Christ."

"It was my grace to the woman who taught me the meaning of grace," said Michelangelo as he stroked her braided hair.

He noticed that her expression had suddenly turned grim. "Dear God, Michelangelo, what do I see? Please, there must be no secrets between us in the heart of Michelangelo."

"No, my darling Vittoria, there are not."

She looked at him with sadness in her dark eyes as he sat down next to her bed.

"Then Michelangelo, please, please—for the love of God—tell me, why do I see that you added my face, with such a frightful countenance, to so sacred a subject?"

Their eyes met for a long moment.

"I can explain, Vittoria."

"You have to, Michelangelo, for my sake—and because this is so very disturbing to me."

Her eyes widened as she pointed near the right hip of Christ on the cross. "And there are the *grotteschi* again, as they were in the chalk study! Dear God, you must explain! You must impart the truth to me once and for all, Michelangelo," she begged, her eyes searching his, a veil of unhappiness shrouding her face.

"If that is possible, I shall do so, my darling, for I do not want the painting to disturb you."

"You must do so, Michelangelo, for it does *greatly* disturb me. For—do you not remember?—upon my seeing the first chalk drawing, I made it clear how much these images disturbed me and implored you not to include them in the painting. Yet it seems you were unmoved by my concerns." Her voice cracked in dismay as she turned away from him.

Michelangelo's face grew sad. "I know, my love, and I deeply apologize that I have not acceded to your concerns. Believe me, Vittoria—I, too, have suffered much regarding whether I should rub these grotesque figures out. Please do not be shocked when I tell you that these faces—yes, including yours—have appeared to me in my dreams for a long time now. They have assaulted me in the midnight hour and before the waking sun, as part of a continuing vision that I now believe points to"—and here the great artist took a deep breath—"the unfolding of events leading up to our Savior's triumphant return."

"Our Savior's return, in your dreams, Michelangelo—and with my face?" That face now turned red with growing irritation. "This is making me suffer greatly. What do all these *grotteschi* mean?" Rising trepidation and anger made her eyes flash as she clasped her trembling hands together.

"My darling Vittoria, pray let me explain." Michelangelo now got up from the bedside and started to look around. "Do you have your copy of the Holy Scriptures?" he asked.

"Yes." Vittoria pointed to a gold inlaid credenza in the adjacent sitting room.

Michelangelo walked into the next room and retrieved her rare, leather-bound Bible handwritten in Latin by Franciscan monks. As he returned, he thumbed through the Old Testament until he came to the seventh chapter of Daniel.

"Here we are. In verse two, Daniel begins, 'In my vision at night I looked, and there before me were the four winds of heaven churning up the great sea. Four great beasts, each different from the others, came up out of the sea. The first was like a lion…'" They gazed at the painting, where there appeared a great lion's face.

He went back to Daniel, reading, "'…and after this I beheld a beast, like a leopard.'" The leopard's head seemed to leap out of the painting at them. He then ran his finger further down the page, and read, "'After that, I looked, and there before me was another beast—'"

"Like to a bear," whispered Vittoria, remembering the scripture. She looked at the painting, and there, yes, was the bear's head, within the leopard's forehead.

"The fourth beast is the most horrible," said Michelangelo. He looked down at the Bible again and continued, "'The fourth beast will be a fourth kingdom on the earth, which will be different from all the other kingdoms, and it will devour the whole earth and tread it down and crush it." Vittoria shivered slightly.

"See this man with the dour profile, the one who emerges from the lion's mouth?" he said. "I have never seen him before except in my dreams, but I ask you—could he be the beast of the Antichrist?" He paused while she reflected on this possibility, studying the man's solemn, emotionless profile.

"Nor do I recognize the second man coming out of the lion's mouth," Michelangelo continued, pointing to a man with two horns protruding from his head, and strange eyes, one of which he shared with the first man. "Could he represent the False Prophet?" he asked. Vittoria's eyes never left the canvas.

Next Michelangelo drew her attention to a hideous, tubercular, cone-shaped demonic face with a bear embedded in one eyelid, a lion embedded in the other. A naked male figure crawled over the demon's mouth as if about to be devoured. "I have never revealed this to anyone before, my dearest Vittoria, but that demon has appeared to me before in my dreams—when I was painting the Haman spandrel in the Sistine."

"The demon is disgusting, yet it is in your Sistine?" Vittoria asked anxiously.

"Yes, for I had dreamt the repulsive demon's face was in the torso of Haman. And now look at this human face." He pointed to the face of a man visible from two angles. Seen from one angle, his hair was combed at an odd slant, and there was a dark shadow on his lip, perhaps a small mustache. His eyes seemed to rage with evil as he emerged from the leopard's head to stare at Christ. From the second angle, the same man had a demonic mask covering most of his face, except for one fearful eye. A death's head emerged from the mouth of the demonic mask, and a single large horn protruded from the mask's forehead. "He also appears in the hair of Esther as she gazes at the torture of Haman in the Sistine."

"But what can it all mean?"

"My dear Vittoria, Haman was a Persian noble who secretly plotted to kill all the Jews in Persia, but he was foiled by Esther, a Jewess, and put to death by the king, who was a good friend of Esther's husband."

"I remember how you depict it so beautifully in the first spandrel, Michelangelo," Vittoria said, nodding.

Michelangelo continued, "And in the second spandrel, we see the story of another woman who saved the people of Israel: Judith beheads the evil Assyrian army general Holofernes, with whom she slept in order to kill him. Holofernes believed his king, Nebuchadnezzar, was God, and he wanted to destroy the Jewish descendants of Abraham—yet unknown to him, Judith was a Jewess."

"These Jewish women, Esther and Judith, were very brave to risk their lives for their people."

"Yes, most certainly, Vittoria, these women saved the Jewish people from annihilation, as in two stories of the Bible, and that is why I portrayed them in the Sistine. Yet my visions raise questions: Does the man's face partially covered by a demonic mask in this painting, *Christ on the Cross*, and appearing in the Haman spandrel, represent a more terrible destroyer of the Jews to come? And who are all these other men, and the demon that appears in both this painting and the Haman spandrel? What do all my dreams mean?"

Chapter 6

AS THE SHORT WINTER DAY faded into darkness, servants lit oil lamps in the palace as did Michelangelo in Vittoria's bedroom. An eerie quiet pervaded the room, and shadows danced along the walls from the lamps' glowing light as he returned to sit beside her and held her hand.

Vittoria broke the silence while looking straight into Michelangelo's weary eyes. "My dearest, darling Michelangelo, you have revitalized me today with your *Christ on the Cross*. I want you to know that."

Michelangelo now saw a warm, bright expression in Vittoria's eyes. He had longed to see her understand the *grotteschi,* rather than be repulsed by them.

"My darling, I am so pleased by what you say, for as you now know, I have deeply pondered the meaning of my dreams as represented in this painting."

"Michelangelo," Vittoria said, touching him softly on the cheek, "I must confess, sadly, that I rubbed out the faces in the *first* chalk drawing you gave me. I realize now that I should not have erased anything, because they were truly by your hand." She brightened then, and said, "I am glad that I never did so with the *second* chalk study you gave me."

Michelangelo stood up and turned towards her with love in his eyes. "Vittoria, is it then correct that you no longer wish for me to remove the *grotteschi* from the painting? You know I want to please you always, and certainly now will remove them if you so desire."

"Yes, that is no longer my wish," Vittoria replied. She reached out for his hand. "Do not rub them, or my image, out of the painting, for they are all by your own hand. And, now that I know their source, I believe it was meant to be." Her breath had become labored.

"Yes, it is meant to be," he said. "Here, in the Gospel of St. Matthew, I believe, is another possible meaning of the *grotteschi*."

"Please read it to me," she said.

"It is from Matthew 24, where our Lord speaks to His apostles of events before His return at the End of the Age."

Michelangelo again sat down next to Vittoria and translated the Latin wording. "'Tell us, Jesus,' the disciples said, 'what will be the signs of your coming and of the end of the age?' Jesus answered, 'There will be earthquakes, pestilences, famine, wars, and rumors of wars…yet take heed that no one deceives you. For many will come in my name, claiming, 'I am the Christ,' and will deceive many."

Michelangelo continued. "And Christ said, 'Many false prophets will rise up and show great signs and wonders so as to deceive many people…for there shall be great tribulation such as has never been seen since the beginning of the world, nor ever shall be.'"

"Do you believe those *grotteschi* are faces of those deceivers to come?" Vittoria asked with visible trepidation.

"Yes, darling, I am truly beginning to believe so—and they will all lead up to the greatest deceiver of all, the Antichrist at the End of Days, who I believe will be deceptively holy—a wolf in sheep's clothing—claiming himself to be a god to the masses who have been deceived and who no longer have faith or believe in our true God," Michelangelo replied.

"And so the faces in the painting are the deceivers that Christ described, and my distraught face reflects the horror to come?" Again, Vittoria labored to breathe.

"Yes, I truly believe so, my Vittoria."

"I now understand your painting, Michelangelo." The lamplight showed the glow in her eyes. "For I, too, have always believed that when we reject God's truth He allows us to embrace all forms of deception, as Christ warns us against. And I also see that in the tribulations of the Last Days, and as a result of our being deceived and having lost faith in Him, God will allow the release of demonic forces like we have never seen before."

Vittoria sighed. "They will be set loose from the Abyss," she continued, "which is their spiritual prison, where they are locked in chains of darkness; and those released will join the demons already roaming free in the world. Together, they will terrorize humanity and wreak their vengeful punishment on mankind through possessing man himself. They will be malevolently brilliant and possess great powers."

"Do you really believe God will allow this horror you describe, Vittoria?"

"Yes, my darling. I always have. In the Old Testament, God warned the Israelites that they would be terrorized if they fell back into their pagan ways. Your vision in the painting could represent those deceivers who become possessed and inspired by these unleashed demonic powers." She reached again for his hand. "For I, too, have had visions of a humanity that will fully choose to serve evil deceptions, false teachings, false gods, and messiahs, instead of our one true God. His first commandment, 'Thou shalt have no false gods before me,' will have been violated in the extreme. Disbelief and a turning away from God will be rampant. Thus, God's release of demonic forces from the Abyss onto Earth in the Last Days will be just."

She struggled, but continued with a certain strength rising in her voice. "And as a result of that release, I believe a deceived world will become increasingly murderous, frightened, confused, and desperate. There will be a rise of demonically possessed, suicidal humans. And certain possessed humans will have great knowledge and be powerful visionaries and hugely captivating leaders who will, in turn, further deceive the masses by justifying their actions in the name of God!"

"I now truly understand, Vittoria, why *your* face is in the painting. For you, too, are warning of the horror to come."

"Yes, my Michelangelo. I, too, now understand why I am in the painting, and your *Christ on the Cross* is now my gift to you as a remembrance of me."

Her voice drifted off as she closed her eyes.

"Please, Vittoria, please do not leave me," he said as tears filled his eyes.

"Oh, my darling Michelangelo, I do love you so."

They embraced and kissed, as he laid her head on the pillow.

She said nothing further. And the man who hammered magnificent sculptures from marble now used his gifted hands simply to stroke her cheeks and hair until she fell soundly asleep.

In the weeks that followed, the pious noblewoman Vittoria Colonna—the Grand Marchesa di Pesca—fell slowly into a coma. She died on February 25, 1547, with Michelangelo at her side.

Vittoria's high funeral mass in the Basilica dei Santi Apostoli, near her home, was led by her friend Cardinal Pole and was followed by interment in the large marble Colonna mausoleum. The funeral drew distinguished mourners from near and far, including many members of European royalty, her close friend Sister Antonia, and her secretary Viscontessa di Muro. Michelangelo Buonarroti ended his loving eulogy with this final statement: "The woman I so loved and admired, Vittoria Colonna, is now at rest in the infinite sanctuary of our great God, having thankfully shared her visions of Him with me."

Yet, as he turned for one last time to look at the resting place of his beloved Vittoria, the creator of timeless masterpieces broke down into uncontrollable sobbing and had to be led away by his friends.

Returning to the Convent of San Silvestro in Venice a week later, Sister Alicia Antonia clutched a sheath close to her. Safely held inside was the second chalk drawing for *Christ on the Cross*—with the *grotteschi* and Vittoria's face intact. Vittoria had given her friend the second chalk study in her final hours, and had included a note detailing what Michelangelo had told her about the strange faces in both the chalk study and the Haman spandrel in the Sistine.

"Marchesa, I am but a simple nun. I should not have something of such importance," Sister Alicia had said to Vittoria when presented with the gift.

"Alicia, you have never been a 'simple nun.' You are the former Baronessa Alicia Antonia, a direct descendant of Conrad IV, King of Germany, Sicily, and Jerusalem," Vittoria said with a smile. "I entrust this to you, and Michelangelo has also agreed for you to have it. You and your good sisters will know what to do with it when the time comes. Keep it safe, for we do not, and cannot, know what the future holds."

As the pious sister walked alone towards the convent in the twilight of the Venetian winter afternoon, she pondered what Vittoria's unusual statement might have meant. "You will know what to do with it when the time comes," she repeated to herself.

Suddenly she felt as if she was not alone. Her soft brown eyes glanced furtively behind her, yet she saw no one—only shadows on the dark walls of the narrow via. "I have become fearful because of this gift," she thought. "Vittoria gave me it to me for a reason, though I really know not why. Protect me, my God, in Jesus Christ's name."

Chapter 7

IT HAD BEEN SEVENTEEN LONG YEARS, nearly to the day, since Michelangelo sat by the bedside of his lovely Vittoria and watched her pass away. Afterwards, he had composed a simple lament in her honor, which began,

> Heaven took through death from out her earthly place
> Nature that never made so fair a face

Now, once again enduring the February cold in Italy, Michelangelo struggled with a fever and cough that grew worse by the day. Two days earlier, in a fit of deep melancholia over Vittoria, he had foolishly decided to walk alone in the large park near his mansion in the midst of a freezing winter rain. He returned that evening chilled to the bone but reasoned that he could allay his ills with a hot bath and cup of warm spiced wine. The next morning he woke up shaking violently.

Later in the day Michelangelo pulled his warmest coat around him and struggled to get to his studio. As he gathered his brushes and pigments, his hands trembled from the pneumonia and fever that were gathering force by the hour.

He strained with shortness of breath as he set a painting on the easel, thinking, "I have lived miserably for the seventeen years since Vittoria departed from my life. My voice has become like that of a wasp caught in a bag of skin and bones. My teeth now rattle like the keys of a broken musical instrument. My face is that of a scarecrow. My ears never cease to buzz. My rattling catarrh drowns me and never lets me sleep."

A new coughing fit caused the feeble old master to bend over, fiery pain surging through his chest. Sweat broke out on his forehead as he pulled himself upright by grabbing the back of a tall chair. Yet he would not retreat to the small bedroom off the studio until he finished this one last task. In spite of the chill that shook his entire frame, Michelangelo unclasped his coat and let it drop to the floor, freeing his arm to make his intended brushstrokes.

At last he was ready. He pulled an oil lamp next to him so he could examine the painting in full light. Before him was his *Christ on the Cross*. He now reached over, dabbed his paintbrush with a clear liquid, and said, "Vittoria, these *grotteschi* troubled you then, as they still trouble me now. I no longer want to see them and shall do you this final grace of removing them. Then, for all time, all who gaze upon this work shall see only the face of our Savior on the cross and your countenance, which I will change to make serene."

It took several minutes of labored breathing and frequent rests before the master was able to finish the initial preparation necessary for removing the faces. Tomorrow, when the clear liquid was dry, he would blacken out the grotesque faces, color over them, and change Vittoria's fearful countenance.

Despite his weakened condition, Michelangelo summoned his strength and was able to let go of the chair and stand on his own once again. "For you, my dear Vittoria," he whispered, as he dipped his brush in a darker paint and delicately wrote, "For my Marchesa," on the bottom right-hand corner of the painting. Satisfied with his efforts, he struggled to move the painting into a vault room off his studio. Then, having returned, he leaned over and blew out the oil lamp. As he wrapped his coat around his shoulders and shuffled out of the room, he found the peace that had eluded him for so long.

Though he did not know it, Michelangelo Buonarroti, one of history's foremost creators of renowned masterpieces, had just completed the final strokes of his last painting, *Christ on the Cross*. In the dim light of the room, near the edge of this final glorious work, the wet paint still gleamed on the canvas. The supreme master with no peer added his initials next to his salutation to the only woman he had ever loved. Those initials would live forever as a true pillar of Western civilization, the initials of one truly graced by the Creator.

The following day, Michelangelo was unable to get out of bed. His fever had worsened, and each breath he took caused his frail chest to heave up and then collapse downward. His eyes were clouded and his forehead was covered with a cold sweat.

"Pietro!" he called in a raspy voice. "Please come, Pietro!"

In a pantry down the hall, Father Pietro Ziani, a trusted assistant who lived in another apartment in Michelangelo's mansion, prepared a hot poultice. "I am coming, Master!" Ziani shouted back. He knew that his master was gravely ill and had prayed late into the night that he would recover.

Though Michelangelo had many assistants during his lifetime, Ziani occupied a special place among those allowed into his inner circle. A short, balding, portly fellow with lined features and darting eyes, Ziani was one of a small number of gifted artisans who worked for, and existed in the shadow of, Michelangelo. A talented painter in his own right, Ziani had worked with the master on certain sections of the *Last Judgment* in the Sistine Chapel. Nicknamed "The Priest" by Michelangelo and his fellow artisans, he was a member of the Catholic order of the Society of Jesus and served the famed artist as confessor, confidant, and direct connection to Father Ignatius Loyola, the founder of the Society of Jesus—or the Jesuits, as they came to be known the world over.

Michelangelo had always wanted to be a member of royalty. He shunned the coarse culture, vulgarity, and blasphemies of the common person, whether rich or poor. He closely associated only with people of refinement, which to him meant mostly members of nobility or of direct noble lineage. Ziani was one of those select few, a titled descendant of his namesake—a leading nobleman of the eleventh century, the forty-second doge, and crowned leader of the Venetian Empire—Pietro Ziani.

Ziani quickly tied up the hot cloths and put them on a plate, then rushed up the stairs to Michelangelo's bedroom. Instead of finding his master in bed, he found him slumped over his desk in the adjoining room, a quill in his hand and a half-finished letter before him.

"Master, what are you doing? You are too ill to be out of bed," he said. He hurried over and began to help Michelangelo sit up. "I must insist—"

Michelangelo—coughing in deep, hoarse tones—motioned for Ziani to stop. Lifting his head up only inches from the table, he managed to scrawl a few more letters onto the page. The priest lifted him into an upright position. Michelangelo looked up at him with appreciation through exhausted, darkened eyes.

"Please," the great painter said, struggling for air, "hold me up while I finish this." Ziani looked at him with a mixture of worry and perplexity, but nodded his assent.

An eternity seemed to pass while Michelangelo's trembling hand scrawled words across the page. Tears came to Ziani's eyes as he watched the enfeebled master.

Finally, after being interrupted by two extended fits of coughing, Michelangelo put the quill down and said, "I can no longer write."

The priest immediately put his arm underneath Michelangelo and lifted him to his feet. Michelangelo, clutching the piece of paper in his hand, groaned with the effort—but step by step, the two men slowly made their way back into the master's bedroom, where Ziani helped Michelangelo into bed and covered him with heavy wool blankets.

"I have prepared your poultice, Master," he said.

"Before that, dear Pietro, I want you to have this." Michelangelo looked intently at Ziani through sunken eyes, lifted up his shaking hand, and gave him the letter. "Please read it carefully and do everything just as it says."

"What is this, Master?" Ziani asked as he took the letter, folded it, and pushed it into the pocket of his robe. "You need not worry. All your accounts are up to date. I've worked feverishly to keep everything in good order." Ziani quickly poured a glass of water and put the glass to Michelangelo's dry lips.

Michelangelo nodded in appreciation. "Pietro, I must confess one last transgression to you," he finally said.

"Please, there is no offense that needs absolution in such an hour."

"No, you are wrong, Pietro. I have failed my Vittoria."

"Master, you did not. You stayed by her side up to the hour she died. No one was ever more faithful."

"This letter—" Michelangelo gasped. "This letter explains it all. Please, Pietro—finish what I cannot."

Ziani looked utterly bewildered. "Of course, Master. If you bid me to, I can do no other—"

"Good," said Michelangelo, smiling. "Now I must rest. I must rest." The great man closed his eyes.

The priest applied the poultice to Michelangelo's chest and wiped the sweat from his master's forehead with a cloth. Those tasks completed, he covered him again and waited until he fell asleep. Then he quietly left the room.

Michelangelo never awoke again. The next day, February 18, 1564, all of Rome mourned to learn that their greatest son of the sixteenth century—and perhaps of all time—was dead. The man who carved a sculpture of Moses so lifelike that he put down his hammer and shouted, "Why won't you speak to me?" would speak no more.

Not, at least, for over four hundred years.

Chapter 8

FEBRUARY 21, 1564
VILLA MICHELANGELO
ROME

He will have a funeral in his honor unequalled
by even emperors and kings.
—Pope Pius IV

The uproar in Rome in the days following the announcement
of Michelangelo's death still had not subsided. The controversy over
where he should be buried erupted when Pope Pius IV announced
that he would personally oversee Michelangelo's interment. Three
days later, the pressure of battling with the pope and nobles on what
arrangements to make had taken its toll on Ziani and the other
members of Michelangelo's inner circle. Ziani entered Michelangelo's
villa an exhausted man. He shut the door behind him and locked
it to avoid the possibility of treasure hunters invading the premises.

The elegant Villa Michelangelo, with its high frescoed ceilings
and many spacious rooms, seemed eerily silent as Ziani fixed himself

some soup and bread in one of its two large kitchens. He sat down at a table and chewed on the hard loaf.

"Imagine—the greatest of artists, wrapped in a mound of quilted cotton bedding to avoid having his body mobbed by the crowds," he mused. "What would the master think of such an indignity? Even after his death, the powers that be continue to fight to control his destiny." He shook his head in both amusement and disgust.

Later, when Ziani went to his quarters to change into something warmer for the night, he noticed the robe he wore the day before Michelangelo died. The corner of a piece of white paper protruded from the side pocket. "Oh, yes—he handed me a letter. How foolish of me to leave it unread for so many days," thought Ziani. "Though it's probably nothing more than instructions to his architects regarding the basilica he had been working on."

Ziani carried the letter into his adjoining private study and, by the light of an oil lamp, read it more carefully.

My faithful Ziani,

My fever and consumption grow worse by the hour. I therefore implore you to complete my unfinished labors. You will find the painting in my studio vault, for you have the combination. There are grotteschi on both sides of the cross. Vittoria and I believe the strange human, animal, and demonic faces are the horrors described in the Book of Daniel, Revelation, and the Gospel of Matthew that will take place before Christ's return. It is said that before His return, restraints will be removed from certain demonic forces imprisoned in the Abyss, which we believe are seen in this painting. These images are from my dreams and they *haunt the painting. As they disturbed my beloved Vittoria, they now terrify me and offer me no peace. Finish the task, please! You will find I have prepared the painting for removal of the images. For the sake of the woman I so loved, and for me, I beg you, please rid them from my sight; blacken them out and*

The letter stopped, and Ziani remembered Michelangelo saying he could write no more. Ziani was stunned. Michelangelo had spoken of such a work many years ago, but he had no idea it was in his vault.

Ziani put down the letter and walked quickly through the villa to the studio. There he found the door to Michelangelo's vault slightly ajar. "He left it open for me?" Ziani thought. With a sense of reverence, he walked into the large closet-like room, holding a candle. Ziani had never been permitted in there. No one had been. There, on a shelf at shoulder level, was a canvas shrouded in white cloth. Ziani gently lifted the painting off the shelf and pulled away the cover.

Shining the candlelight on the canvas, Ziani appreciated Michelangelo's last work, which he was seeing for the first time. "It is so beautiful," he thought, "but so different from the Pietà. Christ is alive here, looking towards heaven, rather than dead and draped in his mother's arms."

He leaned over and studied the background of the painting, but at first saw nothing except two angels in the sky and a skull at the foot of the cross. Where were these *grotteschi* Michelangelo wrote of?

He moved the painting out of the vault and into the light in order to see more clearly. He allowed his eyes to refocus on the bottom right-hand corner. He almost gasped when a woman's face suddenly came into view. It was Vittoria! He carefully studied the face and sighed. It was no mystery why Michelangelo loved her. Who could not be mesmerized by such beauty? Yet in this painting she looked frightened. As Ziani's gaze shifted to the other side of the painting, his countenance suddenly underwent a dramatic change. He had seen the *grotteschi* on both sides of Christ's body. As shadows from the light flickered across the painting, he saw one, two…three, and even more hideous images of faces that appeared to be almost flowing out from one to another. Their very eyes seemed to reek of evil.

Ziani tried to gather his wits. He put the painting on a large stretcher in the room and lit all the lamps, casting out the shadows from the dark room and clearly revealing the *grotteschi*. Michelangelo had mentioned Daniel in his letter, and Ziani knew that Daniel spoke of symbols and images heralding Christ's Second Coming. Studying the painting, he saw immediately three of the four beasts prophesied by Daniel and in Revelation: the leopard, the bear, and the lion.

"But what of all these other faces?" he thought, as he tried to make sense of the rest of the *grotteschi*. The master was terrified by these images—and Ziani could see why. He focused on the face of the man visible from two angles. The man's demonic mask—with a death's head in its mouth, a horn protruding from the forehead—reminded him of Daniel, chapter eight: "Out of one of them came forth a rather small horn which grew exceedingly great towards the south, towards the east, and towards the Beautiful Land." He remembered from his seminary courses that a king—Antiochus IV, who ruled the Seleucid Empire, was cited as having this horn. He also remembered that Antiochus wanted to exterminate the Jews and the nation of Israel in the first century.

"Is this the two-angled face of Antiochus that Daniel speaks of?" thought Ziani. "Or perhaps it is an Antiochus to come in the future?" Then Ziani discovered two other smaller, unrecognizable men's faces in the foreground. Both men were bearded, and their faces intersected the same horn. "Are they related to Antiochus? And are they destroyers, also?" Ziani asked himself.

Ziani began to tremble when he noticed, emerging from the lion's mouth, the man with two horns and strange eyes, one of which he shared with another man. And he remembered Revelation 13: "Then I saw another beast coming out of the earth. He had two horns like a lamb, but he spoke like a dragon. He exercised all the authority of the first beast on his behalf."

Ziani knew that the first beast referred to in Revelation was the Antichrist. Could Michelangelo have had a vision of both the False Prophet and the Antichrist coming out of the head of Daniel's lion? After all, both men shared an eye. And the Antichrist was referred to as the first beast in Revelation and as the fourth beast in the book of Daniel, tying both prophetic books together. "And who is the pus-filled demonic head next to the two men?" he muttered to himself.

To the right of Christ, two other men's faces also shared an eye. One had glaring eyes and the other exposed the teeth of a vampire—aimed at Christ.

"How bizarre all this is!" Ziani said aloud. Frowning, he paced back and forth across the room, wringing his hands. There most certainly seemed to be a chilling visionary message in the *grotteschi*, so he hardly dared to blot them out. Yet what was he to do with the letter? His master had entrusted him to carry out his final directives on Earth. Dare he betray Michelangelo by leaving these faces as they were?

Ziani sat down in a chair, holding Michelangelo's letter in one hand and viewing the painting. His inner agony was almost unbearable—the choice had been entrusted to him. "Is there no other alternative?" he thought. Several minutes passed as he sat with eyes closed, meditating.

An unusual group of Jesuit brothers within the Order now came to Ziani's mind. These brothers felt that they had a special gnosis—a mysterious foreknowledge of the future—known only to them. Unbeknownst to the Jesuit community at large, however, these men were not really Christians, as they said they were. Instead, they believed in certain aspects of Gnosticism, which predated Christianity as the one true faith. The Gnostics believed that Jesus Christ was not the Son of God, but rather a simple human being. They called the creator of the universe the Demiurge. This god, according to the sect, created the world as evil. Furthermore, they believed this evil Demiurge to be the Judeo Christian God, and that a form of an "other good God" existed mysteriously outside the Demiurge-created universe. The members of this group knew each other by the signet ring they each wore, of a lion-headed serpent that signified what they called their *special gnosis* and *association with* the Demiurge.

Ziani, who also frequently questioned the deity of Christ, had seen the ring on these Jesuit brothers' fingers and always wanted to join them to learn more about their special, visionary knowledge. But they ignored him. Now an idea came to him—an idea that could both free him from his agony and possibly, finally, secure his entrance into the group.

"Of course, these *grotteschi* are most truly a very special gnosis. An extraordinary vision of the future for the Society of Jesus," Ziani said aloud. What should he do? To whom should he give his loyalty? Michelangelo had given his instructions to destroy the *grotteschi*—but what would Father Superior Loyola tell him to do?

The priest put down the letter and returned to his own study. There, securely locked in a drawer to which only he held the key, was a secret book given to him and other select early Jesuit members by Jesuit brothers very close to the Order's founder, Ignatius Loyola. The book was called *The Secret Instructions of the Society of Jesus*. Very few Jesuits even knew it existed.

The book's purpose was to provide key Jesuit leaders with a clandestine guide to how the Jesuits could gain absolute power over the political and religious institutions of the day and into the future. The book presented Loyola's vision for stopping the advance of the Protestant Reformation under Martin Luther by restoring the Catholic Church to its former position of total dominance over society and government.

The priest again began pacing, considering his options. He stopped and turned to chapter seventeen of *The Secret Instructions*, "Methods to Exalt the Society." In paragraph three, he read, "We must instill, by persistent teaching, our doctrine with kings and princes. The Catholic faith cannot subsist in the present state, without politics. We must share the affections of the great, and be admitted to their most secret counsels."

"The contents of this painting could someday be used to possibly influence many powerful world leaders, especially if the *grotteschi* really are visions of the future," thought Ziani with a sly smile on his face. "We might be able to alter the future, for we would have knowledge that no one else possesses."

At the end of the chapter in *The Secret Instructions*, Ziani found the heart of the Jesuit's plan to recapture control of society and the Church: "For those who do not love us will fear us."

Ziani closed the book—his decision was made. Michelangelo was dead, but the Jesuits must live. Surely his master would understand that the knowledge of the *grotteschi* would benefit his dear friend Loyola. Ziani remembered Michelangelo once saying that he was willing to build a church for Loyola without charge, just for the sake of their friendship.

"What a fitting gift it would be from Michelangelo to Loyola's order," Ziani told himself. "Although Michelangelo was not a Jesuit, I know he would have agreed that the Order should have a copy of the *grotteschi* in his painting for posterity."

So that night, working alone, Ziani sat down in Michelangelo's studio and scrupulously began to sketch the painting's strange human, demonic, and animal faces onto certain open blank pages in his copy of *The Secret Instructions*. There the *grotteschi* would be preserved, referred to, and passed down for generations to come to help the Jesuits usher in their Golden Age.

With his natural talent and years of practice, Ziani was able to imitate Michelangelo's most delicate strokes. It took him all that night and the next day to complete his *imitazione* of the *grotteschi*, but at last it was done. He also carefully placed Michelangelo's letter inside the book.

With the copy of the master's work completed, Ziani felt a great relief and turned his full attention again to the funeral arrangements for Michelangelo.

Chapter 9

FEBRUARY 23, 1564
VILLA MICHELANGELO
ROME

FOLLOWING THE GRAND FUNERAL in Florence, Ziani quickly returned to Michelangelo's villa to help set the late master's affairs in order. Yet in doing so, he began to believe that Michelangelo would probably have given the actual painting to him and the Jesuits, rather than just a copy of the sketches of the *grotteschi*. Considering that Vittoria was deceased and the contents of the letter had been given only to him, Ziani felt increasingly comfortable with this rationalization. He also knew that there would be only a short window of time before the formal archiving of Michelangelo's works took place.

Ziani realized that Michelangelo's nephew and others would probably prevent him from keeping the painting as a gift, even if he showed them Michelangelo's letter. Michelangelo's relatives were, in Ziani's opinion, greedy secularists. As a result, Ziani came to the conclusion that perhaps the only way he could keep the painting solely for himself and the Jesuits would be to hide it. To be certain that only the Jesuits would forever have this special knowledge of the *grotteschi,* he decided to move the painting from the vault down to his private apartment in the villa immediately. He further decided that he would hide it, for now, by painting a different image over it. He was delighted with his idea.

In his apartment, using his significant knowledge of paints and painting, Ziani began by applying a very heavy coat of special varnish over Michelangelo's painting. This thick varnish would protect the original painting from his subsequent application of layers of paint.

Ziani first, however, completely blackened out all the *grotteschi* Michelangelo so detested, in an effort to reassure his conscience that he was at least acceding to Michelangelo's wishes in this important regard. To accomplish this, Ziani used a special blackening process after first applying another protective coat of specially prepared varnish over the images. He knew that by using this varnish, the *grotteschi* could be uncovered and seen again in the future, if desired. He did not, however, blacken out or change Vittoria's face.

Each subsequent day, when not helping wrap up the estate, Pietro Ziani painted alone, late into the night. He painted a new work of art, using special oil that had a viscosity closer to watercolor used in restoration, so as not to damage the varnish or the painting below it. When he was not painting, he covered the work and put it away in his apartment closet.

However, while he worked to conceal the painting, Ziani's hands shook, as a certain strange sense of foreboding seemed to emanate from the work of art. As a result, he found himself subconsciously changing the subject matter of his developing surface painting. He also found himself increasingly struggling to brush paint onto the canvas. It was as if the painting underneath, *Christ on the Cross* with its blackened sections, resisted being smothered by his every brush-stroke. This only served to strengthen his resolve to cover the original painting. As a Venetian and descendant of a doge of Venice, Ziani called on the nearness of the patron saint of Venice, St. Mark, in his struggle to paint over the original work.

One evening weeks later, Ziani finally and feverishly finished his surface painting, and with each final stroke he felt a sense of relief mixed with a matching touch of unease. Ziani signed the painting and titled it on the back.

"A painting by Ziani encasing a Michelangelo!" he proudly thought as he observed the work. Ziani was truly pleased at what he had done for the Jesuits—and, of course, for himself.

He stood up and backed away from the painting to get the full feeling of it in all its glory. He realized that with this secret gnosis a great destiny awaited both himself and the Order.

However, as he triumphantly stepped back, Ziani tripped and fell. His head slammed hard against the protruding fireplace balustrade behind him, and he crumbled semiconscious into the very large fireplace ablaze behind him.

His robes immediately caught fire as he lay dazed from the blow to his head. He frantically struggled to get up, but was unable to do so. The flames quickly overcame him and smoke engulfed him. His muffled screams were soon silenced, and his body lay prostrate, smoldering like a slowly burning log. Pietro Ziani was incinerated into a twisted, charred, skeletal form.

His painting that concealed Michelangelo's *Christ on the Cross* stood alone, illuminated by the roaring fire. The stark burned-out skull of Ziani stared mournfully at it from empty eye sockets. The reflected light from the flames cast dark, dancing shadows on the walls, and the title that Ziani had so recently added to the back of the canvas shimmered ominously in the candlelight: *St. Mark Defending Venice against Satan.*

Some time thereafter, the painting, along with Ziani's personal effects, was given by the Jesuits to Ziani's next of kin, the Patriarch of Venice. Ziani's copy of *The Secret Instructions* was not among these effects.

One night shortly after Ziani's death, a hooded man in a black robe, with a badly crippled left hand in the form of a claw, carefully put

Ziani's copy of *The Secret Instructions* with the sketches in it and the letter from Michelangelo into *his* personal safe in his room in the Jesuit seminary where he lived. The signet ring of a lion with a serpent's body shone on his ring finger. Before placing the book into his safe, he dipped his ring into hot wax and stamped it as a seal on the inside cover of the book. "The fool. Ziani was never one of us, and now this book is ours…as it should be," he said to himself.

Chapter 10

MARCH 12, 1924
THE FORTRESS PRISON
LANDSBERG, GERMANY

The Jesuits are a military organization, not a religious order...and the aim of this organization is power— power in its most despotic exercise...universal power.
—NAPOLEON BONAPARTE, EMPEROR OF FRANCE

Has there ever been a mortal as beloved as you, my Führer? You were sent to us by God for Germany!
—HERMANN GÖRING, HEAD OF THE SA,
THE NAZI STORM TROOPERS, 1923

A TALL, SLIM, DIGNIFIED MAN in the dark suit of the clergy entered the gloomy confines of the medieval Bavarian Landsberg prison with its vine-covered stone exterior and sharp cornices. The priest had a stern and chiseled face with dark, narrow eyes, and he wore a wide-brimmed black hat. He approached the guard, who was half asleep at his desk, and said in a firm voice, *"Entschuldigen Sie, bitte!"* Excuse me, please!

The young man jerked his head up and immediately spotted the priest's white collar. He jumped to attention, saying, "I beg your pardon, Father."

The well-mannered and erudite priest waved his hand and said, "Not to worry, guard, I am here to see Herr Hitler."

Squinting at the priest, the guard repeated, "Herr Hitler? If you will forgive me, Father. Regulations require that I must ask your name and the reason for your visit before permitting you to see the *Führer.*" The priest was struck by the fact that a guard would refer to the prisoner as "leader" and require special permission to see him.

"I am Father Bernard Stämpfle, a member of the Jesuit Order, and I have come to meet with Herr Hitler and give him confession this day."

The guard, raised as a Catholic himself, quickly understood that he was not talking to an ordinary priest. He sat down and scribbled some notes into the logbook, then stood up again and said, "If you will follow me, Father, I will take you to a meeting room, where you will meet the *Führer*. And then, perhaps…"

"Yes?" Stämpfle raised one eyebrow and gave a wry smile.

"Per–perhaps, Father, you could h–hear my confession," stammered the guard. "I must admit it has been several months—years, actually—since I last said confession."

"Of course, my son; we will deal with that as soon as I am through with my visit."

"Thank you very much, Father." The guard retrieved a set of iron keys from his desk and motioned for the Jesuit to follow him. They walked down the dimly lit, dusty hallway of the old prison towards one of the larger meeting rooms, which the guard opened. The room had one small window. It was barred.

"Wait here, Father."

In recent months, Adolf Hitler's precocious attempt to seize control of the German government through the Munich Beer Hall Putsch had landed him in this prison. Yet Hitler received a lenient sentence. His confinement excluded all hard labor and allowed for comfortable cells as well as daily visits from outsiders he wanted to see. The judge, in this case, apparently believed that Hitler, an Austrian by birth, was not so much a traitor in leading the rebellion as he was simply a "politically mistaken" figure.

However, Hitler's attempt to overthrow the German government caught the attention of the German public and, in particular, certain key members of the Society of Jesus. Among them was Stämpfle, a leading Jesuit intellect who believed, as did others in the Society, that Hitler was a man of destiny. He believed Hitler could serve the Jesuits' purposes in restoring the power of the Catholic Church against the rising popularity of Protestantism.

The guard continued down a dark hallway to Hitler's cell. As Stämpfle waited in the meeting room, he took out his copy of *The Secret Instructions of the Society of Jesus* and reviewed one of the key Jesuit aims extolled by Loyola. "We must be careful to change our politics, conforming to the times, and excite the princes to become friends of ours to mutually make terrible wars so that everywhere the mediation of the Society of Jesus will be implored."

The guard knocked on the open door to Hitler's spacious and comfortable cell, which had a window overlooking a river. Snapping to attention outside and with a straight-arm salute, he said, "*Heil Hitler! Mein Führer*, you have a visitor. His name is Father Bernard Stämpfle, a Jesuit cleric. He says he is here to visit with you and give you confession, sir."

Hitler was seated at a desk, writing. He looked up with a hostile glare, ready to upbraid the young guard for the interruption. Then, with a sneer, he said, "A Jesuit priest, you say? To visit and give *me* confession?"

"Yes, sir," replied the guard sheepishly.

"Give me confession! That is most interesting. I have *nothing* to confess, but if he is here, I will see him," said Hitler, disdain in his voice and a peculiar look in his eyes.

Stämpfle had returned *The Secret Instructions* to his briefcase and was standing at the doorway of the meeting room. As he looked down the long, gloomy hallway, he observed a shadowy figure emerging from the darkness.

Adolf Hitler.

This was the first time that Stämpfle had personally seen the man the German masses called *führer* and whom many, in fact, called "Messiah." As Hitler approached him, Stämpfle saw a man of medium height dressed in a simple brown military uniform devoid of decoration. He had narrow eyes, a large, ugly nose, and a small clipped mustache. His mouth, set in a grimace, characterized his solemn demeanor. A shock of dark brown hair was swept tightly across his receding hairline.

"There is something disturbing about this otherwise common-looking man," Stämpfle thought.

The guard came to attention and, again with a straight-arm salute, shouted, "*Heil Hitler!*"

With that, Hitler waved off the guard and stood directly in front of Stämpfle. The priest was unnerved by what he saw. Hitler stared at him and gritted his bad teeth. Dark circles framed his strange narrow blue-violet eyes. An odd glint now emanated from his pupils, which had become dilated. An unusual malevolence seemed present in his eyes, and they assumed an almost hypnotic quality.

"Herr Hitler, please let me introduce myself, sir," Stämpfle said, extending his hand in greeting. "I am Bernard Stämpfle. I am a Jesuit cleric." As he spoke, Stämpfle felt a certain magnetism compelling him to come to stiff attention in Hitler's presence.

Without shaking Stämpfle's hand, Hitler entered the meeting room, sat down, and motioned for Stämpfle to do likewise.

"I know the Jesuits, but I do not know of you, Stämpfle."

"No, sir, I would not expect you to. The important thing is that the Jesuits know of you."

Hitler grunted at that comment, and his demeanor became even more intimidating. He continued to scrutinize Stämpfle closely, giving the priest the uncomfortable impression that Hitler knew more about him than he led on.

Hitler's pupils dilated again, but this time his eyes suddenly changed from being malevolently hypnotic to those of a cold-blooded predator's. It was as if he were sizing up Stämpfle as quarry to devour. Stämpfle felt distinctly nervous at the strange look in Hitler's eyes and the gritting of his bad teeth. The Jesuit tried to regain his composure.

Clearing his throat, he struggled to begin. "I have been a Jesuit priest for twenty years, Herr Hitler. During that time, I have witnessed the humiliation of our beloved nation and Church. And now I have listened to—I should say, I have been moved by—your speeches. At last, someone is willing to come to the aid of the beleaguered German people."

With that, the Jesuit felt the Austrian's intense, wide-eyed glare push him backwards in his seat. The feeling sent a shiver down Stämpfle's spine.

Hitler spoke in a distant yet measured way, seemingly oblivious to what Stämpfle had just said. "I have studied the hierarchy of the Catholic Church and your Jesuit Order very carefully, Stämpfle. I have learned from the Jesuits. And so did the Bolshevik Lenin, as far as I recall."

"Our sources have said as much, Herr Hitler."

Without acknowledging Stämpfle, Hitler continued. "As such, I plan on emulating much of the Catholic hierarchical structure within my own party. And I plan to model my elite SS units specifically after the Jesuits."

"We are aware of that, and are indeed honored, sir."

Hitler rose and began to pace about the room. "You seem to be aware of many things, Stämpfle. Are you aware that Herr Himmler is a Catholic, too?" His voice rose.

"No, sir."

"Well, you will be," Hitler responded harshly and paced more rapidly around the room, like a caged animal. "Himmler will lead the way in imposing much of your Jesuit organizational structure onto the SS. I know he will be careful to copy the Jesuits exactly, and as such, absolute obedience will be the supreme rule. Every order will be executed without comment."

"Again, we are complimented, sir."

Hitler suddenly stopped, turned, and pointed accusingly at Stämpfle, shouting, "So, if you know so much and are worried about the fate of Germany, do you Jesuits also see how elements of the criminal Jewish conspiracy contrive to destroy the German people, along with me, in order to take over the world? Do you know that, too, Stämpfle?" He stared at the priest with obvious contempt bordering on disgust.

An increasingly fearful Stämpfle, now further taken aback by Hitler's venomous tone, chose his words carefully. "Yes, sir, I wholeheartedly agree with you. Our beloved Fatherland is in dark peril this very hour. That is why I wish to help you."

"You, help me?" Hitler said in a mocking voice. "In what way, other than providing a model for our hierarchy, could the Jesuits help the National Socialists? Are you prepared to take up arms, as we are?"

Stämpfle again chose his words carefully. "Is it not true that you are working on a book telling the world of your struggle?"

"Yes, I am." Hitler stopped and turned towards Stämpfle. "*Mein Kampf* will serve to destroy the evil legends and lies created about me by the gangster Jew press here and throughout Europe. As a result of those lies, an inner voice relentlessly urges me to write my book," said Hitler with rising fury in his voice.

Stämpfle responded cautiously. "I understand this, sir, and because we believe that you are going to rise to inspired world leadership, I am here to offer my services in helping you write of your struggle. It is a message that the German people are starved to hear."

"So, the Jesuits believe I will rise to world leadership?" Hitler jutted his jaw out as his face took on a dark, egotistical look and scornful smile. The late-afternoon shadows danced across his face, forming an eerie mask. Hitler resumed pacing, as if in a trance.

"We know who you are, Herr Hitler," said Stämpfle. "That is why we are willing to put our resources at your disposal."

With that statement, Hitler's face twitched convulsively. His eyes and facial features twisted and contorted in diabolical rage as a bizarre new, screeching voice emanated from him.

"You know *what?*" Hitler roared at Stämpfle. "You *dare* to say you know *who* I am? You bastard priests know nothing of who *I am!*" he snarled. His body shook as he glared furiously at Stämpfle. "Absolutely *nothing!*" He seethed, as saliva coated his darkened teeth and his eyes now turned strangely reptilian.

Stämpfle, aghast, dropped his jaw and rocked precariously in his chair, beginning to fear for his physical safety. Finally, stammering, he blurted out, "D–dear God, s–sir, I must sincerely apologize, Herr Hitler. I meant you absolutely *no* disrespect, sir. I can assure you, sir."

"Then *never* again speak of what you do not know!" Hitler shouted as his body shook.

Stämpfle, profoundly struck by this second, shrill voice directed at him, recognized it as the same voice he had heard in a number of Hitler's public tirades, particularly against the Jews. The almost detached voice was pitched far higher than a man's normal speaking voice, and was filled with terrible rage and hatred. It sounded almost like a primordial scream.

"Please allow me to be clear, Herr Hitler, as to what I meant," he forced himself to continue. "We are convinced, sir, that you are the

Anointed One—the one who will lead Germany out of this Dark Age to a glorious Reich. All of Germany looks to you for its salvation. This is your destiny, sir."

Hitler walked across the room, turned again, and stared grimly at the priest. His anger had subsided. "You are correct, Stämpfle, and it is good that the Jesuits believe that, too, do you understand?"

"Oh, yes, yes, *mein Führer*, most assuredly," Stämpfle stuttered like an excited child.

Hitler was momentarily silent. The Jesuit, his arms trembling, looked up and shouted, "I do! We all do! You have been sent to us for such an hour! With your inspired leadership, Germany and the Catholic Church will regain their former glory—the glory stolen from us throughout five centuries of betrayal and treason. And with that, the Jesuits will accomplish our two major goals: a universal Catholic Church and universal political power under you, in fulfillment of the prophecies of Revelation, as history moves inexorably towards the eventual return of Christ."

"What did you just say, priest? Political power for the Jesuits as history moves towards the return of Jesus Christ?" Hitler said with scorn. "Safe to say, priest, and understand this full well, I—*not* Jesus Christ—am the Messiah of the German nation, and I *alone* will have absolute power."

Stämpfle stared incredulously as Hitler continued, callously and without emotion: "Christ was regarded as a popular leader, like me. Yet even he took a position against the insidious Jews that spawned him. That is how corrupt even he thought they were. The Jews regarded him as the result of an illegitimate relationship, as they do me, and hold us both in similar contempt. Christ's objective was to liberate people from the Jews' strangling oppression and control. My objective is the same."

Then Hitler sat down and leaned forward, staring silently at Stämpfle.

Suddenly he shouted out angrily in a shrill, uncontrolled pitch, "You must see that even the pitiful Christ tried to set himself against the Jew establishment and their totally selfish, deceitful religion with its ridiculous laws." He seethed, his eyes flashing with hatred, his tirade ongoing. "And that is why the Jews crucified him. Did you know that, priest? Do you understand that?" His voice was filled with derision, and his face was contorted again into an ugly mask.

"Well, not exactly in that way, sir," Stämpfle responded haltingly.

Hitler banged his fist on the table. "Well, you *should* know that, because those singular facts about the Jew are not lost on all the clergy throughout Germany and Europe. Why, even Martin Luther himself held a special contempt for the Jews and their religion. In his book *On Jews and Their Lies*, Luther articulated the truth of this 'moral stain' called the Jew."

Pointing and glaring at the priest, Hitler shouted, "The Jesuits and the German people should understand that divine providence has willed that I, and I alone, not Jesus Christ, will carry through the fulfillment of this final objective and the commandment that has been laid upon me."

Hitler again stood up and paced. "Look around you, priest!" he shrieked as he waved his arms, his eyes staring violently into space. "The ignorance of the European masses about the nature of the Jew has made this German nation and all of Europe an easy victim for their bloodsucking greed, sickening decadence, and capitalistic control."

Hitler's fury continued. "But now I am a sudden cleansing light on the Jew, you see, who is revealed as a maggot in a rotting corpse." He stared wickedly at Stämpfle, his ugly teeth bared. "And as such, my destiny is that of a fulfiller of prophecies. I follow my course with the precision and security of a sleepwalker." He grimaced and then stared at the ceiling with an arrogant smile.

Stämpfle was dumbstruck by Hitler's shocking tirade, as well as by the strange second voice emanating from him. The vehemence with which this bizarre, shrill voice expressed Hitler's abhorrence of the Jewish people and loathing of Christ terrified him.

Yet Stämpfle found himself strangely caught up in Hitler's unusual magnetic attraction—as revolting as it was—and shouted, "*Mein Führer*, it was with leaders like you in mind that our founder Loyola preached, 'Go forth and set the world on fire!' Herr Hitler, together with the National Socialists, the Jesuits shall set the world on fire as Loyola wanted us to!"

Hitler folded his arms as he looked at Stämpfle. A perverse smile replaced the hypnotic look and rage of just a moment ago—as if he knew that he now had a controlling influence over the priest.

Hitler remained quiet for several moments. Beads of perspiration covered his forehead. Then, as if another, calmer, person were speaking, he quietly said, "Very well, Stämpfle. You shall help me write *Mein Kampf*."

"I am at once humbled and honored to do so, sir."

"Your Superior General would approve?" Hitler's eyebrow was arched, but the calmer voice remained.

"Of course, sir," Stämpfle replied, still breathing rapidly. "It will be my life's highest honor, *mein Führer*."

"Then you shall return next week, Stämpfle. I will make certain that the prison authorities allow you to come and go as you please. I will see to it that my deputy, Rudolf Hess, cooperates with you, as well. He is in here, too, and has been taking dictation for *Mein Kampf*."

With that, Hitler rose, snapped his heels sharply together, avoided shaking the priest's hand, and said dismissively, "Now you must go."

Stämpfle came to attention and responded with a swift straight-armed salute. "*Heil Hitler*."

Hitler turned and marched out the door, leaving Stämpfle still at attention in the room.

So overcome that he could not speak, the priest fumbled to gather his hat, cloak, and briefcase. He began to open the heavy door as the guard reappeared.

"Father, could you hear my confession?" the guard asked. Stämpfle never responded and never looked back. He walked rapidly down the long corridor and straight out the main entrance into the dark, moonless night. The guard followed him, repeating his request: "Can you hear my confession, Father?"

"Get me Himmler on the telephone," Hitler said to a guard who stood outside his cell.

"Yes, *mein Führer.*"

Shortly after, Heinrich Himmler was on the line.

"Himmler, I want a Jesuit named Bernard Stämpfle and the people he frequently associates with followed. I want their actions reported to me from now on."

"Yes, *mein Führer.*"

Chapter 11

JANUARY 1938
CURIA GENERALIZA
INTERNATIONAL HEADQUARTERS OF
THE SOCIETY OF JESUS
ROME

In fifteen years Hitler has succeeded in restoring Germany to
the most powerful position in Europe. Whatever else might
be thought about these exploits, they are certainly among
the most remarkable in the whole history of the world.
—WINSTON CHURCHILL, 1935

The Jesuits are highly educated men who are prepared
and sworn to start at any moment, and in any direction,
and for any service, commanded by their superior general.
They are bound to no family, community, or country.
—ANONYMOUS

FATHER JOHN LAFARGE fidgeted with his sparse hair as he looked
out at the Eternal City, Rome, through a large, elaborately wrought

window of the Curia. He reflected on the city's rich history and its place in Western civilization, as he awaited with eagerness his audience with the Superior General of the Society of Jesus.

LaFarge, a fifty-eight-year-old Harvard-trained Jesuit scholar from New York City, had just arrived in Rome after a swift transatlantic crossing to Cherbourg on Cunard's luxurious blue ribbon ocean liner the *Queen Mary*. LaFarge loved Italy, was fluent in Italian, and hoped one day to retire there and teach. An urbane man with a slight build and thick black glasses, he had the look of the serious intellectual that he was—an influential figure in the field of race relations in America. He had openly declared that racism is a sin and a heresy. His bold stand attracted the attention of Pope Pius XI in Rome, who had become deeply disturbed by the anti-Semitic legislation imposed in Italy in early 1937 by the fascist regime of Benito Mussolini—*Il Duce*, the Caesar, as Mussolini preferred to be called. Pius XI, in a meeting with Jewish leaders where he heard stories of their growing persecution, broke down and wept, saying, "We are all spiritually Semites."

Pius XI was so impressed by LaFarge's courage and vision that he commissioned him to write a papal encyclical—an official Vatican statement—on the subject of racism, titled *Humani Generis Unitas* (The Unity of the Human Race). LaFarge readily accepted the assignment, and set to work in collaboration with three other Jesuit priests. Now it was to be his honor to deliver the finished product to the desk of Pope Pius XI.

But first, LaFarge would present it for review and approval to the Superior General of the Society of Jesus. The current superior general, one of the "black popes," as they were known in Catholic circles, was Wlodimir Ledochowski, an important Jesuit figure of the time. Before becoming a Jesuit, Ledochowski had been a count and member of Polish nobility residing in Biarritz, France.

"The Superior General will see you now," a Jesuit aide said sharply to LaFarge.

"Thank you so much," LaFarge replied, slightly ill at ease because of the aide's tone and hypnotic look. He picked up his fine Swiss-made black leather briefcase and, pushing back what hair remained on his balding head, followed the aide through the halls of the magnificent Curia.

The headquarters of the Jesuits for centuries, the Curia was within sight of the glistening white-and-gold dome of St. Peter's Basilica, Michelangelo's Sistine Chapel in the Vatican, and all the glorious buildings from the Renaissance era that surrounded it.

When the door opened to the superior general's imposing office suite, Ledochowski was standing with his back to his guest, appearing lost in thought.

"Signor John LaFarge, Superior General," announced the aide.

The top official was startled back into the moment. "What?"

"Signor John LaFarge, Superior General," the aide repeated.

"I must beg your pardon," replied Ledochowski as he turned around. He was a tall, slim man with a refined air and aristocratic features, whose large blue eyes were framed by a pair of expensive horn-rimmed glasses.

"John, I do apologize," said Ledochowski as he reached out with both arms and warmly embraced LaFarge, who returned the embrace. "I was lost in thought. I am sorry, it is indeed a delight and honor to meet with our most outspoken Jesuit in America today."

Standing back and observing LaFarge, Ledochowski smiled and added, "Now, tell me—how have you been?"

"It is so good to see you, Father Superior. I have been fine, thank you. And how have you been?"

"Not so fine, John, but we can discuss that later."

LaFarge gave him a quizzical look.

As both men sat on plush, antique sofas, the superior general nodded to the aide, who nodded back in respect and left the room.

"So, you do us the honor of presenting your encyclical to the Society of Jesus for its approval before giving it to His Holiness. I so very much appreciate your gesture of respect, John."

"Of course, Father Superior, the pleasure is all mine; we are, as they say, Jesuits first and Catholics second," said LaFarge with a wink. With that, he opened his briefcase and took out the hundred-page typewritten document and handed it to the superior general.

The aging official flipped over the cover page and skimmed through the paper, then set it aside. "Of course I will need time to study it in detail, but it looks impressive."

"Thank you, Father Superior."

The superior general got up and walked over to an ornate stained-glass window overlooking one of the Curia's graceful courtyards. After a lengthy pause and a sigh, he turned around and said, "John, do you realize what is going on in Germany with Hitler and his followers now in complete control of the country?"

"I have heard reports, and yes, Father Superior, they are disturbing to all of us. As you know, they are the motivation behind the pope's desire for this encyclical."

"John, what is happening there is much more than just *disturbing*."

"In what way, Father Superior?"

"The Society of Jesus has learned from our brothers in Germany that the Nazis are, at their core, a movement devoid of conscience. Hitler and his inner circle of disciples are, in fact, pathological liars and murderers."

"Liars and murderers?" exclaimed LaFarge, his widening brown eyes magnified by his thick glasses.

The superior general took a deep breath and continued. "Liars, murderers, and worse. From what we now understand, we believe they are totally wrapped up in the occult. At times, an almost out-of-body second voice issues from Hitler, and he has an unusually powerful, spellbinding personality that draws hysterical masses to him."

"Murderers, an out-of-body voice, spellbinding personality, the occult...I am very surprised to hear all this, Father Superior. This is much worse than what we are hearing in America," LaFarge noted with a frown.

"Yes, John, it is *much* worse. Actually, it seems reasonable to believe that the so-called Third Reich and the National Socialists could be nothing more than a political cover for a murderous, occult-based form of religious order rooted in heretical pagan sects. It could be even more sinister than that. Have you seen the newsreels of the Nuremberg rallies?"

"Yes, Father Superior. They are viewed as strange and surreal in America."

The superior general shook his head. "The Order of the SS is at the heart of these bizarre nighttime rituals. Tens of thousands of them march as one, with emotionless faces and robotic precision. Blood-red banners, blinding searchlights, the screaming masses—it would seem the German people have given their very souls over to the Nazis. In Europe, many mystics and occult leaders now believe that Hitler is the 'Anointed One' they have been awaiting."

"Father Superior, this is terrible," responded LaFarge.

"It certainly is, John, but what is even more terrible is that Hitler seems to have an ominous force at work within him that despises all that is Judeo-Christian. His book-burning ceremonies portend a frightening future for us all—particularly for the Jews, but also for Christians. He was recently heard saying, 'We shall wash off the Christian veneer of this nation and bring out a religion peculiar to our race.' Just look at the Nazi swastika, John—it is as if the cross of Jesus Christ has been twisted into a perverse pagan symbol of the ancient Indo Aryans of old."

LaFarge nodded slightly.

"And let me read you something that recently appeared in a leading Berlin paper," Ledochowski continued. He picked up a sheaf of papers from the credenza and adjusted his reading glasses.

"Hitler wrote, 'Religions are all alike, no matter what they call themselves. They have no future—certainly none for the Germans. I may come to terms with the church. Why not? But that will not prevent me from tearing up Christianity's root and branch, and annihilating it in Germany...'"

He skipped ahead. "'For our people, it is decisive whether they acknowledge the Jewish-Christian creed with its effeminate pity ethics, or a strong, heroic belief in God in Nature, God in our own people, in our Aryan destiny, in our pure German blood.' This thinking, John, has resulted in the forced sterilization of five hundred thousand persons who were mentally ill, homosexual, promiscuous, or deformed. And there are now numerous concentration camps in Germany to house these people and others not *acceptable* to the Nazis. Can you believe these words and actions, in a historically civilized nation that has produced such devout Judeo-Christian geniuses in music, mathematics, art, and literature?"

"His paganism is terrifying, Father Superior." LaFarge bowed his head. "Perhaps we have not spoken out strongly enough in our encyclical."

"It is too late for that, John," said the superior general dismissively.

LaFarge looked up, bewildered. "What do you mean, *'too late'*?"

The leader of the Jesuits got up, went over to his desk, and sat, then lowered his head into his hands as if about to offer confession. Raising his head again and looking sadly at LaFarge, he said, "Unfortunately, John, early on, we Jesuits were swept up in this mass hysteria like the others. We were deceived. Even I was somewhat mesmerized by the power of the Nazi movement."

Before LaFarge could respond, the superior general stood up again and walked to the window. "Our leadership was gradually made aware that certain Jesuit brothers found justification for the SS in our principles, and shared our principles with Himmler. Do you know what Himmler's official title is now?"

LaFarge shook his head, "I must confess I do not."

"Herr Himmler is now called Superior General of the Order of the SS by his murderous disciples."

"I am sure we did not realize—"

The superior general raised his hand and said, "Please, John, I wish that were true. But, in effect, we helped the Nazis organize the SS in its early years. Now, looking back, it seems unreal how a certain group of our brothers offered them everything they needed."

Ledochowski's voice broke. Looking up, LaFarge could see his tears and decided to break protocol. He got up, walked over, and put a hand upon the weeping official's shoulders.

Ledochowski continued to struggle both for words and to hold back his tears. "I cannot believe our brothers' actions with these monstrous men. I believe they were so deceived. I am heartsick."

"Surely it is not too late to tell the world, Father Superior," suggested LaFarge. "Perhaps Hitler and Himmler can be stopped if we expose their evil deeds before the public."

The superior general stared in distress at LaFarge. "Events in Europe have taken on a life of their own. And now, I must say, I fear for our lives and for the Order itself."

LaFarge stepped back from Ledochowski, "What? You believe the Society of Jesus itself is in peril?"

The superior general looked at him with deep concern in his eyes. "John, would you take a walk with me in the Curia courtyard? There is more I wish to tell you, but I would feel more certain of the confidentiality of our conversations there."

LaFarge expressed surprise at this request, but acquiesced. "Most certainly, Father Superior."

The two men asked for their black wool overcoats, hats, and scarves, and upon receiving them walked outside into the setting afternoon sun. As they walked, LaFarge noticed Ledochowski's aide watching them intently from the window. Once they had reached a distant corner of the large courtyard, the superior general turned to LaFarge. "John, have you ever heard of one of our brothers by the name of Bernard Stämpfle?"

"I have heard the name, but I cannot place him. Father Superior, before you begin, do you believe the Jesuit quarters are being watched by outsiders?"

"Yes, we could be watched or even infiltrated, especially considering what I am about to tell you."

LaFarge looked back towards the window in which he had seen the aide a moment earlier. The aide was gone.

"Stämpfle was one of our brothers who urged our interaction with the Nazis in order to increase Jesuit influence. He was one of our outstanding writers and leading intellects. He understood *The Secret Instructions* and Loyola's goals better than anyone. Unfortunately, he helped Hitler write *Mein Kampf,* primarily because he believed Hitler would help increase Jesuit authority and end Protestant dominance in Germany."

As the two men talked, the steam from their breath formed two columns of vapor in the frigid courtyard. "At the urging of a select group of our leading brothers, there was a plan for *Mein Kampf* to become a Jesuit master plan for transforming Germany and influencing opinion worldwide through the increasing power of Hitler. This was all consistent with our *Secret Instructions.*"

LaFarge stared at his superior and scratched his forehead in disbelief. "Father Superior, you must forgive me for saying this, and I surely intend no disrespect, but how can we call ourselves Christians and pursue such a course, especially given the blatantly anti-Semitic nature of *Mein Kampf*? It also seems we have totally misjudged Hitler in our quest to increase Jesuit power."

"You need offer no apologies, John. Believe me; I have come to the same conclusions myself. It is why I no longer sleep well at night. Let us walk to my private chapel and study. No one can see us there, and its thick walls render it virtually soundproof."

LaFarge shivered, struck again by Ledochowski's insecurity even within the Curia. "Father Superior, it is getting colder out here in more ways than one."

The priests walked quietly back inside the Curia and proceeded down an ornate, centuries-old hallway to Ledochowski's private chapel and study. The superior general closed the door to the chapel and locked it before proceeding with LaFarge into his study. Then, instead of calling an aide, Ledochowski rubbed his hands together and began to prepare a fire in the study's large stone fireplace.

"Please let me help you, Father Superior," LaFarge insisted as he arranged wood and paper in the fireplace. He then struck a long match and lit the kindling.

"Thank you, John. Now please relax and make yourself comfortable." For a time, both men contemplated the flames that quickly warmed the comfortable, book-filled study.

"In the entire Curia, this study and chapel are my only refuge from the turmoil surrounding us," Ledochowski said with a weary sigh.

Chapter 12

LATE AFTERNOON OF THE SAME DAY
CURIA GENERALIZA
ROME

*If you shall despise my statutes...so that you shall
not obey my commandments, I also will do this
unto you; I will appoint over you terror.*
—LEVITICUS 26:15, 16

*The best political weapon is the weapon of terror.
Cruelty demands respect. Men may hate us. But,
we don't ask for their love; only their fear.*
—HEINRICH HIMMLER, REICHSFÜHRER SS

LAFARGE AND LEDOCHOWSKI now sat close to one another, eyeing each other intently. "And you were saying there is more, Father Superior?"

The older man nodded his head sadly. "I'm afraid so, John. Much more, and we should have seen all this coming. For Stämpfle developed a close, intense relationship with Hitler during the months he worked on *Mein Kampf* at Landsberg Prison."

Ledochowski took a deep breath before continuing. "He told us that Hitler would sometimes go into terrifying trances and claim to hear a voice that Stämpfle could not hear. Hitler said he was in contact with his 'unknown superiors.'"

"*What?* Unknown superiors?"

"Stämpfle told us that Hitler would be working calmly one moment, and then the next moment he would cry out, 'There he is, over in the corner! He's horribly angry at me!' Hitler would then start jumping up and down, howling like an animal."

LaFarge stared at the ceiling, his hands clasped above his head almost as if he were trying to cover his ears. "God save us," he muttered to himself. "Pardon me, Father Superior. Could Hitler be—*possessed*?"

Gravely, with a worried look in his eyes, the superior general said, "Yes, John. Stämpfle believed that Hitler was not only possessed, but that a singularly powerful demon in the form of this 'unknown superior' both controlled and terrorized him. Hitler could be an actual medium for this diabolical thing."

The early darkness of the winter afternoon enveloped the spacious study where the two men sat in the firelight. Ledochowski quietly turned on lamps in the room, which removed the shadows on the wall but could not remove the gloom of sadness and fear that pervaded the room. Sitting down again, he continued.

"And to confirm this theory further, Stämpfle reported that Hitler was always referring to an inner voice urging him on, and that on several occasions, Hitler told him, 'When I am no longer needed, after my mission is accomplished, then shall I be called away.'"

"What did Stämpfle believe Hitler's mission to be?"

"John, I truly shudder at what I am about to tell you. Stämpfle believed that Hitler had been transformed into a truly monstrous successor to certain members of the Ishmael line from Abraham, like the ancient Amaleks, Esau, and Persians, like Haman. These individuals all historically had one mission: the absolute extermination of the descendants of the Abraham line from Isaac and Jacob—namely, the Jews."

Ledochowski now looked at a fearful, anxious LaFarge staring wide-eyed at him through his glasses.

"Hitler's primary mission is to exterminate the Jews?" said LaFarge, still struggling to understand.

"Yes. Completely eradicate them," Ledochowski said somberly. "And our belief is that this demon intends to take matters into its own hands and finish its ancient mission—the liquidation of the Jews—this time through Hitler. This will of course be catastrophic for the Jews, for us, and potentially for the entire world. A war in Europe, besides being terrible in itself, could be the perfect cover for Hitler's evil mission. His destructive powers could be awesome, and he could take on a form of demonic indestructibility in the process."

"May God help us, Father Superior. Do you think Hitler is possessed by Satan himself?" LaFarge asked.

"We actually believe the demon to be something much worse."

"*Worse* than Satan? How can that be possible? Here we are, well into the twentieth century, with cars, planes, and all the things of modern life. Demons and demonic possession is, for most people, the stuff of little red goblins at Halloween parties and biblical fairy tales."

"Yes, John, but consider this—if you wanted your demonic activities to deceive many and remain disguised, would you not want yourself to be viewed as a fairy tale?" countered the superior general. "Or as a joke?" he continued, his blue eyes peering over his glasses at LaFarge.

"You are completely right, Father Superior." LaFarge sighed deeply.

"That is what's going on here, John. We are witnessing only vague indications of a deceptive and horribly powerful demon now at work within Germany."

"Could we be witnessing a release of the demonic *en masse* on Germany," LaFarge wondered aloud, "with these strange rallies and the robotic actions of tens of thousands of men?"

Ledochowski nodded. "It could be that this particular demon has legions of demonic followers. The fact is, John, young Germans have grown up in an era where many people pursue paganism, psychic phenomena, and the occult. And now eight million of these young Germans are members of the Hitler Youth. Their creed is that they *belong* to the *Führer*.

"Himmler himself has told our brothers that he has been 'saved' by a figure of the greatest brilliance—not by Hitler, but by a spirit incarnate in him, *possessing* him."

"My God! Himmler, too?" LaFarge asked.

"Yes, Himmler—and, most likely, Himmler's whole, bloody SS horde. We understand that his SS soldiers undergo occult initiations and pagan ceremonies to replace their Christian faith and names with ancient Germanic names. They also have rites of worship to bring forth 'spiritual forces' believed by them to reside only in their supposed Aryan psyche. We now believe that these 'spiritual forces' of the Nazis are, yes, demonic. Stämpfle thought so, too."

"'Thought,' Father Superior?" LaFarge swallowed. "I notice you have been talking about Stämpfle in the past tense."

The superior general deeply inhaled, exhaled, and then stared sorrowfully at LaFarge. "Because he is dead."

"Dead!" LaFarge exclaimed. The firelight flickered across his fearful countenance as he forcibly exhaled the word.

"Yes. We have learned that Stämpfle was gruesomely tortured and murdered. We believe that Hitler personally ordered the murder of our poor brother Bernard."

"Because he knew too much?"

"Yes, far too much—and he started to report to us things that he had learned about what was transpiring with Hitler and his followers. The Gestapo or SS must have become aware of this and tortured him to find out what he had told, and to whom. And then they killed him."

The superior general continued, his heart heavy with sadness. "We believe that this has led to our being selectively infiltrated throughout Europe by Nazi agents disguised as staff and even clerics."

LaFarge thought of the aide who had made him uneasy when he arrived, who had watched them in the courtyard from the window.

"And thus, we are also convinced that any or all of us are now at risk of being murdered by Hitler through the SS or the Gestapo. Not only could we be suddenly annihilated, but so could the pope himself."

"Surely not even Hitler would—"

The father superior put his hand on the American's shoulder. "Most assuredly he would, John—and this brings me to an important point in our discussion. For the reasons I have explained to you, we dare not infuriate the Nazis further. That is why I am asking you to do something that I know may be quite difficult for you to accept."

"Which is…?"

"I do not want the Vatican to publish your encyclical."

LaFarge could not speak. He looked into the tormented eyes of his superior, and saw a man who had all but given up hope.

"Before you judge me too quickly, John," the superior general continued, "remember what happened to the Jews in the Netherlands when our Catholic bishops spoke out there. It brought them swift and deadly retaliation. The same thing could happen here in Italy and throughout Europe if we speak out against the Third Reich."

"But Father Superior, I have seen in America what happens when the Church does not speak out against racism and bigotry."

"Please, John, spare me *that* comparison! This is not a simple case of racism and bigotry in America. This is a militarized German nation controlled by a demonic, occult leadership and populated by a fanatical, obsessed, nationalistic people. And this leadership has ordered through the Nuremberg Laws that Jews are no longer German citizens and that Germans cannot marry or have sexual relations with Jews. We know these orders are all in preparation for the final separation and extermination of European Jewry and *anything* that stands in its way!"

The superior general took a deep breath and continued. "In any event, there are other reasons for my request." He paused. "Now, what I am to tell you must never be uttered to anyone again. Do you *absolutely* understand?"

LaFarge nodded, but wondered what could be any worse than what he had already heard. Though dinnertime, both prelates had lost their appetites.

"Stämpfle told us that a special copy of our *Secret Instructions of the Society of Jesus* has been among a very close group of Jesuit brothers and passed down to members of this group for the last four hundred years.

"What makes this copy of our *Secret Instructions* unique is that in its pages there are sketches of demonic, sinister faces. Secreted inside the book is a letter alluding to the fact that these faces came to an artist in terrifying visions. And stamped inside the front cover is a wax seal of a lion with a serpent's body."

"How…unusual," said LaFarge.

"You must never tell another soul, John."

"You have my word, Father Superior."

"There is a history here," said Ledochowski. "Remember when you asked whether Hitler might be possessed?"

"Yes, Father Superior," said LaFarge, fatigue mixed with trepidation now evident in his voice.

"I assure you that what I am about to say will sound totally incredible," Ledochowski continued, his piercing blue eyes fixed on LaFarge. "Stämpfle related that the letter was written by the great Michelangelo himself. It reflected his belief that his vision was related to the release of restraints on terrible demonic forces from the Abyss in the End Times."

"*Michelangelo?*" blurted out LaFarge. He couldn't look more perplexed.

"Yes, the great Master Michelangelo. And among all the sketches of faces in the book, there is"—Ledochowski could scarcely bring himself to speak the words out loud—"Adolf Hitler's!"

LaFarge gasped. "Hitler's face, sketched in *our* ancient book of secret instructions, four hundred years ago? You cannot be serious, sir."

"Yes, John, I am deadly serious. And according to Stämpfle, the resemblance to Hitler in the sketch is nothing short of *astonishing*. Hitler's face is shown from two angles. The first angle shows him emerging from the head of a strange leopard, which as you know is not only one of the beasts in Revelation but also a symbol of the German nation."

LaFarge slumped down in his chair, his hand on his head. Crossing himself, he said, "Father Superior, we are surrounded by evil."

"I know, John. I know." Ledochowski put a hand on LaFarge's shoulder and stared intently at him. "Why do you think I cannot sleep? I have so needed to tell someone I can trust."

"Yes, of course, sir. Please, feel free to tell me all. You have my unswerving loyalty to silence, as you know."

And so the superior general passed on to LaFarge all that Stämpfle had told him of the centuries-old sketches: the second angle of Hitler's face, demonically masked, with a long horn emanating from it and reminiscent of that of the ancient ruler Antiochus IV, a would-be destroyer of the Jews; two smaller, bearded faces, along with two other strange faces that seemed to evoke the False Prophet of Revelation and the future Antichrist; the three beasts said in the book of Daniel to appear in the End Times before Christ's return; a cone-shaped demonic face full of pustules, bear and lion upon its eyelids, and a naked man covering its mouth about to be eaten; and finally, a man with the strange eyes of a zealot, sharing an eye with another man with penetrating eyes and vampiric teeth.

LaFarge's jaw had long since dropped, as he stared incredulously at Ledochowski.

Finally, LaFarge spoke. "Dear God. If this weren't coming from you, I would think both the speaker and this information were insane. These demonic images seem to be unspeakably horrific visions by the great Michelangelo. And the only human face of the four that we recognize is Hitler's? The other faces are of the past—or worse, the future…"

Chapter 13

Hitler was a demon, but I realized it too late.
—Erich Räder, Grand Admiral and Commander in Chief,
German Navy under Adolf Hitler

*It is just incomprehensible how those atrocities
came about. Every genius has a demon in him...
You can't blame Hitler...it was just in him.*
—Rudolf Hess, Deputy Führer to Adolf Hitler

Darkness now enshrouded the Curia. The shadowy light from
the fireplace flickered across the superior general's face, suggesting a
scene from Dante's *Inferno*. LaFarge now realized the deep trouble
the Society of Jesus had brought upon itself with its involvement with
the Nazis. He was torn between sympathy for the superior general
on the one hand, and contempt and anger on the other.

"These 'brothers' Ledochowski refers to are not brothers," LaFarge thought. "These are evil men who have completely deceived the Jesuit leadership." He had to question the superior general's wisdom in asking him to keep his encyclical from the pope. "And to top it all off, the Michelangelo sketches and letter, which are simply incredible—and here I am, sworn to secrecy! What have I gotten myself into?" LaFarge's mind raced while Ledochowski continued.

"To make matters even worse, John—we have researched the symbol found inside the cover of the book and we believe we have discovered which specific demon possesses Hitler."

"What?" exclaimed an exasperated LaFarge. "Father Superior, I can't help but feel that we really should inform the Vatican of all this immediately."

"John, you might be right. But there is more I need to tell you."

"Go ahead, sir." LaFarge looked up at the ceiling and grimaced, his frustration visible.

"The lion with the serpent's body is a symbol of a creature named the Demiurge that the Gnostic and Manichean sects believed created the world as evil. These sects predated Christianity and originated in Persia, Egypt, and Babylon."

"I know of them," LaFarge said, nodding. "The Gnostics had all those strange gospels showing, among other things, that Christ had a bizarre relationship with, Mary Magdalene, right?"

"Yes, there's all that silly nonsense of theirs in their gospels, as well as the notion of Christ as a mere man, rather than the Son of God. Their beliefs were ruled as deviant by Constantine's Council of Nicaea," Ledochowski replied. "Yet there is something much more sinister to these deviant beliefs than that!"

"Dare I ask what that might be, Father Superior?"

"The Gnostics and Manicheans were deceived into believing that this so-called Demiurge who created the world as evil was *our* Judeo-Christian God, whom Gnostics refer to as the Jewish God. Mani, a Persian, and the founder of the Manicheans, agreed and said that the devil god who created the world was the Jewish Jehovah. Importantly, however, the Gnostic Demiurge is also known as Samael, the demon whose symbol is the lion with a serpent body stamped inside our *Instructions* book."

"My goodness, Father Superior, those beliefs are both ridiculous and terrifying!"

"They are, John, and what is also terrifying is that Hitler—along with Himmler, Hess, and Rosenberg—embraces those Gnostic beliefs. In fact, those beliefs form the origins of the Nazi party, which grew out of occult Gnostic secret societies, like Thule."

LaFarge's eyes rolled up to gaze at the ceiling.

"Samael in particular has a horrific significance, John. The Gnostic belief in Samael ties to Christian and Judaic Talmudic works, which reference Samael as the Prince of Demons, the Angel of Death, and Venom of God. Jews and Christians alike consider Samael—not Satan—to be the true personification of ruthless killing and geno-cide. Satan, though evil, is wholly different from Samael and more an adversary of man," said Ledochowski.

"Thus, in both Judeo-Christian and Gnostic beliefs, Samael is a known mass murderer," LaFarge muttered.

"Yes, John. And in demon lore, Samael annually calls for the liquidation of the Jews, while brilliantly disguising itself as the Demiurge, which the Gnostics believe is the Jewish God that cre-ated the world evil. Yet by all accounts, it is Samael *alone* who is responsible for bringing upon the people of Israel every hardship that has befallen them."

"You are right. This demon is far more horrible and deceptive—if that is possible—than Satan," LaFarge interjected.

"Yes, it most certainly is. And there is another link to Samael in the material Stämpfle laid eyes upon: Samael is often associated with Asmodeus, the demon of revenge, wrath, and lust, whose symbol is a great bear. The pustule-filled demonic sketch in *The Secret Instructions*, with images of a lion and a bear on each eyelid, represents Samael and Asmodeus. And the naked man being devoured by the demon? This is yet another linkage of Samael with the revengeful Asmodeus. Both could underlie the demonic fourth beast from Daniel that will devour the world—the Antichrist."

"My God, Father Superior, the otherworld face of Samael is in Michelangelo's vision! I now understand what you have concluded from all this history—the Michelangelo letter, the demonic faces, the wax seal in the book."

"Yes, we believe it is the demon Samael, who, with its demonic horde, is now in possession of Hitler and his key followers. And it is consistent with Hitler calling for a Final Solution, the extermination of the Jews. He sighed. "And who do we find is the spiritual force the SS prays to? The self-same Demiurge, Samael!" Ledochowski paused, and then plunged on. "Remember the sketch I mentioned with the demonic mask covering Hitler's face? Stämpfle recounted that it had a death's head in its mouth."

"That is the symbol of the SS."

"Yes, John. And both the demonic mask and the death's head most likely are other signs of Samael, the angel of death."

"So—you believe that Hitler is paving the way for Samael to be fully unleashed in the End Times, Father Superior?"

The superior general nodded gravely. "Yes, John. It would seem that these End Times have already begun with Adolf Hitler."

"Yet what is the reason for this historical intent of Samael to exterminate the Jews?" LaFarge asked.

"It is Samael's ancient quest for revenge against Abraham and all his offspring," Ledochowski explained. "Abraham was the first to reject idolatry and paganism through his covenant with and introduction of our God into the world. Demonic princes like Samael ruled the entire pagan world, as most notably exemplified later by Samael being the patron of the Roman Empire."

"I see, Father Superior. And of course, the Jewish line of Abraham brought forth Jesus Christ, who went to the cross, died in our place, and arose again; thus, the demonic princes lost their death grip on the world," added LaFarge.

"Exactly, John. And finally, it is Jesus Christ who said that upon his return He will cast demons like Samael back into the Abyss for eternity, and they will never more rule the world. The demons *dread* being put into the dark spiritual prison of the Abyss, and Samael hates Christ for this," Ledochowski continued. "Remember in Luke, when Christ removed the demons from the tormented man, how the demons pleaded with Christ not to send them back into the Abyss?"

"I do, Father Superior, I do."

"Furthermore, we believe it is Samael's grand plan that if Hitler does not succeed in destroying all European Jewry, they will flee to their homeland in the Middle East, where Samael can inspire the Ishmael line and the Persians to destroy them, as they have attempted in the past. In fact, Hitler has told certain Middle Eastern leaders that Germany would support Arab liberation from the British but would want to destroy all Jews residing in the Arab sphere."

"That could mean the destruction of the Ishmael line as the Jews fight for survival!" LaFarge exclaimed.

"*Exactly*, John. Total revenge by Samael against all the seed of Abraham."

"Dear God, if what you say comes to pass, this is absolutely brilliant malevolence by the demon Samael, Father Superior."

"It is, John, and with the total deception of all but a handful of us."

"And considering the depictions you mentioned, Father Superior, of the False Prophet and the Antichrist in the End Times: with the Ishmael line potentially fighting to destroy the Jewish line, the person of the Antichrist could be viewed as the perfect savior for all peoples from the turmoil of the major religions—a universal deception of all mankind."

"This potential chain of events is so unbelievably shocking, it is beyond words. It seems that divine justice will be meted out against those who embrace false gods."

With those words LaFarge fell silent for a moment, putting the pieces together in his mind, and then went on, "So, the Jewish people have been persecuted over the centuries because they were thought to be the killers of Christ and non-believers in Christ as the Son of God, when in fact they have been targeted continually for extermination by Samael and his legions—solely because they descended from Abraham, who first believed in our God and because Christ came from the Jewish line."

"It would seem throughout history Samael has taken advantage of the persecution of the Jews by others, including Christians, many of whom believe Jews are from the devil, and has even deceived the Jews themselves in order to hide its own vengeful intentions," answered the superior general.

LaFarge hung his head as he reflected on the contents of the encyclical he and his Jesuit brothers had just completed. While it condemned the doctrine of "a struggle for racial purity" and the harassment being imposed on Jews, it fell short of entirely condemning anti-Semitism. Indeed, it warned of "the spiritual dangers to which contact with the Jew can expose souls."

Then he looked up and asked, "Michelangelo was not a member of our Order, so whose copy of *The Secret Instructions* was this, Father Superior?"

"That is not really known—certainly someone close to Michelangelo. All that is known is that this copy has probably belonged to a specific group of Jesuit brothers for centuries. It has been passed down by them, but was never brought to the attention of the superior generals until now. Terribly, these brothers' identifier seems to be the signet ring of Samael, the lion with the serpent body, just like the wax seal in the book."

"Jesuits who are followers of Samael, Father Superior?"

"Yes. They have always been evil men at heart, disguised as Jesuits awaiting their leader in the sketches, whom they eventually recognized as Hitler."

A look of amazement passed across the American priest's face. "And where is the book now?"

"With Stämpfle dead, it seems that nobody knows where it is or who has it. So now you can see our problem. If Samael, possessing Hitler, unleashes a war with the goal of liquidating the Jews—as I believe he soon will—and our knowledge of these sketches and their significance were to surface, they could be used against us. We are trapped, in a way."

"Trapped? Why do you say that, Father Superior?"

"Hitler will try to annihilate us if we publicly state that he is possessed by Samael, while others will eventually demand an answer as to why the Society of Jesus did not reveal this evil man when we were forewarned about him."

"And no one will believe our protests, no matter how legitimate our reasons may have been," said LaFarge sadly.

"You are correct, John. I have told you all this today for the good of the Jesuits. I truly believe that it is imperative that neither the encyclical nor the knowledge of this copy of *The Secret Instructions* ever reach the hands of Pius XI or, frankly, anyone at all."

LaFarge was silent.

"It is well known in the inner circles that the pope is in grave health. If we delay giving the encyclical to him, it is unlikely that he will ever be able to read it or publish it. This is for his good as well as ours. Do you understand, John?"

LaFarge felt sick as he registered the grim logic of the moment. Reluctantly, he nodded his head in agreement. "And what will future generations say of us if these truths ever become known?"

"They will say that the Jesuits, as one of the world's most educated societies, should have known better," said the Father Superior, pausing. "And I'm afraid they will be correct, though I hope they will see our dilemma. But in any event, the Society of Jesus *must* and *will* survive at all costs, as I am sure you understand. Loyola would want it this way, of that I am sure."

With that, Ledochowski put his arm on LaFarge's shoulder and said, "John, I believe this would be an opportune time to implore the help and protection of the angelic protector of the Jesuit Order."

"Michael the Archangel?"

"It seems both a divine irony and a necessity that we call upon our beloved artist's namesake, Michael the Angel, to guide us and save us in this dire hour, does it not?"

LaFarge nodded silently and retired with Ledochowski to the superior general's chapel. Kneeling down, they recited in unison, "St. Michael the Archangel, defend us in battle, be our protector against the wiles and snares of the devils..."

"Did you transcribe everything the two of them said?" the man in Jesuit habit said to his accomplice quietly in the hushed dark of the attic over the now-empty study.

"Yes, I believe so, although our equipment, being up against a slight crevice in the ceiling, could pick up only so much of their whisperings."

"We must get this to Himmler immediately," the first man urged, as the two began to slowly crawl back through the attic to a trap door in the ceiling of the annexed building.

Three weeks later, Pope Pius XI died.

The Unity of the Human Race was never published, and the pope never learned about the special copy of *The Secret Instructions of the Society of Jesus*, its sketches, or Michelangelo's letter.

Chapter 14

LATE MARCH 1945
WEWELSBURG CASTLE
WEWELSBURG, GERMANY

*The very first essential for success is a perpetually
constant and regular employment of violence.*
—ADOLF HITLER

A LONE MAN in a black SS military uniform stood solemnly in the
dimly lit North Tower of Wewelsburg Castle. An ancient fortress
with a haunted history, it had been personally selected by Heinrich
Himmler prior to the outbreak of World War II to serve as a spiritual retreat for the top leadership, or knights, of the SS. In the tower
were twelve marble columns and twelve marble seats in a circle, one
for each of the knights. Most of the knights were members of the
Totenkopf SS—the unit in charge of the death camps of the Third
Reich, whose black military hats displayed the death's head insignia
of the SS in solid gold.

At the center of the vault room, carved into the floor, a circle with a dark mosaic star called the Black Sun radiated twelve arms. The center of the crypt's ceiling featured a large Nazi swastika. Twelve tall candles illuminated the space, burning at each of the seats encircling the room. The twelve knights routinely performed occult rituals here in worshipping the Demiurge.

The man, SS Gruppenführer Heinrich Müller, the former head of the Gestapo, was the last of the twelve knights still alive. He looked upon a shockingly gruesome scene. Eleven of his fellow knights were seated there bleeding profusely from their heads, blown open from self-inflicted high-caliber bullet wounds. With the advanced Infantry Division of the United States Third Army under the command of General George S. Patton drawing closer by the hour, these eleven knights had made a covenant to commit suicide rather than risk the possibility of capture.

Müller, his hands covered with blood, had carefully propped up each of the eleven dead knights on their blood-soaked stone seats against the circular wall. The men wore long, black, layered robes, now drenched in blood. Each one had a *Totenkopfring*—a skull ring with runic inscriptions—on one hand, a gold ring with a lion-headed serpent's body on the other hand, and an SS dagger with the inscription "My Honor Is Loyalty" at his side.

Müller stared with glazed eyes and a blank expression at the dead men. He had one final task to complete before he became the last knight to die. As he stood before them, his arms outstretched reverently to the swastika on the ceiling, he spoke out loud to the unseen in the room.

"Wake up on the strength of our god, Samael, the Demiurge who sleeps in our interior. For now is the time for our legion to depart these dead human hosts who have served us well. The Jew descendants of Abraham are forever our enemy, and we have swept them away with an iron broom. We shall leave to their God whatever remains of the surviving vermin we did not destroy.

"And the same light that gave rise to the Third Reich *will* return in the future, to be ignited yet again to overcome the light of their God."

Distant screams from below interrupted his incantations. A soldier shouted for Müller to come down.

Müller immediately left the room, hurried down to the basement of the castle, and opened the door. Inside was a black marble altar. It bore the SS insignia in silver letters on the side and contained a collection of rare Gnostic documents on the Demiurge. On the altar, a profusely bleeding, naked man with blond hair, a small round face, and narrow blue eyes was being stretched on a torture rack. He screamed as three soldiers inexorably deformed his body. On his index finger the naked man wore a gold signet ring depicting the lion with a serpent's body.

"How goes it with Richter? Has he confessed to where *The Secret Instructions* book is?" Müller asked with a grim look. The soldiers looked up and said no, he had not, and they felt that he did not have much longer to live.

Albert Richter, a former Jesuit, had served as a full-time member of the SS. He had been assigned to the SS by the leader of the German Jesuit community in Nuremberg.

"Get me the *Führer* on the telephone," Müller told an aide.

Minutes later, a strangely deep, guttural voice on the other end spoke. "It is good to hear your voice again, Müller."

"Heil Hitler." Müller snapped to attention. "It is good to hear your voice again too, *mein Führer*. It is monstrous what is happening to us, *mein Führer*."

"Yes it is, Müller. The German people have betrayed me and thus are no longer worthy of me," said the voice in a more agitated tone. "We gave them a Thousand Year Reich and eliminated virtually all the wretched, bloodsucking Jew sons of Abraham. Yet what do they do? They surrender it all to the Americans, British, Bolsheviks, and remaining Jewish capitalists rather than die. The fools! The scum! They are about to meet their well-earned fate, just like the Jews. Let them perish as the cowards and defeated pigs they are!"

"Yes, *mein Führer*," said Müller sadly. "We have all let you down. I must beg your forgiveness."

"My time here is drawing to a close, Müller. Did you get the book of sketches and the letter yet, or discover its whereabouts from the Jesuit?"

"No, not yet, *mein Führer.*"

"No? What do you mean, 'no'? Torture the insidious bastard using every means possible. Use *any* method! Do you understand? I will not countenance any more failure here, Müller. It is up to us. *We must find and destroy that book!*"

"We have tortured him using every means at our disposal, *mein Führer*, just like Stämpfle. Yet no matter what we have done—drugs, nails into his genitals, and now the rack—he has bled and screamed, but remained otherwise totally silent. It is as if he and Stämpfle before him were in a trance—the ones the Jesuits are notorious for. And now he is near death. He is prepared to die just like Stämpfle did," said Müller.

"I don't care! The book must be found and destroyed. As I told you in Berlin, this you must do, as your last act for me. Do you understand?"

"I do, *mein Führer*. And it will be done. Heil Hitler," shouted the SS knight as he came to attention and extended his arm in a stiff salute. The line went dead.

"The priest is dead," cried out one of the soldiers.

"Shit!" cried Müller. "Damn that fucking priest!" He left the room and hurried back up to the first floor. He stopped momentarily to gaze out of a large ornate glass window on the landing and collect his thoughts as to what to do.

What came next was the window shattering, raining glass everywhere, as a single high-caliber bullet blew a gaping hole in Müller's forehead and went clean through his brain and out the back of his head. Gruppenführer Müller, gushing blood, fell backwards to the floor, dead.

"Looks like I bagged me one of them kraut bastards," a camouflaged sniper with a heavy Southern accent sneered coldly. He spat out a wad of Brown's Mule chew, while adjusting the scope of his high-powered M1903 Springfield from his perch in a tree. Hand carved on the stock of his rifle read the words "Lockhart's Alabama Sharpshooters, CSA." The man was one of an elite commando force who had moved into position in the dense woods near the castle, surrounding it. Known as "O'Brien's Raiders," they were from the United States Office of Strategic Services, a secret global US intelligence service founded in 1942.

One of the senior commando officers shouted into a walkie-talkie, "Stop those damn snipers from firing! We want as many alive in there as possible."

The walkie-talkies crackled again as Major Dan O'Brien gave the instruction they'd been waiting to hear: "Let's go, boys! Get in there now!" Two hundred OSS commandos immediately charged out of the woods from several directions, weapons drawn. They were within three hundred feet of the immense walls of the castle when a massive explosion threw them to the ground.

Bricks, wood, and debris rained down on the group as they hugged the earth and pulled their helmets over their heads. When the first wave of debris had subsided, the commandos glanced up and saw a massive plume of black smoke billowing from the castle's interior. As they started to get up, another shattering explosion struck, throwing them down once more. That blast was followed by two more in close succession. The sky rained down more debris on the unit. When the uninjured men finally struggled to their feet, there was nothing left standing of Wewelsburg Castle but its thick outer walls. Everything inside had been consumed by fire, or soon would be.

A commando cursed as he brushed the debris from his uniform, "We almost had them."

"Look at that!" shouted another commando positioned nearby, pointing towards the sky.

The two men glanced up at the towering flames coming from the very center of the castle. There, a ball of bluish-red fire rose hundreds of feet in the air and hovered over the conflagration. It separated from the rest of the inferno, lingered over the castle for several seconds, and then took on twelve different bizarre shapes before it suddenly disappeared. A commando cocked his helmet back, muttering out loud, "What in hell was that?"

Chapter 15

COLONEL EDWARD BEAUSHELL, the senior officer in charge of a top-secret intelligence unit of the OSS, had just returned to the unit's offices in Norfolk House, on elegant St. James Square. Norfolk House was where Supreme Allied Commander Dwight Eisenhower had planned and launched in secrecy the Normandy invasion less than a year before. Beaushell had just had a late lunch with Allied expeditionary officers, headed by British Major General John Reed, American officers Lieutenant General Andrew Conner, and Colonel Marc Janser at the nearby private East India Club. The men had discussed a strategy on how to find and capture the remaining high-ranking Nazis in Germany. Now with the war in Europe winding down, events were developing with breakneck speed, as American and Russian forces raced to close in on what was left of the collapsing Third Reich.

As Beaushell removed his Burberry trench coat, Andrew Eric Alcott, a young OSS second lieutenant in bio-weapons, called from across the room, "Colonel Beaushell, I think you need to see this cable from one of our commando units in Germany." The lieutenant removed his wire-rimmed glasses, squinting at the black Teletype machine as it clacked away and poured out printed paper.

"Is it about Hitler and Goebbels and the rest of the bad boys holed up in a Berlin bunker?" answered the colonel.

The Teletype machine finally spit out its last line of characters and fell silent. Lieutenant Alcott tore off the page and skimmed its contents. "I'm not talking about that, Colonel. This cable carries the highest secrecy clearance. It's from one of our OSS commando units near Wewelsburg Castle. The castle has just been blown up."

"Wewelsburg?" said the colonel, looking up. "You mean Himmler's house of horrors, where they all dressed up like it was Halloween and pretended they were medieval knights?"

"Yeah, that's the one. Anyway, this report says that highly classified information was given personally to our unit commander by General Reinhard Gehlen prior to the unit's raid on Wewelsburg."

"I know Gehlen." Beaushell began to clean his glasses. "A former very senior official in Nazi intelligence like him would only be dancing with us because he has access to files he knows we want to get our hands on."

"It seems that Gehlen directed our people to try and retrieve a special book at Wewelsburg and to find a Jesuit priest named Richter. The book is apparently several hundred years old and includes—are you ready for this?" Alcott paused, and then continued, braced for skepticism. "Sketches, including an almost-perfect likeness of Hitler, and a letter discussing the sketches, written by—and you are really not going to believe this—Michelangelo."

"Give me that again? A drawing of Hitler several hundred years old? And you mean *the* Michelangelo?"

"That's what it says here," the wide-eyed lieutenant replied as he continued to scan the top-secret memo. "Hitler and Michelangelo."

The lieutenant adjusted his glasses and read from the report, filling the colonel in on the details of the demonic sketches, the letter, and the strange symbol that appeared inside the book's cover.

"It says here the book ended up in the hands of a Jesuit priest, Albert Richter, who was part of the SS and gave personal assistance to Himmler early in the war, to help him organize the SS after the model of the Society of Jesus. The Jesuit hierarchy, right up to the superior general, learned all about this book from a Jesuit named Stämpfle. They concluded that one of the sketches was of a demon mass murderer called Samael. They felt this demon was possessing Hitler."

"You've got to be kidding me," Beaushell said. "Go on."

"Gehlen was made aware of all this Jesuit research and also received transcripts of conversations that had been monitored by the Gestapo and SS through their infiltration of the Jesuits during the war. However, according to Gehlen, all the Jesuit transcripts and research in his and his team's possession had been destroyed without his knowledge, on the direct orders of Hitler himself. It says that Hitler had also personally given the order to Heinrich Müller, the former head of the Gestapo, to find and destroy the book. Gehlen claimed that his knowledge of these sketches and the demonic possession of Hitler was one of the key, but highly secret, reasons that he joined other German generals in trying to assassinate Hitler."

"Lieutenant, we had better be careful talking about stuff like this," said Beaushell with a laugh. "It is possible we would be relieved of duty because of 'severe mental fatigue,' if you get my drift. Where is this Richter fellow and the book?"

"Our boys have learned that Richter was supposedly trying to escape with the book and join up with a woman by the name of Mariel Mendenhall—but if he was in the Wewelsburg Castle at the time of the explosion, he's most likely dead."

"Mendenhall…Mendenhall…where have I heard that name before?" The colonel rubbed his forehead. He jumped up from his desk and walked over to a bank of file cabinets. "Mendenhall, Mendenhall… like the Mendenhall Glacier." Beaushell rapidly thumbed through his files. "Here it is. Let's see what it says."

The room fell silent, save for the sound of the colonel flipping through files as he scanned them.

"I knew it. Several years ago, the OSS considered recruiting her. She was married to a senior Nazi official related to von Papen, the foreign minister of the Third Reich."

"What happened to her husband?" questioned the lieutenant.

"Dead."

"How?"

"Suicide."

"Why do all these bastards kill themselves?" the lieutenant said, and laughed.

"Some kind of party rule when one fails, like falling on your sword." The colonel chuckled. "Anyway, she was one good-looking German blonde, but a tough lady, from a hardscrabble background in Berlin, who wound up owning low-rent apartments in bad neighborhoods. She became wealthy by providing undercover cash for higher-end real estate, buying it at a fraction of its value from rich Jews trying to flee the country. She was transformed into the classic German poster girl for Hitler's 'super race'—beautiful, smart, and successful. She and her husband had one daughter, named Katrina."

"So why did we try to recruit her?"

"She was close to the really bad boys in Berlin, and she thought Hitler, whom she knew personally, was evil."

"So how did she get close to this priest, Richter?" the lieutenant continued. "Going to confession?"

"How the hell do I know, son? Probably girlfriend-boyfriend stuff," Beaushell said, winking.

"Got it, sir."

"Where is she now?" Beaushell queried.

"Our boys don't know for sure, but they believe she's fled Germany."

The colonel put the file back in the cabinet and gave it a hard push shut. "I just don't know about all this. Sketches of Hitler, demons, Michelangelo—it sounds so screwy. Obviously nothing that Hitler planned on having in the Führer Museum that he was going to build and fill with looted masterpieces," he said, and laughed.

"I'll give you that, Colonel," continued the lieutenant, "but there is a lot of really weird stuff oozing out of Germany right now. I mean, concentration camps and gas chambers where mass murders were conducted, horrific medical experiments, the slave labor factories—real evildoings. Maybe Michelangelo saw something like this awful thing coming. He did paint the vision of the Last Judgment."

"Now wait a minute, Lieutenant Alcott. We're in the intelligence business. We are not Nostradamus-type mystics. Hitler by Michelangelo," the colonel muttered. "What's next, Eva Braun by Raphael?"

Then he said, "Well, Lieutenant, we might as well let our man in the Vatican know about all this information. Maybe he can shed some light on it. He works as a Jesuit priest in the diplomatic section of the Holy See."

"Yes, sir, will do."

The colonel walked back to his office, shaking his head. "A demonic mass murderer possessing Hitler?" he thought to himself. "Well, I guess that is one way of explaining the killing of all these Jews we're learning about…"

Chapter 16

LATE JUNE 1945
GRAND HOTEL EDEN
LUGANO, SWITZERLAND

THE FASHIONABLE GRAND HOTEL EDEN, surrounded by splendid gardens and overlooking the beauty of Lake Lugano, sparkled like a jewel in the morning sunlight. In the distance, the Swiss Alps soared into the sky, overshadowing the elegant villas and mansions that dotted the scenic lakeshore. The Swiss flags on the hotel fluttered in the light breeze. Serenity and tranquility had once again returned to this lovely lake town. The end of the war brought an end to the tension and anxiety that had accompanied the flow of Jews being smuggled out of Germany. There were no longer spies from many nations present. Yet, in room 137, the war still raged on. A pretty blue-eyed, blond German woman in a fashionable summer dress rapidly dialed out on the hotel room phone. Earlier she had checked to make sure it was not tapped.

"Josef, where is Albert? Did he get out?" Her excited voice came through the phone line.

"No, Mariel. I am so saddened to bring you the terrible news. They caught up with him trying to escape. He is dead. They killed him at Wewelsburg," said Josef Stroessner, a Jesuit regent in Nuremberg, and a friend of Mariel Mendenhall and Albert Richter.

"Those miserable bastards killed my Albert, even though he had done everything for them," she sobbed.

"Yes, even though, Mariel," Stroessner sadly replied.

"Those murderous scum were such pure evil, Josef. I despised them from the beginning. They will surely reside in hell, where they belong forever!"

A prolonged silence followed, punctuated only by the woman's sobbing.

"Mariel, please, Mariel. I am so very sorry."

"Josef, I am afraid. And now, without Albert…" Her voice trailed off, her tears subsiding.

"There is nothing to worry about now, Mariel. The war is over and they are all dead."

Stroessner knew nothing of the special book of *The Secret Instructions* Albert Richter had given her. "You know he was giving up the Order and that horrible SS for me."

"I know, Mariel. I know."

"But I was so afraid he was giving it all up much too late."

"In the end the SS consumed everybody," said Stroessner. "Mariel, what are you and your daughter going to do now? You are in Switzerland, right?"

"Yes. I am planning to take Katrina to Buenos Aires. I have a new name—Nuller—and a new Argentine passport, and I hope to get a new face so I can begin a new life…without Albert." Her voice was subdued. "My maid is already at my relatives' home in Buenos Aires with all our luggage and belongings. My bodyguard is with us. Maybe eventually we will all go to America. Josef, pray for us, please."

"Of course, Mariel, of course I will."

"Good bye for now. When I am settled in Buenos Aires, I will contact you."

"I will help you anyway I can, Mariel. You will be all right."

Setting down the receiver, she burst into tears and began to open a portable steel safe. From within it, she removed *The Secret Instructions*.

She wanted to destroy the accursed book, but she couldn't. When Albert gave it to her, he said that it was much too important to destroy. She suspected he must have had a premonition of his death, and that he knew the Nazis desperately wanted this book. She could only wonder if they had tortured him into saying what he had done with it. The sketches and the letter could obviously be worth a fortune, but they were like an evil curse. If Michelangelo and his beloved were terrified, why should she not be?

Mariel paced back and forth in the well-appointed suite, holding the book close to her chest, her inner turmoil contrasting starkly with the calm surface of Lake Lugano just outside her window.

"I loved Albert and he loved me, but why did he allow this to happen to him—and now to me?" she thought. "I told him these people were evil early on. The book destroyed him, and it now could destroy me and my dear Katrina."

She carefully fingered the sketches in the book resting in her hands. "The face of Hitler. My God, who could the rest be?" she wondered. "These two bearded men's faces next to Hitler's, the man with the horns, and the man with the vampire teeth. The disgustingly horrible demon's face…I know I should not have this—the authorities should. But whom can I trust, knowing what I know?"

Returning the book to its small safe and placing it in her suitcase, she hoped the worst was not to come. She looked out the window at the lake for the last time, and then, her blue eyes glistening, turned to take her daughter's hand. "Now follow me, and make no noise as we leave. Do you understand, Katrina?"

"Where are we going, Mother?" asked the seven-year-old girl.

"Where you can play and laugh and never know the sound of war again."

"Will we ever see Uncle Friedrich or Aunt Elsa again?" asked the daughter.

"I don't have time for questions like that just now, Katrina dear," she whispered as they got into an empty elevator. "Here now, straighten your hair. Louis has a car and is waiting behind the hotel to take us to our plane."

Mariel Mendenhall deliberately did not make eye contact with anyone as she and her child hurried towards the back of the hotel and went out the employees' exit. There, a BMW sedan waited with her bodyguard at the wheel. Stowing the single suitcase on the floor of the car, and keeping her daughter safely by her side on the backseat, Mariel quickly and quietly shut the door and instructed Louis to drive them away as fast as the car would go.

As Louis pressed the accelerator, she locked the door on her side and was leaning over to lock the other door when she noticed a black car advancing at high speed from behind them. Mariel seethed and uttered, "Damn it to hell!" She immediately reached into her purse and pulled out a high-powered .357 Glock pistol with a silencer.

"Damn it, Louis! Get going! Someone is following us!"

Louis never looked back. He had already yanked the stick shift next to him and hit the accelerator hard. The engine roared louder as the BMW squealed down the narrow street towards the Via Carona.

The black car sped up in pursuit. Mariel quickly and calmly broke the rear window of her car with the gun, as her daughter cried and screamed, "Mommy, what is wrong?"

"Quiet, Katrina. Lay down on the floor immediately," she said sharply, placing the Glock on her crossed arm. Steadying herself firmly on the backseat, she shouted, "Louis, slow down!"

As the black car approached them at top speed, Mariel, squinting, carefully took aim and unloaded several blasts of precision high-caliber rounds at the driver, shattering the car's windshield.

She continued firing away, while screaming for Louis to accelerate, as the bullets from her gun exploded in the head of the driver of the black car, spewing blood everywhere. He slumped over, dead. His hand, bearing a signet ring of a lion's head with serpent's body, still clutched the spinning steering wheel in a death grip. Gunshots from others in the car flew out wildly. As Mariel ducked down, the black car spun into the roadside wall and burst into flames.

Louis shouted, "There are men coming from the front!"

Mariel turned and saw two men running towards the car with guns drawn. "Kill the bastards, Louis! Run them over!" she shrieked as she quickly lowered the side window and crouched down.

Louis floored the accelerator, deftly ducking down while aiming the car directly at the pair. The men's gunshots shattered the BMW's front windshield as Mariel started unloading round after round at the two men. Louis swerved skillfully, narrowly missing another roadside wall and hitting both men directly. As Mariel's car turned the corner, she looked back and saw them sprawled in the street in spreading pools of blood. The black car continued to burn in the distance as people swarmed out of the hotel to investigate. Her bodyguard quickly looked back at Mariel with a wide grin.

"Good job, my faithful Louis. Those shit-filled scum must have thought they were dealing with some *Hausfrau* and her chauffeur," she shouted as they sped down the Via Carona. The BMW then headed for a small airstrip outside Lugano. A private plane was waiting there to take them to Lisbon, where they would board a ship for Argentina.

Mariel comforted Katrina and, taking another clip from her large purse, reloaded her gun. "Josef, you told me the war was over and they were all dead," she thought. "I never believed you for a minute."

Josef Stroessner was anxiously trying to find Mariel at the hotel when he learned that she had checked out. He had to tell her about the call he had received from a Monsignor Stevens at the Vatican Secretary of State's office. Monsignor Stevens was looking for her and had asked repeatedly and angrily if Stroessner had knowledge of her whereabouts. Josef needed to tell Mariel that even though Stevens had personally pressured him, he had told Stevens nothing. Stroessner also wanted to tell her that he had inquired into a Monsignor Stevens at the Vatican—and found that no such person existed.

Chapter 17

IN THE FUTURE
AN ANCIENT ROMAN VILLA
LIBYAN COAST

The future ain't what it used to be.
—Lawrence Peter "Yogi" Berra, Hall of Fame catcher and
manager, New York Yankees

*Demoralize the enemy from within by surprise, terror,
sabotage, assassination. This is the war of the future.*
—Adolf Hitler

*The technocratic era involves the gradual appearance of a
more controlled society dominated by an elite, unrestrained
by traditional values. Continuous surveillance over every
citizen will exist with personal information on all.*
—Zbigniew Brzezinski, Foreign Policy advisor to Barack
Obama and Co-founder of Trilateral Commission

We can no more understand a Russian than a Chinese...
—George S. Patton Jr., Four Star General and Commander,
Third Army, WWII

RICHARD ARENELL sat by his villa's sparkling infinity pool. These days, due to continuous instability in Libya and the Middle East, from the years-earlier Arab Spring, Richard stayed only periodically in this ancient Roman villa on a secluded part of the Mediterranean coast of Libya. He had originally purchased the home years ago as his second residence, as he was very interested in the history and architecture of the region. After acquiring it in a rundown state from the then Libyan government, Richard had restored the large desert-colored villa boasting arched ceilings and ten symmetrical stone pillars. According to records discovered in an archeological dig nearby, this immediate area of the Mediterranean coast had been the frequent playground of Roman senators and the elite during the reign of the Caesars. They had come seeking respite from the heat and politics of the Eternal City. Today, however, because of the politics of Libya and the Middle East, the area surrounding the villa was gated and heavily guarded.

Richard considered first contacting his investment advisor in London through his secure mobile unit, which enabled him to see and speak to anyone anywhere in any language, and then ringing up a Libyan female friend for drinks and dinner later, but he decided to wait until he'd taken an early afternoon swim. He pulled his shirt off, revealing his athletic physique, and was ready to dive into the pool when he looked up and saw something resembling the top of a ship's funnel emerging on the horizon. It was no longer a common sight for large yachts or commercial ships to sail past his villa, given the periodic and well-publicized attacks by high-tech pirates, rebels, and terrorists in the region. What sailed into view was much larger than any ship he had seen recently.

Richard switched his mobile device to zoom in on the ship. His dark blue eyes squinted as he took a closer look in the hot Mediterranean sunlight. Suddenly, one extremely large, dark blue funnel rose higher in the water, as a black-hulled behemoth with a white superstructure came into sharp focus on his screen. It was the size of an ocean liner. A portion of the ship's topmost deck served as a large flight deck, with jet helicopters and seaplanes on it. Below it was a storage area for airplanes, as seen on an aircraft carrier. His system began its calculations, recording the ship's length at one thousand feet and its height at twelve stories—a small floating city.

Richard's system also identified a vast array of sophisticated weaponry, radar, and communications equipment, like those of a warship. Suddenly, his GPS system shut down and his screen went blank. The last bit of information he received was that the ship was called the *Universe Manchuria* and was flying the flag of Mongolia. Richard immediately realized that he was looking at the ship that belonged to Sao Damrey's employer, the highly secretive mega-rich Asian technocrat known only as the "Manchurian."

As a result of Sao's involvement with the Manchurian, Richard had followed the Manchurian's inexorable rise with some interest. The Russian government now provided protection for him after ceding to him complete operating authority over an Outer Manchurian province known as the Jewish Autonomous Oblast. The oblast, which had been a settlement for exiled Russian Jews in the early 1900s, was a Far Eastern province of Russia bordering China. Richard had heard that China had also secretly acknowledged the Manchurian's control of the province. The Manchurian had been granted authority there in exchange for access to his various software firms' developments in advanced cyber-weapons and cyber-espionage, along with financial software using cloud computing, which had dramatically strengthened both Russia's and China's global financial systems. His cyber weapons and espionage software was now for sale to countries "approved" by Russia and China. Among the most coveted military weapons he had made operational was the rail gun. This innovative weapon utilized advanced electromagnetic technology that allowed projectiles to travel at supersonic speed.

Under the Manchurian's control, the oblast had once again become a refuge for hundreds of Russian Jews. This time, however, the Jews were hand-picked brilliant software developers and computer scientists, who joined other select Jewish and non-Jewish computer scientists from around the world in the oblast. Israel feared the Manchurian, whom it accused of "sucking the brains out of Israel" by turning many of its top computer scientists into hugely wealthy mercenaries working for his global software operations in the oblast.

The original basis of the Manchurian's wealth was ULTRA, a patented, secure, highly scalable, cloud-based, global Internet payment system developed by him, which had replaced much of the competition and was now used in virtually all payment transactions. It was thanks to ULTRA that anyone could now, at a fractional cost, move any amount of money and pay for anything in any currency from any device anywhere in the world. All this could be done instantaneously in a very safe, very secure environment, even in this age of cyber-theft and cyber-terrorism. The Manchurian had exclusively licensed ULTRA to the United Nations. It made up the heart of a new and powerfully transformed UN, which had increasing oversight of all global financial regulations on behalf of all its member nations, most importantly, the BRICs: Brazil, Russia, India, and China.

Richard had it on good authority from a very close friend high up in the British government that the Manchurian had also secretly taken control of a major multinational farmland company. With global drought and resulting famine becoming more commonplace, certain Western nations had begun to assert their agricultural dominance over China, in view of China's necessity for agricultural imports, as a weapon against it. Using myriad complex operating and trading front companies, along with covert supply routes, the Manchurian, with China's assistance, was channeling to China as much of his company's produce as possible. Thus the Manchurian helped China dominate smaller food-producing countries in Africa and Asia so that it could feed itself. Millions of people worldwide now unknowingly relied on the Manchurian's empire for their food.

Richard had also learned from his friend of a rumor that there was an even darker side to the Manchurian's agricultural interests with the Chinese. His scientists working in top-secret nanotechnology laboratories were researching how to rearrange the atoms and molecules of common grains and soybeans. The aim was to boost yields from the Manchurian's farms, while dramatically reducing those of his competitors by the Manchurian's rogue seeds "entering" their fields. Apparently he was even supporting research and development of how agricultural commodities could be engineered to contain delayed-release toxins, thus becoming weapons.

The Manchurian was a leading example of a trend in a developing modern Dark Age: a vast business empire becoming a virtual city-state by operating outside traditional national boundaries and employing advanced cloud computing systems, both public and private. Other such virtual city-states were controlled by either mega-rich individuals like the Manchurian or private equity pools of nameless, faceless global institutional capital. The far-reaching tentacles of these city-states, known derisively as "virtual vampire squids," were controlling business empires and smaller nations across the globe. Many of these new city-states had become feudal in nature, replete with their own world-class armaments and large private armies of mercenaries. As a result of one global financial fiasco after another, the world had become sharply divided into two camps: the grotesquely mega rich and the grotesquely poor, while a Darwinian fight for survival was taking place for those in the middle.

As Richard reflected on the Manchurian's wide-ranging global influence, he spotted something else: seven sleek, high-tech destroyers painted gray and black, surrounding the ship. They were all heavily armed. "This is not a security escort, but a small navy," he thought.

His mobile device chimed, and Richard asked it to identify the caller. It responded, "Unknown. Do you still want to clear?"

"Yes. Arenell speaking."

"So, don't you know it's impolite to stare?" He heard a familiar voice. Sao Damrey appeared on the screen, although her exact location was blocked.

"Sao, where are you?"

"I'm seated on a balcony outside my stateroom, looking at a man who is in danger of playing the tourist. Haven't you ever seen a big yacht before?"

"You are on that heavily armed warship-cum–aircraft carrier disguised as an ocean liner, and you're calling it a yacht? That's hysterical, love." Richard laughed, his eyes squinting in the sun as he put on his sunglasses.

"Indeed, I am. Wave, Richard—I can see you clearly." Sao sat in an expensive antique teak deck chair, stunning in a light blue silk lounging outfit, looking through a high-powered satellite-linked device at Richard and his villa. "We are heading towards Lebanon. But right now, I'm requesting permission to come ashore, and also expressing interest in having dinner with you later, SAS Captain Arenell." In a whisper, her green eyes flashing, she added, "Darling, it has been much too long."

In the many years since the September 11th terrorist attack, much had changed for both Richard and Sao. They had drifted back into their separate lives and only saw each other periodically at certain high-end events around the world. They talked intermittently, at Richard's instigation, and always planned to rendezvous somewhere again in the near future. But it seemed to Richard that shortly after 9/11, Sao's world had become solely that of the Manchurian's.

"So, this is the Manchurian's world-famous floating city. I must say, I'm impressed. And do you have your own stateroom on his 'yacht'?" He couldn't help laughing to himself.

"Well, yes I do. Actually, I have my own spacious, fully equipped apartment on board for myself and anyone else I desire to have come join me, like…well, like you, Richard."

"I'd love to see it. The *Universe Manchuria* looks like quite the ship."

"One of the more interesting things about this big boat is that it and its escort ships can become invisible to any device searching for it. They started developing the technology around the turn of the century, and it is now a reality. When the system is turned on, the ship is basically invisible to all forms of electronic and visual spying. It's as if the ship simply isn't there. And then there is the state-of-the-art weaponry. Everyone is positively terrified of our rail guns." Richard now realized what had happened to his system when it tried to input information on the Manchurian's vessel.

"I'd say it's all very impressive, Sao. Nothing but the best for the Manchurian, am I right?"

"Right." Her green eyes sparkled as she broke into a wide smile.

"So, how have you been? We haven't talked in a long while."

"Very busy, Richard—but I want to see you and talk with you. And I have missed you."

"Excuse me, Sao. When exactly did you begin missing me?"

"Oh, Richard, you have always been ready with the quick comeback."

After a momentary distraction, Sao spoke again. "We have received clearance from Libyan authorities to be here, so I can have someone fly me over to your villa. Our pilots can land at your place."

"Sao, am I really supposed to believe that after all these years of barely communicating with each other, you happened to know that I was here and came all this way just to have dinner and chat me up?"

"Richard, you're far too suspicious."

"No, I just remember you far too well."

"We were sailing through this general vicinity on the way to Lebanon, and I was able to check to see if you were here and, voilà, sure enough you were. Anyway, you seemingly have lost your taste for surprises, haven't you, my dear?" Sao continued, dropping her voice. "Do I detect that maybe you don't want to see me?"

"Did I say that?" Richard replied with a feigned quizzical look on his face. "By the way, is the Manchurian onboard?"

"No, he is not."

"Then I'll wait for supper for you to tell me why you suddenly appeared off the coast of Libya. Why don't you come over earlier and I can show you my place."

"What a marvelous idea, Richard! I will see you later on, my dear."

He snapped his mobile device off, after first saving an image of Sao on the screen. Something in the serious look in her green eyes belied the smile on her face and told him to be on guard. "I am sure that she no doubt found me here by using the many spy satellites the Manchurian is rumored to have. It can't be good, knowing she's tied in with that fellow," he thought as he walked back into his villa. Pausing to look over his shoulder, he saw embossed in gold on the ship's black stern: *Universe Manchuria, Ulan Bator.* "The chap is a bloody floating warlord," he muttered as he watched the massive vessel, surrounded by its escorts, continue to sail on into a distant afternoon haze rising from the Mediterranean.

Chapter 18

PALAZZO ANTONIO ANDREA FALCONARA
VENICE

MARIN FALCONARA was a high-living global commodities and derivatives trader with slicked-back blond hair, dark eyes, and a pretty-boy face, who clothed himself in hand-tailored Canali menswear. A suave, decadent European social lion, he favored fast women and faster cars. Unfortunately, the wheels had recently fallen off his lifestyle when he suffered a significant trading setback, which resulted in a devastating personal financial loss. This immediately reduced his social status from lion to lamb, and he decided that he'd had enough of trading and the high life for a while.

Falconara had also had enough of one of the paintings hanging in his immense, exquisitely decorated Renaissance palace. The towering marble edifice called Palazzo Antonio Andrea Falconara, which faced Venice's Grand Canal, had been in his family for centuries. What concerned Falconara was the ominous grayish human skull that had begun to emerge on the surface of a painting hanging on the wall of a side salon. At first, it looked like the paint was partially peeling, but eventually a human skull clearly emerged. As a result, the painting attracted both undue and unwelcome attention from everyone. Falconara had the painting covered in a shroud and moved to a vault in one of the lower rooms of the palazzo, away from public view.

A woman named Fara Grese also shared Falconara's concerns about the painting. A shrewd German, Fara was Falconara's former Lehman Brothers stockbroker in Rome and had for years been his on-again, off-again lover, tolerating Falconara's relationships with other women. A buxom blonde with gray eyes and an attractive face, Fara had also noticed the gradual changes in the painting. Both of them felt a strange sense of foreboding once the skull had fully emerged. When Fara noticed that the painting had been removed from the wall, she queried Falconara, who told her that he planned to call a restorer to get it fixed.

However, from years of collecting and managing his family's art collection, Falconara knew there was much more to this painting than just deterioration and peeling. He realized there could be an earlier work underneath the surface painting, *St. Mark Defending Venice against Satan*, perhaps by the same artist, Pietro Ziani. Falconara also knew about the use of ultraviolet or "black light" to see beneath surface paintings. He contacted a friend at the Correr Civic Museum in Venice to inquire about borrowing such equipment.

Falconara understood that a hidden painting coming completely through to the surface would be a rarity. Most of the time, there would be mere indications of the painting below the surface, as in this case. Yet Falconara also realized that there was generally a good reason for a painting to be painted over—and the need for canvas was not usually it.

Venice's Correr Civic Museum happily provided Falconara with black light equipment, and, late one evening, he descended to the vault room to take a closer look. After unlocking the solid steel vault door and setting the timers, he entered the small, dimly lit room and approached the covered painting. Carefully, he removed the shroud and turned the black light towards the phantom skull.

Falconara soon discovered what seemed to be a painting beneath the surface painting, just as he had suspected. There also seemed to be a heavy film between the two paintings—perhaps varnish, he thought.

"What in hell is this?" he suddenly gasped aloud. As he moved the black light over the area around the skull, he could make out feet nailed to wood, and as he moved the light up the painting further, a ghostly body appeared, and then one of the most recognizable faces in the world suddenly stared out at him.

"Jesus Christ!" Falconara exclaimed. The skull that had shown through originally was at the foot of the cross at the scene of Christ's crucifixion at Golgotha, which meant "the place of the skull."

"This is amazing," he muttered.

Trailing the light slowly back down the painting towards Christ's feet, Falconara could see a woman's shadowy, fearful face to the right of the figure.

Falconara was shaken. "This is really something," he thought. "Who in hell is she?"

He now methodically inspected the entire canvas by attaching the black light to a mounting device, enabling its embedded digital camera to take pictures of the subsurface painting.

He instructed the instrument to scan slowly over the surface. As he watched the scanning process, concern crossed his face. "What is going on here?" he thought.

Falconara could make out angels at either side of Christ's head. He also noticed that sizeable parts of the painting on either side of Christ had been painted over in black. In looking closely at these parts with the black light, he thought that he could make out very faint shadowy forms underneath, encased in black paint, then varnish, and the surface painting. He knew enough to recognize that the use of blackening was significant and seemed to be purposefully done. A disturbing feeling came over him, as if something were looking out at him.

And then he noticed something else: the initials MB artistically rendered.

"Whose initials are these?" he wondered, his face now registering surprise mixed with anxiety.

The ultraviolet black light also revealed the inscription "For my Marchesa," in Latin, near the initials.

He snapped a single, clear picture that recorded the details of the initials for the camera's application to analyze.

"Shit! What is this? I cannot believe it!" Falconara exclaimed when the identity of the initials appeared on the camera's screen. "Michelangelo Buonarroti! Ah, sure. This must be some bullshit hoax."

He rubbed his eyes and shook his head and then peered back at the initials to study them closely. "These initials must have been added," he said to himself. "There is no way—"

Then he remembered how, over centuries, people had found other masterpieces underneath lesser works. "If it was a fake, why would it have been painted over? Holy shit," he muttered as his pulse quickened.

Gasping for air and feeling suddenly claustrophobic, he feverishly covered the painting. He left the vault and closed its door securely behind him; his hands trembled as he set the alarms. A red light flashed, "Warning! Warning!" He now had only sixty seconds to leave the area before alarms would sound at the police department and throughout the palace.

Falconara's dark eyes darted furtively around to ensure that no one was there before he quickly went up the stairs and down the hallway to his library. He shut the door behind him.

It was the dead of night and a terribly haunting feeling came over him. Collapsing into a chair, he thought, "Could it be a painting by Michelangelo? Or could it be just some sophisticated fake?"

He knew of an unfinished Michelangelo painting found years before in the United States that had been valued at $300 million, even though its authenticity was in dispute. It had been done supposedly for Michelangelo's friend Vittoria Colonna. Falconara also remembered a leading Renaissance scholar and fine art dealer from London visiting his collection in Venice and telling him that a world-class Michelangelo painting, if proven real, would be viewed as priceless, as they simply did not exist in private collections.

Fitfully, fearfully, Falconara considered the situation. Here he was, the last heir to an illustrious Venetian family who had discovered something that he knew, if proven real, would have immense ramifications far beyond his own interests. Perhaps his current disastrous financial state was about to take an unimaginably positive turn.

"What should I do?" he thought. "Who should have knowledge of the painting? And if it is real, whose is it? Is it stolen?"

He realized that he could have major problems with provenance and ownership.

Falconara was no fool. Assuming that the work was authentic, he knew that many different people, for many different reasons, would go to any lengths to own a Michelangelo. Especially if it was one containing mysterious unknown subject matter. Who could he trust—if anyone?

He pulled out his mobile device, and at his verbal instruction, an application immediately displayed database information on the Falconara collection. Especially thankful now that he had added every possible security safeguard to his system to prevent outside surveillance, he checked the information on the Ziani surface painting. It was a gift to the Falconara family from the Patriarch of Venice in the early seventeenth century. It had been given in gratitude for their restoration of Saint Rose Marietta, a beautiful Venetian church built in 1420 by an earlier member of the Falconara family for his wife, Helene, a Duchess of Bohemia. The surface painting, *St. Mark Defending Venice against Satan*, portrays Venice as a lovely woman who, with the help of St. Mark, is fending off the seemingly predatory advances of a demonic man. The painter, Ziani, lived in Rome in the mid-1500s. He produced several other minor paintings, as well.

"Ah, yes, here it is," Falconara thought. "Ziani, a Jesuit priest, was also an assistant to Michelangelo in the Sistine and on various other projects.

"For all these years, has Ziani's surface painting protected a supposed Michelangelo from harm? But—why?"

He asked certain questions aloud, and the application researched works of Michelangelo and references to *Christ on the Cross*. Several paintings showed up, but nothing like what he had seen in the vault room. Finally, a reference emerged to a lost painting by Michelangelo.

"Fantastic! Yes, here it is!" A lost painting, *Christ on the Cross*, done for Marchesa Vittoria Colonna, the same woman the painting found in the United States was done for. The dedication he had seen in the painting, "For my Marchesa," seemed to confirm a link. Could the fearful woman's face in the painting have been that of Vittoria Colonna?

Falconara then clicked to a British Museum site referencing the lost *Christ on the Cross* and pulled up the chalk drawing for the painting done for Marchesa Vittoria Colonna. There he also found a cross reference to a statement by a member of the museum's technical team: "The painting resulting from this chalk drawing is lost."

"Oh my God, here it is! Yes! Yes!" he exclaimed, raising his fist in the air, unable to contain his excitement.

Though the British Museum's drawing did not include the woman's face or the black-out sections, Falconara was now convinced that he could possibly have the lost painting of *Christ on the Cross* painted by Michelangelo for the artist's friend, Vittoria Colonna. He tried to maintain a modicum of calm, as he wiped away perspiration covering his forehead.

At three in the morning, Falconara realized that he had a real security problem if this painting was in fact a Michelangelo. This realization kept him wide awake in spite of his mental exhaustion. After going back downstairs to recheck the vault and the alarms, Falconara returned to his huge bedroom suite and restlessly lay down on a large sofa in the adjacent sitting area, while Fara slept in the next room.

Awakened by his movements, Fara wondered why Falconara was up at such an hour. "Are you all right, Marin?" she called from bed. "What are you doing in the sitting room?"

"I feel nauseated, but I will be all right," Marin responded.

Fara, sensing Falconara's agitation, repeated her inquiry as to what was wrong. His nerves frayed, Falconara replied sharply that nothing was wrong. He just felt sick. "Please, Fara," he called to her, "just sleep and leave me alone. I will be all right, I tell you."

"Does your condition have anything to do with the painting, Marin?" She had noticed he seemed upset since he'd moved it away.

Falconara curtly responded that Fara should forget about the painting, as there was no connection between it and his current distress. But Fara knew Falconara to be the picture of self-control and suspected that something was afoot—and she intended to find out what it was.

Falconara's mind raced as he stared at the ceiling. He felt the world closing in on him. He would have to secretly get rid of the Michelangelo. Public knowledge would be disastrous for him, especially in his compromised financial condition. He would have to defend his claim to the painting, and he had no money with which to do so.

And then his thoughts returned to the critical question: "Who can I trust now?" Only Fara entered his mind.

Chapter 19

ARENELL' S ROMAN VILLA
LIBYAN COAST

RICHARD WATCHED as a camouflaged military jet helicopter with a large black "M" on the rotor mount did a flyover several hundred feet above an open grassy area inside his villa's security area. He had earlier notified security of the imminent arrival of the state-of-the-art Chinese-made helicopter, which featured advanced missile defense systems and laser turrets. Slowly, the craft dropped down towards the ground, blowing grass and dirt up in every direction. Once the pilot set the helicopter down and the powerful rotor blades came to a complete stop, a side door opened and a metal staircase unfolded onto the ground. Two armed Asian crew members in crisp white military uniforms moved confidently down the staircase, surveyed the area, and then made sure the helicopter was in a secure and locked position.

One of the crew members gave the thumbs-up to another flight member, and from the bay door a large armored Chinese-made Hummer military vehicle with roof-mounted laser gun turrets emerged and rolled down a ramp; there were two drivers inside. Then a side door of the helicopter opened, and out came a dark-haired beauty with blue-tinted aviator sunglasses, in a striking white Prada summer outfit with a large Chanel bag. Sao Damrey had arrived in Libya. She waved to Richard and turned to the other crewman just inside the door.

"*J'appellerais lorsque je suis prêt à être capté*," she said in perfect French. I will call when I am ready to be picked up.

"Of course, mademoiselle; we will await your call. Your security, of course, will be with you here, and will attend to all your needs as necessary. You will also be watched over by Central Command."

"Yes, I know," Sao said with a sigh.

One of the crewmen helped her down the steps, and she proceeded to greet Richard with open arms. The two embraced and kissed warmly. "Oh, Richard darling, feeling your body so close to mine washes away the many years instantly," Sao whispered, as they strolled away from the helicopter arm in arm to his villa.

"Sao, you look gorgeous. Time has treated you very well. And I still love that perfume you wear."

"Kudos for remembering, old boy. It's still 24 Faubourg, and I wore it especially for you. Yet I thought you only found nuns and other fifteenth-century women with no makeup or fragrance alluring," she replied, laughing.

"I do, but none of them will return my calls."

"Time has treated you well, too, since I last saw you. We are not kids anymore, but you still look great," Sao said, as she eyed his tailored linen slacks, handmade Botticelli loafers, and light-blue Eton linen shirt.

"I dressed for the occasion, as opposed to wearing my usual robes."

They laughed and hugged each other's waists as they walked past his silver twelve-cylinder Maserati Sport Coupe along the winding walkway to the villa's grand entrance. The blue Mediterranean shimmered in the distance.

The driver parked the military vehicle as the helicopter lifted off into the afternoon heat and haze.

"By the way, how chic arriving with your own military escort. Do you have these chaps along with you all the time?"

"They're discreet, Richard—but yes, they come along with my own satellite surveillance connected to Central Command, so we always know what is going on around us, especially when, shall we say, we are in 'less secure' parts of the world."

"That is what the Manchurian wants and that is what is done."

"I really have no say," Sao admitted.

"He is literally keeping his eye on you," Richard said as he looked up at the helicopter disappearing over the horizon.

"He is very protective of me, Richard."

"I am keen to show you my home."

"And I am keen to see it. I assume you enjoy this desert place?"

"Yes, I very much do when I am here, which is much less frequently than I would want. The sense of history interacting with the beauty of the present is compelling."

They entered the spacious villa foyer with its elaborate marble and wooden carvings. "You are still compelling to me, as well. Do you know that, Richard?" Sao leaned down to look more closely at a large blue-and-white Oriental antique on a side table in the foyer. A sea breeze wafted gently through the entryway from double Romanesque doors that stood ajar, leading to an open-air dining area overlooking the sea.

Looking at her, Richard felt the familiar urges of the past to embrace her tightly around her slender waist and playfully caress her lovely derrière.

"Do you still find me compelling, dear?" she asked, consciously leaning over to inspect other antiques, knowing that his eyes were locked on her.

"Unfortunately, too much," Richard thought as he again realized her continual sway over him even after all the years. "Yes, love," he said aloud.

Richard continued to show her through the rooms of the renovated villa, with its Italian-styled modern furniture and airy pastel coloring, interspersed with ancient Greek and Roman artifacts that he had collected over the years. She put her arm around him, as he put his around her, feeling again the intense sensation that only she could give off.

Finishing the tour, the two sat down together on a large, plush sofa on a canopied veranda overlooking the Mediterranean.

"What a lovely place and equally lovely view," Sao murmured as they watched the late afternoon sunlight cast its glow over the waves hitting the shore.

Turning towards her, he said, "You mean of the water, or of you, Sao?"

She now turned provocatively towards him and smiled. "Of me, Richard?"

"Yes, Sao." His smiling eyes focused ardently on her.

With that, Sao loosened the band on her lush black hair and shook her head so that her hair fell luxuriously around her shoulders. She took off her sunglasses to look more intently at Richard, who realized that he was looking into the spectacular green eyes of one of the world's most truly beautiful women. Sao's moist, full lips had parted, and, while still looking intimately at Richard, she slowly unbuttoned her top to partially reveal her natural and perfectly shaped breasts.

"I seem to have trouble keeping my clothes on," she said as she gently pulled Richard towards her.

"Sao, I can't believe I have allowed myself to be separated from you so long," he whispered, as she sensually reclined on the large sofa.

"*Venez ici, amant garçon,*" she said softly, bringing him down on top of her. "Come here, lover boy."

Warmly kissing her smooth lips and soft, sculptured neck, he sensed his strong physical feelings rising up. He firmly caressed her aroused body as their clothes slipped away.

"*Oh, mon cheri Richard, m'ont manqué cela c'est le cas.*" She arched her body and held him tightly, whispering breathlessly into his ear. "Oh, my darling, you feel so good—and so strong in..." she moaned.

The Manchurian's Russian guards were sitting outside of their vehicle in the last heat of the day, as they observed the surrounding area on a satellite surveillance screen.

"They have been in there for hours, Yuri."

"I am sure it takes time to show her the architectural details of the villa," his partner said, and chuckled.

"Along with his personal architecture, I am sure."

The men sniggered raucously.

"She is such a gorgeous piece, isn't she?"

"Boy, you are not kidding. The Manchurian always has the best in the world, doesn't he?"

"He is a man of wealth and taste, that's for sure, but very few have ever even seen him. And she is one of those few."

"You're right, I think she's the only person in the world who really knows him—or at least knows his real name."

Later, the guards watched as Sao and Richard emerged from the villa arm in arm. Sao casually remarked, "You are living in a marvelous antique, my Richard."

"You are right, darling, and, as an antique myself, I feel right at home."

"Not this afternoon, sweetheart. Your welcome was far from antique," Sao reassured him.

"Actually, I must say it was more *unique*."

"Why, I've had dessert before dinner," she whispered, softly kissing his neck.

Richard grinned while helping Sao into the Maserati and then, eyeing her guards, proceeded to the driver's side to get in. Sao lowered her sunglasses and looked over, her green eyes flashing playfully. "You know, honey, you'll have to turn in that great linen wardrobe covering your hot body for a monk's habit when you become a priest. But I am sure the nuns will be as wild over you as I am."

Richard jumped into the car's aircraft-like cockpit and spoke a code that automatically engaged a security code to block GPS surveillance, and the twelve cylinders roared to life. Looking straight ahead, he remarked, "You've got to love the speed of this roadster—and of you, too, love." He glanced at Sao with a wink and broke out into a broad smile. The car bolted onto the main road, followed by the military vehicle at breakneck speed.

She held his hand softly, leaned over, and kissed his cheek. "You're the best, especially when you look at me with those sexy bedroom eyes of yours."

The two drove along the shimmering seaside, with giant cumulus clouds hanging in the distance. After passing elegant, high-walled beachfront homes with heavy security, they entered another world of open-air vegetable markets and young boys herding goats along the road. Even in a modern Libya continually racked by civil war, certain things had not changed from the distant past.

As they sped along, Richard said, "I was worried about you, Sao. Did you know that?"

"You were worried about me?" She raised her eyebrows. "I didn't know you ever thought of me—except, of course, when you prayed for heathens."

"I always pray for my one very hot heathen," he said, with a wide smile and looking directly into her eyes. "Actually, your last contact said that you were going to Kyoto. Do you remember?" He put on his sunglasses to shield his eyes from the glare of the setting sun. "We were thinking of another stay, as we've done in the past, on Antibes at the Hotel du Cap. It was your idea, remember?"

"I remember, darling. It would have been lovely at their private Villa Eleana."

"And then two days later there was an earthquake in Kyoto, and I never heard from you. Forget about the rendezvous—why didn't you at least contact me to tell me you were safe?"

"Honey, I am sorry for not having contacted you; I was in the air flying to Tokyo the day the earthquake happened, and was buried in business issues," she said.

"In any event, I'm glad you weren't buried period. It just seems like there are so many big earthquakes all the time now," Richard remarked. "It's the simultaneous melting and freezing of each of the icecaps, you know. They used to keep the surface of the earth taut like a trampoline, so now the crust's loosening and shifting around, causing more big quakes."

Richard's car automatically veered to avoid a local taxi that had wandered into his lane.

"Whoa! Sorry, love. Fortunately this car drives itself."

"Don't worry, sweetie. I always feel safe with you. You're a tough guy, but you also have this connection to the Big Guy." She pointed her finger towards the sky. "I will *never* forget how we planned to get together at the World Trade Center the morning of the terrorist attack, and then something came up and you had to postpone our meeting until lunch."

"Thank God. I can't believe we were literally saved from certain death in the Windows restaurant by some problem I had to attend to at home," said Richard, shaking his head. "Seeing those planes hit the towers was like watching angels of death."

"Certainly put that argument we'd had into perspective, didn't it?"

"Oh yes, the art exhibit and that enemy of free speech, Giuliani," he said, chuckling. "But then you saw how Giuliani rose to the occasion that horrible day. His actions made him a hero to the world. Why, the Queen made him a bloody knight. Sao, God can raise you up from nothing when you defend Him. He came through for Giuliani, made him a hero in that tragedy, and eventually made sure Bin Laden was dispatched to hell."

"You will never let me forget. Yes, as it turns out you were right about Giuliani—but now, before I die from hunger, where are we heading?" asked Sao.

"There's my dinner club on the Med I think you'll like." Richard stepped on the gas, and the car sped down the coastal highway. Despite her relaxed company and easy-going demeanor and sexuality, Richard continued to wonder what Sao was up to.

"I take it the Manchurian's ship just continues on, and they fly back to get you wherever you are."

"Yes."

Twilight descended on the Libya coast, as Richard swung his car up to the armed security guards at the gated checkpoint entrance to the exclusive private dining and beach club. The club overlooked its own secluded beach on the Mediterranean. Entering the parking area, Sao's bodyguards parked their military vehicle amidst other patrons' bodyguards and heavily armored cars. The air was filled with the intoxicating scent of incense, fresh flowers, and meat roasting on a grill. The club's dining facility was a luxurious open-air setting near the beach, with a tradition of fine Italian and Libyan cuisine. The area glittered with soft white lights. Flowers, dazzling china, and flickering candles graced each table.

"Richard, this is so nice…and romantic," she murmured in his ear and leaned on his broad shoulder.

"Just like home, darling. I'm trying to make coming to Libya worth your while." With a wry smile, he stole a quick kiss on her lips while sliding his arm around her waist.

"Believe me, honey—you already did that for me this afternoon." Her long-lashed green eyes closed and reopened wide again.

Richard walked over to the maître d', a distinguished, middle-aged man wearing a starched white dinner jacket and black tie. Recognizing Richard, he pointed to the outdoor terrace.

"*Mais bien entendu*, Monsieur Arenell. But of course," the maître d' said, and in Arabic sent a waiter to show the party to the table closest to the water.

"*Merci, Akram. Vous avez un club merveilleux ici*," Richard replied.

As they waited for hors d'oeuvres to arrive, Sao, her eyes radiant, leaned forward and touched Richard's hand, casually brushing her leg against his. Her elegant strand of natural Baroda pearls gleamed in the soft candlelight. They were draped over her stylishly low-cut Versace evening dress revealing her ample cleavage.

"So," she said in distinctly feminine tones, "you were saying you missed little old *me*?"

Richard looked at her closely, his eyes showing warmth and caring. "Of course I have missed you."

"I would love to tell him, but I just can't—not yet," thought Sao. "I must know that he truly still loves me before I do." She glanced down, tracing her finger around the rim of her crystal water glass.

The waiter offered Richard a wine list, but he declined. "I believe I know what I want. A bottle of 2004 DRC Montrachet, please."

"*Ah, un superbe Bourgogne blanc*, Monsieur Arenell."

"*Je suis impressionné*, Richard," Sao added.

"I'm glad you're happy with the selection, love."

They took a few minutes to consider the menu and make their selections from among the finest culinary offerings not only in Libya but in the entire region.

"So, if I hadn't been found after the earthquake, you would have been distraught?"

Richard took a drink of water to clear his throat. "I would have been. I would have been *very* upset. You know that. I would think, however, that the Manchurian would be at the top of the list of those who would be distraught."

Sao deliberately touched his foot under the table with hers and said, "Could my Richard be somewhat jealous of my Manchurian?"

"I think he's a fortunate man to have such a beautiful, bright associate as a companion."

"Companion? I don't want to be overly sensitive, Richard, but I hope you are not implying something here." Her eyes narrowed. "What do you think I am? Some sort of 'kept woman'? If that's the case, that really isn't nice, you know. I have earned my position with him through my expertise in art, not through my expertise in bed!"

"I'm sorry, love. I certainly didn't mean to imply anything of the sort."

"However, the Manchurian makes all the sense in the world to me. We both love priceless art and, of course, very fine things, so that is why, yes, I am also his companion."

"Well, let's just say I would love to be your companion, too, one of these days, Sao." His dark blue eyes looked intently into hers.

"I will accept that, Richard, and will say I look forward to it."

"By the way, my dear, I should tell you that I am heading to the States to lecture on Judeo-Christian theology in art at the University of Chicago this summer."

"So…?" she asked with raised eyebrows and tight lips still reflecting her irritation.

"Well, I would love to have you come by. Maybe I would make more sense to you through my lectures."

"Honey, you already lecture me. As a matter of fact, I feel like you are always lecturing me. Anyway, I try to avoid extraneous travel because it is so difficult, even with our private planes, what with all this global terrorism, famine, disease, and regional warfare everywhere. If I didn't have access to my own jet at any time, I would really be concerned about traveling at all."

"The beginning of sorrows," Richard replied. Sao looked at him quizzically. "The terrorism, the wars, the famine and diseases you mention—we're in the 'beginning of sorrows' period, described by

Christ in Matthew 24, which could be ushering in a significant rise in evil before Christ's return."

"Excuse me? The return of Christ! Oh brother, here we go again," Sao said in utter frustration. She pushed her hair away from her face, her exotic eyes flashing; she grimaced. "Stop it, Richard! Here we are, at a romantic seaside club after a passionate afternoon together, and you start discussing the beginning of sorrows, the return of Jesus Christ, and the end of the world...*again*! Just so you know, the Manchurian and I never discuss stuff like this!"

She couldn't conceal her exasperation. "Now, don't get me wrong and start looking cross-eyed at me with those baby blues of yours. Yes, there are global problems; there's social unrest everywhere, assassinations of high-level officials and business leaders, terrorist attacks throughout the world. And yes, there is a Higher Being of some sort out there, but tying the two together? I don't think so. Anyway, I guess I am with the Jews and Muslims on Christ: he is like a great prophet, but a divisive prophet, it seems. Have you considered that perhaps it's Christianity and Christians that have been an impediment to solving the world's problems? As for rising evil, I think evil has been, and always will be, an invention of man. Evil has been around since the beginning," she concluded with conviction in her voice. "Frankly, I am favoring Elijah Nabi."

"Really? Elijah Nabi?" Richard challenged her, clearly taken aback. "I am surprised, but then again, it seems like the fellow's global popularity is increasing every day, doesn't it?"

"Yes, his popularity is increasing—and it should be. He's a wonderfully good person. As you may know, Elijah seems to be the only one who can calm down all these damn Muslims, Christians, and Jews from beating the crap out of each other. The UN loves him, and Iran has cordoned off a part of the country just for him. He's a real peacemaker, a holy kind of guy, which is good. Terrorism even seems to go into a lull whenever he speaks. He embraces the rising power and authority of the UN as being critical for world peace, as opposed to power being concentrated in a single country like the United States."

"I understand he is focused on uniting Christians, Jews, and Muslims into a modern secular society led by his own universal religion of man, consistent with UN mandates. Is that right?" asked Richard.

"Maybe he is, I don't know. All I know is that his words are very comforting to all of us in these uncertain and depressing times."

"You believe in him, Sao?" Richard asked with genuine surprise.

"Yes, I do, in a way. He is critical of 'judgmental Christianity,' as he calls it."

"You mean everyone goes to hell who does not believe in Christ," Richard responded.

"Yes, what's that BS? How do you think the Jewish and Islamic people must feel? I prefer Elijah, because he emphasizes openness and open dialogue among *all* peoples."

"Hopefully Elijah is not just another false messiah taking in everyone because they think he offers them a way of ensuring continued self-entitlement, money, and power," he said, giving her his boyish grin. "Christ warned us of false messiahs and prophets."

"Oh damn, stop already with the Christ stuff, Arenell." She grimaced and stared icily at him. "How did I know you were going to say something like that? Elijah is not like that at all. Why, Elijah likes the Manchurian employing all those Jews in the Oblast."

"The Manchurian knows Elijah?"

"They know of each other, but they have never met. Nobody *meets* the Manchurian."

"And do you know Elijah?"

"Yes, I do—now enough of that. You were talking about me being in Chicago for your lecture. Actually, I might need to be in Chicago about that time for business. I was planning on staying in a town called Lake Geneva, Wisconsin—just outside of Chicago. Do you know Lake Geneva?"

"Not really, just the one in Switzerland."

"Well, it's like a real micro version of the Hamptons, but without the attitude. I like to go there once in a while to visit friends. I own a nice place there; it was a gift from the Manchurian," Sao replied dismissively.

"How did the Manchurian wind up there?"

"He obtained ownership from a private equity group that had bought the place as a corporate retreat. He has a high-interest-rate global real estate finance organization focused primarily on generating defaults from borrowers so he can foreclose on their properties. Remember all those over-leveraged hedge-fund players and stock market billionaires with their castles and residences everywhere that they had to unload? Well, the Manchurian was there, with cash, and he acquired millions of square feet of high-end residential and commercial property all over the world at big discounts that way. He loves financial meltdowns. They create great buying opportunities."

"Generates defaults so he can foreclose? How sporting of him. By the way, does this mean I have your promise that you'll come to Chicago for my lecture?"

Sao slyly smiled at him for a moment, satisfied. "Yes, but in return for—"

The sommelier appeared with the wine. He opened the white burgundy and offered Richard a taste. "It is one of our absolute finest, Monsieur, as you know."

"I know, and it is perfect, I am sure." Richard sniffed the wine's aromatics, as the sommelier filled their glasses.

Shortly after, two waiters arrived at the table holding large trays. One served Richard a plate of steaming Mediterranean vegetables, roasted lamb, and curried rice. The other presented Sao with veal and a rare variety of eggplant, beautifully garnished.

Once the waiters were gone, Richard picked up the conversation again.

"You were saying you would come to my lecture in return for… what?"

Sao took a delicate bite of her veal, and then said quietly, "If you will help me confirm a rumor that I've been following for a few months now."

"Aha," thought Richard, "I knew it. Finally, Signature Sao emerges." Out loud, he asked, "What's up, Sao? I knew there was something behind your visit." Now it was Richard's turn to feel satisfied.

"Oh, please, Richard." She seemed to make a quick check of the other patrons before leaning very close to him and taking his hand. "Through his global art network, the Manchurian has learned that a work by a major Renaissance artist may have recently been uncovered in Europe. It seems this painting has never been on public display. In fact, it's possible that *no one* has ever seen it before. Not for several centuries."

Richard put down his glass and looked intently at her now. "And the reason?"

"Possible *pentimenti* is the most likely explanation," she responded.

"You mean a major Renaissance work under another painting?"

"Possibly, or maybe one that was considered lost, until now."

"Well, that does happen periodically. Any indication of who the artist is?"

"No. But the Manchurian has me working ceaselessly to obtain the greatest art in the world. And he is on to this rumor with a passion." She carefully cut another piece of veal and offered Richard a taste. "He's willing to spend whatever it takes to obtain a masterpiece, and that's what I am working on now."

"You mean so much so that he's even willing to redirect his small navy to find me here on the Libyan coast?" Richard said, tasting the veal from Sao's fork.

"No, Richard. We can find anyone, anywhere, at any time. As I said, the boat was already heading to Lebanon for some reason I know nothing about. I come and go off the boat as I please and when convenient. I have my own apartment, so it's like a home away from home. His flotilla is constantly at sea. It never docks, except periodically for maintenance in its home port on Sakhalin Island, in the Sea of Japan. It is mostly refueled at sea by one of his oil tankers."

"Like a shark—always moving." Richard, laughing, formed a fin with his hand and made a swimming motion in the air.

"Oh, *please*, Arenell. Anyway, here's my idea—if I'm able to locate this painting, I need you, along with my other team members, to rapidly verify its authenticity. I need your brains. Otherwise I would probably leave you to be a monk or 'born again,' or whatever you currently call yourself."

"So today was really about business, not us, wasn't it," Richard said rhetorically, an expression of sadness crossing his face.

"Oh, come on. Will you please *stop* already? Is that what you call this afternoon at your villa?"

"Sao, you never cease to mystify me."

"I still have deep feelings for you," she said simply, her green eyes looking directly into his. "Now, will you help me or not?"

"Despite what you may have observed today, I keep a busy schedule."

"Damn it, Arenell!" An exasperated look came over her face. "The Manchurian is willing to compensate you quite handsomely for your time. Simply name your price."

"At the moment, it isn't a matter of money, but time. I am in the midst of intense preparation for a worldwide lecture series. I'm scheduled to lecture at the University of Amsterdam starting the week of—"

"Please, honey, I'm asking you to help *me*. Please? This is very important to me. If you care for me as much as you say you do, and showed me this afternoon, this is the least you could do."

Richard was struck by the very real anxiousness and urgency in Sao's pleading. "Why pick me, Sao? There are plenty of experts like me in the field."

"Richard, for starters, if this is a major painting with issues surrounding it, expertise, security, speed, confidentiality, and trust become paramount. And I trust you completely."

"Thank you for the compliment." He sat back in his chair and scratched his forehead, glanced up at the ceiling, then closed his eyes for a moment. "All right, let's do this."

Eyeing her closely, he added, "If you do happen to locate this lost painting with *pentimenti*, you can call me. Wherever I am, I will come to wherever you are to examine it. I promise. But only on one condition."

"Whatever you want, blue eyes."

"My condition is that we meet again in Chicago for my lecture."

"You are truly in another world. But I accept your condition."

They finished their meal and gazed out at the dark beach and the Mediterranean. The soft dinner music had shifted to rock as they, along with most of the club patrons, made their way towards the outdoor dance floor.

"Shall I take you back to my villa?" Richard asked halfheartedly, knowing that Sao would unlikely accept now that her real mission was accomplished.

"That's all right. I'll have my guards contact the pilots, and they'll find a place close by here to pick me up. But first, let's walk on the beach. Tonight can still be about us, darling."

"I love you, Sao. I will miss you." Their eyes met and began to glisten.

"I will miss you, too," she said and hugged him as their warm bodies fit perfectly together. Their lips met in a passionate kiss.

With a gentle breeze from the sea meeting the sound of the music emanating from the disco, the two lovers walked down the moonlit path towards a distant sandy peninsula. Their arms were wrapped around each other's waists, and her head rested on his shoulder as they strolled until the seaside club was only a faint light on the shore.

When they were alone, she murmured, "I wish all of this could be so different for you and me, because I really do love you, too."

He gazed into her beautiful uplifted face, gently stroking her luxurious black hair; her exotic green eyes and sensual lips were enhanced by the moon's glow.

"Can we relive this afternoon, darling?" She began kissing his face. Her lips enveloped his, the breeze softly blowing her hair against his cheeks as he caught her captivating fragrance once again. She tenderly began pulling him down onto the soft white sand, the sound of waves breaking lightly on the beach in the background, and a blanket of twinkling stars above.

Chapter 20

CENTRAL INTELLIGENCE AGENCY HEADQUARTERS
LANGLEY, VIRGINIA

I would have never agreed to the formulation of
the Central Intelligence Agency if I had known
it would become the American Gestapo.

—HARRY S. TRUMAN, FORMER PRESIDENT OF THE UNITED STATES

JACQUELINE "JACKIE" FORD—a short, slim, studious brunette, a
member of Phi Beta Kappa with a degree in history from Stanford and
a master's degree in international relations from Johns Hopkins—sat
in her award-filled office in a restricted area within the CIA, scrutiniz-
ing a digital file. An unmarried, middle-aged workaholic, she was a
career senior special agent with the highest security clearance in the
Office of Terrorism Analysis.

A flashing news bulletin came across her computer screen, capturing her attention. It read: "It has been learned that the United
Nations is secretly reviewing a proposal to receive a massive stockpile
of military equipment from the United States in forgiveness of debt
owed by the United States to key UN-member nations. This would

be done to further strengthen the global military presence of the UN in the many parts of the world where there is continuous warfare, rather than relying on individual nations to bring an end to such disturbances."

"That would certainly bolster the UN's position as a major military force in the world," Jackie thought, sipping from her coffee and taking off her glasses to rest her eyes and reflect.

The United States was a superpower in decline—that was for sure. Over the years, she had grown weary of seeing the US and its allies, including France, England, and Japan, steadily retreat, helping to position the UN as the primary police force to the world, with a mandate to reduce conflicts and stabilize failing nations. She was not happy to see over the decades the rise of strong, emerging alliances between countries such as China and Russia, which had formed the Shanghai Cooperative and then brought Iran into their fold. These alliances were led, more often than not, by wise, "street smart" pragmatists, who regularly outmaneuvered the United States in world affairs. In Jackie's opinion, this was due in no small part to a self-righteous, politically correct US State Department led in recent years by a collection of naïve, unqualified secretaries of state. They were mere shadows of former greats like Henry Kissinger.

Acting together, these new emerging superpower countries now provided large-scale financial support to the transformed UN, and so they exerted significant control over its operations. The UN enjoyed such rising military and financial standing in the world that it had become a form of new "one-world government." Global leaders increasingly supported this vision.

As the US continued to incur large deficits funded by debt, it continued to be shorn of its financial status. Now, always on the verge of insolvency, the US had to agree to support UN initiatives. This, along with an educational system so dumbed down it had become a national security threat and a large permanent class of unemployed and underemployed, was why there was social and racial unrest, especially among the young. The United States was caught in an economic "Catch 22." The nation was now at a real disadvantage to achieve the necessary private sector growth to reduce the Federal deficits and create enough jobs, to arrest a falling standard of living. She knew this disaster did not happen overnight.

Jackie had her theories about the root cause: Henry Kissinger had said that the last time America had a true strategic vision was in the period 1945 and 1955. This confirmed her belief that during critical decades of rising foreign competition and global economic change, since the end of Dwight Eisenhower's presidency, who she felt was a truly qualified president for *his time,* the executive branch had been led by a gaggle of politicians from *both* parties who had been elected by, at best, a complacent public and become second-rate presidents with inadequate backgrounds and strategic vision for *their times.*

Deep problems continually plagued the country from significant net job loss to other countries to illegal immigration, stifling regulation and energy dependency. "Strategic vision? What vision?" She said to herself. Now she considered how this vision really had warped with the first black president of the United States. Besides a glaringly inadequate background compared to even his forerunners, two of whom were almost impeached; it seemed this fellow had a distinct socialist bend against capitalism. His campaign slogan of "Forward," was used frequently in socialist and communist ideology. "Well, at least he didn't have the youth singing 'Forward, Forward,' a National Socialist youth song," she laughed to herself. Instead he had been a strong proponent of a powerful UN. His vision was that, "All nations must come together to build a stronger global regime." With a sad end to his administration, she remembered Kissinger saying that this man had been primed to create a "New World Order." If only the US Congress had term limits and wasn't populated by vacuous "empty suit" career politicians, social activists, and multitudes of lawyers of the same ilk from both parties, virtually all of them blind to wastefulness and idiocy, which exacerbated the lack of strategic vision. This self-serving legislative circus had been focused more on funding useless wars, appeasing lobbyists for campaign contributions, and spending wastefully on politically correct social issues, rather than working with the executive branch to have a strategic vision to address the problems of today—decades earlier. As a result, an ever-increasing majority of the population had become dependent on the government.

The failures of government leadership over the decades had left the United States as a culturally divided and dysfunctional democracy with toxic politics and a collapse of civic virtue. "They perceived themselves wise and they were fools," murmured Jackie, suddenly remembering Saint Paul's words to the Romans from a Bible study lesson years ago and now applying it to the branches of government. The American Empire, with its sprawling, bloated government, had become a modern mix of Humpty Dumpty and Edward Gibbon's *The Decline and Fall of the Roman Empire*. She smiled wryly to herself.

Just as Jackie shook herself from her reflections, putting her glasses back on and looking again at the digital file, her computer beeped out an alert. It was her Israeli counterpart in the Mossad, Ari Engel, contacting her to video chat. Ari was a middle-aged, balding family man, who was in considerably poorer shape than he had been years back when he first signed on with the Mossad from the Israeli army's intelligence unit.

Despite their differences, Jackie and Ari shared a common professional role: they were two of the faceless, nameless gears in the global inter-governmental intelligence machine that worked relentlessly to curtail the flow of funding to terrorist groups of all kinds. They did this by searching for the ultimate terrorist funding sources, which increasingly included stolen works of art. Terrorists sold these masterpieces to rogue countries, corporations, and virtual city-states for exorbitant sums of cash. The buyers of the art were willing to make these exorbitant cash payments in exchange for the terrorists protecting them or leaving them alone. Many of these terrorist groups were also secretly aligned with virtual city-states, which utilized them as mercenaries or cyber hackers in the effort to expand their operations.

They said their hellos, and straightaway Jackie knew that something was up. The normally cool and laidback Ari had a nervous energy about him.

"Come on, what is it, Ari?"

"Jackie, you are *not* going to believe what I've just received. It is a most curious thing—frankly, the likes of which I have never seen before," Ari said. "And I could have sworn I'd seen it all." Jackie could see from Ari's surprised expression on her monitor that this was something truly out of the ordinary.

"What, Ari? Tell me."

"The Mossad has just received a very old, still-classified, top-secret OSS report from an unknown source in the Vatican, of all places."

"A report from *our* OSS, the CIA predecessor—and still classified?" Jackie's dubious expression was understandable. "That's incredible, Ari. We must be talking about a document from the 1940s."

"It just came in from our operative in the Vatican, who received it anonymously. Our guy says it would seem that the Vatican—or someone close to the Vatican—has been keeping it secret all this time," said Ari.

Jackie launched a search for background information.

"Ari, I've found a research report that tells me an OSS document, never declassified, surfaced during a deposition in the case of Alperin v. Vatican Bank in 1974. The case, in the District Court for Northern California, dealt with an accounting of World War II assets allegedly looted by Church officials in 1946 from post-war Yugoslavia."

Her words, though fascinating, fell on deaf ears. Ari was completely focused on the report in front of him, oblivious to the fact that Jackie was even talking.

"This is incredible, Jackie, just incredible."

"What is it, Ari?" Jackie was intrigued.

"You are not going to believe this one. This OSS report tells of trying to track down a particular copy of a book titled *The Secret Instructions of the Society of Jesus*. And this book contains sketches of—get this—faces of Adolf Hitler and others, along with a letter from Michelangelo, no less, linking the sketches to one of his paintings."

"Excuse me. Give me that again?" Jackie replied. Ari could see the increasingly amazed look on her face. "The artist Michelangelo?"

"Yep, that's the one. Sketches of faces, Hitler's included."

"Yeah, sure, Ari," Jackie said, smirking. "It has to be a coincidence, someone who looked something like Hitler."

"It doesn't say 'something like,' it says Hitler. Boy, those guys were having too many snorts at the old OSS." Ari laughed out loud. "They must have had some really severe battle fatigue."

"Sure sounds like it. You say this report has just surfaced?"

"Yeah, really, it's like a lost letter that shows up years later. This report's dated 1945 and it just surfaced from the Vatican—and I tell you, it's still marked 'classified.'"

"Well, what's the old saw about truth being stranger than fiction?"

"You're sure right, Jackie. It came to our section directly from our operative. It's as if it literally did not exist from 1945 until today."

"What was the Vatican trying to hide by keeping it secret?" Jackie wondered aloud.

"Well, let me send it to you on channel four," Ari replied, simultaneously sending a copy to Jackie and to his research unit for further analysis.

"Thanks for sending it. Because this arrived at the Mossad first, I have to report a security breach," Jackie added matter-of-factly.

"I'll try to find out more from our Vatican operative," said Ari.

"You check yours first, Ari, before we contact our own operatives there."

"By the way, before I forget, give me the codes on the Egyptian art company with the unusual fine art inventory."

"OK, Ari. Here they come."

Just as Jackie sent the code numbers to Ari, his confidential transmission arrived on her computer screen. Her eyes trailed down a separate screen containing the coded OSS memo.

She pressed the decoder key and began to read the detailed executive summary of an official OSS report of events surrounding the Wewelsburg Castle headquarters of the SS in Germany at the end of World War II. She learned of the contents of the Jesuit book and its links to Reinhard Gehlen, a former leading person in Nazi intelligence; Albert Richter, dead as of the report date; and a German woman named Mariel Mendenhall. She read of the Jesuits' research and their theory that the root of Jewish persecution over the ages was the demon Samael. The research noted that Hitler believed in the anti-Semitic teachings of Gnosticism, which were at the root of the Nazi Party and which acknowledged the existence of the demonic mass murderer Samael. Jackie remembered that the Gnostic idea of Jesus being married and having children by Mary Magdalene had been a major plot point of the book the *DaVinci Code*—an idea she found to be hilarious. But as she came to the end of the report, she could find no humor in the Jesuits' theories that the Nazis would eventually succeed in driving any surviving Jews in Europe back to the Middle East, where they would again face their age-old enemy Samael, and their ultimate eradication.

"Boy, this is really explosive stuff," she thought. "It certainly brings a different perspective to the historical and current problems in the Middle East between the Persians and Arabs—the descendants of Ishmael—and the Jews, the descendants of Jacob since Abraham."

It was undeniable that over the years there had been a rise in antagonism towards Israel. This antagonism emanated primarily from Iran, Arab monarchies, and certain other Arab states backed by Russia and China, who responded to Israel's military and cyber-attacks against its enemies in the Middle East. Worldwide, anti-Semitism was also on the rise, fueled by increasing animosity towards virtual city-states controlled by Jewish high-tech financiers, who were frequently accused of invading what was left of global privacy with their massive operations. Even the perverse Nazi-era "Protocols of Zion," defining the world as controlled by a conspiracy of a few Jewish interests, had been revived. Some of her CIA colleagues had to deal with the resulting terrorist attacks against these financiers and their companies.

And Christianity was also coming under frequent attack with decline of America, the last Judeo Christian empire—not only because of its historical enmity with Islam, but also from certain secular member countries of the UN's Security Council. With now complete linkage of billions of people by the Internet and social media, Christians increasingly compared these secular member countries to the future nations of the Antichrist, who would rule over all using modern technology, as described in the New Testament's Book of Revelation. Jackie was captivated as she read back over the description in the OSS report of the demonic faces and their purported link to Revelation and the Book of Daniel.

She remembered learning in college that Michelangelo supposedly did have visions, which he incorporated into his artworks, such as the Sistine Chapel. But visions of Hitler—and other, unidentified men—possessed by a mass-murdering demon? That was something else entirely. And who were those other men in the sketches? Obviously nobody recognizable to the OSS at the time.

Jackie stared out the window of her office to the flowery gardens outside, her mind racing.

While reading, Jackie had been doodling with the name Ishmael. Suddenly she looked at the page and replaced the *h* with an *a*.

"Oh my God," she whispered.

A chill ran up her spine, and she hastily scratched out the two new words she had created: *I Samael.*

Chapter 21

THE BRITISH MUSEUM
LONDON

ON A TYPICALLY FOGGY AND DAMP London morning, a woman in a black Burberry trench coat and dark sunglasses emerged from a chauffeured black Range Rover and briskly walked into the British Museum.

She had obtained security clearance to see the chalk study of *Christ on the Cross* by Michelangelo for Vittoria Colonna, which had been in the museum's collection since 1895.

After checking through security, the woman entered an elevator that took her up to the Department of Prints and Drawings. Upon announcing herself, the woman was promptly shown to a private viewing room nearby.

She sat quietly while the very valuable drawing was brought to her. A guard stood just outside the room as the aide set the drawing in place.

"Madam, is there anything more we can assist you with?"

"Not at the moment, thank you," she responded.

"Very well, then. The personnel in Prints and Drawings look to be of complete assistance to you," said the aide before leaving the room.

"Then watch while I upload a picture," she said to herself, a barely perceptible sneer crossing her face. She took out her computerized magnifying glass, which featured a concealed digital camera and a transmitting device, and peered through it at the drawing.

"It does look like the faces have been erased," she said softly, as if talking to herself. "Only very dim outlines exist of what would seem to be the faces."

A voice softly emanated from a tiny diamond earring on her ear: "So they were not thoroughly erased?"

"No. It looks as if the faint images could have been faces, but they're blurring out when I enlarge them," the woman quietly replied. "I am capturing and transmitting them to you right now at various enlargements."

"Make sure from your end that the erasures cannot be re-engineered to be brought back to the surface," demanded the voice in her ear. "After you have determined that, you can go."

The woman waited as the forensic system in her magnifying glass analyzed the chalk study. As she waited, she impatiently turned her ring with the lion's head and serpent's body encased in diamonds. In a few minutes, the response came back: the erasures were permanent; the probability of their being clearly recreated was extremely low, but not totally impossible. The erasures had been done unevenly and by fabric, possibly a soft cloth.

She turned and stood up, putting away the innocent-looking magnifying glass.

"Thank you very much," she said to the guard and the aide before exiting.

Leaving the viewing area, she walked down the corridor and took the elevator back to the museum's main entrance. Her car was waiting just outside.

"Who was she?" the guard asked the aide.

"She's some senior governmental type."

"What government?" asked the guard.

"The United Nations," the aide responded.

Chapter 22

PALAZZO ANTONIO ANDREA FALCONARA
VENICE

A FEW DAYS AFTER making his surprising discovery of what lay beneath *St. Mark Defending Venice against Satan*, Marin Falconara finally approached Fara Grese, who stood on one of the large pillared marble balconies of the palazzo. The day was overcast, and she had been watching storm clouds forming in the distance over the Adriatic.

"We must talk." His eyes searched hers as she stood with her back to the Grand Canal. "As you know, Fara, I am under intense pressure."

"Marin, I am going to try to remain calm here, but how the hell do you think I feel?" Fara asked anxiously, avoiding his stare. "You and I have been together for years. We've had good times and bad, but it could all be coming to an end with your financial problems, and nobody knows that better than I do. The party would be over for me, and I could end up broke and on my own."

Fara continued, still too upset to meet Falconara's gaze. "And now, to see a skull materialize from the Ziani painting, and the man I depend on, but who is going down the financial drain, rushing about, taking the painting off the wall, then bullshitting me about restoration—do you think I am a complete idiot, Marin?"

She glared at him with obvious contempt. "It seems like there is a lot of strange stuff going on here, and trust me—I am as sick of it as you are," she added.

Falconara sat down on a balcony seat and massaged his forehead while she spoke. He realized that Fara knew what was going on, and at this stage she was the only person he could trust. She knew everything about him and his problems.

"Yeah, you're right, Fara. We're in the same sinking boat here. But I think I have some good news for a change—which, if handled correctly, could bail us both out, big time." He paused before answering Fara's look of curious disbelief. "And it involves the painting."

"What is it, Marin?"

"It looks to be…it could be…Fara, I think it's a lost Michelangelo painting!"

"Damn you! Is this your idea of a joke, Marin? Believe me, I'm in *no* mood for your jokes." Her eyebrows were arched.

"It's no joke, Fara. The skull we saw is the skull at Golgotha at Christ's feet. According to my research, this could be Michelangelo's lost painting *Christ on the Cross*." He was staring wide-eyed at her.

Falconara did not yet want to reveal to Fara that a woman's face also appeared in the painting, or that some portions had been blacked out. Fara's expression was one of utter shock.

"I saw his initials, Fara. They're very distinctive. It could be worth a huge amount of money, if it's authentic."

"No shit, Marin," she said, looking at him fiercely.

"The fact that it's hidden under another painting could pose a major provenance problem, however," he continued. "This could involve many people claiming ownership, most particularly the museum in the Casa Buonarroti in Florence, which has many of Michelangelo's works. I am sure the museum would claim ownership if they knew about it and could determine whether it was stolen."

"Do you think it was stolen, or that Ziani covered it to protect it from something perhaps?" Fara asked with heightened curiosity.

"Who the hell knows?" He sighed and gazed out over Venice. "In researching Ziani, I found out that he was very close to Michelangelo, lived with him, and died a horrible death by fire in Michelangelo's mansion shortly after Michelangelo himself died."

"Meaning what?"

"Meaning, it was either a gift from Michelangelo to Ziani that went unrecorded because Michelangelo died shortly after giving it to Ziani, or else Ziani simply stole it from Michelangelo's heirs and covered it so that it could not be recognized."

"Of course, everyone will allege it was stolen, right?"

"There would be numerous allegations, I am sure, and I would have to defend against them and my ownership—and with what? I have no money."

"Let's get rid of it, Marin," Fara interrupted.

"I agree, but it will have to be done very carefully—covertly."

"And we should get it out of the palazzo, right?" Fara asked apprehensively.

"Right," Falconara replied.

"Maybe we could store it on your island. It's a virtual fortress with all that high-tech security," she said.

"I was thinking the same thing."

"Whom do we sell it to?" Fara looked at Falconara, her gray eyes narrowing as she thought.

"We need to research a potential buyer, and do it quickly," he replied. "I know of a number of major buyers around the globe who would do just about anything to get their hands on a Michelangelo. I believe our potential buyer could be an aggressive private collector, an institution, or even a country that just wants the painting and could care less about provenance or protocol because they rely on their own expertise and due diligence."

Falconara continued to think about who the potential buyer would be. Finally, he said, "All I know is this. We need to pick only one and go with that buyer. We cannot deal with more than one, because the losers could create trouble. I've read about similar situations in the past, where stolen art—Nazi or terrorist stuff—is discovered. The litigation can go on for years. You begin the process of finding the right buyer. I will get the painting the hell out of here."

Chapter 23

PRIVATE AIRCRAFT FACILITY
SCHIPHOL INTERNATIONAL AIRPORT
AMSTERDAM

RICHARD SAT IN THE luxurious lounge of Schiphol's private jet facility looking out at the various jets parked outside. All were overshadowed by a private Airbus A330 with Chinese identification markings, which was being loaded with golf bags and luggage. A small group of Asian men in casual attire milled around the lounge, laughing and conversing before getting ready to board. Richard reviewed the comments from his lecture at the University of Amsterdam on his mobile device while waiting to be picked up by Sao's plane. Sitting near him was a young man in a blue pin-striped Armani suit having an intense conversation. He used a microcell on his ear, which was designed to keep his end of the conversation quiet as well as garbled to any outsiders using listening devices. Richard noticed that he wore a yarmulke, the traditional skullcap worn by Jewish men.

"Is he captivating our people? You're damn right he is—as a matter of fact, he is captivating the whole damn country," the young man said in hushed but forceful tones. "The prime minister is more worried about him than that Manchurian fellow siphoning off our computer scientists. This guy's much more charismatic. Frankly he's a lot warmer and more loving than any of our own leaders." He paused to listen.

"Of course we are trying to figure out what to do. Do you think we are idiots?" he responded angrily to the voice on the other end of the call. "But we have to be careful. With all the anti-Semitism and 'Protocol of Zion' crap going around, Elijah Nabi is viewed as a comforting and compelling guy who can explain us Jews positively to everyone. His popularity is only increasing among our countrymen, who look to *him* for safety, of all things."

A worried look crossed the young man's face.

"Yes, he is extremely popular everywhere in the world and, yes, he has the backing of the United Nations," he went on. "They fly him around everywhere. I know we cannot trust the UN, but what are we supposed to do, start criticizing Nabi?"

He paused, listening again.

"I know we have at least one of our agents in his organization working to determine what his agenda is. But so far, it seems his only agenda is one of love, world peace, and announcing the coming of his god, who will be Messiah to all. Yes, this could be considered a threat to our established ways, especially with these miracles he's supposedly begun to perform."

His exasperation with the conversation was becoming apparent.

"Is he another Christ? Now come on, how the hell would I know that? If he raises someone from the dead, I guess we'll know—but then what? Hire someone to crucify him?" He laughed out loud before adding, "I'll be at headquarters shortly. I am waiting for our plane but will come right over when we land."

Ending his conversation, the man looked over at Richard.

"Shalom," said Richard. The man returned the greeting with a distinct Israeli accent. He looked Richard over cautiously, and then asked if he was Jewish.

"My father is." Richard shrugged. "As he used to say, 'We Jews are just like everyone else, only more so.'"

The man smiled grimly and nodded.

"What brings you to Holland? Here on business?" Richard inquired.

"Yes."

"Let me introduce myself. I'm Richard Arenell."

"Nice to meet you. I'm Alon Eban."

"Eban? Wasn't that a famous Israeli diplomat from the distant past?"

"You are thinking of a long-gone relative named Abba Eban. He was Israel's ambassador to the United Nations in the 1970s. He was well known in the world for his outstanding command of the English language," said the young Israeli with a sigh.

"Israel could probably use your relative's wonderful wisdom and common sense again today, what with the arrival of Elijah Nabi as Israel's self-appointed savior," Richard offered.

"Do you know about him?" asked Eban suspiciously.

"Of course, doesn't everyone? There's something about the man's appeal that disturbs me, though I can't put my finger on it. It's probably just that I am wary of overtly popular people who always seem, eventually, to disappoint," Richard explained.

"Mr. Arenell, your plane has just landed," a lounge assistant informed him.

Richard nodded. "How does the Israeli government feel about him? Do you know?" Richard asked, gathering his belongings for the flight.

"I have no idea," said Eban dismissively, looking away.

"Well, hopefully he's one of the good guys, because he's rapidly becoming the central figure of his own religion."

"We will see, I guess," said Eban.

The young Israeli stood up and uttered the familiar Jewish phrase, "Next year in Jerusalem, Richard Arenell."

"Yes, next year in Jerusalem, Alon Eban."

With that, Eban turned and walked over to the flight desk, as a UN satellite recorded his movements.

"We are being advised by our satellite that Eban is finally leaving," said a man from a remote United Nations location.

"Good, make sure it continues to track him. It was very difficult," another man replied, "but our agent in the flight facility believes he has successfully intercepted at least some of Eban's conversation."

Chapter 24

BOEING BUSINESS JET
EN ROUTE TO CHICAGO

RICHARD SPOTTED A SPECIAL long-range stretched version of the Boeing Business Jet, which could travel up to the speed of sound, pull up to a gate. Its lights were flashing and the Manchurian's markings— M 371—were distinctive in black on the jet's tail. Gazing at the jet's immaculate silver-and-white fuselage gleaming in the sunlight, Richard noticed unusual bulges on the jet's sides, which he knew hid the portals for the plane's missile defense system.

"You will be boarding via the forward entrance, Mr. Arenell," the gate assistant informed him.

Sao waited for him just inside the forward door, wearing flight slippers and a sheer, loose-fitting blue silk outfit. Her hair was in an impromptu chignon for the flight.

She felt the familiar surge of excitement when she saw Richard walking down the gangway towards the plane's entrance, with his smiling dark blue eyes and dimpled grin.

"Oh, Richard darling, I have missed you so!" She greeted him with a warm hug around the neck and a kiss as he entered the plane.

"Tall, dark, and handsome as ever," she whispered in his ear and nestled her body close into his.

"It has been dreadful without you, too, beautiful," he said, and laughed. He hugged her, lifting her off her feet, and kissed her.

"Let us know when you want the wheels up, Ms. Damrey," announced the flight attendant over a speaker.

"We can go now," she replied.

Within a few minutes, the large jet was taxiing out to the runway.

Richard and Sao took their seats close together on a plush sofa. They were automatically strapped in. The hushed murmur of the powerful jet engines blended perfectly with the soft background mood music in the ultra-soundproof interior of the luxury aircraft. This custom-built jet featured a small gym, and besides being able to fly at the speed of sound, it could also fly at altitudes considerably above those of conventional jets. There were two spacious residential apartments, one at each end of the plane. Everything onboard was discreetly bolted down, and seat belts were tucked out of sight but automatically available everywhere. The plane's two apartments were opulent, replete with teak paneling, magnificent art, gold fixtures, antique French furniture, and Persian rugs. There was also a conference room in the middle of the plane, between the two apartments. Information and communication was monitored there, with constant feeds coming in from every significant media and intelligence source in the world.

The jet was airborne soon after Richard boarded. They were heading west over the Atlantic in perfect weather, so the seat belts automatically released shortly after takeoff.

"Did you have any problems with security?" Sao asked as she sipped her tea from a delicate Sevres cup.

"You must be kidding." Richard laughed. "With virtual ID, the authorities have everything on frequent flyers like us, including our personal genome maps.

"It does come in handy, though," he admitted. "There was someone with my name on a watch list in Canada. A quick biometric scan and I was cleared to fly. They ushered me right through to the waiting area for passengers on private planes."

"And does this form of transportation to Chicago meet with your approval?" Sao asked with a flirtatious wink.

Richard looked around, admiring the plush surroundings. "I say it would be difficult to buy any first-class upgrade to this. Is there anyone else on board, or is it just you and me?"

"Just you and me, babe," she said playfully, touching his nose. "This plane is primarily for my use. There is a separate apartment in the back of the plane so executives with the Manchurian's businesses, or my friends, can travel undisturbed if they're going my way."

"Impressive. The chap is like an octopus. How many jets does he have?"

"I prefer 'Renaissance man,' my dear. As for jets, I have to admit I've lost count—he has one of the world's largest fleets of private jets, and one of the leasing companies he controls has some of the largest private jets in the world. He also has a fleet of state-of-the-art fighter planes with mercenary pilots, which he provides to countries so they can ramp up quickly to blow each other up." She laughed out loud. "We refer to his fleets as the 'Manchurian Air Force.'"

"I am sure aircraft manufacturers must adore him!"

"They sure do, along with the usual crowd of weapons dealers and merchants of death dealing in nukes and bio-weapons," she confirmed, looking at him over her cup of tea.

"That's really a bit edgy, love."

"Not really, Richard. When you deal in global weapons like he does, dealers and countries show up. They are kind of like a club."

"How charming, an old boys' club. In any case, the last time I heard from you, you said that you had something important to tell me. You've made progress in finding the lost masterpiece, I take it?"

"We will get to that a bit later, honey. First, why don't we order dinner?"

"Splendid," said Richard. "I haven't eaten since this morning."

Sao reached over and pushed a button next to her chair and said, "Geraldo?"

"*Oui, madam?*" replied the voice through an unseen speaker.

"*Nous va dîner maintenant.*" We'll have dinner now.

Almost instantly, two flight attendants dressed in crisp blue steward uniforms appeared and set the table in the formal dining room. Simultaneously, Geraldo entered their cabin and asked to take their appetizer order. Their *dîner* featured *tomates à la provençale* and *coq au vin blanc*, perfectly complemented by a Reserve Sauvignon Blanc from Vanessa M Vineyards, one of Australia's premier labels and owned by the Manchurian.

After dinner, the two settled onto a spacious sofa in the jet's elegantly appointed living room. The flight attendants had prepared steaming cups of Indonesian coffee and *chocolat noir biscotti*, and had turned the ambient lighting down to a more subdued level.

"So, when will I get to meet our host in person?" Richard asked.

"First, one does not *meet* the Manchurian in person. Second, whenever he feels a person would be of benefit to him, trust me, he rings me up." Sao stretched her legs across Richard's lap.

"That must mean that I'm of no current benefit to him," Richard surmised. He began to massage Sao's legs.

"You are so easily injured, sweetie," teased Sao. "If your involvement in our project wasn't important to its success, you would be flying with me to Chicago this evening, but in the next apartment." She laughed. "Just kidding, you sexy devil, so don't get offended."

Sao dabbed the sides of her mouth with a napkin as she nibbled on a biscotti.

"What's important is that the Manchurian recently told me that if, in fact, I do secure this rumored masterpiece through a private sale, a significant bonus—twenty percent of the total purchase price—will be coming my way. If the painting costs, say, three hundred million, I will receive sixty million dollars as a bonus. The arithmetic is so easy, isn't it?" she said with a smile.

"Fancy that, love. What does that work out to hourly?" he said, teasing her good-naturedly.

"Always the jokester, Arenell; but that is why I can't let him down—and I can't do it alone." She looked directly into his dark blue eyes. "And, by the way, I believe in a bonus system for you, too. Do you get my point?"

"Yes, I do—congratulations in advance, and thanks for thinking about me." Richard smiled and set his cup of coffee on a side table, deftly leaning over to kiss Sao in the same movement.

"Now do you want to tell me what progress you've made in locating this lost masterpiece?" he asked.

"By masterpiece, do you mean in finding you again, darling, or the painting?"

Richard smiled. "Actually, I could assume in finding me."

"I found you, and as a result I must say we shared special moments in Libya." She touched his face softly. "Didn't we?"

"Yes, we did, and I think we both came to realize that we can live with our differences. I am what I am, and you are what you are, but our caring for each other always seems to transcend our differences," Richard said, as he softly kissed her hand.

"I know I will tell him soon," she thought, "but he must feel completely comfortable with our relationship. I am not being fair by not telling him."

"Pardon me, Ms. Damrey," Geraldo said, entering the room. "A call has been intercepted by Central Command for you. They say it is urgent."

"Who is it?"

"A woman regarding a painting that she believes you are aware of. You have exactly two minutes to talk to her. Should I have the call routed to the plane?"

"Absolutely," said Sao.

"It's the painting, Richard!" Breaking into a grin, she quickly rose from the sofa and hurried to the conference room down the hall.

A short time later, Sao reappeared, beaming.

"We have it in our sights. It's the Old Master, all right, the one I was just telling you about." There was genuine excitement in her voice. "It resides in Europe with a guy who has a collection, and he needs to sell it immediately—financial issues or something. She talked and I listened. This is great!"

Sao did a little dance and leaned down to kiss Richard, her hair tumbling loose from its chignon onto his face as their lips met.

"Who's the woman, and who's the Old Master?" Richard asked, smiling broadly at her happiness.

"The woman is the owner's assistant. She said she is positive the Manchurian will want the painting, and they want him to have it, because the Manchurian's reputation precedes him. You see, everybody—collectors who want to sell, and the like—will always wait for the Manchurian to show up. They know that when he wants a painting, he will beat the best offer of anybody in the world. He acts very quickly and simply doesn't care if there are issues surrounding a painting. He has no problem with litigation—his only concern is getting actual possession." Richard looked impressed. "How rare!" she thought.

"Honey, I am going to get you to Chicago for your lecture and have my meetings. We can meet up in Lake Geneva. Then, I am going to head back to Europe to meet this painting's owner."

The sky outside was growing dark and Richard glanced at his watch; it would still be a few hours before they reached Chicago as they were not flying at supersonic speed. He did not want to remind her of her promise to attend his lecture, as he realized this point was probably moot. In any case, he did not want to interject touchy subjects now, with Sao so excited and happy. She couldn't contain the reason for her excitement any longer.

"Richard, you are now of definite benefit to the Manchurian—and you are about to meet him!" She leaned over and kissed him again, her eyes sparkling like emeralds.

"Geraldo, please tell Central Command to get me the Manchurian, and tell him it's very important," she called out to a hidden intercom. "As if it would be anything else," she added quietly to Richard. "Come. We have a specially equipped conference room in which to talk with him." Sao moved swiftly to the conference room down the hall. "She is something to behold and now an audience with his royal highness," Richard thought, rising from the sofa and stretching. "I need to tell her I am doing this for her, otherwise she can have her mystery man."

Entering the plane's spacious, windowless, paneled conference and communication room, Richard was truly amazed at what he saw. At the center of the room, as if floating in space, was a form of virtual environment: a huge, transparent floor-to-ceiling, highly detailed digital grid of the world in three dimensions, displaying all its countries, regions, cities, and topography. The marvel of modern technology was surrounded by cockpit seats for viewing.

"You know we can zoom in and see the smallest, multidimensional detail of any target, in real time," said Sao to Richard, then faced the screen and said, in a firmer tone, "Chicago."

A screen emerged from the grid in space, showing an aerial view of Chicago, the highways pulsing with cars heading in and out of the city.

"May I?" Richard asked, and Sao nodded. "Swift Hall, University of Chicago."

There on a screen before him was the very building where he would soon be lecturing; he could see individual students mingling on the front stairs in the last of the afternoon light. "Why, I can see what one of the ladies is reading," Richard said, chuckling.

"Of course you can," replied Sao. "The screens can instantaneously display any level of detail along with any quantitative or qualitative information you want. This allows us to immediately create multi-dimensional financial or strategic models. And the system can interpret verbal commands in multiple languages and respond in the same language."

"Now this is what is called keeping tabs on things," Richard said with a laugh. "Google maps are prehistoric, eh? I assume all the colors I see have some significance to the Manchurian?"

"Richard, you are so yesterday sometimes. Yes, certain digital codes represent his different operations around the world," Sao explained, then said a code. With that, the entire system disappeared into the ceiling, and a conference table and chairs unfolded from the floor. The lights automatically dimmed, then returned to full power.

"That indicates the room has been scanned successfully," explained Sao.

"The room recognized us?"

"Yes, honey, otherwise there would have been a system shutdown at the beginning." As she spoke, Richard remembered how his system had shut down when he tried to access information on the Manchurian's ship in Libya. "The Manchurian has created his own form of artificial intelligence security. Because he has his own cloud communication and satellites, the system is virtually impenetrable by cyber-terrorists. All his businesses operate on it."

Sao said another code, and then, "Where specifically is he?"

A system voice answered from out of thin air, "He is on the *Universe*. He will be with you in a moment."

"Are you sure he is there?" Richard asked.

"Not really. No one is ever sure *where* he is. It's like he is everywhere and nowhere," Sao answered. "Only the system you just heard really knows. Everybody interfaces with the system, which he alone controls. He can see us, but we cannot see him."

"He never uses video for calls?" Richard was amazed by the technology surrounding him. "The invisible chap is a bloody wizard," he thought, laughing to himself.

"Manchurian, how are you?" Sao had seen a signal light up, and she motioned to Richard to stop talking.

"I am fine, my dear Sao." The Manchurian's voice came out of the air as if he were in the room. "And my Sao is fine?"

"Yes, thank you, sir.

"Manchurian, as you can see, I have Richard Arenell here with us. Richard, as you'll recall I mentioned, is a leading expert in the science of art diagnostics and authentication, with an excellent reputation in the Old Masters."

"I know all there is to know about Mr. Arenell. Good evening."

Richard looked cautiously at Sao. "Good evening to you, sir." He instinctively looked for the source of the Manchurian's voice, before realizing the detached voice wasn't originating from any single point in the room. "It is a pleasure to finally meet you, sir. I have heard so much about you from Sao and, of course, from the rest of the world."

The Manchurian's accent was unidentifiable, and his voice carried a calm air of absolute certainty as he said, "Do not believe everything you hear from the world, Mr. Arenell—only what you hear from Sao."

Sao interrupted. "Manchurian, I think we have the lost masterpiece in our sight. I received a call from the assistant of a gentleman who resides in Europe. He owns the painting and wants to sell it to us in short order. The owner has financial issues. There are also provenance issues with the painting because, the assistant confirms, the painting itself is beneath a surface painting by another artist. The assistant did all the talking and it was very fast—she was clearly aware of and trying to avoid our sight, sound, and identity detectors. I could only listen. When I finish my meetings in Chicago, which will include a conversation with our competitors' representatives, I will fly back to Europe. The owner's assistant will notify me as to where to meet. She said to give her three days."

"Sao, does she seem to know what she is doing?" asked the Manchurian. "And did we get any surveillance track on her identity or location or her mobile device? Did we lock her to a satellite going forward?"

"She was sophisticated enough to know that we could immediately lock in on her and identify her. She had advanced anti-surveillance equipment defending her. She also had scrambler devices on her, and she was done before our people could bypass the devices. We do know the specific location she was calling from in southern France, and, by the sound of her voice, we were able to determine an approximate physical profile."

"Not able to lock in a satellite trace, though?"

"No. She had that blocked, and wrapped up the conversation before we could override it and lock her in again. The fact is, she was very secretive, but she confirmed the ghosting effect in the painting. All of which leads me to believe that we could be dealing with a truly major painting. Richard, what do you think?" She looked to him, hoping he would know to agree with her assessment. He didn't let her down.

"I would agree, Sao. Paintings that have been covered up have historically been found to be important. Common sense dictates that someone would only want to protect or hide a painting if it is valuable. Of course, if the painting *is* valuable, that can lead to provenance problems. And the circumstances associated with why the original painting was covered over can pose challenges, as well. An additional downside is the condition of the painting that has been painted over—unless it was done correctly, you could have a true restoration challenge on your hands, as you know.

"The fact that the painting is ghosting means that something is amiss in the pigment, and thus the over-painting process itself could have had negative effects on the underlying artwork. Did the assistant give any indication of what was appearing?"

"No," replied Sao.

"So we don't have much to go on in that regard," Richard commented. "However, from what we do know—and I'm just speculating here, sir—we could potentially be dealing with a lost painting by a major master as Sao said."

Emboldened by the continuing silence, Richard went on to suggest how to proceed. "Sao, you should do an immediate search of all currently lost paintings by major artists. Actually, most of the great painters have had lost paintings, and a number have been found over the years. Works by Raphael, DaVinci, and other lesser artists, such as Caravaggio, have all been found. The works of Michelangelo—both his paintings and his drawings—have been the most difficult to find of all.

"Of course, sir, you know better than anyone the value of a Michelangelo, because you own certain drawings by Michelangelo that are worth extremely significant sums."

"Yes, we know, Richard, and we have already done what you suggested," said Sao testily.

"I read about a small wooden Christ figure by Michelangelo found in 1963 that recently traded for one hundred and fifty million dollars," Richard added. "There was an unfinished painting of Jesus and Mary found in New York back in 2010 that would seem to be by Michelangelo and had a value of three hundred million ascribed to it. Of course, it would be worth significantly more today, though there is still some controversy surrounding its authenticity."

There was a moment of silence, which the Manchurian broke by asking, "Mr. Arenell, would you please consider being employed by us immediately as an advisor?"

"I would be happy to consider it, sir."

"That means he will," said Sao, with a wink and grin to Richard. "Mr. Arenell?"

"She is right, sir," Richard said aloud, while thinking to himself, "Damn, she always reads my mind."

"Thank you, Mr. Arenell."

"Sao, I want all the leading independent experts on Old Master paintings immediately retained but not made aware of anything as yet. The potential competition has good authentication teams, so I want to render all key outside advisors unavailable to them. We want this transaction to move quickly, and even though the seller seems to want us to buy it, we all know information can be leaked and competitors can try to move in on us.

"For your information, Mr. Arenell, Sao is heading to the States to meet directly with representatives of our two major global art competitors," said the Manchurian. "We need to negotiate an arrangement with them because they are almost as passionate as I am about acquiring major art, and they have recently become a problem for me. If this painting is a major work, they could become a significant problem."

"May I ask who they are, sir?"

"You may, Richard, but with a complete understanding of the highly confidential nature of this information and the damage it could cause everyone if leaked," Sao interjected, staring at him.

"Of course, Sao," Richard immediately responded.

The Manchurian answered with an air of derision in his voice. "The first is a certain high-level Saudi prince named Turki al Taqiy, who purchases his art anonymously through myriad fronts. We have learned that, because of me, he has had to align with a secretive virtual city-state called Blackpearl. This city-state, which started as a large US private-equity firm, now controls several small countries as well as a giant Brazilian agricultural consortium. Both entities, the prince and the Blackpearl consortium, are almost certain to bid against me for major works in both private and public sales. They all have limits, but they will make me pay, because they know I have no limits, and when I want a painting, I get it. I assume you have heard of them?"

"Yes, they are well known in major art circles, although as you said, they operate through myriad anonymous front companies and buying agents in order to protect their identities."

"I have learned that they now want to win, and have decided to join forces against me. There are also a few very wealthy Chinese trying to organize a consortium along with a rogue Russian mega-billionaire, a particularly obscene, crazy fellow who really believes that he is in our league, though he is actually too over-leveraged to be a threat. I'm not worried about him, but this unholy alliance of the Saudi prince and the city-state could not have come at a worse time. Of course, there is a downside for all these characters—although they know I do not have a limit, they are always concerned that I could drop out one day, leaving them with an outrageous accepted bid. I have already financially damaged the Russian fool by doing that very thing during fierce bidding for a Renoir. He ended up having to grossly overpay for it when I did not outbid him."

The Manchurian now directed his comments to Sao. "Have our team of experts available to move immediately, Sao, and introduce Mr. Arenell to them. They are in various parts of the world, and I would like all of them to assemble at one of our locations in Europe and be put on stand-by."

"Yes, sir."

"For your information, Mr. Arenell—"

"Sir, please feel free to call me Richard."

"Thank you for that courtesy, Richard. For your information, we believe that we are one of the most prepared—if not *the* most prepared—art authentication organizations in the world. Our equipment is equal to, or better than, that found at any major museum. This allows us to purchase the finest paintings on Earth, rapidly, efficiently, and with complete confidence. We have the most advanced equipment, specially made for me, and have experts in each technique, from computerized X-ray and infrared reflectography to chemical analysis of paint and canvas. We also have advanced painting subtraction techniques uniquely designed to discern and separate multiple X-ray images of paintings beneath the surface of other paintings."

"Impressive, sir."

Richard noticed Sao smiling at him.

"If this painting is on par with a Raphael or a DaVinci, what sort of figure are we talking about, Richard?"

"Solid nine figures, I would say," Sao offered.

"Richard?"

"It's definitely in that range, sir. Aside from quality issues and the like, we know that major museum pieces by Impressionists and Modernists are now in the three hundred to five hundred million US dollar range based on insurance values. The *Mona Lisa* is valued at close to two billion US dollars for insurance by the Louvre. As you know, sir, if this is a clean, significant work by a major master, we start in the solid nine-figure range and often go up from there."

"I understand," said the Manchurian.

"And of course, there are the issues of provenance, sir."

"Of course, that is why I have a worldwide battery of attorneys specializing in those matters. We have dealt with such issues previously, and make financial arrangements with the seller until provenance and ownership issues are resolved. I always prefer to defend a work in my possession against claimants, rather than outside of it."

He shifted his attention. "Sao, please keep me informed of any developments. I *want* to get this particular painting, and I am fully prepared to do whatever is necessary to make that happen. I will stop at *nothing* to get it—and I will be most *upset* if I don't," the Manchurian added with, for the first time, a mildly threatening tone.

"Of course, sir, we totally understand," said Sao. Richard knew her well enough to read the barely perceptible apprehension on her face.

"That's all for now," the Manchurian said in closing.

"Goodnight, sir," they both replied. The Manchurian had already disengaged.

"Your employer seemed a bit edgy, love. Maybe he is more knowledgeable than we think about this particular work of art," Richard remarked as they walked out of the conference room.

"He gets that way at times," she admitted. "Darling, let's go into the lounge. I want to show you the plane's star machine. The walls and ceiling of the plane effectively disappear in that room, and we'll be able to watch all the stars outside and more, just like on the beach in Libya again. OK?"

"It sounds lovely, my dear," said Richard, putting his arm around her waist and pulling her close.

The Boeing, now cruising at eight hundred miles an hour at fifty thousand feet, its identifying lights flashing, headed west through the calm night skies towards the United States, under constant surveillance from the Manchurian's Central Command satellites.

Chapter 25

THE INSTITUTE FOR PUBLIC ENLIGHTENMENT AND PEACE
ROME

The world is now more…prepared to march towards a world
government. The supranational sovereignty of the intellectual
elite and world bankers is surely preferable to national
auto-determination as practiced in past centuries.
—DAVID ROCKEFELLER, FORMER CHAIRMAN OF CHASE MANHATTAN
BANK AND FOUNDER OF THE TRILATERAL COMMISSION

EDUARD RAVA WAS ABOUT to place a call to Fara Grese. A former leading official in the Jesuit hierarchy in Germany, Rava was now one of the senior fellows at the Institute for Public Enlightenment and Peace, an elite global think tank. This powerful organization was on the level of other groups, such as the Trilateral Commission, that advocated a strong New One-World Order.

The institute occupied a magnificent pink-and-white marble mansion in Rome, the former Villa von Waldeck. The villa was once owned by a German princess, but during World War II a branch of Josef Goebbels's Third Reich Ministry of Public Enlightenment and Propaganda in Italy occupied it. A German sculpture of a black leopard served as an imposing centerpiece in the courtyard.

The institute's membership was kept secret, though it was believed to include a wide range of extraordinarily wealthy patrons worldwide, along with representatives of certain member nations of the United Nations Security Council. All members were elected by secret ballot. The membership was known to have a deep, wide network of connections throughout the world. This network included the heads of major companies in every business sector, primarily media and financial, along with former heads of state, including former secretary-generals and presidents of the United Nations. The institute had very modern, secular leanings, and it was rumored to be covertly anti-Israel and anti-Christian. It was also an avid supporter of the "peace-keeping" one-world doctrines of the United Nations.

Rava had known Fara for many years before she met Marin Falconara, and had gotten to know Falconara through her. They were all members of high society in Venice and Rome. Rava pressed a small video monitor in his mobile device with his index finger— the same finger graced by his signet ring bearing a lion's head on a serpent's body.

A butler at Palazzo Falconara answered on a mobile video, which displayed a live image of Rava.

"May I speak to Fara Grese, please?"

"May I tell her who is calling, sir?"

"Yes. This is Eduard Rava. She knows who I am."

"Thank you, sir."

Fara came on screen almost immediately. "Eduard, how are you? I trust you're well?" She carried her portable device over to a chair and sat down.

"Very fine, my dear Fara. And you? It has been a while."

"These are very interesting times for me, Eduard."

"I presume especially in the area of fine art disposition, Fara?"

"What do you mean by that, Eduard?" Rava noticed Fara tense up and couldn't miss her angry stare.

"Fara, I plan on being in Venice in two days and would like to meet with you."

"Pardon me, Eduard, but what the hell did you mean by that comment about fine art?"

"Please, Fara, let us meet, and I will tell you then."

"I want to know right now, damn it. What did you mean, Eduard?" Fara switched off the video on her device so that Eduard could no longer see her, but her voice remained both angry and nervous.

"Why did you turn off the video, Fara?"

"Because I damn well felt like it, Eduard."

"Please, Fara. Calm down. You and I go way back and have always had many common interests. I would not want to have to relate to Falconara what those common interests are. And as you also know, being close to the UN, we are always provided with the information we need in order to further global enlightenment and peace."

Despite the darkened video screen and Fara's momentary silence, the tension was palpable.

"Cut the shit about global enlightenment and peace, Eduard. You must truly think I am an idiot. What are you telling me—that I need to meet with you in Venice as soon as possible?"

"Yes, Fara, that would be very good. And please keep this conversation to yourself for the time being, until we meet."

"I will let you know the time and place, Eduard."

"I knew I could count on you."

Fara ended the call. Fear and anxiety had transformed her face. "The son of a bitch knows about the painting and is trying to extort me. How did that happen?" she thought. "I know what he must be thinking about in connection with the painting."

Chapter 26

THE BAHA'I TEMPLE
WILMETTE, ILLINOIS

*The nations are ready to give the kingdoms of the world to any
one man who will offer us a solution to our world's problems.*
—ARNOLD TOYNBEE, BRITISH HISTORIAN

*Evangelist Pat Robertson has said…we should have a world
government, but only when Christ arrives…to achieve world
order before that time is the work of the devil. Well, join
me, I'm glad to sit here at the right hand of Satan.*
—WALTER CRONKITE, FAMOUS BROADCAST ANCHOR FOR CBS NEWS

ON THIS LATE SPRING DAY only a few sailboats rocked gently
in a Lake Michigan harbor ten miles north of downtown Chicago,
in the upscale North Shore suburb of Wilmette. The boats were all
that remained of a once-thriving private yacht club, now closed due
to lack of membership—a clear reflection of the economic realities of
twenty-first century America. Not far away, however, pandemonium
was breaking out.

The commotion centered on the imposing 137-foot Baha'i Temple, known as the Mother Temple of the West for the Baha'i faith. The normally quiet, tree-lined streets surrounding the temple were blanketed with hundreds of thousands of people waiting to view the coming of a special man.

The massive white temple with nine sides and an ornate dome symbolized the unity of all the world's major religions. One of those major religions was the Baha'i faith itself, founded by Bahá'u'lláh, a Persian born to nobility in the nineteenth century. Baha, as he was known, had claimed to be the latest manifestation of God at the time, and a prophet just like the earlier prophets Abraham, Moses, Christ, Mohammad, Krishna, Zoroaster, and Buddha.

This bright spring day, however, was like no other, because today a new prophet would appear—a man proclaimed by many to be the latest manifestation of God. His name was Elijah Nabi. After being welcomed by Baha'i officials, Nabi would speak directly to the people of the world, living in a state of permanent unrest in this new Dark Age. They had lost faith and confidence in the world's secular governmental and religious leaders and yearned for a renewal of the peace, security, and prosperity of the past.

This was a rare public appearance for Elijah Nabi. Normally the omnipresent Nabi communicated to the world only through global media and social networking systems, never in person. Now a world-wide audience estimated to be several billion strong would watch his arrival and speech simultaneously, on every communication device imaginable.

Impassioned chants rose from the masses gathered in anticipation of Nabi's arrival:"Oh, Prophet Elijah, oh, Prophet Elijah," "Speak to us the truth!" and "Restore our faith like no other can."

Nabi—a powerfully magnetic, charismatic figure—possessed great knowledge and vision. He was also said to perform miracles. Originally mistaken as one of the prophets of God known in Revelation as the Two Witnesses, this person named Elijah was neither from an Islamic, Christian, or Jewish faith, nor from any other religious tradition. Nabi instead forged his own faith and spirituality, and was now one of the most recognized people on Earth. He had written a hugely popular, bestselling e-book, which, along with the miracles he had performed, had brought him widespread recognition and considerable fortune. Entitled *A Road to Universal Spirituality, Peace, and Prosperity,* his book was a guide to unlimited potential for human beings in thought and action. Nabi's thinking and beliefs were consistent with the UN's one-world government objectives, thus the UN provided him complete support at all levels.

Nabi was seen as a patron, scholar, humanitarian, and spiritualist who believed in human goodness. People of all faiths throughout the world loved Nabi's warm smile and his mesmeric personality. He had billions of "friends" on social media networks worldwide, and his pronouncements were followed by an equal number on a daily basis. His soothing voice projected hope to a world depressed by the violent times of the new Dark Age. Nabi had now come to the heartland of America in order to attend private meetings and to speak his message of world unity, peace, and spirituality.

Richard had seen Nabi's tumultuous arrival in Chicago on his mobile device. With his lecture preparation completed at the University of Chicago, Richard went to the North Shore on a helicopter to a waiting car all arranged by Sao. He briefly visited his literary friend, Roberta Rubin, at her famous Book Stall bookstore in Winnetka and then headed to the gathering to see this worldwide personality that Sao herself believed in. To his surprise, Sao managed to obtain electronic credentials allowing him entry to the event, personally approved by one of Nabi's assistants.

"It pays to know this fellow," Richard reflected, as he stepped out of his town car.

Once he was confirmed to be Richard Arenell and, more importantly, a personal friend of Sao Damrey, he was graciously admitted to a cordoned-off section of the magnificent interior of the Baha'i Temple reserved for select media representatives and VIPs. Richard looked up at the soaring, twelve-story interior of delicate lacework carved in marble. The light from the building's many windows reflected off the gleaming interior surfaces. On the ceiling were the words "God Is Most Glorious."

Richard was standing near a guarded section close to where Nabi would be speaking. He heard the unmistakable sound of jet helicopters approaching.

Outside, everyone watched as Nabi's light blue armed United Nations jet helicopter and two guard helicopters circled high around the temple, then slowly descended to a secured landing pad next to it. Hundreds of local police, state police, and plainclothes UN security guards surrounded the entire area.

Elijah Nabi emerged onto a red carpet wearing lustrous white robes, white slippers, and a small white-and-gold skullcap said to symbolize the great mystery of radiance, light, and glory.

Richard watched with fascination as an ear-splitting roar of approval and energy consumed the building. It sounded as if a rock star were stepping on stage. Nabi had arrived and was entering the temple.

And there was the same chant, repeated over and over: "Speak your truth, Elijah, like no other can."

What Richard observed was a man of medium height with a warm, welcoming smile exposing perfect white teeth. He had dark hair and a pale complexion, smooth facial features, and deeply penetrating eyes. Hundreds inside the temple, and hundreds of thousands more outside, screamed, "Elijah Nabi has arrived!" Richard figured a number of the people in the assembled crowd knew, as he did, that *nabi* was the Hebrew word for prophet.

National, state, and city officials were the first to speak, officially welcoming the international celebrity.

"We want to hear the truth from Elijah Nabi, not you," people yelled. The multitudes began to angrily chant his name and stamp their feet. Immediately silenced by the hostile uproar from the masses, the officials and politicians abandoned their welcome speeches and motioned for Nabi to take over.

Richard closed his eyes and rubbed his forehead at the loud shrieks emanating from the swarms of people. Both inside and outside the temple, the crowd exploded with thunderous applause and cheering as officials and members of the clergy either embraced or knelt before Elijah Nabi, one after another. Richard thought to himself about the Old Testament verse from Deuteronomy about idolatry. The group then joined hands with a smiling Nabi, who looked out at the throng as he raised his arms in a show of unity intended for the media.

The officials and clergy returned to their seats, and complete silence fell inside the cool, white marble edifice. Outside, the crowd became quiet, watching and listening, transfixed. Many of them carried a device that picked up a transmission from inside the temple and projected a virtual-reality screen in the space in front of the viewer. Nabi's words could be instantly translated into virtually every one of the world's languages and dialects, for people who were viewing locally and around the world.

"I love you, my brothers and sisters of our one world," Nabi said in English. "I love you!" he shouted out again, fully extending his arms in the air. This gesture was met immediately by thunderous applause.

"I greet you in the name of *my* Messiah from God, who when he comes will be the messiah for *all* and blind to the differences among those followers of Allah and Jehovah, Buddha and Krishna, the Great Spirit and the Galilean Christ. I greet you on behalf of my Messiah from God, who will show us all the highest spirituality and goodness, and will demonstrate to all true love without qualification.

"For this wonderful Messiah, I am not worthy of carrying his sandals."

After that passionate opening statement, there was a moment of silence before the crowds once again erupted into resounding and continuous applause.

Millions of secular people believed Nabi was not the prophet Elijah of the Old Testament, but a forerunner of their Messiah to come. Richard, however, was surprised to hear Nabi paraphrase John the Baptist, who had said that he, John, was not worthy of carrying Christ's sandals.

"My brothers and sisters, you are no doubt inspired, as I am, by this magnificent house of worship of the Baha'i. With its nine sides depicting the essential unity of all the world's great faiths, it is testimony to the fact that God, through my Messiah to come, will guide us into ever-ascending levels of spiritual knowledge, enabling us to gain wisdom equal with his own, as man grows to be like God and to achieve the true human liberation and eternal life that God wants for all of us."

"What was that he just said?" Richard wondered in disbelief. He recognized these as the three-fold points of ancient paganism, in existence since before the birth of Christ.

Nabi continued. "No longer should the Jew fear the Muslim, nor Christian fear Hindu, nor Buddhist fear Sikh, for man will be entering into a New Enlightenment, an age of global unity and order, a one-world religion as my Messiah from God becomes all the world's Messiah."

His words were met with another round of nearly deafening applause, as Richard again shook his head in disbelief.

Nabi spoke for another twenty minutes on restoring prosperity, saving the environment and endangered species, fostering peace through global economic initiatives for the disadvantaged, and promoting advanced birth control methods dictated by the United Nations. He also outlined his unique plan for the nation of Israel to become a United Nations protectorate for its own security. The crowd stood transfixed by the compelling power of his personality and oratorical skill.

Once his speech was over, there was time for prearranged questions. His aide read the first: "What about governmental and business corruption in all countries of the world? This has always been a major problem, which has led to significant financial loss worldwide."

Nabi nodded his agreement. "It is as the questioner said. But with the major advancements in biometric identification, as is being done in India and China, and financial software techniques, the UN, in conjunction with the world's major countries and financial institutions, is proceeding with developing a comprehensive system that will be able to identify every single person definitively and track every monetary transaction that takes place on the planet. All world citizens will eventually be required to have all of their information invisibly embedded on their hands. Corruption will become virtually impossible under a system of such exact and instantaneous identification and monitoring. No one will be able to divert funds, for example, because it will be impossible to hide such transactions in the completely transparent financial marketplace of the future. This is as it should be in a world economic system that benefits all. It is a small price to pay for the end of corruption and deprivation."

Richard thought, "The UN will know my monetary transactions from anywhere on Earth? With complete knowledge comes complete control." He cynically laughed to himself.

The expansion of e-terrorism had already ushered in an era of nearly complete loss of privacy. Governments, along with the UN, tasked with bringing "peace" to the world, had unlimited access to an enormous amount of data on everything and everyone in order to fight terrorism and quell the extensive social unrest worldwide. It was no wonder the secular common man had lost faith in these political leaders assembled here and had grown afraid of what was happening to the world. People increasingly believed that something ominous was ready to befall both the planet and the human race. Others, believing in scripture, feared that widespread technology had created an incredible dependency on a false god tethered to electricity for power. In any event, Richard knew all too well that there was no place to hide—unless one were wealthy enough to afford the latest private networks and cloud technology to keep one's communications, identity, and location private.

A reporter interrupted the next question by shouting, "Specifically who is your Messiah—Jesus Christ? And if not Jesus, then who?"

Nabi looked at his aide, who angrily began to read the next pre-arranged question. Before he could do so, Nabi shook his head and said, "I will answer my brother's question."

There was absolute quiet as the crowd realized the reporter had violated the questioning process and was now being surrounded, as a precaution, by UN security personnel.

Nabi answered by saying, "My Messiah is the truly Anointed One and is not Christ. For unlike the Galilean Christ with his judgments and parables, which have divided men over history, my Messiah from God will unite all harmoniously with his perfect relativism, which, many times, is all that distinguishes between what is good and what is evil.

"In a world striving for eternal peace, there can be no room for eternal punishment. For my Messiah, when he appears on Earth, will be seen as the perfect man—unlike Christ, with his insistence on his absolute uniqueness as God and his being separate from man. My Messiah from God will also be among the living, for all the prophets, including Christ, are no longer among the living. And let no one deceive you. They never will be again." A wide smile spread across Nabi's face.

There was a sudden, reflective pause, but then the mesmerized audience broke into raucous cheers and applause once again, and chanted, "Long live Elijah Nabi!"

With that, Nabi waved off further questions and said, "Thank you, my faithful ones." Clasping his hands in prayer, he looked towards the heavens and strode out of the temple. A large contingent of armed UN guards now suddenly appeared and formed a phalanx three-men deep surrounding Nabi, so that he could no longer be seen, as he walked out the door. His private UN jet was standing by at a nearby airport to take him to New York.

As Richard left the temple, amid the noise of departing helicopters and police sirens, he looked back on it and the tracery on its towers. Intertwined there, he recognized the symbols of many of the world's religions, including the cross, the star and crescent, and the Star of David. Yet what particularly caught his eye were the ancient pagan symbols having arms bent at right angles, which became the twisted cross that had, in modern times, come to symbolize Adolf Hitler and Nazism.

The next day, the world watched again as Elijah Nabi, greeted by yet another deafening round of applause, addressed a standing-room-only audience at the United Nations General Assembly.

Nabi shouted and, waving his arms, said, "Let me begin, members of the General Assembly, with a saying from Paul-Henri Spaak, your first president. This wise man said, 'We do not want another committee. We have too many already. What we want is a man of sufficient stature to hold the allegiance of all the people and to lift us up. Send us such a man, and whether he is from God or the devil, we will receive him.'"

Then, at the top of his lungs, Nabi cried out, "Let me then say to all of you in the world—I bring good news! The wish of the United Nations for that man to come who will hold the allegiance of all people will be answered before this generation passes away."

His ringing statement was met with a standing ovation as the gathered crowd erupted in wild applause. Nabi stood with his arms outstretched. His gleaming white teeth were framed by a broad and charismatic smile, as the masses before him chanted over and over again, "Hail Elijah Nabi, hail Elijah Nabi forever!"

A commentator remarked that he had not seen such a response at the UN General Assembly since a time long ago when Mahmoud Ahmadinejad had spoken there. Afterwards, Ahmadinejad said that while he was addressing the assembly he had "felt a halo over his head." The commentator went on to say that assembly members that day had been seemingly hypnotized and transfixed by the Iranian leader's oratory. The reason for their entranced state was that they had been under the control of a "hidden presence," according to Ahmadinejad.

Chapter 27

LAKE GENEVA, WISCONSIN

WEARING HER FAVORITE Escada jeans and Chanel flats, Sao sat alone in the late afternoon on the large columned veranda of an estate known as Heatherhurst, on the shores of Lake Geneva that the Manchurian had gifted to her because she liked to go there. Earlier in the afternoon, to unwind from intense, back-to-back morning meetings in Chicago, Sao had taken a ride down a long, winding road called Snake on a locally made vintage Stateline motorcycle, her hair flowing behind her from under a bandana. She rode from the estate to the quaint upscale resort town of Lake Geneva, then around the south shore of the large lake and back to the property. The town was only seventy miles north of Chicago, yet it always seemed one step removed from world turmoil. It was still a favorite place of very wealthy Chicagoans, with their magnificent summer "cottages" dating back to the 1800s.

Sao was expecting the Manchurian's art competitors to arrive shortly. After meeting with them, she looked forward to a relaxing dinner at the estate with Richard, her close friends from Palm Beach and Paris, Eugene Kite and Nicole Gerard, who, along with her Lake

Geneva friends the Fhillips and Friedmans, all owned residences on the lake.

In the distant past, Heatherhurst—named after the daughter of the original owner, a dynamic Chicago insurance company entrepreneur—had been the site of glittering formal galas given by him before he tragically died from brain cancer. Located in the exclusive area of the lake known as the Gold Coast, the twenty-acre property had as its centerpiece an imposing Colonial Revival–style mansion featuring fifteen bedrooms, large formal rooms, and an enormous chandeliered ballroom with giant murals. An expansive lawn, dotted with verdant gardens, surrounded the Snake Road property and swept down to the lake. The compound was built in 1929, just before the Great Depression. For the most part, the estate was generally only occupied by cleaning crews and resident caretakers. The Manchurian had never been there.

The jet seaplane of the art competitors' representatives landed on the lake and proceeded to the estate's pier complex. The late-afternoon sun reflected a golden glow on the lake's still waters as Sao watched the seaplane come to a stop and the man and woman disembark. She walked down to greet them just as they started up a tiled walkway in her direction.

"Welcome to Heatherhurst and greetings from the Manchurian to both of you. It is good to see you again," Sao called out. "But not necessarily under these circumstances," she silently added.

"Greetings to you and to the Manchurian, from our clients," answered the woman.

"We look forward to seeing you again in Europe after our brief meeting here," said the other.

"Absolutely, I want to thank you both for taking the time to stop and meet with me on your way into the city."

One of the advisors, a very attractive redhead named Felicia Betancourt, was a famous Mexican artist in her own right as well as an owner of a prominent fine arts advisory business and art gallery based in Zurich, Switzerland. She was Saudi prince Turki al Taqiy's chief advisor on major art acquisitions.

The other man, Mr. Laen Cotkey, ran a large global agricultural and energy commodities fund based in Luxembourg. The fund's major investor was a Brazilian agricultural consortium, controlled by Blackpearl, one of the world's more enigmatic virtual city-states. Blackpearl had effectively taken control of several smaller, insolvent African and Eastern European nations through the purchase of their outstanding debt at deep discounts. They then installed their people as new leadership so the countries could avert bankruptcy, and they took security interests in anything of value in each country. One of Blackpearl's affiliates was also a major art buyer, and Cotkey, being a significant collector in his own right, served as advisor on these purchases. Blackpearl and the Saudi prince were now aligning against the Manchurian to break his single-handed control of the purchasing of major artworks.

The advisors and Sao sat on the veranda, and, after an exchange of pleasantries, the Saudi prince's representative came quickly to the point. "Sao, it seems this alignment of ours is creating a problem for the Manchurian."

"No, Felicia, not really," said Sao, meeting her eyes calmly and unemotionally. "The Manchurian still maintains his no-upper-limit policy on the price he is willing to pay for art of major significance. That significance, of course, is his alone to decide. But I think you realize from his past purchases where he stands on works that are considered by experts to be significant."

"We do," the Saudi representative confirmed.

"Of course, with your alignment and stated goal of defeating the Manchurian, we will be creating potentially huge, unwarranted windfalls for sellers, who will more easily create bidding wars."

Neither advisor disputed Sao's assessment of the situation.

"The Manchurian wants you to know that he is intimidated by no one and will not change his purchase policy because of your alignment. However, he is potentially open—as I am sure your clients are—to some compromise on the matter as it relates to certain types of significant art acquisitions."

"What does the Manchurian propose?" asked Cotkey.

"He would first determine if a specific painting fell into the category of major significance we are talking about. If it did, he would notify you and your clients and would invoke the following: namely, that your clients, at no cost to them, would have the work of art on consignment for their personal use, for specific periods of time, in perpetuity. They would also have the right of first refusal if the Manchurian ever sold the work. In consideration of this arrangement, your clients would agree to refrain from bidding on the work of art. In effect, your clients would be able to have the artwork for their limited personal use without any expenditure of money."

"And this arrangement would apply exclusively to our clients?" Betancourt asked.

"That is correct."

"What about the Russian?"

"The Manchurian believes—if you will excuse my language—that the Russian is an over-leveraged ass who is a legend only in his own mind."

Both advisors laughed aloud. Sao smiled.

"The Manchurian knows that your clients, like him, have a special knowledge and sincere passion for very significant masterpieces."

"Sao, does the Manchurian foresee a specific situation where this agreement might come into effect?"

"Not currently, per se, but potentially in the near future." She lowered her eyes.

Cotkey then said, "We wanted to meet with you, Sao, and establish a dialogue since we were literally flying over the area. We thank you for your proposal. Naturally, we will need to discuss it with our clients to explore whether it is something they would consider. It is different from what we were anticipating, as you probably realize."

"If it is a proposal we like, we will draft a response addressing what we would be looking for as far as specifics are concerned," Betancourt added. "Again, we wanted to take the opportunity to meet with you on this important matter in person. And I believe I can speak for both of us in saying we appreciate the Manchurian's proposal."

Cotkey interrupted, looking towards the piers. "I see your guests are arriving already."

"Yes, they are friends of mine coming here for dinner. I'm so sorry you won't be able to join us. You've come all this way for so brief a meeting."

"Thank you again, Sao," said Betancourt, "but we have commitments that we need to get back to in Chicago. We really should be on our way."

As Sao escorted the two advisors down to the lake, she saw her friends' classic antique wooden boats docking at Heatherhurst's piers, with the help of attendants. She was waving to the arriving guests when out of the corner of her eye she saw Richard appear on the veranda.

She watched as the advisors' jet seaplane taxied away, powered down the lake, and lifted off.

As Sao strolled back towards the mansion, the ground suddenly trembled. The trembling quickly grew into more violent shaking. Sao felt a deep, rocking sensation and then watched the mansion gently rolling, as if it were floating on waves. Richard instinctively moved away from the mansion and towards Sao. The undulating ground caused him to move as if he were drunk or in a boat on choppy water.

One of Sao's friends shouted, "Earthquake!"

"Dear God, we are going to die!" another of them screamed.

"I believe it's your New Madrid fault acting up again, love," Richard shouted out as he reached Sao, who had stumbled up the lawn as it rocked under her feet.

The earthquake was over nearly as quickly as it had begun.

Grabbing Sao by the arm, Richard said calmly, "We must move to higher ground immediately—there could be a big wave from the lake."

"These earthquakes never stop! They're everywhere, Richard—even here," Sao cried, holding on to him as they headed uphill towards the mansion.

Sao's guests weren't far behind, running across the expanse of lawn as the first of many rolling aftershocks hit. Almost immediately, a thunderous huge wave rose dramatically from the turbulent lake and headed towards shore, slamming the docked boats into the crumbling piers and furiously washing up water and boat debris onto the lawn towards the fleeing guests.

Chapter 28

PALAZZO ANTONIO ANDREA FALCONARA
VENICE

Venice…the masque of Italy
—Lord Byron

Sao proceeded swiftly to a waiting car that was to transport her to the Grand Canal in Venice. She had just arrived via her jet, flying nonstop from Chicago, after dropping Richard off for his lecture. At the Grand Canal, she would be met by a watercraft that would take her to the Palazzo Antonio Andrea Falconara for a face-to-face meeting with Fara Grese. While there, she hoped to confirm her suspicion about who had painted the masterpiece and learn important information about the painting. This way she and the Manchurian could decide whether to proceed with its purchase.

On the flight over, she had been in discussions with the Manchurian regarding the logistics of the process if they decided to go forward. They felt that they had sufficiently diverted the attention of the Saudi prince and Blackpearl with their "alignment" scheme delivered by Sao. The Manchurian would now have just enough time to purchase the painting without their interference. Both she and the Manchurian knew the window of opportunity was extremely narrow to complete the purchase before their competitors found out about the deception. They were willing to deal with the expected fallout.

Sao could feel her adrenaline pumping as she and her two armed bodyguards were driven away from the private air terminal. This was truly the most exciting opportunity of her professional life—purchasing what could be a major lost masterpiece.

As the car entered Venice proper and headed towards the Grand Canal, Sao's feelings for this still-magnificent city soared. She loved Venice and knew it well, having spent many summers there with her father.

Falconara's sleek Riva inboard boat, with its uniformed captain, was waiting for Sao. She and her bodyguards boarded the large mahogany craft and were seated in plush blue leather seats in the aft as the boat quietly moved out into the canal. Magnificent palaces on either side of the water shimmered in the morning sunlight like a Canaletto painting, and gondoliers smiled and waved at Sao, crying out, *"Ché bella donna,"* as Falconara's boat went by.

On the starboard side a narrow picturesque canal leading off the Grand Canal slowly came into view. She knew the canal led to one of her father's homes, a charming villa at Via Fantasia 41. Suddenly Sao had pangs of warm memories of her father, mixed with sadness. Her father, now deceased, had been a brilliant financier who was very proud of her.

As the Riva gently glided to a stop in front of their destination, Sao was struck by the Palazzo Falconara's imposing multi-story marble and stone facade, signifying a once-glorious Venetian empire—one of the longest-reigning empires in human history. It was these celebrated palaces that still made Venice one of the most brilliant architectural achievements on Earth.

At the same time, Sao also noticed a grim-faced woman with blonde hair at the canal entrance to the palazzo. She was dressed in black, and Sao recognized her in spite of the large black sunglasses she wore.

"Fara Grese, I presume?"

"Yes, I am Fara Grese. And you are Sao Damrey."

"That's correct. It is good to meet you."

Fara showed no emotion and did not return Sao's greeting. "Ms. Damrey. If you would not mind, please step inside here and submit to our biometric process, as we discussed. Your bodyguards will remain outside, please."

"That is fine, Fara."

Sao walked into a small booth just inside the palazzo's canal entrance. The booth's door shut, and within seconds Sao emerged on the other side, having completed the screening process.

"Thank you. Please follow me."

With an air of rising expectation, Sao walked quickly up the staircase, across a huge high ceilinged marble foyer, and down a flight of stairs into a dimly lit vault in the lower recesses of the palazzo. Fara instructed her to wait, while she proceeded forward and, entering a series of codes from her mobile device, unlocked the vault.

Entering the brightly lit vault, Sao's heart skipped a beat. She fought the urge to gasp.

"Oh my God," she whispered under her breath. Her green eyes widened as she beheld a digital image of a painting on a screen.

She instantly recognized it, from her research, as Michelangelo's lost painting *Christ on the Cross*. His initials were clearly visible at the bottom.

Sao stared at the screen in complete silence, fully comprehending what this discovery meant. "A Michelangelo! This is the greatest of treasures, and just as we had hoped it would be," she thought. Trying to remain composed, she realized, "Everything I've learned now ties together."

Though the digital image was not a perfect reproduction of the painting, Sao was immediately struck by how alive the figure of

Christ looked—triumphant, not in despair. Sao wondered to herself if this could be a true, visionary representation by Michelangelo of the crucifixion of Christ.

"And who is the woman in the painting, Fara?"

"We believe her to be Vittoria Colonna, for whom Michelangelo did the painting."

"She looks terrified."

Fara remained silent.

"'To my Marchesa'—interesting," Sao commented as she noticed the inscription. "There is a study of this in the British Museum."

"Yes, there is," said Fara.

"Fara, you and Falconara have my compliments for managing to make this digital image of the painting while it remains hidden by the surface painting."

"Thank you. It was difficult and is by no means perfect, but it clearly shows a Michelangelo."

"The surface painting is by whom?"

"It is a Ziani, but he is of no particular consequence."

"Tell me, do you have any idea what lies beneath the blackened areas of the painting?"

"We do not, but we understand the Manchurian has the equipment and techniques to determine that."

"Yes, he does."

"I cannot believe what I am seeing, and these blackened-out parts seem ill-omened," thought Sao. "Could there be any link between what I have learned and this painting? It is too close to be a coincidence."

Fara Grese stood silently, staring dourly at Sao from behind her dark sunglasses.

Chapter 29

UNIVERSE MANCHURIA
OFF THE VENETIAN COAST

LIKE A MASSIVE GHOST SHIP, *Universe Manchuria* emerged from a low-level fog and, with its flotilla of seven destroyers, slowly came to anchor in the Adriatic Sea forty miles off Venice. The captain, Robert Urgo, was a former, decorated vice-admiral and commander of a guided missile cruiser group in the United States Navy. He had just brought the giant ship and its escorts safely through huge waves and turbulent seas caused by a significant underwater earthquake en route.

Sao and Marin Falconara, whom she had met earlier, were being transported in a *Universe* jet helicopter to an appointment with the Manchurian. Sao was still amazed by what she had seen in Venice. She believed the painting would be proven to be an authentic Michelangelo, and the Manchurian agreed with her that there was enough evidence to move forward with the process of required due diligence before purchasing the work.

Falconara glanced out through the window as the helicopter slowly approached the *Universe* and carefully landed on its flight deck.

"Unreal—this is a small navy," Falconara thought as he observed the destroyers surrounding the ship.

As they waited for the rotors to come to a complete stop, an officer in a spotless white naval uniform opened the door and greeted them with a smile. "Welcome home, Ms. Damrey. It is good to see you again, as always."

"Cheng, it is good to see you, too! Meet Marin Falconara," Sao said, pushing back her windblown hair. "Marin, this is First Officer Cheng Mah, who is in charge of the ship's aircraft facilities section."

"My pleasure, Mr. Falconara, welcome aboard." Cheng gave a crisp salute.

"Thank you, Cheng," said Falconara, taking in the length of the massive ship.

The wind blew in sharp gusts as they proceeded across the vast deck, past tied-down jet helicopters and seaplanes, and into the ship's interior.

As they walked down a semi-enclosed deck, Falconara noticed the ship's seemingly endless teak flooring, framed by white metal walls and large lifeboats. There were brass and gold fixtures everywhere, and every inch of the vessel was spotless and shining. They went quickly to an elevator, where Sao, who knew the ship's layout well, pressed the button to go down to a main salon.

"This is spectacular, Sao. It is like being on one of the great ocean liners of the past. Truly befitting the man who will own a Michelangelo painting," said Falconara.

"Yes, it is, Marin," Sao casually replied.

Falconara was casually dressed in a double-breasted blue blazer, fine linen shirt, gabardine slacks, and Gucci loafers. He remarked that he was impressed by even the large elevator itself, with its mahogany interior, magnificent paintings, crystal chandelier, and Persian rug over teak flooring.

They stepped out of the elevator, and Sao led Falconara to a large salon, which provided them a view of one of the ship's three

Olympic-sized swimming pools, with a giant bar and lounge area overlooking the sea.

There, two uniformed waiters welcomed them and offered to take their drink orders.

Antique French furnishings and tapestries tastefully decorated the salon, along with softly lit masterpieces by Titian and Tiepolo, and palace-sized Persian rugs covering its floor. A beautiful hand-carved Louis XIV conference table focused the eye on the center of the salon, and a large chandelier of intricate Swarovski crystal hung overhead. Lavish displays of fresh flowers were everywhere.

Suddenly a clear voice spoke. Falconara could not see the source of the sound. It was as if it came from directly in front of them, and yet out of nowhere. "Welcome aboard, Mr. Falconara. Hello, Sao. Please make yourselves comfortable at the conference table."

It was the Manchurian's disembodied voice.

If Falconara was surprised, he was good at maintaining an appearance of calm. "Good day to you, sir," he responded. "Your ship is exceptional. Where does today find you? Obviously you are not here, although it sounds as if you are at the table with us."

"Thank you, Mr. Falconara."

"Please call me Marin, sir."

"Fine, Marin. My location is not relevant. I can see you clearly, though, and am ably represented in person by Sao."

The Manchurian quickly turned his attention to the matter at hand. "Before we get down to business, I should notify you that one of my attorneys is also on this call and transcribing the discussion. His purpose is to expeditiously draw up an agreement between us in regard to the painting—if, in fact, we can come to an agreement. Is that satisfactory with you, Marin, understanding that you wanted no one here other than yourself?"

"Perfectly satisfactory, and I thank you, sir. As you know, I have personally chosen to sell the painting to you."

"I must say that we are truly gratified by your doing so, Marin. We will execute an agreement immediately once we have authenticated what we all truly believe is a Michelangelo. This is a momentous occasion, of course, for all of us."

"I have had the painting moved to a highly secure location, for obvious reasons, awaiting your final due diligence."

"Very good, Marin. And now I understand you are asking seven hundred million in US dollars for the Michelangelo?"

"Yes sir, I am." He gulped. "As you know, a Michelangelo painting is, for all intents and purposes, priceless. But, in my opinion, the direct link between this work and Michelangelo's very close friend Vittoria Colonna brings additional value, as do other seemingly hidden aspects of the work."

"I will accept the price, Marin. However, the due diligence issues arising from the fact that the work is underneath a surface painting will need to be resolved to my satisfaction. Furthermore, as you mention, there are significant hidden portions outside of the Christ figure that are so thoroughly blackened out that they will require special equipment to be seen and cleaned with any precision. This entire process must be completed to my satisfaction before I give my final approval to complete the transaction."

"But of course, sir," Falconara confirmed, reluctantly nodding his head.

"I also understand that you have not done anything to determine what is underneath the blackened-out parts. Nor have you had the underlying painting authenticated by any third party, because of your reluctance to move the painting to a third-party conservator."

"You are correct, sir," Falconara responded, nervously pushing back his blond hair, frowning as his lips tightened.

"That is good, Marin. Furthermore, we understand there is a likely provenance issue—namely, that unless we can document that the painting was either a gift to Ziani or sold to him by Michelangelo, its ownership will likely be challenged by the

Michelangelo Museum, the direct repository of the Michelangelo estate, if they find out about it."

"That is also correct, sir," Falconara said, looking directly at Sao, concern in his dark eyes.

"I am not concerned about any legal actions the museum will undertake, as they will prove to be futile for a number of reasons. Naturally, we will strive internally to document matters and negate any such claims if they arise from the museum upon them becoming aware of the painting." The Manchurian paused before continuing. "I further understand that you have financial difficulties at the present time, Marin."

"You, unfortunately, are correct there, too, sir." Falconara bowed his head and clasped his hands together.

"I understand that three hundred million dollars would resolve your current financial difficulties."

"Yes, sir. You have good sources of information."

"Here is my proposal then. Charles, will you outline it for us?"

Charles Freisler, a leading international fine arts legal specialist based in Paris, presented the details of an agreement that would take place in stages, subject to due diligence satisfactory to the Manchurian. The first stage called for the Manchurian to lend Falconara three hundred million dollars immediately, with no interest and no principal payments. This loan would be secured by only the painting, which would be in the Manchurian's sole possession. The agreement further spelled out all the various contingency issues that could arise and what would be done to mitigate them so as to remit the remaining four hundred million dollars due to Falconara, which would be held in escrow for Falconara's benefit.

When Freisler had finished, the Manchurian asked if Falconara found the agreement satisfactory.

"Yes, sir, but I would like another two days to review the loan and purchase agreement and think about any further issues. In the meantime, let us proceed with your due diligence on the painting.

Please provide me with the agreements as soon as possible. Is that satisfactory to you, sir?"

"Yes, it is, Marin. I thank you for coming here to meet with us. Sao, do you have anything to add?"

"Nothing at the moment, other than that our team is ready to begin the due diligence."

"Then let us proceed. Thank you, Marin. The agreements are securely on their way to you as we speak. Charles will provide instructions on how to access the document. The agreements will be between you and one of my entities. Which entity is it, Charles?"

"Sir, we have yet to work out the final deal points, but it will be with one of your thoroughly insulated legal structures, and we will notify Mr. Falconara what the structure will be in short order."

"Thank you, Charles," said the Manchurian, "and thank you again, Marin, for meeting with us."

"Thank you, sir." Falconara took a deep breath and finally exhaled.

Chapter 30

CENTRAL INTELLIGENCE AGENCY HEADQUARTERS
LANGLEY, VIRGINIA

JACKIE FORD spoke anxiously on her mobile video to Peter Nauert, a deputy director in the National Clandestine Section of the CIA and her superior for this mission.

"Yes, Peter, the Mossad has matched the identities."

"You're sure?" Nauert gave her a serious look from the screen.

"Yes, I am sure. Ari has contacted us and confirmed that she was living in Buenos Aires under the name of Nuller, but that she was actually the missing German lady-friend of Jesuit priest and SS member Albert Richter, all right—Mariel Mendenhall. She died years ago, but her daughter, Katrina Mendenhall Nuller, is still alive.

"As you know, Peter, I've tried to explain to everyone that the old post-war OSS report should not be discounted. It might not be at the top of our hit list here at the CIA, but it sure is at the Mossad—of course, it has greater relevance there, because of the Hitler connection. They absolutely do not think the report is a hoax or a fairy tale. They're intent on finding and retrieving *The Secret Instructions* book with the sketches and the Michelangelo letter."

"I hope you're right and this is real, Jackie. I don't want to be made a fool of. We already have had enough trouble around here with constant false terrorist leads and wild goose chases ginned up by all the paranoid jackasses and political appointee hacks that have been involved in running the agency. At least our current head, Les Wilson, is qualified."

"Well, Peter, the Mossad certainly thinks it's for real, and they're no dummies. And they don't like to waste time. We know Katrina is still alive and that she is living in Buenos Aires. She is in her own house, using the assumed name Katrina Nuller. Therefore, I am requesting permission to join the Mossad in Buenos Aires to see if she has *The Secret Instructions* in her possession or if she knows where it is."

Nauert was silent, his brow furrowed. He looked as if he was trying to figure something out.

"I know you think this is all crazy, Peter, but think about this," Jackie went on, trying to conceal her frustration. "Our reports tell us that both Mariel and Katrina had fairly extensive plastic surgery in the past. Why would they go to such lengths to disguise their identities if they had nothing to hide?"

"Jackie, you have my permission," said Nauert, though he hardly looked convinced.

"Thank you, Peter."

Later in the day, using a secure communication channel, Jackie relayed the news to the Mossad. "Yes, Ari, I have permission to make the trip, and I look forward to meeting up with you in Buenos Aires."

"Good, Jackie. By the way, we have learned there could be other operatives trying to find the book."

"Who are they, Ari?"

"Unfortunately, we believe they are operatives from the United Nations."

"The UN? Shit, I wonder what the hell they're up to."

This added a whole new dimension to the search, Jackie thought as she entered an access code in order to contact Nauert with this new information.

"Yeah, shit is right. This confirms the reality of the book," Ari said.

"The question is: what do they know that we don't?"

A world apart from Ari Engel and Jackie Ford, Marin Falconara decided to return to Venice before proceeding to his island, where the painting was safely stored, to await the arrival of the Manchurian's team. Once in Venice, however, he discovered that Fara was gone from the palazzo, having left no information as to her whereabouts. He attempted to reach her, without success, and grew concerned as to what she might be doing. Instinct told him to get back to the island and the painting. He set out immediately.

It was early evening. Thunder and lightning in the distance indicated the approach of a bad storm; Falconara, an accomplished aviator, circled his jet helicopter over the rugged island fortress in preparation for landing. He was unpleasantly surprised to see a jet seaplane bobbing gently in the water, tied to one of the island's docking stations. There should not be anyone on the island. With a sickening sinking feeling, he realized that something could be terribly amiss. The location of the island and the fact that he owned it was unknown to everyone but himself and only one other person: Fara Grese.

Falconara figured whoever was there was likely to be armed. He circled his helicopter again and engaged its long-range, heat-seeking infrared scope to see if he could detect any human movement. Criss-crossing the island, the computerized scope reported that it detected no one outdoors and that the seaplane had no occupants. This implied that any people were inside the building, and thus out of the infrared detector's range. Falconara's unease grew.

He landed at the heliport, on the other side of the island from the docked seaplane. Falconara had come well prepared for any contingencies. He was armed with a high-tech laser gun fitted with an infrared beacon and precision target-sensing capabilities.

Falconara's first order of business was to check the unoccupied jet seaplane. The computerized timing meter indicated that the engine had been shut off two days ago. "Whoever is here has been here for days," he realized, and groaned inwardly.

Falconara used an application on his mobile device to check the seaplane's ownership. The resulting report indicated that the owner was an obscure Chinese company headquartered in Shanghai. "Could this have something to do with the Manchurian?" he wondered. He and Fara had been interfacing with the Manchurian's people in anticipation of the due diligence. Was a double-cross going on by the Manchurian? Was Fara involved? What about Damrey? Falconara realized that if these were Manchurian operatives at work here, he was trapped and could not call the authorities.

Strong gusts of wind across the island signaled the incoming storm, as Falconara hurriedly voice-entered the access code to unlock the main building's exterior door. Once inside, Falconara found that the electronic security doors at the bottom of the stairs had been compromised. The next stage of his security system, a large door leading into the innermost secure area, was open as well. He realized that whoever was on the island could be in the vault where the painting was stored. Moving quietly towards the vault with his gun engaged, he was shocked to discover that all the additional doors leading to it were open. Moving quickly and silently, he arrived at the open door to the anteroom of the vault.

However, instead of seeing the vault door, as he was expecting, he was amazed to find himself face-to-face with a door he'd only seen demonstrated when the system had been installed—the "doomsday door." Falconara alone knew of its existence, and it could be opened or closed only by means of a coding instrument in his sole possession.

The doomsday door, constructed of ultra-thick, blast-proof specialty steel and concrete, was normally concealed in a ceiling cavity. That it was down could mean only one thing: the intruders had electronically hacked the final door to the vault, not knowing that the hidden door was programmed to drop immediately through the ceiling behind them once the vault had been penetrated. The process took just seconds. They would be sealed inside the vault with the masterpiece they sought.

Falconara realized that he did not have the coding instrument to raise the door—it was back in his helicopter.

Outside, the sky darkened with the threat of rain. Falconara's infrared light cast a strange glow on his anxious face as he made his way back to his helicopter. Cursing his situation, he quickly found the coding instrument and returned to the fortress entrance, as rain began to pour down.

When Falconara was just outside the doomsday door, he activated the coding device with an instantaneous DNA scan of his fingertip. The door slowly began to rise.

The first thing he noticed was a faint odor emanating from inside the vault, at first stale, and then foul. When the door was a few inches above the ground, he stopped it momentarily and listened for danger, but heard nothing. Raising the door a bit further and still hearing nothing, he checked his infrared pistol for heat signals. Nothing. He raised the door fully to its usual hidden position in the ceiling and then disengaged it so that it couldn't close on him. A crumbling sound from inside the vault startled him.

"What was that?" he murmured to himself as he moved forward carefully into the darkness of the chamber. The interior motion-activated lights came on with his movement. A moment later, his scream echoed through the fortress. Before him, he made out the ghastly remains of Fara Grese, his pilot, three armed men, and what he assumed were two computer technicians from the type of equipment they were slumped over. They were all lying near the entrance.

It was clear that they had experienced a horrible death by suffocation. Their grotesquely twisted, purplish faces stared at the ceiling in agony, lifeless eyeballs bulging from their sockets, blue tongues and mouths open wide as they had struggled for their last gasps of air. Their hands were bloodied from their frenzied, but ultimately futile, efforts to claw open the metal door. They were more mummified than decomposed, due to the special humidity-controlled atmosphere of the chamber.

Falconara's initial shock had quickly transformed into anger. "Ha, I knew it—serves these fucking bastards right," he said bitterly.

The scene before him confirmed his intuition: Fara's true loyalty was not to him, but to his pilot from New York. Falconara had become convinced that the two were sleeping together. "The bitch was too greedy in the end. She sure screwed up her lover-boy, all right," he thought, and then, "But I wonder who got her to try and double-cross me?" And there, in the shadows of the vault, was the Golgotha skull, now clearly visible through the peeling painting, its empty eye sockets peering out over the grisly scene of death. He spat on the bodies in a final sign of contempt and then covered his nose from the stench.

Falconara realized that he could not notify the authorities, for doing so would open up the entire matter and stall the sale of the painting. He felt trapped. Believing that the painting was cursed, he now obsessed over getting rid of it immediately. Later, he could pay underworld professionals, those who make people disappear, to dispose of the bodies.

Falconara furtively looked around and then carefully moved the masterpiece out of the first vault and into a second one outfitted with the same security measures.

After securing the painting in its new location, Falconara returned to the first vault. Leaving the bodies where he found them, he reset the doomsday door so that it would close while he left and shut the entrance door to the vault behind him.

"This accursed painting! Who was behind all this? The Manchurian or someone else?" he asked himself. Anger at his situation consumed him and he swore out loud.

The doomsday door slammed shut, turning the sealed vault into a tomb.

Chapter 31

BUENOS AIRES, ARGENTINA

"ARE YOU AND the Mossad certain of the woman's identity?" asked Beauchamp "Champ" Daviss, the CIA chief in Argentina who was stationed in the US embassy as an embassy official.

"They are absolutely certain it's her, Champ," Jackie replied. "This woman is Katrina, the daughter of Mariel Mendenhall."

"You can assure me, Jackie, that you and the Mossad have done your homework on this woman?"

"They have, and we have, too. Nauert wouldn't have had me come down here unless he believed this operation was essential."

"I understand, and of course I have confidence in Peter's judgment, but frankly the whole thing is quite unusual, if you ask me."

"I am not asking you," Jackie thought, trying not to show her irritation.

"The Mossad has all the appropriate covers?" asked the chief.

"Completely, and for the purposes of this mission, we are Argentine security agents."

"Right. You speak Spanish, don't you, Jackie?"

"Fluently, Champ."

"Get the book. Do whatever it takes, Jackie." Daviss smiled and extended his hand to shake hers.

Jackie stood, smiling, and shook his hand. "Will do—and thank you for your support."

Back in the embassy's main hallway, she used a special top-secret device to connect with Ari. "Ari, this is Ford," she said. "Where and when do we meet?"

She listened to his reply.

"You're right, Ari—perhaps you and I will have the dubious honor of seeing the face of the next Hitler before anyone else does."

Later that night, the gray gravel crunched under the tires of a specially equipped black stretch SUV with Argentine government plates as it rolled to a stop outside a small stone residence. It was 10:30 p.m. and the outlying Buenos Aires neighborhood of Ensenada was deserted.

The blacked-out SUV carried four of the Mossad's operatives in Argentina, along with Jackie and Ari. All the technology necessary for the mission, including hidden-object and secret global data-transmittal equipment, was on board, along with an array of advanced security detection devices.

Ari had met Jackie earlier in the lobby of the nearby boutique Hotel Pasquale Salvatore on Avenida Amber. Jackie had been given all the necessary papers to establish their team as agents of Internal Security—the Argentine equivalent of the United States FBI.

The driver of the SUV, Ricardo Padilla, was an Argentine Jew and Mossad operative. He turned to Ari, waiting for instructions.

"Ricardo, you and your men search the house for any hidden vault, while we talk to Katrina," Ari instructed him, then turned to address another operative. "Manuel, you remain in the SUV. We understand there's no one here except Katrina and the housekeeper. We need to incapacitate the housekeeper."

Ricardo added, "All alarms were neutralized earlier. We can just pop the door."

"Right," said Ari. "*Vamos!* Let's go!"

Padilla and two men wasted no time making their way to the front door and opening it. They were immediately confronted by a small, frightened young woman with jet-black hair and eyes. She stared at them in shock as she was sprayed in the face with an extremely powerful knock-out drug just as she tried to scream. She was caught by one of the agents as she immediately slumped to the floor. The remaining team members quickly emerged from the SUV and moved past the prostrate housekeeper on their way to various rooms in the house.

"Nuller's upstairs," someone whispered.

Jackie moved silently upstairs and went quickly down the darkened hallway until she located Katrina's room. She opened the door and turned on the crystal light fixture overhead, to see an older woman with a homely, wrinkled face, who lay sound asleep, propped up on two pillows.

Jackie instantly reached down, applied a seal to Katrina's mouth, clamped restraints on her wrists, and locked her to the old brass headboard of her bed. Nuller immediately awoke and tried to scream, terrified to discover that she could neither speak nor move.

"Frau Katrina Mendenhall Nuller," Jackie began, addressing the woman by both her real and assumed name, "*Ich muss mit Ihnen sprechen*. I must speak with you."

Nuller struggled to sit up. She looked stunned at her circumstances and began to cry. In clear German, Jackie said, "We are Argentine Internal Security agents and we need to have *The Secret Instructions* book and we need it now. We are searching your home, but I want you to tell me the book's location immediately."

The terrified woman's eyes betrayed the fact that she knew what Jackie was talking about. "Frau Nuller," Jackie said quietly now in Spanish, "there is nothing to fear. We have not come here to harm you. Trust me. We only wish to have the book. Will you show us where it is?"

After a moment, Nuller meekly shook her head side to side. No. Her eyes grew wide with fright once again as Jackie said, "That is not good, Frau. You must cooperate with us immediately. Please, Frau Nuller. We are not here to harm you. We are Argentine agents working on behalf of our government in search of the book. Your house will be turned upside down and inside out in our search if you do not cooperate. Do you understand?"

Jackie leaned over Nuller, staring into her frightened eyes. "Please, Frau Nuller, hesitate no longer if you know where the book is. If you will just tell us where we can find it, we will leave your home in a matter of minutes. I promise you."

Just then, a loud thud sounded on the ceiling and the light fixture rattled. The woman looked up and began sobbing uncontrollably.

"Please calm down," said Jackie. "Frau Nuller, we just want you to tell us where we can find the book that belonged to your mother. The book's secret is safe with us if you will just cooperate."

Still no response.

"Where is the book, Katrina? You need to show us!" Jackie said through clenched teeth, her frustration rising.

Nuller turned away, desperately struggling to decide what she should do.

"Katrina, I can only protect you so much longer. You must tell me where it is so I can take it away. I assure you that doing so will eliminate a great danger to you. Will you now show me where it is?"

Ari came into the room, and Jackie discreetly nodded at him. He spoke to Jackie in English.

"Is she cooperating with you, or do we need to give her something?"

Nuller glanced over at him with even greater fear in her eyes.

Jackie put her hand on the woman's shoulder. "Please, Frau Nuller, I want to help you. Just tell me where the book is and I'll make sure he doesn't touch you."

"Well?" Ari said in a louder voice. "What is your answer, Nuller?"

"Please, time is running out," whispered Jackie to the woman. "Just tell me where it is and I'll get him and the others to leave. I promise."

"If you will please stand aside, I will inject her." Ari motioned for Jackie to step out of the way as he started to walk towards the bed, but Jackie stayed put.

"Please, Frau Nuller. Please let me help you, before it's too late."

Ari was next to the bed when the woman finally nodded in the affirmative.

"You will show us, Katrina?" Jackie asked.

She nodded again.

"I am going to remove your mouth seal. Please, if you know what's good for you, do not say a word until we ask you." Jackie turned around and nodded at Ari.

Ari scowled at the woman as he told Jackie, "I will be back shortly to see if she has kept her word."

"She will," said Jackie. "Now please, just give us a minute alone." And then she removed the mouth seal and the wrist restraints.

Ari glared at the woman one last time, then turned and exited the room. A look of relief came over the woman's face as she gazed up at the ceiling and sighed. She put her face into the goose-down quilt and quietly sobbed.

Then, with all the energy she could summon, she whispered, "Take it out of here. Take it away from me. I never want to see it again—do you hear me?"

"Yes, of course. Tell me where it is and I will remove it immediately." Jackie got up and started looking around the room. "Show me where it is and we will leave at once."

The woman slowly raised one arm and pointed to an ornate silver jewelry box on her dresser. "There—you will find it there."

Jackie immediately went to the dresser and opened the box. She dug around inside and only found a diamond necklace, a silver bracelet, and a key. She turned around. "There is no book, but there is this key. What does it open?"

The woman pointed to a closet at the far end of the room. Jackie walked quickly to the closed closet door. "Is this the key to the closet?" she asked.

"No. Inside...inside the closet."

Jackie stepped inside the walk-in closet and turned on the light. She brushed aside old coats, dresses, and sweaters in search of a safe or lock box.

A moment later she walked out of the closet and said, "Are you sure it's here, Katrina? I can't find anything."

"Look beneath your feet...the floorboards directly under the light fixture," she said, weakly waving her hand and again burying her head in the quilt.

Jackie first looked up at the fixture, and then down. There, in the stained oak flooring, she noticed several boards with minute cuts at either end. Before calling Ari, who had all the search equipment, she looked around for something to help her pry the floorboards loose. She noticed a set of keys on the dresser. She worked the end of one key into the seam between two of the floorboards. Slowly, one end lifted up.

In short order, Jackie was able to remove the entire cover. She stared down into a crude compartment about two feet deep. At the bottom of it lay an old case made of tarnished steel. A thick covering of dust partially concealed the inscription on the cover: "Richter–Schutzstaffel Stabswache–Nuremberg." Jackie carefully removed the case from the hole, murmuring, "Ah, yes, Richter—SS Protective Echelon Staff—Nuremberg."

She carried the box out of the closet and set it on the dresser. Nuller turned away at the sight of it. The case was secured with an old silver padlock. Jackie tried to insert the key she had found in the jewelry box, but the lock was rusted in places. She pulled a tube of lipstick from her pocket and rubbed it on the edge of the old key. At last, it slid into the lock, which broke open.

Just then, Padilla walked into the room, Ari following behind him. "My men and I have completed our search, and we have found a vault but nothing in—" Padilla stopped mid-sentence and looked at the steel box. "Aha, what have we discovered here?"

Jackie took a deep breath and then opened the box. She was instantly met with a strong, acrid odor. There, covered with dust, its title barely legible, was a cracked leather-bound book in Latin: *The Secret Instructions of the Society of Jesus.*

Nuller's trembling voice came from behind Jackie. "That cursed book has brought my family nothing but suffering. Nothing but suffering—mark my words—from the day Albert Richter gave it to my mother. It has not been touched since my mother died, and I do not ever want to see it again. Take it and get the hell out of here, you bastards."

Jackie turned around calmly and said, "Frau Nuller, I thank you for your cooperation. We shall leave your property in a matter of minutes. I would suggest that you tell no one of this evening's activities. I would direct your servant to do the same. Your housekeeper is sound asleep, but she is fine and will awaken in a few hours.

"But if you are ever asked, simply say that the book was stolen from you," added Jackie before leaving. "And may you now enjoy well-deserved peace."

"Peace? I have known no peace since I was a young girl."

"I can assure you that you have nothing to fear from us," Jackie said.

"Then I shall tell *you* something," Nuller ominously replied.

Jackie turned to face Nuller from where she stood in the doorway, casting a dark shadow into the room.

"You have everything to fear from that wretched book; it is cursed." Nuller spat out the words, her eyes filled with rage. "Now get out." Nuller pointed a gnarled and trembling finger at Jackie.

When she heard the SUV pull away from her home, Nuller walked down the staircase to check on her housekeeper. Her eyes widened in horror upon seeing the young woman lying in a pool of blood. As Nuller was about to scream, she heard a noise behind her. Looking around, she gurgled and gasped for her last breath as a powerful clamp grasped her neck, snapping it in two.

Chapter 32

ISLE OF CAPRI
ITALY

A NAKED MAN AND WOMAN were sitting up in bed in a darkened room of the man's house overlooking the Mediterranean on the Isle of Capri. He spoke rapidly in German, using a microcell in his ear, nervously fingering his signet ring with the lion's head and serpent's body.

"Yes, she and her bastard friends totally failed in their attempt to get the painting, and yes, they are all dead."

He listened anxiously to the voice on the other end of the conversation.

"I don't know where it is, but I assume it is still on the island," he offered in an attempt to placate his caller.

"I know you are angry. So am I. Please do not harm me. I tried my best to serve you, sir." Then, "Are you there, sir? Are you there, sir?"

The call went dead.

The man turned to his companion. "I know too much. I never should have attempted to serve him on this mission. I need to hide quickly, before they find me."

"What about me?" the woman asked, frightened.

"Come with me right now. Hurry—get dressed."

As he turned to give his lover a kiss and an embrace, they heard a noise and turned towards the window. Their stares were met by a volley of silenced high-caliber bullets, shattering the window and riddling the faces of Eduard Rava and the adulterous wife of a UN official. Blown backwards onto the bed, they lay there bathed in blood. Their horribly disfigured faces gazed lifelessly into space.

Chapter 33

BUENOS AIRES, ARGENTINA

BREAKING THE SILENCE of the Argentine night, the SUV carrying Jackie, Ari, and *The Book of Secret Instructions* raced down the road. Their destination was a private airstrip outside Buenos Aires. There, an Israeli government aircraft disguised as a private jet waited to take them out of Argentina and directly to Israel.

Jackie and Ari rode in the rear of the SUV, which housed all the digital-transmission equipment. Jackie was about to make an initial assessment of the book, sketches, and letter, before transmitting a coded report securely to waiting officials in Tel Aviv and Langley. Ari had just engaged the high-security video satellite link between their governments.

"Good evening to all of you, and congratulations on a successful mission so far," the Mossad and CIA officials said as the secure video screens went live.

Ari and Jackie could see their counterparts in both locations. "Good evening to all of you as well," said Ari.

"Sorry to keep you up so late in Tel Aviv," added Jackie.

The Israeli officials spoke first. "We understand that the book has been found but that it was not where we initially thought it would be."

Ari replied, "That's correct, sir. Jackie is removing the book from its box as we speak."

Everyone watched in tense anticipation as Jackie, wearing white archivist's gloves, slowly lifted the antique book out of the box.

"I want to be careful, gentlemen. This is obviously very fragile, and I am concerned about its condition." The tension in the SUV mounted. Jackie set the book down on a special examining tray and very carefully opened the cover.

"Oh my God, would you look at this!" she exclaimed. "Here is the wax seal of the lion with the serpent's body—and here is the Michelangelo letter, all right."

"The overhead is ready to transmit the book to us, Jackie," Tel Aviv noted calmly.

"Right away," Jackie replied.

"All you have to do is open the book to each page, and the scan will do the rest," a voice from Tel Aviv confirmed.

Jackie opened the book to scan the first page of sketches. "There is Hitler. Ari, look!"

Jackie inspected the sketch of Hitler as Ari leaned over.

"We are not getting good imagery yet," said the voice from Tel Aviv.

"You will not believe who else I can make out. I can't—"

Her sentence was ended with a blinding light followed by a massive explosion and a burst of flames as the SUV was blown into jagged bits of steel.

The video screens in Langley and Tel Aviv instantaneously went dark. The quiet Argentine neighborhood was seared and shaken by the blast, and the scene was violently illuminated by fire. Cartwheeling pieces of metal, tires, and human body parts rained down over Ensenada. Dogs barked and the street came alive as horrified, screaming neighbors poured out of their houses to witness the disaster.

Jackie's decapitated head, bloody and burnt, lay on its side against the street curb. Her bulging eyeballs were frozen in terror, her mouth contorted in a silent scream. She was now a grotesque spectator to the failure of the mission, and to the destruction of *The Secret Instructions of the Society of Jesus.*

Pandemonium broke out at CIA and Mossad headquarters.

"Moshe, are you saying they were blown up?" Nauert shouted to Moshe Edelman via the video link. Edelman was a senior deputy in the Mossad's Collection Department responsible for covert activities in Argentina. Edelman, in turn, was screaming at his subordinates for answers. The darkened video screens reflected back the shocked expressions of both governmental intelligence units.

"They have been completely destroyed," Edelman confirmed. "The last data transmitted from the SUV indicates that a missile attack was detected. We should know more shortly."

"How the hell did this happen? There must be a major leak somewhere in one or both of our organizations," Nauert said.

"This mission was carried out at the highest level of secrecy at both of our agencies, Peter," Edelman responded.

"Bullshit secrecy! Everyone is dead!" Nauert exploded.

"Certain agencies of the UN were aware of the book and were allegedly also seeking it," said Edelman, looking up.

"I am aware of that," Nauert retorted angrily. "Whoever it was obviously wanted the book destroyed and had a damn good plan of execution. The SUV was supposedly shielded against this kind of an attack. Something either penetrated the shield or disabled it."

"This seems to confirm that there truly is something to those sketches and the Michelangelo letter," Edelman added soberly.

"Boy, you're a damned master of understatement, Moshe. Of course there is. We've moved out of the realm of fairy tales. And Jackie and Ari just lost their lives proving it."

"And we've lost two great agents and a significant part of our internal operations in Argentina. Damn it!" Edelman fumed. "Padilla and his team did a good job in getting the search organized."

"Give me a break, Moshe. Our efforts at execution were a failure, considering the outcome."

A brief moment of exasperated silence followed, after which all that could be heard were voices calling out instructions to computers to extract any critical bits of data from the SUV's on-board systems before they, too, were destroyed.

Nauert spoke first. "What do we know about this possible UN involvement?"

"Not much. Unfortunately Jackie and Ari knew the most," said Edelman.

"We're receiving a call for you, sir."

"Who is it?" Edelman asked.

"It's a call from Mike Afrik, one of our special field agents."

"Yes. Afrik, this is Edelman…What!" Edelman patched Nauert into the call. "We have just learned from one of our Argentine operatives that Katrina Mendenhall Nuller and her housekeeper have been found dead, their necks crushed."

Later, Edelman contacted a key covert agent in the field via a top-secret line.

"We need to make you aware that both Ford and Engel are dead, along with the whole team. Nuller is also dead at the hands of an unknown killer. *The Secret Instructions,* its sketches, and the letter from Michelangelo have been destroyed, as well. We are trying to determine who is responsible for this disaster, but you need to be exceptionally careful, as I'm sure you understand. Our security has been severely breached, and the leak could have originated from the inside. We are following up on a connection between the information you have provided us and the UN agencies that we believe were seeking the book. We cannot have your cover broken, and we will do all that is necessary to protect it."

The agent responded, "Obviously, I am in an extremely bad position now, Edelman. The security leaks must be stopped. Do you damn well understand? I mean *stopped*—no excuses will be tolerated. Find out who is leaking information and *eliminate* them immediately."

Chapter 34

UNIVERSE MANCHURIA
INTERNATIONAL WATERS
MEDITERRANEAN SEA

THE *UNIVERSE MANCHURIA*, its many lights dimmed this early evening, slowly came to a full stop and anchored in international waters in the Mediterranean, at 35° longitude, 17° latitude.

The ship and its escorts were hundreds of miles from Falconara's island. The vessel's extensive array of anti-detection equipment—including its mega-metals and super-lens invisibility shields—was activated, making it impossible for anyone to detect the *Universe*. Meanwhile, using the Manchurian's global satellite-detection equipment, an elliptical perimeter had been established hundreds of miles out, encompassing both the ship and the island; the ship was able to detect the smallest movement anywhere within that perimeter. Even if another vessel had an invisibility shield of its own, the *Universe* would be able to detect it. The destroyer escorts also had their invisibility shields on as a matter of course. That night, there was only one report of random ship traffic in the region, nothing out of the ordinary.

Throughout the day, the *Universe* had been abuzz with long-range jet helicopters and jet seaplanes delivering the Manchurian's due-diligence team and forensic equipment from initial staging areas in Europe. The entire coordination was military in its precision, expertly handled by the Manchurian's logistics personnel.

Sao and Richard were on a helicopter en route to the ship. Richard had been flown in from London to Messina on Sao's jet a day earlier so the two could rendezvous at an intimate boutique hotel before heading to the ship.

Sao had brought Richard up to speed on recent events, including the agreement with Falconara. She and the entire team had been supplied with the Manchurian's most advanced communications equipment, including personal invisibility shields, which rendered them unrecognizable to snooping satellites and other spy equipment.

"I have never been this excited in my life over a masterpiece." Sao's green eyes were shining. No one but Richard could have sensed another, darker, emotion in Sao's face.

"But...?"

"There is so much that is good about this painting," she said, "but I also detect something that could bode trouble."

"What do you mean?"

"I know you haven't seen it, but the blackened-out portions of the work have an aura of...foreboding that is truly unnerving."

"How does the Manchurian feel?"

"Dispassionate, as usual. He just wants this painting no matter what. The Manchurian has paintings by every other great painter in the world—but he only has drawings by Michelangelo."

"Where is he now?"

"I don't know, but he will be observing everything in his inimitable way, secretly and invisibly."

A call routed to the helicopter interrupted Sao. It was from Marin Falconara.

"When are you going to be here, Sao?"

"Marin, are you all right? You sound anxious. Has anything happened?"

"Sao, I can't elaborate, but I have run out of time. You must come now with your experts or forget about this painting. I need this done *without delay*," he thundered.

"We'll be on our way shortly. We are all assembling on the *Universe* in preparation for going to the island. But what is the problem, Marin?" Sao put the conversation on a speaker so Richard could hear Falconara, as well. She looked apprehensively at Richard.

"You don't want to know," he said.

"What do you mean, Marin?" Her irritation was apparent. "Is there something I *need* to know?"

"Not really, other than the fact that I have real personal problems and they're becoming unbearable. We need to authenticate and complete the transaction this evening."

"Is it safe to come there or not? Are either you or the painting in danger, Marin?"

"It's nothing like that, Sao—it's all right. We just need to get on with this. It has taken far too long already, though it's not your fault. It's mine."

"Trust me, Marin. It will be done." Sao ended the call.

"Let's get on with it," Richard said brusquely. "We'll have armed guards with us, right?"

"Absolutely, a full contingent is ready to go. By the way, are you armed, Richard?"

"Excuse me? No, but I am beginning to think I should be."

"We have weaponry for you, if you want it as a precaution," said Sao.

"Why, I forgot to pack my flak jacket, old girl." He laughed out loud.

"Always the joker, Arenell," she said, and grinned at the moment of levity.

Sao and Richard observed a beehive of activity as their jet helicopter set down on the flight deck of the *Universe*. In one corner of the deck, a team of specialists loaded art analysis equipment into helicopters, while guards and other technicians assembled elsewhere on deck, awaiting Sao's arrival.

Richard stepped out of the helicopter first. "Introduce me to the team, Sao, and then let us check everything out and we'll be gone straightaway."

"Right."

Two men in black jumpsuits approached them. Sao made the introductions. "Reinhold and Albert, please meet Richard Arenell."

"Good evening, gentlemen. It is good to finally meet you."

Both men displayed the air of seasoned professionals, their expressions reflecting the seriousness of the project as they shook hands with Richard.

"Reinhold Rubirosa, from Monte Carlo, is in charge of various scanning equipment, including the X-ray, infrared reflectography, and ultraviolet," Sao explained to Richard. "His two assistants, supervised by Albert Hussein, from Beirut, are in charge of our chemical analysis equipment for canvas and paints. All this gear gives us the ability to separate one painting from another, whether above or beneath. The image of each painting will then be displayed side by side on our screens.

"Additionally, Richard, Albert is a world-class art restorer and investigator, and Reinhold is also an expert, like you, in the interpretation of paintings. His responsibility is to work with you to make a final determination of authenticity. Both men are under permanent contract to the Manchurian."

"Outstanding, gentlemen," said Richard.

"Thank you, Mr. Arenell," Rubirosa replied. "The Manchurian provides us with the best equipment in the world."

"Gentlemen, please call me Richard."

"Richard will be leading the charge on interpreting the painting and its meaning, as well as determining its authenticity," Sao interjected. "He realizes, of course, that we all need to be in agreement when it comes to authenticity. He respects the fact that we are skilled art historians and technicians, as well. As you know, the key for the Manchurian, and for the determination of the final price, is to fully authenticate the painting as an original Michelangelo, done solely by his hand. If there were other artists from Michelangelo's studio involved, we need to know that. It does not mean that the Manchurian would not buy the painting—because he would. It would just obviously influence the final price he would be willing to pay."

"With our collective expertise, I am confident we will determine the painting's authenticity, Sao," Hussein said.

"Shall we get on with it?" Richard asked.

"Once you and I change into our jumpsuits, Richard, we'll be ready to go."

They headed below to change, emerging moments later in black jumpsuits. With a wave off from the crew on the flight deck, they boarded the jet helicopters loaded with the appraisal gear. As the copters lifted off sequentially into the twilight, Richard adjusted his special version German Mauser C-1000 computerized gun, fully equipped with sensors to guide bullets to a far-off moving target with pinpoint accuracy.

"Ah, the exciting world of fine art with Sao," Richard thought. "What sort of pickle have I gotten myself into here? I need a Mauser for an art appraisal because people would literally kill for a Michelangelo."

A thousand miles away, a Saudi Arabian government jet, bristling with anti-missile weaponry, was flying at the speed of sound across the Atlantic to Riyadh. The jet was connected by a high-security private satellite communication network to a conference room in London, overlooking Saint Paul's Cathedral. The participants in the videoconference were coming online and beginning to speak.

"Felicia, are you heading to meet with the prince on this?" asked Laen Cotkey, the Blackpearl representative.

"Yes I am, Laen," Felicia Betancourt replied. "And I understand, like you, that the Manchurian was picked and the painting could be a Michelangelo. We did not even have a chance to talk to the owner. What's his name—Falconara?"

"That's correct," Cotkey said, grimacing. "The Manchurian co-opted the entire deal through his deception delivered by Damrey."

"I don't have to tell you that the prince is furious at being double-crossed by those sons of bitches. Damrey communicated to me that there could be a potential deal with us, as had been discussed, on what we now know is a Michelangelo. She explicitly said that we should hold off on pursuing such a deal if we were aware of it," said Betancourt, anger obvious in her dark eyes.

"Same here, Felicia. My client is infuriated."

"As a professional courtesy, the prince holds up for just a minute, just one damn minute, and the bastard locks it up using Damrey as a foil—damn him."

"You know, Felicia, this is just the Manchurian's type of transaction, too—a lot of hair on it and provenance issues to boot. Believe me, we are as pissed off as you."

"You can't give the damn bastard even a second, let alone the time we did."

"Do you know what it's going for, Felicia?"

"Over a half billion US, I understand."

"I heard three quarters of a billion," Laen said.

"Well, we could play individually in that price range and certainly acting together. The prince would personally pay that much for a Michelangelo."

"We both know the Manchurian's moving fast on this. How do we stop him or derail the process?" interjected Cotkey.

"I am arriving soon in Riyadh. After I meet with the prince, I will plug you guys in and we'll figure out what our next steps should be. In the meantime, we need to get your people in Europe to track down Falconara. Make direct contact with him using whatever means necessary. I'll have the prince's people try to do the same. I can assure you the prince wants that painting and will go to any length to get it—and I mean *any* length."

"And so will Blackpearl. We'll get right on this."

Cotkey cut out from the videoconference and looked at his associates in the room. "I wonder what Felicia means when she says the prince will go to *any* length…"

Chapter 35

FALCONARA ISLAND
OFF THE VENETIAN COAST

DARKNESS ENSHROUDED Falconara's island fortress as the Manchurian's three large jet helicopters drew near. Falconara, watching through night-vision equipment, received a predetermined signal from Sao on his mobile device. The front of the island was instantly illuminated by huge searchlights located on the helicopters.

The seaplane belonging to Fara Grese and her ill-fated companions rocked gently on the opposite side of the island. Falconara had managed to contact the Manchurian through the Manchurian's attorneys and had come to the conclusion that the Manchurian was not behind Fara's attempt to get the painting. He had no idea who was. All he wanted to do now was just close the transaction with the Manchurian and get the money.

Falconara anxiously peered out from the interior of the fortress. He hoped it was Sao who had signaled and not an impostor. When he saw both her and Richard emerge from one of the helicopters, he breathed a heavy sigh of relief.

Turning off his night-vision equipment, he set the doomsday door code on the second vault with a scan of his fingertip. He had been prepared to seal the second vault and all areas leading into it if it had been anyone else.

To calm himself, Falconara breathed in deeply, slowly exhaled, and took a tranquilizer pill. He then moved quickly through a hidden exit out to the helipad area to greet the contingent preparing to unload the equipment from the helicopters under armed guard.

"Sao, it's so good to see that you have finally made it!" he shouted out over the din of the helicopter blades.

"Marin, it is good to see you, too. Meet Richard Arenell, who is co-managing this process with me."

"Marin Falconara—it is good to finally meet you." Richard smiled, extending his hand. Falconara seemed nervous and avoided making eye contact.

"Likewise, I have heard a lot about you. Please call me Marin."

"And please call me Richard."

"You have a deal. If I may, Sao, I'd like to know who's who in this contingent, and who is going to be doing what, before we proceed."

"No problem." Sao motioned for Hussein and Rubirosa to come over. While the two men approached, Sao and Richard observed that the shadowy island fortress before them was quite large. The main walled structure was built into a black, rocky, moss-covered landscape. There was only one visible entrance, in the distance, and it looked difficult to reach. Ancient cannon mounts and rusted World War II anti-aircraft gun platforms built into the side of the fortification were evidence of the various stages of the fortress's life.

The wind was blowing hard. Sao pushed her hair away from her eyes as she introduced Falconara to Rubirosa and Hussein. Richard headed back to the helicopters and divided the guards and other personnel into small squads. Of the ten well-armed guards, he assigned six to remain outside with the three helicopters and assigned the remaining four to the team entering the vault. The technicians assigned to Rubirosa and Hussein began bringing the equipment cases forward.

"We will now go down," Falconara said. Suddenly the rocky ground opened up before them, revealing a secret underground entrance to the fortress. "A modern convenience, preferable to the long hike up the hill," Falconara quipped as he pointed to the distant entrance.

"Very good, Marin." Sao took a deep breath and the seriousness of the moment registered on everyone's faces.

As they descended the illuminated stairs, Falconara opened the first of several doors leading to the lower-level vault area.

"I am impressed with your security here, Marin. When did you stake a claim to this island?" Sao asked.

"It has actually been in my family for centuries. It was first used as a place of refuge from the barbarians at the end of the Roman Empire. In fact, Venice was created by Christian Romans, like my distant ancestors, who fled the barbarians with the fall of Rome. The fortress was also used in the late Middle Ages to provide shelter from the attacks against Venice, and then during World War II, as a hiding place for valuables—and lately as a highly secure location for valuables in our own treacherous times. Needless to say, I consider the painting in question to be exceedingly valuable."

They had arrived at the vault area. Falconara cast a furtive glance at the first vault, which contained the disintegrating remains of Fara and her accomplices. He then turned quickly to his left and proceeded to the second vault's entrance.

"This way, please."

The entourage stopped and watched as Falconara, using his decoding instrument, opened the front entryway to reveal a separate door. He mentioned nothing of the doomsday door, which he had set on fast close.

He opened the final door. There, in the vault's faint light and bathed in eerie shadows was *St. Mark Defending Venice against Satan* revealing the work of Michaelangelo underneath.

Everyone, with the exception of Falconara, stood in silent awe. An unnatural glow from the light in the room seemed to illuminate the fully exposed Golgotha skull. Its dark, vacant sockets stared menacingly out at the assembled group. Ziani's painting cracked and flaked, revealing the skull and the colors and textures of the wooden cross of the painting beneath.

"Creepy," Sao thought.

"So everybody, here at long last we finally have our hoped-for Michelangelo." Richard's satisfied tone broke the silence. Smiles, as if on cue, broke out among the participants.

But Falconara tersely interrupted, shifting the mood. "Would everyone just stand where they are for a moment? Before proceeding further, I need to tell you about security in this area. There is adequate space for you to move and set up equipment around the painting. However, angled shafts of light will soon be switched on to outline the perimeter within which you can move freely. Please respect that perimeter, or there will be great difficulty for all of us."

"Please explain," Richard insisted.

"What exactly do you mean by 'great difficulty,' Marin?" Sao added, showing signs of irritation. Stress became apparent on the faces of all the personnel in the cramped vault.

"This room's interior is entirely coded and digitized. The security system allows for movement only in the space defined by the angles of light. If the painting is moved, or if someone attempts to go outside of the area defined by the light, or should something happen to me, the doomsday door will shut."

This enraged Sao. "The what! A doomsday door! What in hell is going on here, Marin?" Her eyes flashed as she glared at Falconara.

"I will explain, Sao. Please do not get excited," Falconara responded calmly.

"Please do, Marin. Because I am getting excited, and we damn well need a thorough explanation before we proceed any further."

"This arrangement simply means that, although I do not have my own guards"—he motioned to the Manchurian's guards in the room—"this room guards for me. Do you have a problem with that, Sao?" asked Falconara, matching her intense stare.

Sao looked at Richard with concern. Richard seemed to be studying the interior, while everyone else looked around with uneasy expressions.

"Don't worry, people. I will create enough space for the equipment to be set up and for the review to be completed with ease. I will light the perimeter areas to show you what I mean. I will then explain how the door operates."

Rays of light now encircled the painting like a halo. The team was allowed to approach the artwork with equipment and inspect it closely.

"If there is any movement of the painting, a security issue will arise. We will all be locked in this vault by an unseen door that will close rapidly. At that point, the door can only be released if I recode it. This ensures that nothing can happen to me," Falconara said, a sly smile playing at the corners of his mouth.

"Marin, we need to speak to the Manchurian about this before we proceed."

"I have already notified him," Falconara curtly informed Sao.

"I am here, Sao." The Manchurian's voice immediately filled the room, interrupting Falconara.

"Manchurian, what is going on here?" Sao asked with a quizzical look on her face.

"Good evening, sir. Where do we find you this evening? Can you see us in this room?" Falconara asked.

"Yes, I am with you and can see you. Sao, we have taken the necessary steps to work with Falconara, who notified us of the monitoring oversight and the issue of the door. We have checked it out and will be monitoring the situation continuously throughout the evening."

"If something untoward was to happen and the door closed, would there be a way out for us?" Richard interjected.

"Our team outside has the ability to open the door within sixty minutes," the Manchurian responded. "There is more than enough air for that period, and we could always drill through to allow air if we needed additional time for any reason. Everything has been calculated, Richard. Additionally, the Italian authorities will be automatically notified by a special signaling device in Falconara's possession. This is in case the painting is moved without his permission or something happens to him."

"Thank you, Manchurian. We would not want to proceed until these issues were worked out to both your and our satisfaction," said Richard.

"Manchurian, are you absolutely certain that our team is protected?" Sao asked clearly and firmly, but with obvious uneasiness in her voice.

"Of course, Sao, otherwise you would have never been allowed to proceed."

"May we now begin the due diligence? Time is wasting," urged Falconara.

"Is everyone comfortable with the Manchurian's assurances?" asked Sao.

Affirmative nods came from everyone present, amid worried glances.

Noticing Sao's grimace, Richard smiled and whispered into her ear in his clear English accent, "I believe hazardous duty pay would be spot on for all of us, my love."

Sao nodded in the affirmative.

Chapter 36

LATE EVENING
FALCONARA ISLAND

THE FIRST PIECES OF EQUIPMENT put into place by the technicians and crew were large, high-intensity digital lamps with special
filaments that did not risk damaging delicate artwork. The lamps provided extraordinary clarity to the finest detail of the surface painting.

"Remarkable, Sao," said Falconara. He observed a whole new
perspective to Ziani's painting. The white skull and wood of the
cross in the underlying painting showed a covering of clear varnish.

The team hooked up an on-site advanced computerized subtraction device to the Manchurian's vast cloud computing system. This
apparatus was uniquely designed to discern and separate all images
of an underlying painting obscured by a surface painting. Attached
to this device was another piece of equipment that could examine
the brush technique and conceptual development of a work of art in
order to determine a forgery.

The team then added apparatus for chemical analysis. This equipment was designed to analyze paint and canvas, and to date paintings
by determining the age of wood, canvas, and pigment.

The last two digital devices to be put into place were a reflecto-graphic apparatus and an infrared-radiation device identical to ones at the Metropolitan Museum of Art in New York. Together, they would allow the team to explore in detail what lay beneath the surface of the painting including the blackened areas.

The four digital devices also acted as virtual reality displays that allowed the four tests and analyses to be viewed simultaneously. The combined analyses would produce a final, comprehensive report on the painting. A fifth digital display would show the two distinct paintings side by side.

Hussein's technicians were involved in the dating of the surface pigments, wood, and the canvas from both the back and the front of the painting.

"Richard, it looks like we are all set up to proceed," said Reinhold Rubirosa.

"OK, Reinhold, let's get the two paintings separated and up on the display."

Rubirosa started to work the master computer console that governed all the equipment. Dead silence pervaded the room, filled with equal measures of high expectations and uneasiness. Minutes passed in hushed silence. All eyes focused on the fifth screen.

A strange chaotic struggle ensued on the display. It was as if something were trying to prevent the Michelangelo painting from emerging out of centuries of darkness. The image flickered, at first appearing partially, then momentarily appearing fully, before disappearing into the darkness as if pulled back by some unseen force. The display went dark for a while and everyone in the room sensed failure. Then, as if the unseen force took over, the painting reappeared, only to disappear and reappear agonizingly, over and over again. Suddenly, struggling in one final effort to overcome the darkness, like a beautiful wave, *Christ on the Cross* finally splashed over the lighted display in all its grandeur. Michelangelo's initials gleamed radiantly. The effort to bring the masterpiece into the modern world had been successful.

Instantly the silent tension was broken by a cacophony of screams, shouts, and praise echoing throughout the vault. The spirit of Michelangelo himself seemed to have entered the room.

"Dear God, would you look at that!" Sao screamed, jumping up and down.

Richard, smiling his boyish grin, raised his fist in the air exclaiming, "Yes!" as Sao hugged him.

Applause reverberated throughout the vault.

"Yes, yes!" yelled Falconara. "There is the image I first made out under the black light and in the digital reproduction. But it is so much clearer now!"

"I can't believe what I am seeing," Rubirosa chimed in.

"And look at how really blackened out certain parts are," said Hussein.

"Manchurian, this is unbelievable!" exclaimed Sao, beaming. "It is really here! Manchurian, can you see it clearly?"

"Yes, Sao," he replied in his characteristically calm, matter-of-fact way.

After the outbursts of joy, the vault suddenly turned quiet again. All the participants found themselves studying Michelangelo's magnificent work. The only noise in the room was the hum of the digital displays.

Christ's face appeared amazingly lifelike, gazing up towards the sky. The pigments used to render his flesh were remarkably vivid and poignant, even under the yellowing varnish.

"The painting was probably originally coated with a natural resin varnish," Richard explained, breaking the silence. "Michelangelo is known to have usually applied heavy varnish to make his paintings look glossier and the colors more saturated. Unfortunately, over time, the thick varnish layer has probably deteriorated due to being covered by the surface painting."

Rubirosa concurred. "I agree, Richard. It looks as if the varnish has become yellowed and hazy beneath, making the painting appear encased in yellow plastic. Because of oxidation and other chemical reactions over time, the varnish has become less soluble, which might be a problem. It could prove more difficult for the conservator to remove."

"Jesus Christ looks so human—like any one of us in this room," one of the technicians said in a tone of awe.

Another aide remarked, "What beautiful flesh tones...and his face and eyes are so expressive, looking heavenward."

"Even though on the cross, Christ looks triumphant!" said Hussein.

Yet no sooner were those words spoken than the extensive blackened areas seemed to also come alive. They glistened in the light against a shadowy background, as a disconcerting patina of glowering darkness now ominously surrounded the figure of Christ. There was only silence among the vault's occupants at this development, but unease was evident on their faces as their attention shifted to the woman's face and her terrified expression, which had become more pronounced with the enlargement.

"Do you see her?" said Falconara excitedly. "She is Vittoria Colonna. He dedicated the painting to her next to his name."

"You're right, Marin. It is Vittoria Colonna. She commissioned this painting all right. The chalk study that Michelangelo prepared for her is in the British Museum," Sao added.

"Yes, but the chalk drawing in the museum does not show her face—or for that matter any of the blackened-out parts," Falconara remarked.

"You are right, Marin, the sketch only shows Christ on the cross, the angels, and the skull against dark chalk swirls," Richard confirmed. Here before them was the most-painted figure in human history, Jesus Christ, a true work by a master of the ages. It was worth hundreds of millions—but major parts of it were blackened out. Why? "Now we must finally see behind the blacked-out parts. Reinhold, are we ready? Can we do it, old chap?" Richard's voice reflected calm determination.

"Yes, we can," Rubirosa affirmed, smiling confidently at Richard. "But it will have to be expertly done in very tight quadrants and further subdivided using our high-intensity focal plane array technology. I know you can do it, Richard."

"Thank you, Reinhold," he replied.

"What does this version of the focal plane array exactly do again, Reinhold?" asked Sao.

"It optimizes viewing in the infrared bandwidth. So Richard will not only be able to see beneath the surface painting but also further enhance viewing in the infrared bandwidth to see under the blackened parts."

"It seems that we not only have the blacked-out areas to deal with but also the varnish underneath those areas. Potentially there may be more than one layer of varnish," Richard reminded the group. "Before we begin with the array, what have you determined about the wood, pigment, and canvas, Albert?"

"Both the wood and canvas are from the period of Michelangelo. Without question the analysis of the pigments also ties the work back to the 1550s. The pigments are from the same period, but there are two different pigments associated with the blackening process."

"Really, what do you mean, Albert?" Richard evinced surprise.

"Same time period, but two different painters involved. There are definitely two different hands. One painter, it seems Michelangelo himself, was responsible for the conditioning, which was applied before the blackening solution. The blackening solution, however, was worked on by a different painter. Yet both were done in very close temporal proximity."

"Are the brushstrokes on the main canvas consistent with preliminary drawings made on the canvas before painting?"

"Yes, we can see Michelangelo's initial sketches made prior to the application of the paint. We also see there are no strokes from any other hand but Michelangelo's. Additionally, the initials are distinctly his and painted by him. Using our database, we have analyzed the stroke angles. They are all consistent with Michelangelo's. So it would appear that the painting was touched only by Michelangelo, with the exception of the final blackening process," Hussein concluded.

"And thus there is a second hand at work in the process?"

"Yes, Richard, it would seem that someone other than Michelangelo blackened over that which Michelangelo had prepared," Hussein confirmed.

"You are positive that Michelangelo conditioned the painting and then someone else blackened over his work?" Richard wanted confirmation for this hypothesis.

"Yes, it certainly seems that way. Actually, it looks as if someone tried to *reverse* Michelangelo's initial conditioning process, but then the same strokes eventually re-blackened it."

"Interesting," said Richard. "I have to wonder if it was Ziani, prior to painting over the Michelangelo."

"Gentlemen, let us proceed please," the Manchurian tersely interrupted.

"Richard, just so you understand, you will be looking at the painting only through the microscope. We will be able to capture single-point measurements as well as enlarge images of the painting," Rubirosa instructed.

"Understood," Richard replied. "Are you confident I'll be able to see under the blackened part using tight, quadrant-by-quadrant and single-point measurements?"

"Yes, though you must work very slowly. Since you'll be looking through a microscope, if you move too quickly, the images could become blurred and the transfer to the other displays could be slowed."

The tension was palpable. The moment of truth of what lay behind the blackened areas had finally arrived. Rubirosa stepped behind the console and stood facing the painting to begin the process. Silence filled the room as Richard squinted into the microscope. "Nothing can come of nothing, so here we go. I can take a digital picture and then hopefully place it up on the displays."

"Correct, Richard."

Richard began. "I am going to need more intensity, Reinhold. This black goo is on really thick."

Rubirosa slowly raised the level of intensity. "I want to take it easy, Richard, so the intensity—"

All of a sudden Richard's body jolted and he shouted out, "Hold it, Reinhold! I *cannot* believe what I am seeing. This is truly incredible."

"Richard, what is it?" Sao cried out.

"This is astonishing!"

"Damn it, Richard, what is it? Tell us!"

"It is the *face*...clearly visible from two angles...of *Adolf Hitler*."

Loud gasps and shrieks filled the room.

Sao moved to Richard's side and softly touched his shoulder.

"Hold on, Sao, I need to adjust this better." He kept his face pressed to the microscope's eyepiece.

"Richard, are you sure?" Sao asked.

"Are you sure, Arenell?" the Manchurian echoed calmly.

"Yes—damn well sure. This is positively astounding. Reinhold, let me adjust, OK?"

"Yes, Richard. I'm moving the controls back over to you now."

Richard spoke again, this time with cool certainty in spite of his amazement. "I am looking at a mask, a demonic mask. A horn protrudes from it, covering part of Hitler's head. There is a death's head in the mouth of the demonic mask. And—you're going to think I've lost my bloody mind—but I am also looking at the face of Osama Bin Laden! The horn protruding from the demonic mask forms part of Bin Laden's forehead, like a turban. I can also see Mahmoud Ahmadinejad. It's his head, shown at an angle with Bin Laden's forehead!"

"Stop it, Richard! You have got to be kidding. Hitler, Bin Laden, and Ahmadinejad?" snapped Sao.

"What the hell is going on here?" Falconara said.

"It would seem like hell is *exactly* what is going on here," Richard retorted.

"Richard, please stop and put it up on the screen…please," Sao pleaded.

"I'm trying, Sao. Try to keep calm, love." He continued studying the faces. "It's almost like an optical illusion. They are all part of a leopard-like head. Hitler's mouth forms one of the eyes of the leopard. There is also a bear's head embedded in the leopard's head. And a lion's head in the leopard's mouth and something below that—"

Sao spoke tersely to Richard. "Damn it, Richard, please stop talking and get them up on the screen now!"

"Settle down, will you, Sao? I am trying to. Reinhold, I need to adjust again. Now, Reinhold—put them up if you can."

The assemblage stared at the display. Suddenly, like a ghastly protuberance rising out of the darkness of the grave, the double-angled pale face of Adolf Hitler menacingly emerged onto the glowing display. From one angle, his grim face exposed one malevolent eye. Yet from the other angle, that eye appeared terrified. A repulsive, demonic mask covered most of his face. It had evil eyes and a gaping, misshapen mouth holding a death's head in it. One elongated horn protruded from the forehead of the demonic mask. The horn formed a forehead over the emerging, smaller face of Bin Laden and the even smaller face of Ahmadinejad. All three faces appeared encased within a fierce, leopard-like animal's forehead. A bear's head, which shared an eye with the leopard, emerged from the leopard's forehead. Finally, a lion's head protruded from the leopard's mouth. All were displayed on the screen for everyone to see.

It didn't seem to matter that Richard had forewarned them: The images had reduced everyone in the room to stunned silence, their eyes wide, mouths agape. An air of dread now pervaded the vault. Everyone cast furtive glances at one another in the claustrophobic space as the frightening images appeared to look back at them.

Richard spoke first, as he stepped back from the equipment. "This is the most incredible thing I have ever seen or, for that matter, any of us has probably ever seen or will ever see in our lifetime."

Still no one said a word.

At last, a low voice spoke.

"Son of a bitch, I cannot believe this, either." Falconara broke the silence. "I told you I felt something horribly dark about this painting, and now I see why. Maybe I can understand all these bizarre animals, but how on earth did Michelangelo have a vision of Hitler, Bin Laden, and Ahmadinejad?"

Sao looked intently at the painting, as if something had been confirmed for her.

"Manchurian," Richard inquired, "I assume you can clearly see what we are seeing here?"

"Yes, of course, Richard. What do you make of all this?"

"Michelangelo was certainly a visionary, but this vision is far more extraordinary and remarkable than anyone could possibly have imagined. I bloody well wish he were here to tell us."

"Well, he's not, Richard, so—interpretation, please." The Manchurian's tone was somber and terse. Richard responded in kind.

"The demonic mask on Hitler's face seemingly denotes possession—the 'face of evil.' The death's head in the mouth symbolizes death and is the 'language' of the demon, and thus, of Hitler. The crossing and forming of Bin Laden's forehead, as well as the face of Ahmadinejad angled into Bin Laden's forehead, clearly implies a singular evil connection and the language of death among them. All of these men, of course, share a hatred of the Jews, as well as a common purpose: their annihilation. The demon's horn connecting Hitler to Bin Laden and Ahmadinejad could also represent the demonic inspiration or possession of these men as a direct outgrowth of Hitler's evil intent against the Jews."

The Manchurian remained silent, so Richard continued. "As I remember from scripture, the enlarging horn is a symbol in the Old Testament Book of Daniel describing Antiochus IV, a Persian who considered himself God. He wanted to destroy the Jews in the first century because of their belief in their God."

"Hitler is then a modern representation of Antiochus. Bin Laden and Ahmadinejad, formed by the horn, are outgrowths of that," Sao broke in. "Who would you surmise the demon is, Richard—Satan?"

"At this point, I'm not really sure who the specific demon might be, but whoever it is signifies death to the Jews."

Richard thought for a moment, and then continued with his interpretation.

"The fact that all the men are drawn within the limits of the head of this leopard-like animal must also be significant. All the animals are from Revelation, but the leopard is most important. In Revelation, chapter thirteen, verse two, John of Patmos says, 'And the beast which I saw was like unto a leopard and his feet were as the feet of a bear and his mouth as the mouth of a lion: and the dragon gave him his power, his seat, and his great authority.' Again, we can discern the bear's head in the leopard's forehead, and the lion's head protruding from the leopard's mouth. The dragon, of course, is demonic. The fact that the lion and bear are depicted within the leopard clearly indicates that Michelangelo's vision is tied *both* to the End Times in Revelation and to the enemies of the Jews.

"My rationale is that these three animals also represent empires that dominated the Holy Land after the fall of Judah and that remain the enemies of Jews and even Christians today. The lion represents Babylon, the modern Iraq. The bear is Medo-Persia, or Iran. And the leopard is Syria. Of course, the leopard was also the symbol of the German Reich, and thus it serves as a bridge connecting Hitler's evil in Germany to the End Times and these other countries today."

Richard's interpretation served to focus his thoughts and settle everyone's nerves. The team regained a reassuring sense of professional composure from his analysis.

"The composite creature of the bear and lion in the leopard is not God's creation. God created everything after its kind; there are no mixed creatures in God's creation. Hence, one may assume the leopard beast is of the demonic realm and represents the three universal empires in Daniel, chapter seven, verses four to seven, that had 'the mouth of a lion,' 'the feet of a bear,' and was 'like a leopard.' The three images of Hitler, Bin Laden, and Ahmadinejad also specifically constitute Daniel's demonic realm—the precursors of this dreadful beast yet to come and thus tied to the three animals of Revelation denoting Iraq, Iran, and Syria. These countries *could*, in fact, form the *seat* of the world empire of the Antichrist, the dreadful final beast to come. Of course, the Antichrist, possessed by the demonic, will bring on the destruction of the Jews and the Christians alike, Armageddon, the End Times, and the return of Christ."

The room was silent, with everyone caught up in Richard's interpretation, until Sao asked, "Manchurian, what do we do now?"

There was no answer.

Rubirosa finally broke the silence. "Richard, we are obviously dealing with a painting with remarkable insights into the signs of Revelation and the potential seat of the Antichrist. I remember Ahmadinejad saying Iran and Syria will create a new world order. If I understand you correctly, all this is tied to the return of Christ, right?"

"Absolutely—along with the triumph of Christ."

"What do you mean by the triumph of Christ?" the Manchurian now interjected testily.

"What I mean, sir, is that, with Christ's triumph over death as seen here, followed by his return, there will be the final triumph of good over evil. Christ will expel all the demonic evil spirits inhabiting Earth and send them back into the Abyss. The demonic abhor being sent back to the Abyss. I believe this to be the underlying meaning of Michelangelo's vision as depicted in this work."

In the deep silence that followed, a troubling thought crossed Sao's mind: "I can only wonder what the other blackened parts will reveal."

Chapter 37

MIDNIGHT
FALCONARA ISLAND

"HUSSEIN, ARE YOU *positive* that these blackened areas date from the mid-1500s?" the Manchurian asked. "The equipment is giving you an accurate read?"

"Yes, sir, the canvas beneath is untouched. The weave dates check out accordingly."

"Manchurian, what do we do now?" Sao again asked impatiently.

"Please be quiet, Sao. Proceed with the analysis, Richard."

Richard moved back to the microscope and peered into the heavily blackened parts of the painting. "I am scanning down to the second quadrant, but it is really blurring out. I think I'm seeing—yes, two more men's faces appear to be emerging from the lion's head."

"Other faces, Arenell?" Falconara exclaimed in disbelief.

"I can't recognize them. Why are the images blurring out, Reinhold?"

"I can't tell as yet, Richard."

"Can you bring them up on a display?"

"I'll try," Rubirosa replied. "What do they look like, Richard?"

"It's hard to say. They are too blurred. One appears to have horns. It looks like two heads coming out of the lion's mouth. The one with horns could be the False Prophet. Possibly the other face could be the Antichrist himself, but who knows? I can't be sure."

"What in hell is *this*?" he wondered to himself, then continued to speak: "I think what I am seeing now might actually be the demonic dragon from Revelation. The demon has hideous eyes and abscesses—pustules—like smallpox. One of the demon's eyelids shows a bear's head. The other is a lion's head. And there's a naked man being consumed by the demon's mouth."

"That is vile, Richard," Sao interrupted with disgust.

"Just get the damn things up on the display, Arenell. We're wasting time," Falconara insisted.

"Damn!" Richard moaned, his words weighted with frustration.

"What's wrong, Richard?" Sao asked.

"Now I see nothing."

The anxiety in the room became palpable again.

"Reinhold, we have a problem, don't we?"

"Yes, we well might, Richard."

"Is anything coming up on the display?"

"Nothing yet, Richard."

"Could it be jammed? I mean, I'm capturing images, but nothing seems to be registering."

"There's a problem on the console," Rubirosa announced. "A blurring effect has apparently crept into the digital upload, according to the feedback I'm getting from clarity readings."

"Why would that happen?"

"I can't tell, Richard."

"Can you fix it?" Sao asked.

"I am trying, Sao," Rubirosa answered, "but this is very strange. This shouldn't be happening at all. I don't know—it almost seems like there's some kind of interference."

"Manchurian," Sao asked, "is there too much high tech going on here?"

There was no response.

Everyone in the vault grew more agitated and fearful by the minute, eager to end the analysis and get out of these cramped quarters. Even the most composed among them fidgeted, while those less self-assured seemed ready to abandon the project immediately and escape the confines of the vault.

"While you're trying to get things straightened out, Reinhold, I'm going to move across to the other side straightaway." Richard adjusted the position of the microscope. "Moving to the upper quadrant to the right of Christ's head, just below…Let me take an angle shot… Hold it…Reinhold, there's another face, but I can't move down to it. Is the equipment malfunctioning?"

"Should we bring in backup equipment?" Hussein suggested.

"Can you get this picture for me, Reinhold?"

"No, I am trying to fix the damn thing!" Rubirosa responded tensely, irritated by the barrage of questions.

Richard peered into the scope. "Another facial image is nearly visible, Reinhold."

"Richard, nothing is responding."

The entire group fell silent, anxiously waiting for Richard to speak.

Suddenly the Manchurian interrupted sharply: "We are detecting significant intrusion from four different directions in a wide space surrounding the island."

"You are detecting *what*?" screamed Falconara.

"What do you mean, Manchurian?" Rubirosa shouted.

Sao had a bewildered look on her face. "Manchurian, *what* is going on here?"

There was only silence.

"Answer me!" she screamed, losing her composure.

Richard seemed oblivious to the commotion, reacting only to what he saw through the scope. "Whose face could this possibly be—with vampire teeth?" he wondered.

"Our satellite and movement detectors, which are surrounding the island at some distance, are indicating very large numbers of seamless invisibility shields. There is major, unrecognized movement into the surveillance space from four different directions," said the Manchurian quickly, but calmly.

"What does this mean for us, Manchurian?" Falconara asked in panic.

"You will be notified in a moment."

Oblivious to the growing panic around him, Richard checked in again with Rubirosa. "Can you get anything that I am seeing to come up on the screen?"

"No, Richard."

"My outer perimeter personnel are now being attacked by very significant forces," the Manchurian reported.

Falconara realized he needed to get out of there with the painting.

"Whoever they are, these forces are moving rapidly towards the island," the Manchurian explained. "You must all remove yourselves and the painting immediately to our helicopters. I repeat: We are detecting a very large hostile force approaching at considerable speed. Evacuate to the helicopters immediately."

"What the fuck is going on out there? We are supposed to be protected," screamed Falconara. "Where are you, you invisible bastard! Are you trying to trick me?"

The room exploded into fearful cries: "Are we going to die here?" yelled a technician. "Manchurian, help us!" shouted Hussein.

There was no response from the Manchurian as the pandemonium grew into full panic within the vault. Suddenly Falconara pushed Richard out of the way and lunged for the painting. He grabbed it with one hand, while using the other to unload a round from his automatic pistol at the two guards nearest to him.

Everyone now tried to follow the other two guards, who escaped out of the vault and up the stairs. Gunfire and shouting echoed throughout the vault as people tripped and fell over the equipment, as well as one another, to avoid getting shot.

One guard went down from Falconara's shot, while the other guard fired back, accidentally hitting one of the escaping technicians. Sao yelled to Richard, "The door, the door!" as she saw the doomsday door begin its descent.

Richard and Sao ran and dived underneath the closing door. Falconara fired at the remaining guard, and then turned towards the closing door.

The vault's lighting flickered. The digital displays and equipment collapsed, further enshrouding the remaining personnel desperately trying to escape before the door closed.

Before the second guard fell, mortally wounded, he managed to fire a final round, hitting Falconara in the back. Screaming in pain, Falconara attempted to get through the closing door with the painting, but fell as an explosion shook the inside of the vault.

The doomsday door slammed shut, crushing the feet of the prostrate Falconara as he howled in agony. His shrieks mixed with further explosions and the cries of those trapped in the chaos of the sealed vault room. Sao and Richard staggered into the hallway and quickly looked back to see Falconara, pinned just outside the closed door.

"Get the painting, Richard!" Sao shouted.

Falconara wailed in pain, clinging to the painting. His contorted face and blond hair were covered with blood, as he struggled to aim his gun at Richard. "You will *never* get my painting, you fucking bastard," he yelled out.

Sao leaped forward and knocked the gun out of Falconara's hand with a fast karate kick and then, in the same fluid motion, executed a powerful stomp-kick to the back of his neck. Falconara gave a final groan and lay face down, silent and bleeding profusely. Richard, his automatic pistol drawn, grabbed the painting away from Falconara's death grip.

The pair heard large explosions, gunfire, and men shouting from the direction of the front of the island, where the helicopters were parked.

"Follow me, Sao," Richard shouted as he headed towards the rear of the island through the vault's back entrance, which Falconara had pointed out earlier.

As they emerged, the two lovers were met by scorching sheets of fire from shadowy figures running towards them with flamethrowers. In spite of the intense heat and flames, Richard immediately got in front of Sao and unloaded a storm of automatic fire at the moving targets. The attackers fell to the ground, engulfed in flames from their own weapons.

Sao sidestepped a burning body and screamed to Richard to head for what seemed to be an aircraft behind the fortress. Richard, clutching the painting, ran after her. Sheets of fire rained from the sky on everything below, and floodlights illuminated the scene. For a brief moment, Richard made out scores of flaming and incinerated airborne black objects falling out of the sky. The same black objects, which he suddenly realized were humans, moved towards both him and Sao before the area went dark again. The advancing horde had shot out the floodlights.

"Get them!" one of the invaders commanded.

Richard was unloading a round at the descending shadows when he felt multiple, sharp pains penetrate his head and body. He felt himself lose consciousness—along with his grip on the painting.

"I've been shot," he realized. The last thing he heard was Sao's frantic cry, "Richard!"

And then everything went dark.

Chapter 38

UNDISCLOSED LOCATION
MANCHURIA

THE SENIOR LEADERS of the Manchurian's satellite intelligence and surveillance teams had been glumly viewing the devastation on Falconara's island and were now reporting their observations to the unseen Manchurian.

"We have watched the disaster unfolding, sir. We can confirm that the island is entirely on fire and completely devastated."

"Is there any movement in the region?"

"No sir. The island is ablaze and the intense heat will prohibit anyone from getting close for some time."

"Are there *any* signs of life?" The Manchurian asked somberly.

"It is a total conflagration, sir. No signs of life, just flames. Our satellites observed our rail guns incinerating many of the attackers in the air, but a good number of attackers were able to avoid being killed. They applied a powerful accelerant from both the air and ground as the attack was under way. Before they left, they lit the island on fire."

The Manchurian now realized the full extent to which his operations on the island had been woefully undermanned. His personnel relayed the fact that the attack force seemed fully aware of the Manchurian's surveillance operations. Thus they attacked in the dead of night with highly sophisticated invisibility shields and satellite-deflecting night-vision equipment of their own. They executed a number of maneuvers so as to avoid detection and attack by the *Universe*'s weaponry until they were nearly at the island. By then it was too late for the Manchurian to launch a comprehensive counter-attack.

Satellite detection from other global entities immediately flashed views of the unfolding disaster around the world. Italian authorities had been made aware of the battle on the remote private island and were the first to arrive on the fiery scene. They had learned that Marin Falconara owned the island.

Those few parts of the island not already completely destroyed by the blaze fueled the fire. Huge balls of flame shot into the sky, and the Italian authorities were helpless to extinguish the blaze. The authorities reported the disappearance and presumed deaths of Falconara and his girlfriend. Rumors circulated about a valuable work of art on the island being sought by the mega-billionaire Manchurian. There was no way to confirm this, as global authorities knew that the Manchurian, as Russia's Presidential Plenipotentiary of the Jewish Oblast, was fully insulated from all inquiry unless initiated by the Russian government.

The Manchurian was alone and enshrouded in total darkness, viewing a virtual reality display. The flow of intelligence output was interwoven with a three-dimensional timeline of people and topography in complete detail. He could see the entire island, both inside and out, the view determined by his voice commands. All the imagery had been either retrieved or reconstructed by his global intelligence and surveillance personnel using his artificial intelligence systems. With all this technology, the Manchurian was still unprepared for what had happened. He had been so entirely obsessed with the Michelangelo painting and consumed with the details of purchasing it that he had foolishly disregarded what his intelligence had told him well before the attack: there was a distinct probability that his competitors or others could have learned about the painting and were planning an attack.

The whole situation was foreign to him. The Manchurian had little experience with defeat.

"Was the Michelangelo destroyed in the fire?" he wondered. What had happened to Sao and Arenell? Were they dead, like the others? Or was this all a grand ruse? Had he been double-crossed by all of them?

He knew that Sao and Richard had escaped from the vault. He also knew Falconara and the painting got out. But then the place started blowing up, and he lost all vision of the inside of the fortress, while on the outside his satellites also had difficulty because of all the invisibility shields.

Whoever the attackers were, they were capable of stealth flying at high speeds, nearly at sea level. The Manchurian's intelligence showed that the initial wave was subsequently reinforced by a large squadron of invisibly shielded aircraft, probably drone jet helicopters. Furthermore, the Manchurian's intelligence indicated that the blurring of the screens, which had interrupted their viewing of the painting, was the work of this assault force. Somehow they were aware of the stage the Manchurian's experts had been at in the due diligence process. This suggested that there might be an attacker's agent in the Manchurian's ranks, but his intelligence reported that the attack had most likely been executed through the attacker's own sophisticated real-time detection methods.

His intelligence also disclosed that someone had secretly placed high-tech explosive devices within the vault. These were connected to the doomsday door and had evidently been placed there after the security sweep performed by the Manchurian's agents. "Could it be that Falconara was prepared to die with the painting and take everyone with him if something went wrong?" the Manchurian wondered. "Or did someone else have the opportunity and motive to rig the vault?"

The answer from his intelligence was that if Falconara could not get out, he would have been prepared to commit suicide and kill everyone.

Although his people were able to capture images from the painting prior to the attack, they had been unable to transmit anything, including the detailed and comprehensive analysis of the painting. All the equipment was destroyed, as was the critical satellite linkage to the cloud backup system. Thus everything pertaining to the painting was completely lost.

The Manchurian's intelligence system quickly concluded that this attack was a masterfully executed military operation. The attack came from carefully hidden bases that were established despite his satellite surveillance. Only a very sophisticated major power—a country, virtual city-state, or terrorist group—with both significant detection and anti-detection capabilities could have done this. Which major power—or combination of powers—was it?

According to his intelligence, the prince and Blackpearl would not resort to such extreme measures to get the painting, even though the Manchurian had deceived them. They also did not have enough time to prepare for such an attack. His intelligence told him that it was an antagonist who had been made aware of the Manchurian's preparations well in advance, and who had time to prepare a successful counter-mission, possibly in collusion with the prince and the virtual city-state. It was someone capable of knowing everything, someone who commanded a major power. And given the interference encountered before the attack, the Manchurian's intelligence concluded that it was someone who did not want any more faces in the painting revealed. For reasons of his own, the Manchurian knew that his intelligence was right in that regard.

The Manchurian received data and armament analysis that showed that more than one force was involved. An assessment was then made of the most likely combination of countries, virtual city-states, and terrorist organizations that could have launched the attack. Unfortunately, that exercise proved inconclusive, pending final analysis. Any number of combinations of powerful enemies could have acted against him, making this enemy extraordinarily formidable and elusive.

The command system interrupted the Manchurian's thoughts. "Sir, the system has received a call from the prime minister of Israel. They say they need to talk with you immediately. Also, the Russian premier wants to talk with you as soon as you are ready."

"The Israeli prime minister wants to talk to me?" thought the Manchurian.

Chapter 39

UNKNOWN LOCATION
KHUZESTAN, IRAN

RICHARD AWOKE GROGGY, lying on a magnificent antique Persian rug in what seemed to be a lush, manicured garden. A large canopy of palms shaded the area around him, which was blanketed in similar rugs. He quickly realized that, although his hands and feet were loose, he could not move them. "The best I can hope for is that a magnetic immobilization device has been used on me," he thought bitterly. He was in a stupor from being shot and struggled to think of what type of stun device had been used to shoot him.

Though alone, he had an undeniable feeling that he was under some form of surveillance.

Before him, a huge altar wrought of solid gold rose from the ground. In the distance, Richard could make out a triangular sculpture of gold and silver with an inverted cross in its center. The entire piece appeared to be suspended in midair.

Richard sensed that the garden was part of a much larger compound, although from his current location he could see little other than palm trees, foliage, and endless blue sky.

The air was warm and dry, and a gentle breeze was blowing. Richard shouted Sao's name, once, and then again, and again. He heard no response.

He recounted the firefight in the darkness of Falconara's island. He assumed that the attackers had some form of individual invisibility shields and personal flying equipment from the way they had appeared out of thin air.

What he witnessed in the vault was now magnified in his mind as he recalled the incredible turn of events that landed him in this unknown garden compound. Hitler, Bin Laden, Ahmadinejad, and two more blurred men's faces coming out of the lion's mouth. One of those faces had horns. Could they have really been the face of the False Prophet and Antichrist? There was also another blurred face with vampiric teeth. And then there was the image of a terrified Vittoria Colonna. Richard also remembered the repulsive, demonic face with the naked man being devoured.

Had he seen that demonic face before? Wondering and still struggling to think clearly, Richard realized that whoever had pinned him down on this rug had a reason for keeping him alive. What could that reason be? He tried to sort out what might have happened to Sao and the painting, but fatigue took over and he closed his eyes and nodded off again.

And then it came to him and he awoke with a start. "I think I know where I have seen the demonic face." As this thought crossed his mind, Richard looked up. On the other side of the altar he saw a dour-faced man in flowing robes trimmed with black and gold, a burnoose covering his head, mirrored sunglasses concealing his eyes. This man with no eyes stood with his arms crossed in front of the golden sculpture. "Who is that?" Richard wondered. "And why is he staring at me?"

Chapter 40

THE SAME DAY
TEL AVIV, ISRAEL

AT THE SAME TIME that Richard was confronted by the robed man, a top-secret videoconference had begun in a special underground Israeli government compound on the outskirts of Tel Aviv. The meeting was between the prime minister and deputy prime minister of Israel, their staffs, and the president and vice president of the United States. The US leaders were located in the Situation Room of the White House, along with their respective chiefs of staff. The heads of the Mossad and the CIA were also linked into the videoconference.

"Donald, we are pleased that you and the vice president, along with your staffs, could meet with us on such short notice," said the Israeli prime minister.

"Thank you, Asher. The feeling is mutual," replied the US president.

"As you know, Donald, we are all here to discuss a potential link between the loss of our respective civilian and military intelligence personnel on a special assignment in Argentina and the loss two days ago of the Manchurian's personnel on the private Venetian island owned by an Italian citizen, Marin Falconara, now deceased. We believe both incidents are linked and that they involve the lost Michelangelo painting *Christ on the Cross.*

"The Manchurian has declined to speak with us, but we have learned about the total loss of his personnel. This has been a complete disaster for him. His entire team, along with some of the best art-analysis machinery in the world, was utterly destroyed. We believe that whoever or whatever attacked him was a highly professional military force backed in whole or in part by a major world power."

The US vice president interrupted. "Mr. Prime Minister, we would not agree with the conclusion that the attackers necessarily involved a major power."

"Your reasons being, sir?" the prime minister responded, clearly surprised.

"Well, frankly, these days, mega-rich individuals like the Manchurian and large virtual city-states all have the ability not only to employ large numbers of their own mercenary military personnel, but also to access advanced armaments available from around the world, including nuclear and biological weapons. Thus, any number of entities working alone or in conjunction with others could theoretically mount a large, well-organized attack against the Manchurian and us—all it takes is money."

There was silence from all in attendance at this statement.

"In any event, we have learned that underneath the blackened portions of the Michelangelo painting was not only Hitler's face, as in the sketches, but also the faces of the late terrorist Osama Bin Laden and Mahmoud Ahmadinejad, our longtime anti-Semite foe and still a major factor in Iranian leadership. In addition, there were other faces, but they became digitally blurred as the attack began."

Finally, the US president asked the Israeli prime minister, "So, Asher, what's your take on all this?"

"Well, Donald"—he looked directly into the president's eyes—"presuming the attackers blurred the faces, we suspect the attackers themselves might be linked to those faces. And given the faces we already know about—Hitler, Bin Laden, Ahmadinejad—it's no great leap of faith to assume that the blurred faces could be those of people who also bear no fondness for the Jews.

"We must, therefore, deduce that this force that attacked the Manchurian could also be hostile to the Jews and, thus, Israel. It seems reasonable to assume that this attack force was also aware of everything that has been going on—the Jesuit book, the sketches, and Michelangelo's letter. In fact, this same force could be directly responsible for the destruction of the book of sketches, the letter, and either the destruction or theft of the painting—their motive being to keep the world unaware of the content of this particular masterpiece."

"Your thoughts, Prime Minister, as to who might be responsible?" the US vice president asked.

"The United Nations, either acting alone or in concert with some other powerful force. We are sure of it," interrupted Zohar Berman, the head of the Mossad.

Turning to Berman, who was ready to respond to any questions, the prime minister calmly asked, "I know we have always mistrusted the UN's intentions, Zohar, but how do you come to that conclusion?"

"Sir, as we all know, the UN has now become a virtual independent world power with ever-increasing military capabilities. They are currently exercising their power, unchecked, to realize their own agenda. And we know that part of their agenda is a nefarious one against Israel in particular. Hyperbole intended."

"What is their specific nefarious agenda?" challenged the prime minister.

"How in hell do you conclude they are involved?" the US president echoed skeptically. Then he addressed the head of the CIA: "And what do you think, Les?"

"Mr. President, we have discussed this with Berman and agree with his assessment."

"Go ahead, Berman," said the Israeli prime minister.

Clearing his throat, Berman took up the challenge. "Gentlemen, even before we started on our mission with the CIA to obtain the Jesuit book, the Mossad had learned of the existence of certain unnamed secular organizations with distant Nazi origins and confirmed anti-Semitic and anti-Christian beliefs. These rogue organizations are financially backed and shielded from discovery by the UN. We later found out they were looking for the Jesuit book and, we can now also assume, the painting."

"You're sure of this, Berman?" asked the US president, looking doubtful.

"I am virtually certain, sir."

"Do you have any specifics on these so-called rogue organizations?"

"Not really, other than the fact that, although the UN presents the face of an international peacekeeping force to the world, which we have never trusted, we have known for years that it is also the center of international spying and clandestine operations. Out of this activity, certain rogue organizations with an ominous dark side have developed within militarized units of the UN. This dark side is neo-Nazi, anti-Semitic, and anti-Christian. This dark side of the UN has been brought to our attention only recently, but, unfortunately, it is expanding rapidly not only into the senior leadership of the UN, but also via covert, strategic alliances with terrorist organizations, certain virtual city-states, and the development within the UN of its own secret police force."

"You have got to be kidding. A secret police force—you mean like the old Nazi Gestapo?"

"Yes, sir—and equipped with state-of-the-art high-tech capabilities."

"Well, if what you say is correct, then we have an even bigger problem with these UN bastards than we thought," concluded the prime minister. "Frankly, if it were not for the fact that the Manchurian was the target of this attack, I would think *he* was behind all of this. His control of the Jewish oblast—with all those Jewish scientists—deeply concerns us. Hearing this about the UN certainly adds to our mistrust of them. I mean, as you all know, many of our citizens actually favor the idea of Israel becoming a damn protectorate of the UN, as espoused by Elijah Nabi, who has the UN's backing."

The apprehensive looks on the faces of the conference participants reflected the disturbing nature of the theory put forth by Berman.

"One final link also seems to tie together all the facts and beliefs articulated here today and presents a further problem for all of us," the prime minister continued.

"There is more to this situation, Asher?" said the US president.

"Yes, Donald. Unfortunately, there is. As you know, CIA agent Jackie Ford and our Ari Engel developed this whole idea of securing the Jesuit book based on the OSS memorandum we received. We are all aware of the contents of this memorandum, but I want to focus on one aspect of it, namely, the demon Samael.

"As we know from the memorandum, it is believed that Samael seized the opportunity to possess the anti-Semitic Hitler directly in order to more effectively eradicate European Jewry with his rise to power. That would leave the Ishmael line in the Middle East, along with the Persians, to destroy the remaining Jews fleeing Europe. This, in fact, has happened over time, through Bin Laden, Ahmadinejad types, and others inspired by Samael, all of which continues to this day.

"But here's the link I would like to establish: We have learned that in the painting, besides Hitler's demonic face, another repulsive demonic face appears. This demonic face is covered with smallpox, and its eyelids have a bear's head encased in one and a lion's head in the other. A naked man is in the process of being eaten by the demon."

"That is disgusting, Asher. And frankly, hearing the whole story, it all seems damn surreal and supernatural to me. Especially the way you present it," said the US president.

"I agree, Donald. But let us not forget the supernatural and supernatural events are an intricate part of the history and heritage of the Jewish people, as the original chosen people. However, what is truly unsettling in this case is that our intelligence has revealed that the demon with those eyelids in the painting depicts two demons. Samael is represented by the lion's head, while the demon Asmodeus, the Great Bear—the demon of merciless revenge, wrath, and lust—is represented by the bear's head."

"You mean you believe there could be two demons, now combined in one, stalking the Jews?"

"Yes, Donald, and in a final, inauspicious footnote to all of this, if you replace the *h* in *Ishmael* with an *a,* you get *I Samael.*" Could the *a* stand for *Asmodeus within Samael?*"

The room fell utterly silent.

Chapter 41

UNKNOWN LOCATION
KHUZESTAN, IRAN

*I call Christianity the one great curse, the one great intrinsic
depravity...I call it the one immortal blemish of mankind.*
—Friedrich Nietzsche, German philosopher

*Be strong in the Lord and the strength of His might...that you
may be able to stand against the schemes of the devil...*
—Ephesians 6:10–11

THE DESERT WINDS BLEW SOFTLY around the man with flowing
robes and mirrored sunglasses as he watched Richard from a distance.
Upon waking, Richard had managed, with difficulty, to sit upright
on the Persian rug, though his arms and legs were still rendered
immobile. With an animal instinct, he felt compelled to silently pray
to himself, "Jesus Christ, protect me from this man."

"Jesus Christ protect you, you slimy excrement?" the robed man
screamed; he approached menacingly from the periphery of Richard's
vision.

Servants appeared out of nowhere and quickly brought forth a throne of solid gold. The man sat down in front of Richard, his ornate slippers almost touching Richard's face. The man then crossed his legs and, after farting loudly at Richard, spoke.

"You have been rendered an immobile, putrid hulk from worshipping Jesus Christ and inhaling his words, do you know that? As for Christ, his dead, crucified body belongs floating in a large jar of my urine, encased there for eternity as a specimen of diseased feces."

As the man spoke, Richard focused on his reflection in the man's mirrored glasses. The man kicked Richard down to the ground.

"Where is Sao Damrey, who are you, and why have I been brought here?" Richard spoke defiantly, struggling into a sitting position again.

"There is no Sao Damrey here and you have seen what was not yours to see, so you must now be sacrificed, in keeping with your Christian nature of martyrdom."

He laughed hysterically, then shouted at Richard, "And you have a beautiful body, which I shall enjoy performing unique sexual and sacramental rites on, whether you are alive or dead. I shall drink your blood as my sacramental wine of life and eat your brains and organs for good health." He laughed maniacally again. "And the fire upon the altar on which your hollowed-out body will be sacrificed will be a sign of my true love for Jesus Christ." The man snarled. "For know this, Christian excrement: I have consumed the blood of many of your kind. Poor pathetic people—even as I possess their thoughts and make them mine, they remain splendidly unaware of their own destruction."

He laughed wildly and feverishly, exposing glistening, vampiric teeth. Revolted, Richard recognized him as the blurred face with the vampire teeth in the painting.

"Yes, you are facing that man," the robed man sneered.

Though Richard was now certain that his captor could read his mind, he could not stop a vision from entering his head of the man's teeth tearing at him, of the man drinking his blood and then eating him like a cannibal.

At this, his captor motioned to a servant, who proceeded towards Richard with what looked like a burnt, charred canvas. Richard suddenly realized that this was all that remained of Michelangelo's *Christ on the Cross*. The servant hung the canvas around Richard's neck.

"Behold the crucified Christ...the King of the Jews!" screamed the robed man as he spat at the charred canvas. "Crucify forever the bastard Christ who removed the joy from our world and reduced the supremacy of man that my followers and I have fostered! Deny Christ three times, you loathsome scum, and you shall truly be saved...from me!" He laughed feverishly.

Richard stared sadly down at the charred remains of the painting hanging from his neck. The only figure left was Christ on the cross. All the other figures had been burned away.

Richard proclaimed, "You could not burn away Christ and you never will!"

The man kicked him in the face, issuing a warning. "Be very careful of how you speak to me." Then, to his servants, he added, "Turn Christ's pathetic face away from me at once. You know I can't stand to look at the miserable bastard."

Richard, his face bleeding, had fallen backwards. Servants hauled him back up and repositioned the charred canvas so that it draped over his back.

The robed man looked smugly satisfied by his servants' swift execution of his command. "I see you believe you know who I am," he said confidently, carefully folding his hands together. The bleeding Richard was reflected in his sunglasses.

"Has he read my mind again?" Richard thought to himself.

"Yes, I have read your mind, you wretched fool, because in me all knowledge resides. My name is Knowledge," he arrogantly declared, touching the top of Richard's bowed, bloody head with his slipper.

"You are the face in the painting with vampire teeth. You are possessed."

The man's fiendish gaze stared at Richard from behind his glasses.

Richard suddenly felt an inner spirit rise within him, a strength he never knew, to directly address the demon within this possessed man. Words surged powerfully through his mind as he spoke.

"I do not fear you, demon, as you possess this hapless soul, because I can see in you everything that has happened in this world today. I know that you possess us through deception, penetrating us as an inner voice through all our senses. And in deceiving and blinding as many humans as possible, with as many false gods as possible, you intend to carry us back with you to the Abyss to which you will eventually be returned by Jesus Christ.

"Yet we have the free will to choose not to be deceived and blinded by you. I know we can be delivered from your evil through our reliance on the true God and His son, Jesus Christ. And even though your perverse actions are against God, all of us—including even you—serve the will of God.

"For you are nothing but a doomed perversion of good. And Jesus Christ, by His death and resurrection, broke your hold on this world. And upon His return, you and your demonic horde, along with your followers, will be cast into the Abyss for eternity. You know it, and you hate Christ for it.

"And, yes, you can kill me as you intend, but you cannot destroy me, for I have eternal life with God through Jesus Christ."

Richard's gaze dropped as he finished, and he found himself gasping for air.

"You dare to vomit insipid scripture upon me, you drunken whoring piece of shit? And I should beg for mercy to the Most High like all the rest?" He laughed fanatically again, and again kicked Richard hard in the head. "I beg for mercy from no one!"

Richard, his face covered with blood, felt the same inner spirit arise in him again, and he remained conscious.

"For many despise Christ as much as I do, so yes, they will follow me," the man said, and laughed coldly, "all the way to their graves."

"Christ, I ask you to protect me from this evil before me," Richard repeated in his mind.

The man's mouth began to open and shut robotically, once again making visible the vampire teeth that so closely resembled those in the painting.

"He prays for protection again!" He broke into another icy peal of laughter and then stopped abruptly, saying grimly, "You say you know who I am? You know *nothing* about who I am, you fucking Christian slime. For you are *nothing*. It is only those who lust for power, riches, beauty, and the glamour of this life who know me. And I raise them up for the entire world to behold, envy, and idolize. I caress their beautiful bodies continuously, as golden chalices of my love. I have seduced them and filled their love of themselves with my drugs, which have always been the true expression of my love as they fornicate in my presence. For they know I will do anything for them, and they for me.

"Yet it is a pity—for they, too, can become fools if they arrogantly think their thoughts and accomplishments are from themselves alone and not from me. Why, I have trapped them in their own brilliance! Yet at least they are not the poor, deformed, ugly, retarded, and rejected—all of whom are unworthy to live and whom I make sure are exterminated by those I love and deceive. For I am the greatest of deceivers, and it is I and I alone of whom it is written in scripture, 'He shall deceive even the very elect.'"

Richard cried out again in bold response, "Christ's disciples had power and authority over you. And they have passed this authority to me and all the followers of Jesus Christ to make you subject to us."

The demon replied, his sharp teeth protruding menacingly, "*I* subject to *you*?" He shrieked inhumanly, "I am subject to *no one*!"

Richard then watched as four nude male servants carried in a naked young woman with a pretty face and beautiful body on a massive solid gold platter and placed her on the altar. She screamed and squirmed desperately in attempts to get off it. Richard saw that she, too, was helpless, her limbs immobilized.

The man rose from his chair and walked over to the woman and exclaimed, "Ah yes, do you see this sacred feast of prostitution that has been lovingly brought before me?" She continued her blood-curdling screams. Richard watched as the man, his back to Richard, opened his robes and began pulling the woman towards him. Her legs dangled from the altar as he leaned onto her body and put his mouth on her neck. Her screaming turned into moans of pleasure, and her body and legs undulated in orgasmic throbs, as the man sexually penetrated her and then sunk his teeth into her neck. Finished, he knelt before her limp, open legs draped over the altar.

Revulsion filled Richard at what he saw. His thoughts turned to Sao. Could the same thing have happened to her? When the man got up and turned away from his victim, Richard could see his captor's mouth covered with blood. The woman, bleeding profusely from the neck, lay silent and still on the altar. A servant rushed over with a linen cloth and delicately cleaned the man's mouth and teeth. Richard watched as the servants lifted the dying woman from the bloodstained altar, placed her back onto the platter, and carried her away.

Turning towards Richard, the man screamed, "Oh, please have pity on me, for my lust is insatiable. Yet remember, it is written, is it not, in the dear Lord's Prayer, 'Give us this day our daily bread.' She was my daily bread, and she gave it to me well!" He smiled sadistically. "I will enjoy feasting on her delicious remains later. Fortunately, my murderous twin will have nothing of these fleshly delights, so they are all mine!"

Richard, nauseated, thought back on the demonic face with a lion and a bear on each eyelid. "A murderous twin?" he muttered.

The man addressed his servants: "Remove this useless vermin from my sight, gag him, and crown him with thorns. Prepare him for his Christian sacrifice."

Four more naked male servants appeared and carried Richard away by his legs and arms; he was bleeding and beaten, and the charred painting of *Christ on the Cross* still hung from his neck. They took him into a tiled open area lined with palm trees and surrounded by ornate mosaic walls. A peaceful scene surrounded him, yet in the middle of the area loomed a strange altar that resembled a stone pyre. Looking around, Richard saw no one. He shouted out for Sao. He could hear only the rustling of the trees. A dark-robed man suddenly appeared, and Richard looked at him coldly. Before he could do anything, the man quickly grabbed his arm. Richard felt a pinch and then overwhelming grogginess, as he collapsed onto the ground unconscious. His head was then crowned with thorns.

Chapter 42

UNDISCLOSED LOCATION
ISRAEL

*Warfare is the way of deception, Go forth
when they will not expect it.*
—Sun Tzu, *Art of War*

Far from where Richard lay captive, Lieutenant General
Richard Chambers of the 24th Special Tactics Unit of the United
States Air Force, dressed in Israeli air force fatigues, stood next to an
unmarked jet transport plane on a dusty runway in a remote Israeli
desert location. Chewing on a cigar, Chambers conferred with his
team of US technology experts, who had just arrived on the transport. Under a satellite invisibility shield, the team was readying the
technology to be used in a planned attack by Israel.

A squadron of American-made unmarked Israeli air force F22
advanced fighter planes that had been modified into drones were
engaged with invisibility shields and laser missiles and positioned for
take-off. Minutes earlier, an unmarked American-made B-2 stealth
bomber, now also part of the Israeli air force and piloted by Israelis,

had lifted off. The B-2 was equipped with laser bombs and laser guns. A hospital transport and an Israeli military jet transport filled with elite Israeli Sayeret Matkal Special Forces units also waited in the background to take off. Capable of flying at very high speeds and landing without a runway, they were to follow behind the drone fighters. All the aircraft had the ability to penetrate the most sophisticated and heavily defended targets with their American technology in place.

Chambers's team had been running checks on all the aircraft technology, especially the invisibility shields, the American-made state-of-the-art infrared wave technology, and undetectable communication code. American software had also been installed on the planes to link them to electromagnetic waves around them, enabling them not only to fly effortlessly almost at sea level but also to blend in with the geography itself. The planes thus avoided any form of detection from the ground, while their shields defied all satellite monitoring from the air. The technology would effectively auto-pilot all the aircraft to their final attack coordinates.

The president of the United States and Chambers were in direct communication using special encryption devices. The president asked pointedly, "Dick, can we be completely confident that this covert action is going to go off without a hitch? We always take a significant risk when allowing the Israelis to use our technology in these attacks."

"Sir, go off without a hitch? I know you must be kidding," Chambers said, smiling and continuing to chew hard on his cigar. "You know you can always count on my boys for precise execution when the chips are down. I love the Israeli air force execution, but as you know, they are simply more effective when we help manage all our technology while they are in attack mode.

"And I have our best talent here, headed by Colonel Chris Heller along with Major Jeff Bambas and his team. They will be fully deployed in case the shit hits the fan and things get dicey out there. Pardon my language, Mr. President."

"Dick, you know you can always clearly state your position to me," the president said, and laughed.

"And you know, sir, I have always leveled with you on these special missions you ask us to perform. And as usual, and again pardon my language sir, the sons of bitches we attack never know what hit 'em."

"I know, Dick, I know, and I expect the same follow-through here."

"Done, sir. You won't lose any sleep on this one." With that, Chambers and the president disengaged. Chambers lit his cigar and adjusted his sunglasses against the blazing desert sun.

"I love the way you clarify things to the President, Dick," Heller chided, having overheard the conversation. "Hey, the CIC talks straight, no bullshit. I like that. OK, now let's get all our asses in the air and make sure—"

The roar of the Israeli fighters taking off drowned out the rest of their conversation.

Chapter 43

CHOQA ZANBIL
KHUZESTAN, IRAN

LONG SHADOWS from the sun's rays emanated from the towering ziggurat of Khuzestan's Choqa Zanbil. In antiquity the giant tiered pyramid had been dedicated to the worship of pagan gods with horns protruding from their foreheads. Ancient swastika symbols on artifacts and shards in the vicinity of the ziggurat attested to distant Indo-Aryan cultures that once occupied this Persian region.

Today, however, the revitalized ziggurat was the center of a new desert community. Skillful use of modern technology supported magnificent grounds, hanging gardens, reflecting pools, luxurious homes and apartments, and a beautifully restored canal built during the Elamite period. Choqa Zanbil had been bequeathed by Iran to Elijah Nabi and designated a United Nations protectorate.

At the foot of the ziggurat, a lavish celebration was drawing to a close. Waiters in flowing white robes and golden headdresses served the honored guests, who were making toasts of the finest wines and champagnes from Baccarat crystal designed for Napoleon. The exclusive guest list represented the ultra-rich and powerful of the sectarian and non-sectarian world. Prelates and religious leaders from every major religion, the heads of the United Nations past and present, all the members of the UN Security Council, and ambassadors to the UN, including those from the United States and Israel, mingled with global business, entertainment, and media moguls. In light of Nabi's plan for the UN to turn Israel into a special global protectorate, even the religious and non-governmental leaders from Israel were there.

A few days earlier, the world's elite had come, by private and government jets, from all over the globe to this ancient kingdom, which was home to Nabi and his close followers. They had been welcomed to Nabi's expansive and luxurious community to celebrate and attend meetings on the beginning of a new, global, secular religion that would be endorsed by the UN and headed by Nabi. By now, so many people throughout the world worshipped Nabi that governments either wanted to take notice of him or were forced to do so by the incessant political pressure of their citizens.

The assembled guests now eagerly awaited Nabi's appearance and parting words. He finally arrived clad in his well-known flowing white robe with elaborate gold trim and his familiar gold skullcap. After briefly thanking all who had come, he addressed the assembled throng of dignitaries.

"My dearest friends, I am so humbled by your presence here and your outpouring of good wishes. Our new one-world religion is under way, and I am honored by the role the United Nations has asked me to assume in its development.

"It is important to remember that it is not me, but the spirit of the coming Messiah, who imbues me with strength. From obscurity indicative of his nature, the Messiah's arrival on the world scene will be accompanied by miracles, signs, and wonders. For my Islamic brothers, I truly believe he will be seen as your messiah. For my Jewish brethren, he will confirm the messianic covenant with the Jewish people that I am here to proclaim. And finally, for my Christian friends, he will be like the return of the Christ, but will not be Christ, for Christ is dead. And finally, our messiah from God will be greater than any god who has ever walked the earth." His blue-violet eyes lit up with pleasure as he surveyed the smiling faces of the distinguished attendees before him.

"My good brothers and sisters, we now conclude your visit. Your planes and my own are waiting to take you back to your home countries. I wish you, as always, a speedy and safe journey."

After a standing ovation, the attendees bid Nabi and each other farewell and waited to be transported to their planes. A large motorcade, led by Nabi's staff and UN military personnel, took the guests to a private airfield some distance from the ziggurat compound.

Chapter 44

CHOQA ZANBIL
KHUZESTAN, IRAN

RICHARD REGAINED CONSCIOUSNESS and felt a strange metal gag around his mouth. He coughed on his own blood, which was dripping down his face from the beatings and crown of thorns. He did not know where he was. He struggled to raise his head and focus his tired eyes, but when he did, sheer rage consumed him.

He saw Sao, standing silently at a distance, talking to a robed man. She was as calm and beautiful as ever.

"Sao," he tried to scream, but the gag muffled his voice. She looked in his direction, stared at him, and turned away. Her normally sparkling emerald eyes were emotionless.

"Are you drugged? Are you one of them?" Richard roared furiously as the gag muted his shouts. "Speak to me!"

"I can't believe what I am seeing. Is she one of them?" he thought, rolling on the ground in pain. The crown of thorns only cut harder as he struggled to free himself of it.

Sao walked out of view, without responding to Richard's attempted screams.

"You have deceived all of us!" he thought. "Is the painting destroyed and everyone dead because of you?"

His anger was churning in the agony of remembering their shared past. Flashbacks of his history with her consumed his mind. "Good God, how could she have so completely deceived me?" he railed at himself.

Then, as if caught in an unfolding nightmare, Richard watched as Sao approached from a distance with none other than Elijah Nabi.

"She is a damn follower of Nabi!" He was sickened by the thought.

Richard now realized that he should have suspected something when Sao first mentioned over dinner in Libya that she had met Nabi and believed in his message.

Could she be Nabi's lover, too? Had she betrayed everyone, including even the Manchurian, to get the painting for Nabi—or was it for the horrific demonic man in the painting?

Richard dropped his bloody head in crushing dismay. He knew that with the charred canvas on his back, his crown of thorns, a bloody face, and the gag on his mouth, he was a pitiful figure for her to behold.

Nabi and Sao now paused in the courtyard to talk. Richard watched as Sao kissed Nabi on the cheek then approached him, prostrate on the ground, visibly in pain.

As they came nearer, Richard's eyes, reflecting the anguish he felt, again met Sao's. She showed no emotion whatsoever; it was as if she didn't even know him.

Out of nowhere an armed servant handed Nabi a long, razor-sharp saber. Sao remained expressionless as she stood next to Nabi in front of Richard. She spoke to him at last.

"You have been very foolish, Richard, very foolish. I have been with Elijah from the beginning, because only his thoughtful words bring peace and hope to this troubled world. There is no one else who can do this—and certainly not you and your Christ. Your words and

Christ's words are no longer compatible with peace in this world, as I have repeatedly told you.

"Yet you would not believe me. You and your kind spread only condemnation and confrontation. You are the enemy of the faithful and those of us who truly desire peace. Only Elijah represents the voice of peace, reason, and understanding. And therefore, Richard, even you must now see that you are an enemy of Elijah with your beliefs."

"She speaks the truth, Richard Arenell," Nabi interjected. "Now you must die for your Christ. Sao, would you please complete the martyrdom of this poor soul?" he asked, with a satisfied smile. "Of course," she coldly replied.

Richard was dumbstruck as he now realized the full extent of Sao's deceit and that she, not Nabi, would be the one to execute the demonic man's order to sacrifice him. Richard fiercely stared first at Sao and then at Nabi, whose eyes looked into the distance with complete disinterest. "Nabi the holy person," Richard thought with contempt, as Nabi handed the saber to Sao.

Richard simply could not believe what was happening to him. He looked up into Sao's face one last time. His dark blue eyes reflected his profound sadness, torment, and shock. Her face was blank as she stared wide-eyed right through him. Richard dropped his head and saw his blood dripping to the ground. He was consumed by overwhelming sorrow at the thought that he was now to die at the hands of the woman he loved.

Yet Richard was driven to lift his head one more time. He saw the saber slowly rising, and whispered, "May the evil ones before me be forever blinded in the name of Jesus Christ! Lord God, forgive my sins and have mercy on my soul."

As he spoke those words, the first wave of Israeli fighters rapidly and invisibly approached their destination. Their target came into visual range.

Richard could no longer look. He gritted his teeth and dropped his thorn-covered head, closing his eyes for the final time.

As he did, his ears filled with blood-curdling screams.

In an instant, Richard felt a shower of blood spray him as Elijah Nabi's cleanly decapitated head fell to the ground and rolled in front of him. His servant's severed head followed almost immediately. Nabi's bulging blue-violet eyes, still reflecting his total shock and surprise, stared lifelessly at Richard. Nabi had been hit so hard by Sao's precision saber strike to his neck that it had shattered his perfect dental work. Sharp vampiric teeth, now clearly exposed, glistened in a mouth full of blood.

Thunderous explosions and a barrage of firepower sounded in the distance. Sao dropped the bloodied saber and deactivated Richard's magnetic constraints in one move. Richard threw the metal gag aside as Sao pulled an automatic pistol from her pocket. Pointing to the decapitated servant, she shouted, "Take his weapon and follow me!" Richard grabbed the servant's weapon and, wincing in pain, removed his crown of thorns and smashed them into Nabi's bloody face. Shouting out in angry exhilaration, "You have lost your head over her, too, you demonic bastard."

Seconds later, two of Nabi's elite UN praetorian guards rounded the corner of a building and took aim at Sao, running ahead. But before they knew what hit them, they fell to the ground dead, their bodies riddled by a ferocious barrage of bullets from Richard, who shot with pinpoint accuracy.

Chapter 45

CHOQA ZANBIL
KHUZESTAN, IRAN

I am the Lord thy God. Thou shalt have no other gods before me.
—THE FIRST COMMANDMENT, EXODUS 20:1–3

THE ATTACK ON ELIJAH NABI'S community was carried out with exacting precision. The Israeli attack force had flown over several countries, as well as into Iranian airspace, with complete invisibility and secrecy. Their stealth bomber delivered the first blow—a deadly high-energy laser carpet bombing of the entire Choqa Zanbil area, executed with complete effectiveness. The B-2, after dropping its payload, headed back to Israel. The B-2 was immediately followed by the Israeli drone fighters, which fiercely bombed and strafed the community. Hundreds of robed men and women, attempting to flee the bombing, were instantly killed. All the fighters, with their jet engines muffled, circled up and silently back for another air assault. The attack transport and hospital craft had stopped in midair and rapidly descended. The elite Israeli Sayeret Matkal Special Forces unit quickly disembarked, firing at anything that moved. Total chaos reigned.

"Prime Minister!" an aide screamed to the Israeli leader. "We believe we have achieved a complete surprise. And it looks like our timing was perfect."

The aide was correct: Nabi's main forces and the UN military personnel had been taken completely by surprise, as they were all at the distant airfield escorting the guests and dignitaries onto their planes.

The last plane filled with guests had lifted off just before the attack. At that strategic moment, Nabi's forces were surprised, confused, and completely unprepared to be mowed down by drone fighters and the overwhelming firepower of the Sayeret Matkal units.

With Sao in the lead, Richard, who still had the charred painting around his neck, raced across a garden towards the relative safety of a distant wall. As they ran, they could hear incoming fire from the attacking Israeli units. Deadly spray bombs exploded in the distance, vaporizing everything in their path with a blast of thousands of deadly laser beams in a 360-degree circle.

Nabi's guard units rushed to the scene and aimed handheld missiles at the Israeli fighter planes, but they were no match for the laser barrage. A spray bomb exploded, sending shrapnel, plaster, and body parts high into the air. The fighters above continued to strafe as Israeli ground forces engaged in close-range firing with the arriving Nabi and United Nations personnel.

The two lovers moved quickly along the compound wall towards the sound of shooting. Richard pushed Sao down as three helmeted UN men rounded a corner, shooting at them. Sao fired from the ground as Richard shielded her and unloaded rounds of fire from his own weapon. The men dropped, mortally wounded, but Richard suddenly felt a sharp pain from a bullet entering his leg. Still, he got up and staggered forward.

In her peripheral vision, Sao noticed two men in an open window aiming guns at Richard's back. She screamed for Richard to get down as she fired at the men, hitting them both. Richard watched one of the men fall from the window. However, the other man managed to unload a final round at the pair before he died. To Richard's horror, Sao cried out and crumpled to the ground. Ignoring the bleeding from his own gunshot wound and the wounds to his head, Richard crawled towards Sao.

Blood oozed from her lower left side. Summoning adrenaline strength, Richard lifted her up and, limping, moved her as gently as possible away from the most intense fighting. Sao raised her hand to his cheek and clutched his arm hard with her other hand.

"I love you so," she whispered, gently touching his bloodied, sweaty, dirt-covered face.

Richard tore off his shirt and used it to wrap her side and apply pressure over her wound. "Oh, my darling, I so love you," said Richard, stroking her hair. "I cannot believe what you have done."

"I am so very sorry for what you've been put through," she gasped, "but it had to be done this way. The sadistic bastard wanted me to prove my love for him by killing you—otherwise you would have been killed by his forces back on the island." Sao looked into Richard's eyes, now glistening with tears. "There's so much I need to tell you, my love." Excruciating pain contorted her face.

"Yes, yes, my darling, but please try not to move now," Richard implored.

"It hurts so, on my left side," she said, her green eyes glazing over.

Richard cradled Sao tenderly. He had to get help for her immediately.

But there was no break in the assault. He shouted for help as bullets flew by. An interminable minute later, the firing subsided; he lifted her again, just as a contingent of soldiers raced directly towards them. He recognized their uniforms as those of the Israeli Sayeret Matkal.

"We're with Damrey," the lead commander said into a microcell in his helmet. Then, turning to Richard, he added, "And you are Richard Arenell?"

"Yes. Thank God you are here!" Richard said, as a Special Forces doctor moved in to attend to Sao.

"Looks like a severe gunshot wound to the left pelvis area. We need to get the bleeding stopped immediately," the doctor called out as he broke open his medical field container and other medics arrived on the scene to administer aid.

"The hospital transport will be here in a minute," shouted the unit commander.

"I am one of them," Sao whispered to Richard as the doctor applied a special compound to the wound and a medic prepared a blood transfusion machine.

"Special Forces?" Richard asked.

"I am a member of the Mossad, attached to them," she said calmly.

Richard was dumbstruck and responded only by kissing her and continuing to comfort her as the doctor worked on her. "Darling, you saved my life and are forever a brave hero to all of us in killing off that demonic bastard."

"Stopping Nabi was my mission, even more important than securing the painting," she replied hoarsely.

"Please rest now, my love," Richard whispered into Sao's ear. She nodded and closed her eyes.

"Have you stopped the bleeding, doctor?" Richard anxiously asked the physician.

"I have, but we'll need to operate immediately. You're bleeding too, Arenell."

"Forget me—attend to her."

Suddenly the Nabi compound fell largely silent. For a moment, all they could hear was the desert wind rustling the palm fronds. The silence was broken by a team of medics arriving with motorized cushioned stretchers. They gently lifted Sao onto one stretcher and Richard onto the other.

The vertical-lift hospital jet transport had landed close by.

The Special Forces doctor's voice could be heard over the din of the incoming aircraft. "It looks like she is going into shock. Let's move, damn it!"

Chapter 46

UNITED NATIONS EUROPEAN HEADQUARTERS
GENEVA, SWITZERLAND

SATELLITES FROM ALL the major nations and virtually all global news organizations had immediately picked up the assault on Nabi's compound and facilities. They had begun transmitting pictures of the attack to shocked viewers worldwide. The secretary-general of the United Nations, en route to Geneva from the Nabi celebration, immediately prepared to dispatch additional UN military personnel to the community from nearby bases. Other countries in the region also put their military forces on alert. Every type of media communication device and social network in the world screamed the headlines to the world.

"Elijah Nabi's large UN-protected community at Choqa Zanbil, Iran, came under intense attack by Israeli forces today using American-made fighters and a B-2 stealth bomber. It is a still unconfirmed belief that the United States Air Force provided technological assistance but no fighting forces. Nabi's fate and the reason for the attack are still unknown."

Billions of people around the world were in stunned outrage. Social networks, blogs, and all forms of instant messaging were flooded with pictures, comments, and discussion on the attack. Various heads of state, as well as business and religious leaders, had been promptly notified as they returned from the meeting with Nabi.

The secretary-general of the United Nations and the president of its Assembly issued a joint statement from Switzerland:

"In a day that will live in the annals of time, Elijah Nabi and his compound have been attacked by the military forces of Israel, with support from the United States of America. It is absolutely inconceivable to us that Israel would attack the one person, along with his loyal followers, who have called for Israel's protection by the United Nations. This apparently premeditated attack on Elijah Nabi, the most successful leader in bringing long sought-after peace to the Middle East, requires an immediate and thorough explanation from Israel and the United States before the United Nations Security Council. We are now faced with an international crisis of the greatest magnitude. Military forces of the United Nations worldwide are on the highest alert to protect our world from any further unprovoked attacks. We want to assure the world community longing for peace that the United Nations will commence immediate military operations against Israel and the United States if any further attacks ensue, for any reason, against any member of our global community."

Meanwhile, at a hastily convened international videoconference, the prime ministers of Great Britain, Japan, and France were simultaneously shouting at the president of the United States.

"Mr. President, what has been going on with the United States and Israel?" the prime minister of Japan demanded.

"Gentlemen, the prime minister of Israel will soon be making a formal statement to the world explaining the reason for this attack."

"Forget the damned Israeli PM. We want to hear from you! What in hell is going on here, Donald? And where is Nabi?" said the British prime minister.

"We understand he is dead, Spencer," replied the president.

"Dead! You cannot be serious, sir," the French prime minister exclaimed.

"Yes, I am quite serious. Nabi is dead," the president repeated.

The British prime minister raved: "Donald, this must be a tactless and bizarre joke. Do you have *any* idea the impact this is going to have on billions of people in countries around the world—including mine, France, Japan, and yours if he is dead?"

The French prime minister shouted, "Billions of people adore—hell, they worship—this fellow!"

"I guess they better get over it, gentlemen, because as my vice president from Arkansas put it, 'His cage may still be a turnin', but this squirrel done died,'" the tired president cynically responded.

Chapter 47

ON BOARD AN ISRAELI HOSPITAL JET
EN ROUTE TO TEL AVIV

THE FULLY EQUIPPED hospital jet transport—carrying Sao, Richard, and a number of other wounded—left the Nabi community, protected by a contingent of drone fighter escorts. A massive fireball totally destroyed what remained of the community as the remaining drone fighters and Israeli Special Forces swiftly departed.

Sao struggled to speak. Richard was at her side. His bleeding had been stopped, but the bullet was still in his leg and he was in agony. However, he wanted the medics' full attention on Sao. "Please rest, my love, and please don't say anything," he whispered, holding her head close to him as the medics prepped her for surgery while transfusing her with a special blood compound for shock and blood loss.

"We have brought her back, Richard. She's very strong," one of the medical staff said, when suddenly the plane lurched and dropped from severe turbulence, throwing the team and their preparations into disarray.

Sao turned to Richard, clutched his arm, and spoke haltingly. "He was going to destroy my people," she said, her eyes glazing over. "And I think his 'messiah' is the Antichrist."

"Yes, my darling," Richard said. He suddenly choked up as he thought, "Is she going to die?"

"Nabi had fallen obsessively in love with me, and I learned his true nature. I also secretly learned about his plan to have the UN eliminate Israel once it was a protectorate of the UN. I informed the Mossad. They knew that he and the UN had been behind the deaths of Israeli and American agents in Argentina, and they wanted him eliminated."

"So he was also behind the attack on Falconara's island?"

"Yes, with the UN. When things started to go wrong there, I just knew it was his people at work." She winced in pain.

"Did he know you were on the island?"

"Yes. He wanted the painting and wanted me to get it to him after the Manchurian bought it. But in the end he attacked rather than relying on me. I am sure he began to suspect me and wanted to test me by having me kill you."

She was a triple agent—the Mossad, Nabi, the Manchurian—Richard realized.

She gasped for breath and then went quiet for a moment.

In spite of her weakness, she was determined to speak. "My Richard, I don't know if I'll make it, and I'm so sorry I've kept this from you. We have a child together." She looked intently into his eyes for his reaction.

His jaw dropped in disbelief, yet in spite of his complete surprise, Richard happily said, "Darling, this is so wonderful, but why did you never tell me? Where…?"

"With my mother in Israel. Our daughter is beautiful. Her name is Judith."

Richard, still stunned, now realized the full extent of the multiple secret lives Sao had been leading. And then, seeing the questioning look on her face, mixed with intense physical pain, he reassured her of his devotion to her and to the daughter he had never met.

"My darling, you will live, and we will be together with our daughter," he said as he kissed her. She smiled weakly and closed her eyes in exhaustion.

Two medics approached. "We must go now, sir."

Richard kissed Sao again tenderly. Tears filled his eyes as she struggled to say, "Richard, pray to Jesus Christ for me. I have come to see why you believe in him."

"I will, my darling, I will!"

Sao and Richard exchanged one last, sorrowful glance as her hand slipped away from his and the operating room door closed between them.

Richard slumped into a seat and silently prayed: "Please save her, good God in Jesus Christ's name. I love her so."

He buried his face in his hands.

Chapter 48

THE SEATS OF GOVERNMENT
JERUSALEM AND WASHINGTON

THE WORLD HAD NEVER SEEN such an outpouring of grief for any one individual. Billions of people convulsed from sadness to despair over the death of Elijah Nabi. Many followers could not go on without their charismatic leader, choosing instead to end their own lives out of grief. It was as if a part of them had died with him.

At first, massive prayer vigils were held everywhere around the globe, and hundreds of thousands of spontaneous shrines of candles, flowers, and messages appeared. But as the mourning continued, there emerged well-organized protests—sometimes up to a million people strong—rallying against Israel and Israeli-related organizations worldwide. Anti-Semitism grew to a fever pitch.

In the United States, millions of people were also in mourning. Evidence presented before a bellicose and bombastic Congress indicated that certain covert units of the United States Air Force, secretly operating with the knowledge of only the president and vice president, provided technological assistance to the Israelis in their attack on Nabi. Numerous anti-Israel and anti-Semitic factions both in and out of Congress confronted the few remaining Jewish members of Congress. These members vehemently denied any involvement and blamed the attack on the president, vice president, and Israeli government leaders.

Even in Israel, hundreds of thousands of secular Jews mourned the death of Nabi and called for the resignation of the prime minister and his entire cabinet.

The global financial markets, roiled by events, were in a high state of turmoil. The stock market's Volatility Index hit all-time highs.

The UN called a special emergency session of the Security Council. It formally condemned the actions of Israel and the United States. Many member nations called for immediate economic sanctions and possible military reprisal against both Israel and the United States. Israel remained on high alert and now ominously threatened nuclear retaliation if attacked. The United States also implied severe consequences if there was an attack against either it or Israel.

The US president, in Washington, and the Israeli prime minister, in Jerusalem, along with their staffs, conferred via live secure video link.

"Unfortunately, the painting has been virtually destroyed by Nabi's people," said the Israeli prime minister, his face filling the president's screen. His exhaustion was transmitted clearly along with his words. "I mean completely destroyed, Donald, except for the figure of Christ on the cross."

"I know, Asher. And…?"

"And, because it seems like everything that could go wrong did go wrong, Sao Damrey has died, due to sudden unexpected complications from her emergency surgery after the attack at Nabi's compound."

Neither head of state could look more disconsolate.

"Furthermore, Donald, I have been told that Damrey's secret digital upload of the painting, destined for us, was blocked by an elaborate security monitoring device at Nabi's compound. It was a miracle that she was not exposed while trying to film it."

"Oh, crap, Asher," groaned the president. "This is absolutely horrible. And on top of it all, we have lost that brave Damrey woman and all her information. None of this is what I wanted to hear, damn it!"

"Believe me, I know, Donald. The loss of Damrey is devastating to all of us."

"What about the Nabi remains?"

"Nabi's remains have totally disappeared," said the prime minister.

"What? How?"

"He was incinerated in a huge fireball set off by his own people shortly after the attack. They then committed suicide. Nothing remains at the site but a tremendous burned-out hole."

The president was silent.

"Mr. President, we need to determine the best course of action from here." The camera pulled back to include the prime minister's chief of staff, who continued, "In that regard, sir, what we know is the following: Richard Arenell, who was also Damrey's companion, got the charred remains of the painting, which is now in our possession."

"And it was Arenell who was confronted alone during his capture by a demonic man with vampiric teeth who turned out to be Nabi. He had managed to disguise his teeth and his identity to the public all this time." The prime minister's chief of staff stated the bizarre details as fact. "These are the same vampire teeth Arenell first saw in a blurred-out face in the painting on Falconara's island, just before the attack by Nabi's people. He then saw the vampire teeth in Nabi's decapitated head, protruding from broken dentures that had been covering them. They had been smashed when Damrey decapitated him."

"While Damrey was in Nabi's compound and his people were cleaning the painting, she saw his face in it, baring his vampire teeth at Christ. She communicated that to us, and it was the final justification for our attack," added the prime minister.

"Additionally," continued the Israeli chief of staff, "Damrey passed on that she saw other human faces, though not clearly. This was most probably the reason Nabi destroyed the painting. He did not want any of those faces, including his own, disclosed."

"Unfortunately, with the painting destroyed except for the Christ figure, and with Sao Damrey gone, we now need to try to present this case to the world, based on connecting what we know from Arenell, our agents, and through historical documents," said the prime minister. "Everyone in the world knows that Israel will attack those it perceives as a real threat. But rumors of covert technological assistance from the United States are also very disturbing to everyone, so we will have to deal with those, too."

"You don't have to tell *me*," said an exasperated US president. "This is terrible. There is really no tangible evidence. Without being able to produce the painting itself or the Jesuit book, it'll be a hard sell."

"Yes, Donald, we understand that, but what Arenell and Damrey saw, experienced, and communicated to us about Nabi confirms what we, as Israel's leaders, suspected all along—namely, that Nabi was intent on Israel being made a protectorate of the UN so that in time it could be destroyed."

"Correct, Asher," said the president, "but the UN will deny all of this unless we get more evidence. Plus, a lot of American citizens—as well as the many idiot members in our Congress—are now being bullshitted by the secular press into believing that powerful Christian factions close to the vice president and myself, and in particular the top Christian leaders in all branches of the US military, conspired to have Nabi destroyed because he condemned Christ. And to top it off, that we used the Israelis as our surrogates."

"Oh brother! That's ridiculous."

"You're telling me it's ridiculous? I have to face a multitude of these nonsensical characters daily," moaned the president.

"Unfortunately, events have not turned out as we'd hoped they would, so now we find ourselves faced with a skeptical world that adored—damn, worshipped—the deceptive, demonic bastard. We will have to do the best with what we have," the prime minister sadly concluded.

Following the conference, the Israeli prime minister placed a video call to Richard Arenell.

"Richard, words simply cannot express how devastated we all are at Sao's passing. Yet we are truly happy to learn that you and she had a child together."

"Asher, I cannot possibly relate the awful sadness I feel at losing her. I loved her so. She saved all our lives in eliminating Nabi and was shot while firing at assailants who were going to kill me. She literally saved my life twice," Richard said mournfully, his face reflecting the sadness he felt.

"I know—believe me, Richard, I know," said the Israeli prime minister, attempting to console him.

"I will never forget how she looked when they brought me in, Asher—so beautiful, so at peace. And I felt so bad for the doctors, they were devastated, for they had tried so hard. Everything that could go wrong did go wrong. As you know, they had no choice but to operate. With all the turbulence, the damn surgery went very poorly. The bullet, I understand, also caused more internal damage than they first realized, damn it. The resulting complications proved to be just too much."

"Be assured, Richard, Sao is a great heroine to the Jewish people, in the likeness of Esther and Judith, our great heroines of the past who prevailed against those who would destroy us. She will be honored accordingly. Plans for her memorial are already being discussed. This is such a tragic loss for all of us."

Richard simply bowed his head.

Meanwhile, in a secure meeting room at the United Nations offices in Zurich, two senior UN officials spoke in hushed tones.

The first man asked, "Is he safe, or will he be exposed? Will there be more planned 'accidents' and 'suicides' over Nabi's death to stop those who know of him from being forced to reveal him?"

"Yes, it will be done, but you should know it could be only a matter of time before he—along with us—is revealed," answered the other man.

"You could be right. However, we are in the midst of a concerted effort to stop that from happening," the first man responded, tapping his ring, with its lion and serpent's body, against the table in agitation.

Chapter 49

CONVENT OF SAN SILVESTRO
VENICE

A MEMBER OF THE construction crew hired to secure the foundations at the Convent of San Silvestro peered into an open cavity in a wall that had just been uncovered deep in the convent's foundation.

"Ciò che l'inferno è questo," he thought. What in hell is this?

"Leonardo, come here! There is some kind of hidden room or vault here I want you to see," he called in his choppy southern-Italian dialect to the head of the construction crew.

"If we don't support this thing, a cave-in could occur at any time. The whole place could fall into the canal," Leonardo, his boss, said. Upon seeing the cavity, Leonardo's concerns quickly turned into curiosity. "This looks like some kind of ancient structure."

"Damn, the place looks like the Roman catacombs. What was it—an old burial vault for the nuns?" said the man who had called Leonardo over.

"I wonder if the sisters even know it exists," said another member of the crew, who had come over to look. "It appears untouched, and it's obviously ancient."

345

"We should notify the nuns as to what we have found," Leonardo said as he placed a call to the mother superior of the convent.

"Sister Margareta Maria?"

"Yes, sir," a voice answered on the other end of the line.

"This is Leonardo, the head of the construction crew working here. Sister, we have found what appears to be an ancient vault in the foundation of the convent that we wanted to make you aware of. It could be in danger of collapse."

"I will come right down, sir."

In the early-morning hours in a remote part of Israel, Richard stood watching the rain fall. Deep beneath his feet was a top-secret facility protected around the clock by extensive satellite shields, surveillance equipment, and Special Forces guards. Sao's body, preserved in a special chemical wrap, had been placed in an underground mortuary in the facility. Eventually, a private ceremony was to be held in Tel Aviv for her, and she would be laid permanently to rest once a memorial was constructed in her honor.

In the meantime, a brief Jewish ceremony had been held in the facility; only Richard and a few military personnel had attended. The small ceremony was held in secret due to the continuing international uproar surrounding the death of Elijah Nabi. The world had come to learn that Sao Damrey was a Mossad secret agent and Nabi's assassin. His followers damned her for this, even in death. There was deep and legitimate concern that if the location of her body were known at this time, Nabi fanatics would desecrate it.

Richard stood alone in the rain, inconsolable outside the underground facility's entrance, having viewed Sao for the last time.

Nearby, a jet helicopter landed, and a man got out wearing military garb and a yarmulke. He strode towards Richard, whose back was turned. Placing his hand on Richard's shoulder, he said, "It is next year in Jerusalem, and I am here, Richard."

Richard turned around and saw the face he recognized from his meeting in the airport in Amsterdam.

"Alon Eban!" Richard said with surprise.

"Yes, Richard, it is me."

They warmly shook hands.

"Alon, thank you so much for coming."

"It is my great honor, Richard. I am with the Israeli government and am acting as their official representative here today."

"Really, I didn't know that. What position do you occupy, Alon?"

"I am a deputy director of the Israel Security Agency, Shin Bet, which is part of Israeli intelligence. We work closely with the Mossad. Sao had been working over the years with the Mossad, when she was needed, primarily at first in keeping an eye on the Manchurian. He is at the center of a totally compartmentalized structure, so it is virtually impossible for anyone to know much of what he is up to."

"Do you know what her real relationship was to him, Alon?"

"In a way we do. We understand they shared a close relationship, especially after Sao's father died. She was loyal to him in that she never told us what 'close' meant—though, of course, we had our assumptions. We left it alone, because she remained loyal to us in that the Manchurian never learned about our relationship with her."

"And Nabi?"

"That was different. She had been engaged a while back to scope out who Nabi really was and what he was up to. Both we at Shin Bet and the Mossad were suspicious of the deceptive son of a bitch right from the start. Sao's objective was definitely to get close to him, and she did an incredibly good job of it. Nabi was totally taken by her. He knew that she was Jewish, but it was like he was blinded by his passion for her."

"She was as brave and smart as she was a ravishing beauty. She was shot saving my life."

"Of course, Richard, and words cannot express how truly sorry I am—we all are—for your loss. It is our loss, too. You should know that Sao Damrey is now a great heroine to the vast majority of Jewish people. You must take comfort in the fact that you and this remarkable woman had a child together."

"I take great comfort in that, Alon. And I hope the world will come to know what Nabi was, that he intended to destroy Israel, and that Sao saved her people from annihilation. Ironically, she named our daughter Judith." He turned his gaze to the entrance of the underground facility, where Sao's body lay in the mortuary.

"You must go on, Richard, as difficult as it is. We must all go on, for Sao, who gave her life to destroy Nabi, who in turn was planning to destroy us. He was brilliantly deceptive, demonic and truly deserved to die."

"Believe me, I understand, Alon. Nabi was a truly horrific person, a vampire and a cannibal, possessed by Samael and Asmodeus. He could read minds, and there was no question that he was intending to kill me. But, in the end, evil can be blinded by God if it is God's will, and thus Nabi never saw his death coming—certainly not from Sao. She saved my life twice, and I realize she was *my life*. And now she is gone." His eyes glistened.

Just then both men heard a noise and looked around to see a smaller Israeli military helicopter land. A moment later, a nun emerged, her white habit gently blowing in the wind. The effect was striking: it appeared that she had the wings of an angel. Aided by one of the military pilots, she made her way to Richard and Eban.

Meanwhile, across the Mediterranean from Israel in a graceful, elegant, and secluded sanctuary, a dense stand of tall trees swayed in the soft breeze. The trees cast a dark shadow on the large French chateau high atop a hill overlooking the village of Cap Ferrat, on the Cote d' Azur. The author Somerset Maugham once described Cap Ferrat as a "sunny place for shady people."

A man with dark, silver-streaked hair and large, malevolent eyes quietly put down a rare, antique book he had been reading, the prurient *Droll Stories* of Balzac. He raised his head as if he sensed something, and gazed out at the magnificent sweeping view of the Mediterranean.

His gleaming blue-violet eyes turned even more menacing as he peered through the library's ornate French doors to the sea beyond. He got up and walked onto the balcony in order to take a closer look.

"Heim!" the man angrily roared at the top of his lungs. "Get in here!" he screamed again, staring at the horizon, his eyes bulging and his teeth grinding.

The man's aged medical doctor walked as quickly as he could up the broad marble staircase to the library. At the entrance to the room, he called out, "Master, what has happened?"

The man glared at his doctor. "There is something amiss out there," he said, pointing to the sea. "I know it. We are being revealed *again*!" His sinister, lined face contorted in rage. "Those filthy Christian bastards have uncovered us again and we are no longer safe," the man added to himself, muttering obscenities.

"Have security get me to my plane and prepare to come with me," he commanded. Then he retreated through the library and went down the staircase at a rapid pace.

The doctor called the man's security without delay.

Chapter 50

UNDISCLOSED LOCATION
ISRAEL

THE SERIOUS-LOOKING NUN approached Eban and Richard carrying a large steel case.

"Mr. Richard Arenell?" she asked, looking from one man's face to the other.

Surprised, Eban asked, "Sister, what are you doing here? And how did you get through security?"

"Who told you to find me here?" Richard added.

"Mr. Arenell, I can only say it is by the grace of God that I found you. And now, here I am. That is all that matters."

Richard and Eban stared at each other apprehensively. The nun's presence represented a serious breach of security. "Sister, we need to understand how you got here—on one of our military helicopters, no less," Eban insisted as respectfully as he could.

"My name is Sister Margareta Maria," the woman said quietly. "I am the Mother Superior of the Convent of San Silvestro in Venice, Italy. Vittoria Colonna was a dear friend of my very distant ancestor Sister Alicia Antonia of our convent."

Richard looked intently at her, and then asked in amazement, "Vittoria Colonna of the *Christ on the Cross* painting?"

"Yes, the Vittoria Colonna of the painting," she confirmed, ignoring Eban's requests that she explain her presence. "I need to show you something very important, and that is why I am here. I trust only you." The nun glanced nervously at Eban.

"Sister, let me introduce Alon Eban, the deputy director of an Israeli intelligence unit."

The nun immediately relaxed, and spoke quickly but clearly: "In this case, I have a sketch of the faces of the most evil ones and strange animals from Revelation, along with the face of Vittoria. They are surrounding Our Lord, Jesus Christ, and were drawn for Vittoria by Michelangelo's own hand as a second chalk study for his painting *Christ on the Cross*. There is also a note from Vittoria telling of something to do with Michelangelo and the Sistine, but unfortunately the note is terribly faded and torn."

Richard and Eban looked at each other in complete disbelief as the Sister continued.

"As it turns out, Vittoria gave this second drawing to her good friend Sister Alicia, who was a member of our convent at the time of Vittoria's passing. Vittoria was a beloved patron of our convent. Sister Alicia also left a short note with the drawing relating the details of receiving it."

"There were *two* chalk drawings?" Richard said. "I know the one in the British Museum…"

"Yes, the first one, which doesn't show the faces, is in the British Museum. It seems that this second drawing, and the notes, have been in our convent in Venice for all these centuries, hidden in an underground vault."

Richard held his breath as Sister Margareta Maria removed a pair of large, plain archival folders from the steel case she carried. Both men were speechless as she held before them an old drawing, well preserved and quite clear. She calmly pointed out the human faces. "There is Elijah Nabi, with vampire teeth; and there are the two images of Adolf Hitler. And here are Osama Bin Laden and Mahmoud Ahmadinejad. And then there is this unknown figure." She pointed to an unknown man who shared an eye with Nabi.

"And here, two more faces coming out of the lion's mouth— both look like they were sculpted from stone, one with horns and one shown in profile. We do not recognize these men, either. Nor do we recognize this demon's face next to them. And there is Vittoria's anguished face. And here are the notes."

"Prime Minister, you are simply not going to believe what both Arenell and I are looking at," an incredulous Eban shouted into his mobile device.

Chapter 51

ON BOARD AN ISRAELI MILITARY TRANSPORT
EN ROUTE TO JERUSALEM

IT WAS NOT LONG before a large vertical-lift Israeli military jet transport touched down near the mortuary that held Sao Damrey's body. Numerous Israeli military gunships circled overhead, their laser guns and invisibility shields engaged. Two special satellites, as well as drone spy-craft, watched closely for any movement in the entire region. The transport itself also had its shield engaged and carried a full complement of military guard personnel, as well as a world-class contingent of specialized art forensic experts and equipment.

Richard, Eban, and Sister Margareta Maria, with her steel-encased archival folder now placed inside a highly secure container, were led onto the high-tech transport.

"Gentlemen, Sister, good afternoon," Deputy Prime Minister Moses Ariel greeted them as they entered the plane.

"Moses, it is a surprise to see you here," said Eban.

"Alon, this matter is of the utmost importance to us. The prime minister wants this authentication process to be done immediately, en route to Jerusalem," Ariel explained. "We fear that if hostile forces learn of the existence of this second chalk study and the notes, they will attempt to destroy them, as they have everything else."

He paused, and then addressed the nun. "Sister Margareta, I hope you understand the significant risks involved here to the drawing?"

"Sir, whatever you need to do so that the world can finally see it is entirely all right with me. You have the absolute support of our convent and the authority from me to do as you wish with the study," she replied.

"Thank you so much, Sister. Speaking on behalf of Israel I cannot tell you how grateful we are for you and your sisters' selfless magnanimity in this crisis. Our world is terrorized, and once again the Jewish people are targeted for destruction by the forces of evil. The extent of this effort is just being revealed as we uncover the true nature and overarching mission of Elijah Nabi. It is truly a miracle from God that the vault containing this drawing was discovered when it was."

"Most *truly* a miracle, sir, and one for which we should all be eternally grateful," Sister Margareta Maria said, and bowed her head.

"We are eternally grateful, sister. Our people will now get you safely back to your convent immediately. I again cannot thank you enough for your help here. It will never be forgotten by Israel," Ariel responded.

After the nun departed, leaving behind the drawing and notes in their protective case, the plane lifted off. Richard stood alone and took one last look out the plane's window at the heavily guarded facility. Twilight enveloped the building.

"Oh my darling, I will love you and miss you forever, and I will love and care for our daughter forever," he silently promised.

On board the transport, the forensic team began inspecting the drawing and the note from Vittoria. Though quite fragile, the chalk drawing was still in good condition, thanks to the dark and nearly airtight conditions it had been kept in, undisturbed, over the centuries.

The drawing was placed in position for computerized infrared carbon-dating equipment to examine the paper. Specialized authentication equipment identified all the other features of the drawing. The illegible note was subjected to various forms of radiography to determine what the faded parts might reveal.

For everyone on board, time passed unbearably slowly as the specialists went about their designated tasks. In the midst of the weighty silence, Eban received a message.

"We are now being informed that hostile forces associated with the United Nations are frantically searching for the chalk drawing," Eban reported, a note of tension in his voice. "Damn it, how could they know about it?"

"There is obviously a major leak somewhere," the deputy prime minister replied. "We're going to need to change our plan." He appeared to be turning something over in his mind. "Where are we at in the authentication process?" he said quickly.

"We have transmitted scans of the drawing and notes to Jerusalem, and the authentication confirmation is coming in," replied the lead art forensic specialist, his eyes glued to a computer screen.

The deputy prime minister turned to Richard and said, "Richard, I am going to ask you to do something, but I will understand if you choose not to do it."

"What is that, sir?" Richard asked, surprised by the strange request.

"This material must be preserved at all costs. What I propose is that we drop you, with the drawing and the notes, to a secret underground location. We have already developed a range of backup plans in case a problem like this arose, so we are prepared for this contingency. Your SAS experience is invaluable to us now if you choose to do this."

Richard looked away, considering the request. He thought of Judith waiting for him to return safely to Israel. He thought, too, of Sao and the ultimate sacrifice she had made for her people.

"Richard, I need your answer right now, because we are closing in on the site."

"I will do whatever is necessary, sir."

"Prepare Arenell to be dropped," the deputy prime minister commanded.

Richard was hardly prepared for what being "dropped" would entail. Guards quickly assembled around him and took him to a separate room, where they placed him in a sleek, compact, computerized glider. He was told that the glider would propel itself safely away from the transport plane into a magnetic field created by a powerful guidance system at the hidden site below. If all systems worked properly, Richard would be safely delivered to the ground. If they didn't, Richard could land the craft himself using a separate guidance system, which they quickly ran through with him. "Got it," he replied brusquely.

As darkness fell, the leader of the fighter squadron escorting the transport jet plane coded in, saying, "We have received information that there are enemy combatants entering Israeli airspace at our coordinates. We ask permission to engage and destroy them by all necessary means. Ground missiles are also being deployed."

From the transport plane, the deputy prime minister responded, "Permission granted for all necessary actions against them. Do we know who they are?"

"We believe they are UN forces. They've been monitoring us closely."

"They want to destroy the drawing, so we will have no physical proof," Eban replied. "We need to drop Arenell and then get away from here as quickly as possible."

The lead art forensic specialist provided the update they'd been anxiously waiting to hear. "All our authentication techniques check out, Ariel."

"You are sure?"

"We are positive, sir."

The plane erupted into a roar of approval from everyone on board.

"Transmit the findings to Jerusalem and get ready to drop Arenell now."

The drawing and notes were brought into the next room and placed in a protective cylinder within the glider that encased Richard.

"They are waiting for you, Richard." Then turning to the deputy prime minister, Eban said, "Our timing so far is perfect, Ariel."

The plane began its rapid descent through the darkness.

"Are we receiving our people's coding from the ground?"

"Yes, we are one minute from the drop."

"Ready the glider and transition the control to countdown."

Software systems took over all operations and began the precise countdown. The bay doors of the plane opened.

Suddenly a powerful laser beam from the ground illuminated the belly of the plane. Richard's glider slowly propelled itself onto an electromagnetic track leading directly to the hidden location below. The laser went out, and the jet transport ascended and headed towards Jerusalem.

The commander of the fighter squadron escorting the transport jet radioed in. "Be advised our fighters and missiles have successfully destroyed the attacking combat—" His words were cut off before he could finish, as he witnessed the explosion of the transport plane and its disintegration in midair in front of him.

"The transport plane just blew up in front of us!"

"I don't know what happened, but I saw a laser light," said another pilot.

"The enemy was behind us. We destroyed them," said another, dumbfounded.

"There must have been a bomb on board!"

"How could this have happened to us?" The commander exclaimed in despair.

Chapter 52

ISRAELI GOVERNMENT HEADQUARTERS
JERUSALEM

DAWN BROKE EARLY at 3 Kaplan Street, Qiryat Ben-Gurion. The office complex of the Israeli prime minister was a scene of frenzied commotion. The prime minister's press secretary, John Grossman, a former New Hampshire book publisher and graduate of Harvard Business School—his eyes red, his face tear-stained—convened a special meeting of the press in the Government Press Office, prior to the address the prime minister would be giving later in the morning.

Clearing his throat, Grossman announced with overwhelming sadness, "The prime minister of Israel will soon explain to the citizens of the world, and at the request of many governments, why Elijah Nabi's community was attacked and he was assassinated.

"Furthermore, he will tell you how the nation of Israel was attacked by Nabi's agents and operatives, in concert with military personnel from the United Nations, as recently as yesterday. A suicidal attack by a covert UN operative destroyed one of our transport planes. In so doing, it took the lives of our deputy prime minister, a deputy intelligence head, and others acting unselfishly in the best interest of Israel and of the world at large.

"The nation of Israel will not rest until these murderers are brought to justice. We continue to remain on the highest nuclear response alert. The United Nations has been formally warned of the following: Israel is now prepared to use any and all of its weapons, including nuclear and biological, situated around the world, against UN establishments if the UN—or any other hostile nation, acting either on the UN's behalf or independently—attacks again."

After a moment of stunned silence, questions from a standing-room-only audience of international reporters bombarded the press secretary both in person and via videoconference.

"Israel is prepared to use nuclear force, and you have these weapons around the world?"

"Absolutely, and I will take no further questions on that subject."

"Why do you believe the plane was destroyed by agents of Nabi and the United Nations?"

"Was the United States involved any further here?"

Grossman silenced them. "I will have no further comments until after the prime minister speaks."

At the same time as the meeting in Jerusalem, a top-secret communication was under way among certain United Nations military officers in Europe.

"We were able to destroy those Zionist bastards who had the chalk study!" an elated voice screamed to a UN peer in Germany.

A smug voice chimed in: "The plane was blown up by one of our people, disguised as a specialist, who carried a nano-liquid bomb inside him!"

"Wonderful!"

"Then the actual chalk study is destroyed?"

"Yes, we are sure of it."

A short time later, in a heavily guarded facility off Florence Gold Road in the Chelsea section of Jerusalem, a glum prime minister stood at an imposing podium. A large blue-and-white menorah with an olive branch, the emblem of the State of Israel, was behind him.

The president and vice president of the United States and their staffs had gathered in a West Wing conference room to view his historic speech.

"Thank God, we believe we finally have the goods on the evil bastards, Mr. President."

"Are you sure, French?" the president asked, turning to his vice president for an answer.

"Yes, at last, Donald. This time we are sure—as you will see."

Global news feeds streaming from hundreds of agencies around the world now all focused on the Israeli prime minister. "My fellow citizens and citizens of the world," he began, haltingly. "I can assure you that what I am about to tell you will be considered beyond belief, but I can also assure you it is undeniably true. What you will see and hear from me today will explain much of the sorrow that has singularly befallen not only the Jewish people over time—right to the present day—but also all the citizens of this world. Tragically, this sorrow is far from over.

"This account begins with Michelangelo Buonarroti, one of the greatest painters of all time, and two chalk drawings that he produced in preparation for what has turned out to be a chilling revelation in his last painting, *Christ on the Cross.*

"I have in my hands one of the two chalk studies for that painting." The prime minister held the drawing up for the world to see. "This centuries-old drawing has been tested by our government to prove its authenticity, and the results will be made available shortly."

The prime minister told the puzzled crowd about the first chalk drawing, which was in the British Museum, and the tortuous journey spanning almost five hundred years that had brought the second drawing to his hand this day. He revealed to the world the even more elaborate and tragedy-filled story of the painting *Christ on the Cross*, and the Jesuit book containing sketches from the painting and Michelangelo's note.

"Outrageously, both the painting and the book were recently destroyed by Elijah Nabi and his followers in two separate attacks. All that remains of these historically significant and priceless works is the charred canvas of the painting, on which only the figure of Christ can now be seen.

"Yes, my fellow citizens, the supposedly peace-loving Elijah Nabi, who has been worshipped by billions in so many quarters of this world, destroyed these works. In this abhorrent act, Nabi collaborated with secret military personnel from the supposedly peace-keeping United Nations. As recently as yesterday, Nabi's followers and their UN supporters tried unsuccessfully to destroy this second original Michelangelo chalk study for the painting, which I now hold in my hands.

"I must inform you with great sadness that Nabi's followers' outrageous attack resulted in the loss of a number of our wonderfully talented and good countrymen. These selfless countrymen of ours were attempting to deliver this chalk drawing safely into my hands. They made the ultimate sacrifice to reveal what we now know about these works of art and Michelangelo's vision within them. I give you my personal assurance that these heroes, along with Sao Damrey, our singularly remarkable brave Jewish heroine, who also gave her life in the defense of Israel, will be remembered by a special monument at the Wall of Honor in the Garden of the Righteous at Vad Yeshem in Jerusalem.

"Now, surely you are wondering why a supposedly good man such as Elijah Nabi, and his presumed peace-loving followers, and even the United Nations, would go to such lengths to destroy these works by the great Michelangelo.

"The reason is simple. They all contained clear imagery of the faces of a number of men who, though unrecognizable in Michelangelo's time, are widely recognizable today.

"And one of those faces was that of Elijah Nabi."

A growing commotion filled the auditorium of the Government Press Office. Security personnel asked for quiet from the crowd of reporters as the prime minister continued.

"Elijah Nabi is pictured with three other recognizable faces in Michelangelo's visionary work: Adolph Hitler, Osama Bin Laden, and Mahmoud Ahmadinejad."

There was a loud communal gasp, followed by insistent murmuring from the crowd.

"And what do all of these men have in common? They have a monumental, unswerving hatred of Jews and an insatiable desire to eradicate all Jewish people from the face of the earth.

"We also strongly believe that all the men I have cited were either directly possessed—yes, I said *possessed*—or at the very least powerfully inspired by a singular horrific demon that we believe has stalked the Jewish people since the time of Abraham and who has never ceased annually calling for our annihilation. This demon's face is pictured in the chalk study I have here, the painting, and the Jesuit book of sketches.

"This demon's name is Samael—a mysterious and terrifying demon known historically as a merciless, genocidal, demonic mass murderer by both Christians and Jews. The cult of Gnostic believers, prevalent in the world today, claim that Samael is *our* Jewish God who created the world as evil. Yet it should be understood by all that this brilliantly malevolent and highly deceptive demon Samael is *not* our Jewish God but is, in fact, the Angel of Death and the Venom of God. Samael would arise in full force in the End Times, which many Christians, including our own Orthodox Jews, believe we are in today. And, as you will see from the chalk study, we believe Samael's latest—but not last—possession was Elijah Nabi himself.

"Yet the world says that Elijah Nabi was a wise and holy man. I am here today to absolutely dispel this most dangerous of misconceptions. We must all understand that this demon, Samael, has no form and is, in fact, a maker of form. Thus, Samael can change rapidly from one form into another or possess others. And thus the demon can be a handsome man, a beautiful woman, a powerful animal, or anything it wants to be—including a seemingly wise, holy person.

"Samael most recently took exactly that form when he possessed Elijah Nabi. And working through Nabi, Samael deceived the world. Samael's unwavering plan was to have Nabi manipulate the puppets at the United Nations into working with him to destroy Israel and finish the extermination begun by Adolf Hitler. In fact, Nabi has been quoted as secretly saying, 'Now the remaining Jewish vermin will be liquidated through my trap of holiness and loving kindness, which I have set for them.'

"That trap was to have Israel first become a 'protectorate' of the United Nations—as Nabi so proudly proclaimed—and then eventually be destroyed by the same body's military in a 'socially necessary' act approved by Elijah Nabi. And that is the reason Sao Damrey assassinated Nabi."

There was dead silence in the auditorium at the Government Press Office and across the world as countless people watched simulcasts.

"So, with this chilling revelation, let me continue and bring you back to the beginnings of World War II, where the first knowledge of this dreadful vision by Michelangelo—the vision that spawned this horrific revelation—began..."

In a UN location in Germany, two voices screamed in a violent rage.

"We have not destroyed the drawing after all!"

"We have failed!"

"And now we have been revealed to the entire world by these hordes of Zionist and Christian bastards!"

Chapter 53

LAKE COMO
NORTHERN ITALY

AN EXHAUSTED RICHARD ARENELL, his face deeply etched with grief and fatigue, climbed out of a privately marked Israeli military jet helicopter that had carried him to a helipad on an estate secretly owned by the Israeli government. He walked alone down a manicured path towards the Villa Millucille, from the Renaissance period. The villa overlooked Lake Como, one of the most beautiful lakes in northern Italy. As an Israeli government facility, the estate was heavily guarded and fortified with security systems and high-tech armaments hidden everywhere. However, it was soon to be closed, along with other non-military Israeli facilities worldwide, due to the danger posed to these facilities after the Nabi attack.

Richard paused to look across the shimmering lake surrounded by the Italian Alps and saw the elegant white-and-gold Hotel Villa d'Este on the distant shore. He fondly remembered the romantic weeks he had spent there with Sao at the beginning of their relationship. Losing her was still unbearable to him. And though there had been a brief feeling of elation when he was honored, along with Sister

Margareta Maria, for helping to deliver the chalk study to the Israeli government, he continued to mourn not only the loss of Sao, but also the loss of Alon Eban and the others who had died in the explosion of the transport plane. He looked away, letting out a deep melancholy sigh as he remembered how close he came to death on the plane.

Yet, as he approached the villa's grand entrance, a warm light entered his mind's eye, and a true happiness and excitement arose in his heavy heart. Richard Arenell was about to meet his daughter, Judith.

The door to the mansion silently swung open as he approached. A plainclothes Israeli security guard stationed at the doorway greeted him. "Welcome, Mr. Arenell. Please come in, sir."

"Thank you," Richard responded, stepping inside.

He passed through a biometric security booth and into a formal entrance hall with golden chandeliers and elegant floral arrangements. Beyond the hall, a spacious room offered a spectacular view of the lake through floor-to-ceiling Italianate windows.

"Please make yourself comfortable in the great room, Mr. Arenell," a military attaché said, motioning down the hall. "May I have one of our staff bring you something to drink while you wait, sir? You will be joined shortly by Ms. Damrey's mother. She has just arrived with your daughter."

Richard's heart leapt at the power of those two simple words "your daughter."

Declining the offer of refreshment, Richard proceeded to the great room and sat down on a Queen Anne sofa and gazed out at the lake.

He took a deep breath and felt a sense of amazement come over him. Here he was about to meet his daughter by the woman he loved—who, it would seem, had also been loved by one of the richest, most mysterious men in the world, as well as Elijah Nabi himself.

Even though Richard had felt that he knew Sao and they shared a special bond, he realized he really had not known her at all. He wasn't alone. It seemed that no one quite knew *everything* about Sao Damrey. A spectacularly beautiful and exotic woman, who was intelligent, sophisticated, and worldly—and an *amoureuse* and Israeli spy who could kill if necessary. Richard consoled himself with the thought that Sao had only let Nabi love her in order to eliminate him, that she had used her seductive talents ultimately as a heroic defender of Israel. "A truly unique and remarkable person," he thought. And she was a mother, the mother of his child. "What an honor to have known her as well as I did. Who could ever replace her?" he wondered to himself.

His reverie was interrupted by words he would never forget.

"Richard, meet your daughter, Judith."

He looked up, and there before him was his lovely daughter wearing a simple dress, with a demure smile on her sad face. Her green eyes, cheekbones, and dark hair were decidedly Sao's, but her dimples were Richard's alone. Next to her stood a woman who was unmistakably Sao's mother: a stunning Venezuelan woman with lush, dark hair and large, almond-shaped green eyes exactly like her daughter's. The resemblance across three generations was striking.

Richard rose to greet Judith, his eyes glistening. For a moment, they both simply looked at each other—family they'd never met.

"Judith, you look just like your mother," he said, as Judith began to cry. "I feel so fortunate to be your father." They embraced, holding each other tight. "I love you so, Judith," Richard said through his own tears.

In reply, he heard the most wondrous words that a man who had just become a father could ever hear. "Daddy, I love you, too, and so did Mom. She told me so many times." Judith buried her head in her father's chest as he held her close and she continued to cry.

Minutes passed as the two just held each other tightly.

"Oh, my lovely Judith, there is so much I want to know and to tell you. I want to give you the happiest life imaginable," Richard said as he finally released her and held her at arm's length for a moment. He looked over to Sao's mother. There was not a dry eye in the room as he walked over to embrace her.

"Oh, Richard, this is such a bittersweet moment. Please let me introduce myself. I am Adara Damrey. I miss Sao so much, yet Judith and you finally being together is just the way Sao would have wanted it." Deep emotion and strain showed in Adara's eyes as she began to cry.

For Richard, it was surreal: meeting a daughter he had never known, a complete stranger, while also realizing how incompletely he knew Sao herself. And now she was gone.

"Please sit down," Richard said, ushering Adara and Judith towards the sofa.

"There is so much to ask you both. Frankly, so much has happened over the last year that it's become a bit of a blur to me," he said, his blue eyes briefly glazing over.

"Perfectly understandable, Richard," Adara said, and Judith nodded somberly in agreement.

They sat in the formal living room, with the lake and mountainous backdrop behind them. Judith, close to her father, smiled at him weakly. Richard was tremendously relieved that she seemed to like him. Obviously, Sao had made it clear to Judith who her father was and had painted him in a positive light.

Addressing Adara, Richard asked, "Did you know Sao was a member of the Mossad working with the Israeli Special Forces?"

"No, I didn't, Richard. I had not even the slightest idea," Adara answered. "We only knew that she worked for the Manchurian. We learned about her involvement with Nabi and the Mossad along with everyone else, after Nabi died. However, as a result of working for the Manchurian, Sao became extraordinarily wealthy in her own right. You will be informed shortly of the particulars of a very significant trust fund for Judith. It is managed by a team of advisors, personally selected by Sao at her private bank, Eszterhazen & Cie. Banquiers in Geneva, Switzerland.

"The Israeli government has also told me to inform you that Judith will be supplied a substantial income for her needs in perpetuity from a separate trust established by them in Sao's memory. She will also have the personal use at all times of Israeli government aircraft and, given the circumstances, will be supplied for the foreseeable future with a contingent of plainclothes Israeli secret service. This protection will also apply to you, not only as her father, but also for your heroic service to Israel."

"How gracious of them," Richard said, a bit overwhelmed by this news.

Richard looked again at his daughter, who still had a sad smile on her face upon hearing the words of her grandmother.

"Adara, thank you so much for helping Judith through this terrible time," Richard said, then turned to address his daughter. "Judith, nothing would make me happier than for you to join me at my home in London—but of course that is entirely up to you." Judith turned to her grandmother and smiled.

Adara said, "We've done a lot of talking about this, Richard. Judith does want to come and live with you." Judith beamed and nodded her head. "She wants to get to know her father, leave the past behind, start fresh…" Adara said, her voice catching at the end.

"Judith, I love you and so look forward to taking good care of you in our new life together," Richard assured his daughter. Adara turned to Richard and said, "I will ship all of Judith's belongings to your residence immediately. I will also make arrangements to meet again about Sao's personal effects." Her voice quivered.

"I can't thank you enough, Adara." Richard's lips tightened in a grimace and his eyes dropped at the mention of Sao's personal effects.

"I will take my leave now, so the two of you can talk and get to know each other." The three of them rose, and Adara hugged Judith tightly then put her hand out to Richard.

"Thank you for all you have done for Judith," he said, clasping her hand in turn.

"Thank you from me, too, Grandmother. I love you so," Judith chimed in with wide green eyes and a sparkling smile.

"She is just like her mother, as you will find out, Richard—very smart, very athletic, and, of course, very charming and beautiful. And now I can see you in her, too."

"Thank you, Adara. We look forward to seeing you soon." His dark blue eyes met hers, gratitude mixed with sadness, before she turned to leave.

Shortly after, Richard and Judith proceeded out of the villa as well, walking to a car that would take them to a private airport near Como.

"Your grandmother has been good to you, hasn't she, Judith?"

"Yes, I love her so much, but I miss Mom terribly."

"I do, too," Richard said. "I do, too."

Chapter 54

UNITED NATIONS EUROPEAN HEADQUARTERS
GENEVA, SWITZERLAND

*In later times some will depart…by giving heed to doctrines of
demons through the pretensions of liars whose consciences are seared.*
—1 TIMOTHY 4:1–2

RICHARD AND HIS DAUGHTER, now heavily guarded, re-entered
a world awash in reproductions of the second chalk study for *Christ
on the Cross* with all the human, animal and demonic images in plain
view. Digital images had gone viral within minutes of the Israeli prime
minister's press conference, and hard copies were displayed everywhere.
Social networking and media in all forms, discussion groups, blogs,
and messaging at all levels worldwide interpreted what the drawing
and its faces meant for the future. Who did the unrecognized faces
belong to? What were all the connections between these men and
Hitler, Bin Laden, and Ahmadinejad? Were they from the future or
the present day, or were they unknown men of the past? Were they
the False Prophet and Antichrist or other would-be destroyers of the
Jewish people? An international manhunt for the unidentified men

in the sketch had been launched by the United States, assisted by Interpol and the few countries aligned with Israel.

The world had been surprised by the unusual press conference suddenly called by the United Nations after the Israeli prime minister's. The president of the UN began by stating that the UN had no interest in discussing the drawing or looking for the unknown men whose faces appeared in it. He went on to say that the UN absolutely disagreed with the popular interpretation of the drawing's subject matter, its history, and its impact on the future. The UN believed it to be an extraordinarily elaborate fraud, he said, irrespective of the proof the Israelis offered, including the story of its "convenient" discovery in the convent. The deception, according to the UN president, was part of a high-level global Christian conspiracy led by the president and vice president of the United States and their key military leaders, all of whom were Christians, to denigrate the enlightened universal religion created by Elijah Nabi and supported by the UN.

When asked by the press whether Nabi was demonic, as he was portrayed by Israel, the UN president answered with a categorical "no." The fact that Nabi was pictured with vampire teeth pointed towards Christ was certainly the fraudsters' idea to try and make Nabi appear evil, but the perpetrators of this hoax could not overcome the inherent goodness of Nabi. The UN president went on to say that Nabi's disagreement with Christ's followers was that they believed Christ was the Son of God, a point that Jewish and Islamic people alike believed to be false.

The UN president argued that when the global Christian faction behind this hoax realized that their fraudulent chalk drawing was unlikely to erode the foundations of Nabi's new religion, they had no option left but to kill him and his closest followers. They used the leaders of the Israeli government and its armed forces as pawns because they feared Nabi's power as much as the Christians'.

The UN president insisted that the entire discussion of demonic possession by Samael was ridiculous. It was nothing more than an attempt to smear Nabi and others, including the UN itself, with ancient religious superstitions that were irrelevant and patently ignorant in modern times.

He concluded his address by saying that Nabi had never felt anything but loving kindness towards the Jewish people and had urged the UN to protect them. Reports that the deceased Sao Damrey, a Mossad agent, along with Israel's Christian co-conspirators, knew otherwise was pure fabrication and part of the conspiracy.

When asked by the press whether Nabi's forces had hired UN mercenaries and received covert UN help to destroy the original Jesuit book of sketches and the painting, the UN president adamantly denied all involvement. Instead, he accused the Judeo-Christian conspirators of destroying the works in order to frame Nabi and the UN as part of their plot to destroy him. The UN president claimed the Israeli government's possession of the charred remains of the painting was proof of its involvement. He demanded the canvas be repatriated to the Michelangelo Museum in Florence, its rightful owner.

From the private airport near Como, Richard and Judith boarded a privately marked, high-security Israeli military Gulfstream jet that would take them to a secure residence in Israel. Once on board, they discussed Judith and Sao's life together. His daughter had been describing their happy times when Judith made an innocent comment to her father—a comment that shook him to his core.

"You know, I saw one of the images from the chalk drawing before it went viral—a man's face. Only it looked different to the drawing, more like a painting. Mom was looking at it on her mobile device when I was with her on her friend's yacht, just before she died." Saying this, sadness crossed the young woman's face yet again.

"What do you mean, dear? When were you with your mother before she died—and whose yacht were you on?" Richard looked incredulously at his daughter, trying to make sense of what she had just said.

A short time later, the Israeli prime minister was interrupted during a meeting with his key advisors on the United Nations press conference. A signal in the conference room registered an urgent call from Richard Arenell.

"Mr. Prime Minister, Richard Arenell is on one of our planes heading back to Israel with his daughter, but he says he needs to speak with you urgently about what his daughter has just revealed to him about Sao Damrey."

"Put him through immediately on the secure video channel."

"Go ahead, Mr. Prime Minister."

"Richard, it is so good to see you."

"It is good to see you, too, Asher."

"Please speak freely, Richard—as you can see, my key advisors are all here. We're all eager to hear what you have to say."

Richard, who was in an office on the plane and away from his daughter, explained to the assembled group what Judith had seen on Sao's device.

"Gentlemen, given everything that has happened, Judith's sense of chronology could be somewhat confused, so I almost hesitate to say this. Apparently, Judith was with Sao when she was viewing an image on her device of the part of the *Christ on the Cross* painting that shows the face of the unknown man who shares an eye with Nabi. And, gentlemen, I can't believe I am saying this, but from the timeline Judith has reconstructed for me, it seems that this may have happened *after* we all presumed Sao was dead!"

The complete silence that momentarily filled the room was broken by the prime minister suddenly yelling at one of his aides.

"Get Zohar Berman and his Mossad lieutenants in here immediately!"

Pandemonium ensued as aides rushed to contact the Mossad.

"Richard, do you really think—" the incredulous prime minister began.

Richard interrupted him. "I frankly don't exactly know what to think, Asher. I am going to talk with Judith again, but I thought you should know at once, because my instincts tell me I could be right."

"Absolutely, Richard, we are on it now."

Chapter 55

ON BOARD AN ISRAELI JET
EN ROUTE TO ISRAEL

THE ISRAELI AIRCRAFT had reached its cruising altitude. Having moved quickly into international airspace, the jet was now joined by heavily armed Israeli fighter escorts. Richard had returned, and now looked closely at Judith. Her mother's green eyes looked back at him. He gave her a reassuring smile and said, "Judith, I would like you and me to go over the things you told me again very carefully, alright?"

Richard suddenly felt surprise and elation, but also anger; his eyes narrowed. He took a deep breath to calm himself and looked out the jet's window at the fighter escorts off its wing. What could really be going on here? He did not want to jump to conclusions, but memories of Sao's secret agendas resurfaced in his mind.

Judith again related how her mother came to Judith's private school in Switzerland to pick her up and take her away by helicopter to a large yacht in the Atlantic Ocean. Her mom had her bodyguards with her, as always. Judith didn't even recognize her mother at first, because she had blond hair. She had flicked the long blond locks and tapped her big dark Escada sunglasses and asked what Judith thought of her new look for the season. Richard couldn't help but smile wryly—it certainly sounded like Sao.

"You know what was kind of weird now that I think about it?" Judith said. "The bodyguards were speaking Hebrew. I don't really remember any of Mom's bodyguards speaking Hebrew before."

"Mossad or Sayeret Matkal?" Richard wondered to himself uneasily.

"Did your mother happen to say whose yacht it was?" Richard asked.

"To be honest, I didn't pay all that much attention," said Judith. "I wish I had now. But we were always going to someone's yacht or estate or villa somewhere. Her friend wasn't there—it was just us, together." A wistful look came over Judith's face, and she wiped a tear away from her cheek.

Richard nodded and clasped her hand reassuringly. "Was it later, after Mom had left you back at school, that you learned she had died?" he asked.

"Yes."

Richard knew that although Sao's death had been reported immediately to key governmental authorities, there was some lapse of time before her death became known to the public—even to Sao's mother and Judith.

"Where was your grandmother when you were on the yacht, dear?"

"She was in Israel, at her house."

When Sao took her out of school, she'd said it was because she needed to go away for a while and wanted to spend some time with Judith before she left. By the time they arrived on the yacht, it was late and Judith went to bed. Soon after, she'd woken up with a bad headache and went to find Sao to see if she had some aspirin. Her mother was in the yacht's living room, staring so intently at her camera that she didn't even hear Judith approach. Her mother was always assessing one artwork or another, so at the time Judith thought nothing of what her mother was looking at: a painting of a man's face with malevolent eyes, the same man she now saw everywhere in reproductions of the chalk drawing, sharing an eye with Elijah Nabi.

The next day, Judith and Sao just relaxed together and swam in the yacht's swimming pool. They did the same the day after that, and then she and Sao, with her security detail, boarded the vessel's jet helicopter, which dropped Judith off back at school. Judith said Sao told her she might not be in touch for a while but not to worry. She also asked her daughter not to mention their being together to anyone, especially Sao's mother. "We don't want anyone getting jealous, do we?" she said to Judith, winking.

"She didn't even want me taking a picture of her, in case anyone found out," Judith told Richard. "I sneaked a shot of her new look. She was gorgeous, wearing this big chic hat the whole time—you would never have recognized her. I wish I could show you, but she made me delete it."

Richard was simultaneously thrilled and upset given the timeline Judith described. It sounded as though Sao was actually alive while he, her family, the Israel government, and millions of Israeli people were deeply grief-stricken over her death.

"Why would she not even tell me or the Israeli prime minister?" he thought. "There had better be a damn good reason." Yet his anger quickly dissipated and gave way again to exhilaration of the distinct possibility that Sao might be alive. "I love her so," he murmured.

His daughter turned to stare out the jet's window. Richard stifled the urge to tell her the news that he knew she wanted to hear as much as he did. The idea that Sao was alive was more plausible every time he considered it, but he didn't dare risk saying anything to Judith until he was absolutely certain. For the moment, he would have to keep his thoughts to himself. "How was she able to take a picture of one of the unknown men when supposedly her ability to had been thwarted by Nabi's security system? What could be happening here that would preclude her from letting me and the Israeli leadership know she was alive? It's always a mystery with Sao," he thought, as Judith turned away from the window, leaned against her father, and closed her eyes.

Chapter 56

OFFICE OF THE ISRAELI PRIME MINISTER
JERUSALEM

"BERMAN, I WANT TO KNOW—and I want to damn well know *now*—what in God's name has been going on here between you and Sao Damrey!" The prime minister's face was contorted in rage, and he was banging on the table in the conference room with both fists. The target of his vitriolic outburst was none other than Zohar Berman, the director of the Mossad.

"We understand she could be alive!" shouted the prime minister. "For shit's sake, man, what could be going on in your heads that would prevent even *me,* the damn leader of this country, from knowing about this? Who are you guys working for anyway?"

"Asher, I apologize profusely, sir," the red-faced Berman quickly, but calmly, replied. "Yet with all due respect sir, we in the Mossad have been outraged about what seem like regular security leaks from governmental offices outside of the Mossad causing great damage to our operations and loss of key personnel. The destruction of the transport plane was only one such example, but frankly, sir, it was the last straw. It was critical that in Damrey's case the utmost secrecy be employed, and if you'll let me explain, I am sure you will see why."

"It better be good, Zohar!"

"You are correct, Asher. She is alive," Berman said. "Her death was perfectly staged by our Sayeret Matkal doctors after they operated on her. Thank God her wound was not as serious as first thought, because of the high-tech anti-ballistic protection she was wearing. As a result, her recovery was rapid. But frankly, their methods for simulating Sao's death were brilliant, if I must say so myself. We did this for two reasons. First, so that she could continue to operate clandestinely for us. And second, of even greater importance, to protect her. Given the highly charged atmosphere surrounding Nabi's death, we believed Sao would be in immediate, grave danger of being killed by Nabi's supporters and the UN, who would be preoccupied looking for her unless they were convinced she had died. As it is, we know they are hunting for her burial site."

"Her burial site? They are the scum of the earth. And against whom is she operating in these covert activities, Zohar?"

"Against the Manchurian and the unknown man whose face was revealed in the chalk drawing sharing an eye with Nabi."

"What? The Manchurian! What does all this mean, Zohar?"

"Asher, what it means is that she was able to secretly photograph the face of the unknown man who shares an eye with Nabi, using one of our micro cameras located in a contact lens she was wearing. She did it at Nabi's compound, while his personnel were cleaning away the surface painting and analyzing the Michelangelo painting. Soon after, they destroyed the painting, leaving only the charred Christ on the cross. Either they were unable to destroy Christ's figure or chose not to, in order to accuse us of fraud, as they have done.

"As we all know, Nabi's security system destroyed all the other pictures she took except this singular image. Miraculously, it survived—as she found out, *after* the fact."

The prime minister and his staff listened in amazement as Berman continued. "And it doesn't end there. Damrey recognized the man who in the painting shared an eye with Nabi. He was associated in some way with the Manchurian. She had seen him periodically over the years in private meetings with the Manchurian."

The prime minister shook his head in amazement. "She saw this man with the Manchurian, who refuses to meet anyone else in person?"

"Yes, this singular unknown man sharing an eye with Nabi."

"Well, who in hell is he? Does she know?"

"No," said Berman. "She learned of him sometime before Sister Margareta Maria brought us the chalk drawing. We are virtually sure he also has an association with Nabi, pictured as he is sharing one common eye with Nabi in the drawing."

"Was Sao with anybody else we should know about while she was on the yacht?" asked the prime minister.

"No. The yacht is actually one of our armed naval vessels disguised as a yacht. Sao was heavily guarded by Sayeret Makal commandos and naval personnel. In addition, both she and the yacht were constantly under invisibility shields. Damrey wanted to be with her daughter one more time before she left to hunt the unknown man for us. She planned to start by meeting with the Manchurian," said the Mossad chief.

"Where is she now, Zohar?"

"Unfortunately, that is a problem, sir. At the moment, we don't quite know. We have lost contact with her. She insisted that it was better for her to act alone in this mission, at least until she made contact with the Manchurian and she could learn more. He is all but invisible, and only Sao has any real access to him."

"You've lost all contact? Shit, Zohar! How the hell can that be? I thought we were in the surveillance business. With all our cutting-edge capability, this is unacceptable."

"I know, sir," Berman said sheepishly, his face reddening once again.

"She could be in real trouble. How can she elude our detection, Zohar?"

"She has the ability to evade all detection, including ours, and might want to if she believes that she is within the Manchurian's surveillance. Frankly, his systems could be better than ours, and she needs to evade all detection in order to evade his," the Mossad chief said with candor.

The prime minister had run out of patience. "I don't want to hear any more excuses, Zohar. You need to find Sao Damrey, and you need to find her *now*!"

The prime minister got up from the conference table and walked out of the room while saying to an aide, "Inform Arenell immediately of what we know, and tell him I want his help in finding Damrey. We could be fast running out of miracles here!"

Much of the world was still mourning the loss of Elijah Nabi. Israel and the United States continued to experience pressure and intimidation from the United Nations, which was taking advantage of the generally weakened condition of both nations to encourage sanctions against them. Covert terrorist operations increased, unchecked, against both nations. A cloud of heightened anxiety spread over an already terrorized and depressed world, which now found itself on the brink of war—one that would likely include the use of nuclear and biological weapons.

Transported to a secure Israeli residence, which was under constant surveillance using every security measure Israel could provide, Richard and his daughter were treated as if they were heads of state.

Once inside this temporary home, Richard received a top-secret message from one of the prime minister's aides explaining what had transpired with Berman. It concluded with, "Richard, you need to help us determine what is going on and help locate Sao. The Mossad will interface with you at once."

As he packed a bag for himself and one for Judith, he thought, "Sao loves her people, but what she has been doing is so dangerous, and now, with the Mossad having lost track of her, anything can happen."

Richard, Judith, and their security detail were picked up and taken by military jet back to Jerusalem.

"I will be gone for a while, Judith."

"Daddy, please be careful," Judith said anxiously.

"Please don't worry, darling. Everything will be all right and I'll be home again soon."

Upon arrival in Jerusalem, Judith was taken to her grandmother's home, which was now also under around-the-clock surveillance. As difficult as it was for Richard to leave his crying daughter, he knew he was needed like never before.

While Richard was saying his farewell to Judith, it was late afternoon in a quiet corner of the French Riviera. A customized silver Aston Martin DBS twelve-cylinder coupe with a lone driver took the sharp curves on the corniches high above the Mediterranean with perfect precision. The car passed swiftly through a number of jewel-like towns clinging to the cliffs above the shores. The bulletproof, bombproof car was equipped with advanced weaponry and the most sophisticated anti-surveillance equipment on Earth. It was invisible to all forms of GPS and other satellite detection devices.

Later, in a new Mossad underground compound in an undisclosed location, the acting deputy prime minister and two senior members of the Mossad briefed Richard on the search for Sao. Worry was written all over the faces of everyone present.

"You've lost complete contact with her? How can that be?" Richard asked.

"We believe Sao is either in such danger that she cannot respond, or that she is simply trying to avoid danger and therefore wants to remain totally hidden from any interception," replied the Mossad official. "We know she would communicate with us if she could do so safely—she has the most sophisticated technology available, which she used to communicate with us when she was with Nabi. We know the equipment works. What we don't know is whether she is up against something even more powerful."

"Meaning the Manchurian?" asked Richard.

"Yes. Sao is trying to meet with him."

Richard grimaced.

"Gentlemen, my concerns are that Sao, being the brave and dedicated woman she is, may underestimate the very significant danger she could be in," he said. "Yes, Sao is the only person with direct access to the Manchurian, and she does have extraordinary influence over him. But given all that has transpired, even Sao could really be out on a limb with him now."

Chapter 57

ON BOARD A PRIVATE JET
EN ROUTE TO CAP D'ANTIBES,
FRANCE

There was another angel in the seventh heaven different in appearance from all the others and of very frightful mien. Thereupon Moses prayed to God, "Oh may it be Thy will, my God, not to let me fall into the hands of this angel."
—The Ascension of Moses: The Legend of the Jews

A SMARTLY ATTIRED MAN with dark, silver-streaked hair sat alone in his large, lavishly appointed long-range Dassault private jet. The plane had flown nonstop since its departure from Blumenau, Brazil, and was nearing Cap Ferrat, on the French Riviera. His strangely malevolent, blue-violet eyes peered out the jet's window at the white cumulous clouds, which framed a brilliant early twilight of pink, blue, and gold.

A solid gold and diamond signet ring with a lion's head and serpent's body glistened on his finger in the fading light. His mouth formed a sneer, and he ground his teeth.

"It is such a pity how, in the end, my key chess pieces have always failed me in my struggle with the Most High to exterminate the Jew," he thought. "And now that fornicating bastard Nabi has failed me, too. My lascivious twin and I found such gratification and excitement in him, as opposed to this body we are once again consigned to share. Yet not for long, for my human face has been exposed by those miserable nuns. I will now have to enter into a new form and identity. How clever of the Most High to send the Archangel Michael, my eternal adversary, to Michelangelo in his dreams."

He muttered expletives and his face twitched with increasing agitation, then contorted into a scowl.

"My elegant move to have the United Nations make Israel a 'protectorate' and then eradicate the Jewish maggots once and for all was truly enlightened. This chess game I have been forced to undertake would have finally ended, with a sudden checkmate against the Most High.

"Yet even with all my inspiration and insight—infusing Nabi with the power to enable him to gain the unquestioning support of the compliant fools at the United Nations—the bastard, like others before him, was seduced by a voluptuous whore. A Jewish whore, no less!

"Using that whore against me was a rather calculating and cunning move by the Most High, but I saw it coming! I warned Nabi so many times in his dreams: 'Beware of the Jewish whore. She will destroy you!' Still he would not heed my warnings! For instead of glorifying me through obedience, the insipid turd used my power to glorify himself through his disobedience. Oh, how he was overcome by the sheer ecstasy of rutting the Jewish whore, to my eventual detriment. He was blinded to her ways, and in the end the wretched scum deserved to lose his head at her hands!"

His menacing eyes narrowed, reflecting all-consuming disgust and disdain.

"My zealous Ishmaelite and Persian followers have been willing disciples for my legions to use to accomplish our goal. Yet for all their successes against the parasites, none has yet risen to the supremely powerful level of Hitler. Only Hitler, my most powerful chess piece ever, fervently tried to be obedient to me and my plans to the end. I knew he would, and that is why I picked him out of the excrement and exalted him, through my supremacy, to both deceive and control the masses while destroying the Jew for me."

A fiendish smile crossed the man's face exposing his glistening teeth.

"He allowed me and my legions complete possession and influence over him and his followers. We nearly accomplished both the eradication of the Jew and control of the world, as in the past. How truly marvelous a time! How mighty a chess piece he was for me! He reigned over his followers as a true superman; and, with the authority I gave him, through the banner of the twisted cross, millions were destroyed who dared stand in our way. Through him, our seduction of the Germans and entrapment of the Jew were all embracing, until it was too late for both of them. It was we, not the Most High, who were worshipped and glorified through Hitler by all Germans in their magnificent decadence. Why it was just as in Roman times, when that empire was ours and we were patrons to the Caesars, before the wretched Christ came to Earth—as a Jew, no less—to save the world from us."

A frown crossed the man's face.

"Sadly, in the end, even my dear Hitler failed me, too. I have unfortunately learned, through the loss of these key pieces, that I must always be on guard against the devious moves of the Most High. For when my actions drove the Jew vermin out of Europe towards their enemies in the Middle East, He countered by guiding them to create Israel and end the Diaspora.

"Oh, how the Most High makes me suffer! Israel's creation is a precursor to Christ's return to challenge our control of the world and to cast us back into the Abyss. And now Nabi's failure has resulted in my having to develop new moves against the Most High, once again using the enemies of the Jews as my pawns.

"For the Most High knows that I am relentless and will counter His every move by inspiring the Ishmaelite, as I have done since their beginning, to again strive to eliminate the Jew and thus themselves, thereby putting an end to all the seeds of Abraham. For we will forever condemn Abraham for what he has done to us by introducing the Most High to our world.

"I must cease my reflections. There is no use in looking back on what could have been. I must now contend with the reality of today. For the Most High has exposed me and my disciples through the drawing of his nauseating son. That leaves only a few final moves for me before our messiah arises to lead us and our world to the final confrontation with Christ. And one of those final moves is the Manchurian."

The man's white Egyptian cat, with its striking blue-violet eyes, leapt onto his lap. He stroked it, while peering out with venomous hate in his eyes at a distant rainbow of color bursting forth from a far-off storm. "Scripture says that the will of the Most High is done in heaven and on earth," he mused. "Does the will of the Most High prevent us from totally liquidating the Jew and the Ishmaelite?"

Suddenly, with his fists clenched, the man exploded in rage. He looked up to the heavens and screamed obscenities, then roared, "Scripture, not us, shall be damned to the Abyss, as will Christ and his followers, the Jews and the Ishmaelites! In the End, I will succeed in eliminating them *all* from my sight! Do you understand? You will not prevail against me in this, my final mission to destroy and devour the sons of Abraham."

Then, like a lion, the man licked away the foaming saliva from his lips and closed his eyes.

Darkness engulfed Jerusalem as Richard, protected by high-security monitoring, strode through a well-guarded walkway and into the prime minister's office for a night meeting with him and his staff. After going through security screening, he was ushered into the prime minister's office. The prime minister greeted Richard with warm embraces, as did his senior aide.

"Richard, we and the United States are still trying to develop a final plan as to what to do about the United Nations. It engages in these vitriolic verbal attacks and covert physical attacks against our interests worldwide through the use of mercenaries. And now we have that mysterious, unknown man being linked to the Manchurian by Sao. And who is this man? God only knows."

The prime minister gathered his thoughts before proceeding.

"Anyway, Richard, you have been briefed by our people."

"Yes, I have, Asher, and I agree that we must—and we *will*—find her. She has simply taken too much upon herself in attempting to find the unknown man. I believe her acting alone in trying to meet with the Manchurian is risky. The fact that she has not contacted anyone is highly unusual, and I think it indicates the danger she must be facing. She also might be relying too heavily on what she believes is her still-intimate relationship with the Manchurian."

"You are right, Richard."

"Sir, I am also here with a request."

"Anything, Richard, what is it?"

"It concerns the remains of the painting in your possession—the charred canvas fragment of *Christ on the Cross*."

Chapter 58

PALACE OF THE RED TILES
CAP D'ANTIBES, FRANCE

*And even in the last combat with the ancient foe, armed solely
with faith, the heart still, from long habit, on Christ shall call.*
—VITTORIA COLONNA

*Submit yourselves therefore to God. Resist the
devil and he will flee from you.*
—JAMES 4:7

THE SILVER ASTON MARTIN began a slow, final descent from the
highest of the Riviera corniches to the elegant French resort town of
Antibes and on to the exclusive peninsula of Cap d'Antibes. Moving
past the Villa Vera, a celebrated mansion with extraordinarily lush
gardens and cascading waterfalls, the car passed walled estates and
the famed Hotel du Cap as it headed towards a secluded part of the
forested isthmus.

Sparkling antique street lamps flickered as night enveloped the
surrounding area. In the distance, the shadowy Palace of the Red Tiles

loomed, its massive columns, Venetian roof, and medieval chimneys set off by surrounding acres of well-tended land.

The Aston Martin continued down a dark, narrow road, which led to the estate's entrance. The car proceeded through a massive iron gate into a large paved courtyard and came to a stop.

Sao Damrey looked through the windshield at the palatial edifice shrouded in darkness.

"He said he wanted to meet me here, yet it appears to be deserted," she thought.

Just at that moment, otherworldly, gleaming lights seemed to shoot through the palace.

"What in hell was that?" she asked herself.

Sao looked in the rearview mirror and realized that the gate at the courtyard's entrance had silently closed behind her. The palace's large double doors of red iron slowly swung open, revealing a dimly lit foyer.

Sao froze. Had she allowed herself to fall into a trap? She immediately turned on the car's powerful high beams and transmitted her location in a Mayday signal. A flashing message on the car's console lit up: outbound transmission failure.

The car's headlights revealed a marble foyer accented with opulent gold and onyx. An imposing grand staircase covered with a rich Aubusson carpet led to a dimly lit second floor. A tall, shadowy figure suddenly appeared in the gloom at the top of the stairs.

"You have risen from the dead, Sao!" an oddly shrill, yet familiar-sounding, voice resounded.

Sao spoke through the car's speakers, "Manchurian, is that you?"

"Yes, of course it is me. Please, come in," a now pleasant voice replied as the Manchurian descended the staircase. As he came to the palace entrance, she saw that it was him. A Caucasian man with a face like a mask made of stone, very dark, mysterious eyes, a Roman nose, and thin lips blocked the light from the foyer, casting a shadow on the entrance.

"Let there be light!" The Manchurian laughed loudly, as additional interior lights automatically came on. "You can shut off your high beams, Sao—you are blinding me."

"What is going on here, Manchurian?" she calmly asked, still hesitant to leave the relative safety of the Aston Martin. "Are you alone?"

Sao opened the car's wide-angle laser-gun ports.

"Of course I am alone, as I said I would be."

"You have blocked my signals."

"Who are you signaling, Sao? You, of all people, should know that signal-blocking is part of my security system, having dealt with me all these years. Now, please come inside."

Sao stepped out of the car. She was equipped with a pocket-sized, very powerful laser-guided Pfeifer-Zeliska 600 Nitro handgun and was wearing a high-tech, invisible full-body and facial laser and bulletproof shield.

An Israeli reconnaissance satellite transmitted a highly secure coded message: "Signal received from interceptor D1."

"Transmit D1 location," a system computer responded.

The satellite responded, "D1 location signal blocked. Unable to verify location; still searching."

The Manchurian walked into an ornate side salon and seated himself on a large sofa at the end of the room, motioning for Sao to sit down near him. She followed him in and did as he indicated.

"Sao, you asked to see me, yet I am sure you know that I am terribly upset with you. You have grievously disobeyed me and caused me great loss. You realize that, I am sure," he said in a low voice.

"You were not only Nabi's lover; you were also working with him to get the painting away from me, weren't you? And you were also working with the Israelis in their plan to assassinate Nabi. You have been a busy woman." A look of profound contempt now slowly enveloped the Manchurian's face.

"After all I have done for you. Your response was to create a disaster for me, while causing the deaths of many innocent people. And all for the Jews, as it turns out," he said, openly glaring at her with hostility.

"Yes, Manchurian—all for the Jews," Sao countered. "I was in a position to help my people. For Elijah Nabi was a demonic Pied Piper. He deceived many Israeli citizens into demanding that Israel become a protectorate of the United Nations, for its own good, when his sole purpose was to have the UN eventually destroy Israel. His mission was to annihilate the Jewish people and, of course, destroy any evidence—the Jesuit book, the chalk drawing, and Michelangelo's work—linking him to Hitler and the other infamous anti-Semitic figures." She paused before adding, "But you already know all of this, don't you, Manchurian?"

A moment of silence passed before he responded: "Were you aware of the Nabi attack against me on the island, Sao? Did you help him plan it?"

"It was not an attack against you. Nabi was determined to destroy the painting, regardless of me or anyone else who wanted it—including you. However, I do not wish to discuss this any further. For just as you have become aware of my relationships, I have become aware of a number of very disturbing developments as well regarding a particular relationship of yours, which is why I requested this meeting.

"I am aware that the very few people other than me who know your identity have all died since the drawing by Michelangelo was displayed to the world. No one, not even the Israelis, knows what you and I know: that one of the unknown men emerging from the lion's mouth in the drawing shows an uncanny resemblance to you. You knew that, and that is why *you* wanted the painting so badly. That development, along with a particular relationship of yours, seems to link Nabi's plans to destroy Israel with another plan to destroy your Jewish scientists in the oblast. Am I making myself clear, Manchurian? You know of the relationship, I am sure, and of these plans, don't you?"

Dead silence was the only response.

"I personally know that the unknown man sharing an eye with Nabi has been with you since the beginning of your rise to wealth and power. I believe this man is possessed by a demon whose ultimate aim has always been to destroy the Jewish people, now through both Nabi and you.

"I know this demonic monster for what it is—a mass-murdering manipulator, a deceiver that has been using its supernatural intelligence and power to control Nabi, you, and in fact many of us, like so many puppets on a string. And this demonic thing has become even more horrifically powerful and more capable of wreaking havoc in these dark and chaotic End Times before the return of Christ.

"I believe you know full well of whom I speak: the demon Samael, the Angel of Death and Venom of God.

"You must now tell me of his plan and your involvement, Manchurian. And you must tell me, are you one of the men emerging from the lion's mouth in the painting? I can assure you these developments do not bode well for you—but, because of our long, close relationship, I will try my best to quell the Israelis' fury at you. I have not disclosed to them that one of the faces in the painting is yours. But I can assure you that they will find the demonic man and destroy him before he destroys Israel."

"My, my, Sao Damrey—Israel's great heroine—who do you think you are talking to?" The Manchurian looked at Sao, his eyes now suddenly reflecting a deeply sinister malevolence she had never seen before.

"You are nothing but a filthy Jewish whore!" An obscenely shrill, hissing voice filled the room with an inhuman sound.

"So, I am a filthy Jewish whore, am I? You have never called me that," responded Sao, looking surprised. "Who are you really, Manchurian?"

A white cat with blue-violet eyes appeared out of nowhere to rub against the Manchurian's sofa.

"There is something very different about him," Sao thought as she was drawn to the Manchurian's eyes, which had now changed color and seemed to mirror the cat's, not only in their fiendish expression but in their remarkable blue-violet color, as well. "And I have never seen him with a cat!" she thought.

"Yes, there is something very different about the Manchurian," an unfamiliar voice now screamed from the Manchurian's mouth.

Shock gripped Sao as she stared at him. She reached for her gun as the Manchurian lunged at her like a huge predatory animal; letting out horrifying howls.

The gun fired wildly as an overwhelming force hit her. The gun dropped to the floor. A shrill voice screamed from out of the Manchurian's mouth. "You cannot kill me, you fucking Jewish whore, for I live forever and I am here for a very special occasion—to kill and devour you!"

His face had become violently contorted, as if it was being deformed from the inside. A putrid stench permeated the room. Sao screamed in terror as the Manchurian's long arms and incredibly strong hands and legs enveloped her like a python. The two fell to the floor. Sao tried desperately to breathe, heaving and squirming flat on her back, her body arched but trapped. The Manchurian's hands tore feverishly at her clothes as he slithered like a reptile on top of her. His gruesome, twisted face loomed over hers. She shrieked again as she felt his body crush her with a deadly grip. No longer able to gasp for breath, her naked body exposed, she went limp and the room darkened as she slipped into unconsciousness.

The last thing Sao saw before she passed out was the Manchurian's face horrifically transformed into the demonic one she had seen in the Michelangelo painting. It had hideous tubercular lesions and protruding, icy blue-violet eyes; upon one eyelid was the face of a lion, while upon the other was the face of a bear. The Manchurian's mouth had become hideously distended and dripped with bloody pus, which trickled around his now glistening sharp fangs. The mouth full of fangs began slowly closing around her exposed neck.

Suddenly, a screeching voice emanated from the Manchurian's mouth as he turned to look towards the entrance to the room. He screamed out, "What do you want with *me*, Man of God?"

"In the name of Jesus Christ and by the power of the Holy Spirit, I command you, Samael: Release the woman and be gone from my sight!" His thunderous command loudly echoed throughout the palace as Richard walked defiantly towards the Manchurian. The charred *Christ on the Cross* painting hung from Richard's neck, and he held it steadfastly in front of him.

The demonic face had immediately disappeared and now the Manchurian's ghastly deformed face glared at Richard. For a moment, Sao's twisted, prostrate body remained wrapped in the Manchurian's vice-like grip. But upon hearing Richard's command, he slithered off Sao and headed towards Richard, leaving Sao bleeding and unconscious on the marble floor.

The Manchurian glided towards Richard like a huge snake. Fetid foam, flecked with blood, oozed from around his gleaming, repulsive eyes. His mouth was open and distended.

"I beg you, don't torture me with that image of Jesus Christ," the inhuman voice screeched out from the Manchurian, followed by a violent, scalding blast of heat and the toxic smell of putrefaction. The blast filled the room and swirled around Richard, burning him, gagging him, and nearly knocking him to the ground. The Manchurian slinked rapidly forward.

Richard yelled in pain but stood fast, shouting, "In the name of Jesus Christ and by the power of the Holy Spirit, I command you, Samael: be gone from my sight!"

A resolute Richard moved slowly and steadily forward, holding the charred canvas steadfastly in front of him. The Manchurian's macabre blue-violet eyes were fixed solely on Christ as he slithered over to Richard. Suddenly, to Richard's horror, the Manchurian rose up. He lunged powerfully and robotically forward and knocked the image of Jesus Christ from Richard's hands; it swung around his neck. The intense sickening smell became overpowering as the Manchurian's crushing arms and hands enveloped Richard in a death grip, pulling him downwards. Richard fought with all his strength to resist the pull, while again taking hold of Christ's image and thrusting it directly before the Manchurian's appalling eyes.

Richard, unable to breathe and feeling himself buckling under, roared at the top of his lungs one last time, "In the name of Jesus Christ and by the power of the Holy Spirit, I command you, Samael: be gone from my sight!"

At once, awful inhuman howls and hissing, followed by pus mixed with blood and scalding heat, spewed from the Manchurian's mouth. A rancid smell swirled around the room and choked Richard, who shielded himself with the image of Christ. And then, abruptly, the Manchurian's body fell like a rag doll at Richard's feet. Sensing what was about to happen, Richard quickly ran over to Sao's still unconscious body and threw himself on top of her.

He held the canvas with the image of Christ over both of them as intense heat filled the room, incinerating everything. It whirled around and over them but did not touch them or the canvas. Other rooms throughout the palace began shaking. All the windows were blasted out. The floors buckled and began collapsing. The palace ceilings cracked open, exposing the night sky above. A gigantic, twisting flame of searing heat now rose from the Manchurian's blistering, disintegrating remains. The flame escaped through the hole in the ceiling and, taking all the heat with it, soared above the Palace of the Red Tiles. Richard, still covering Sao's unconscious body and himself with the image of Christ, remained in a prone position, untouched by the heat and scorching debris falling all around them.

He whispered, "I thank you, my Lord God through Jesus Christ, for casting out the demon Samael and delivering us from his evil."

Israeli commandos, who remained in the courtyard around two jet helicopters, awaiting Richard's signal, watched the dreadful unfolding horror of the shaking palace and its windows blowing out as it collapsed. The impact threw them to the ground as suddenly an enormous miles-high column of twisting flame, studded with millions of glaring evil blue-violet eyes, ascended into the sky above the palace and as quickly disappeared into the night sky with a thunderous roar.

The commandos erupted in a chorus of shouts and expletives as they entered what was left of the ruined palace.

Chapter 59

1546
PALACE OF THE COLONNA CESARINI
ROME

The true work of art is but a shadow of the divine perfection.
—Michelangelo Buonarroti

Michelangelo Buonarroti and Vittoria Colonna walked hand in hand down the marble steps from the sweeping terrace of her Palace of the Colonna Cesarini to the park-like setting of its extensive formal gardens. The private grounds had been expertly designed for Vittoria by the noted botanist Prince Federico Cesi. Geometric flowering beds and soaring shade trees surrounded the couple. Sitting together on a finely carved marble bench, Michelangelo and Vittoria gazed at the ornately sculpted fountains, which drew their water from an underground spring. Vittoria always delighted in showing Michelangelo the new specimens of flowers and plants that the prince had recommended for her enjoyment.

Michelangelo held Vittoria's hand. His dark eyes looked mysteriously into her lovely, serene face as he leaned over and softly kissed her.

"My dearest Vittoria, it is so wonderful to be alone together on this beautiful day here in your magnificent gardens. We are away, for at least a moment in time, from the coarse, maddening world in which we live—a world that continually pulls at us and sadly pulls us too far apart," he sighed.

"Oh yes, my dearest, the demands on you by the powerful are constant," she whispered, "yet you know I love you so and I love the way you kiss me."

"I am so happy, my beloved," the great master responded, "for it is in these special gardens of yours, surrounded by all that is wonderful in God's flowering creation, that my love for you wells up and overflows like water from these majestic fountains." They embraced each other and gently kissed.

Later, walking back towards the terrace, Michelangelo declared, "As a sign of my enduring love, my darling, I am about to begin a painting for you. It will depict Christ on the cross, as I know how our savior is so dear to you. I will first do a chalk drawing of it for your approval."

"Oh, my Michelangelo, what a wonderful expression of your affection you give to me." Vittoria lightly dabbed a tear away from her eye with her handkerchief as they ascended the stairs. "I so love you for doing this for me. I know your painting will be a sign of strength and devotion forever. What shall be its name?"

"It is my intention to call it simply *Christ on the Cross*. For we are but temporary, while from the cross, Jesus Christ's protection and devotion to all of us is eternal."

Chapter 60

DECAPOLIS REGION
SEA OF GALILEE

*The fear of God is the beginning of wisdom and the
knowledge of the holy is understanding.*
—PROVERBS 9:10

CENTURIES LATER, and worlds apart, the charred canvas fragment
of *Christ on the Cross*, the last painting of Michelangelo, on which
only the image of Jesus Christ remained, hung majestically across the
back of a small, jewel-like chapel. The chapel, overlooking the Sea
of Galilee, belonged to an Italian order of Franciscan nuns. Here, in
what had been known in ancient times as the Decapolis region, Jesus
Christ performed the miracle of removing demons from a tormented
man, walked on water, and spoke the Beatitudes that are still recited
daily in places of worship throughout the world.

Yet on this day, a full contingent of military guards and a fleet of
Israeli army vehicles—with missiles, rail guns, and invisibility shields
engaged—were stationed at a discreet distance around the chapel.

A formation of Israeli fighter planes circled in the blue skies overhead as a GPS surveillance satellite monitored the entire area.

"I now pronounce you man and wife," the presiding prelate, Jaime Fonoll, the Archbishop of San Juan, Puerto Rico and a close friend of Richard, announced. Israeli officials, led by the prime minister, along with the couple's family and friends, clapped and cheered with unbridled enthusiasm.

Sao was beautiful in her mother's delicate handmade lace wedding dress. On her bodice, she wore a small service ribbon identifying her as a State Warrior of Israel. Richard, in elegant formal attire, displayed the service ribbon of a State Warrior of Israel on his lapel. Joy and happiness in their eyes, Richard and Sao exchanged their first kiss as husband and wife. Judith cheerfully hugged both of them.

Tears and exclamations of delight filled the historic chapel as Richard and Sao Arenell, smiling warmly, their daughter between them, walked down the aisle and out of the church into the sunshine of their new life together. There, surrounded by heartfelt cheers and spirited clapping from well-wishers, Archbishop Fonoll handed them a very valuable ancient scroll as a wedding present. He said that it was from the French side of his family and had been a former possession of Napoleon Bonaparte. Fonoll then offered his blessing on their union: "May the peace, love, and protection of Almighty God and our Lord and Savior Jesus Christ be with you forever, Richard, Sao, and Judith." And moving his hand in the motion of the cross, he said, "*In nomine Patris, et Filii, et Spiritus Sancti.* Amen."

Turning to each other, Sao and Richard smiled, kissed, and opened the scroll, which read,

> *I am Alpha and Omega, the Beginning and the End, the First and the Last. Blessed are they that do His commandments that they may have the right to the Tree of Life and may enter in through the gates of the City. For without are dogs and sorcerers, whoremongers and murderers, idolaters and*

whosoever loveth and maketh a lie. For I, Jesus, have sent mine angel to testify unto you these things in the churches. I am the root and offspring of David and the bright and morning star.
—THE REVELATION OF ST. JOHN THE DIVINE 22:13–16

Judith, reading by her mother's side, shivered momentarily. She looked around to see if anyone else had felt the sudden chill breeze that had left goose bumps on her skin. On the hill overlooking the chapel was a poisonous *tzefa* snake. Its ice blue-violet reptilian eyes locked on to hers, and the snake opened its mouth to reveal sharp fangs and a forked tongue before it silently slipped into the shadows.

Author's Note

THE BOOK THAT YOU HAVE just read is fiction interwoven with historical and current facts. The historical facts in the book include the following:

- Michelangelo presented a chalk drawing as a study for a proposed painting of *Christ on the Cross* to noblewoman Vittoria Colonna, which, subject to her approval, he would paint for her.

- The chalk drawing presented to Colonna is currently in the British Museum.

- The painting of *Christ on the Cross* is lost according to documents in the British Museum.

Also among the current facts are the following:

- The author has in his possession a digital image of the chalk study downloaded from a leading virtual database of European painting and sculpture.

- This copy reveals significantly greater detail in the chalk drawing than is visible in the drawing held at the British Museum.

- This greater detail was revealed when the author enlarged the drawing on his computer.

- The detail in the enlarged image of the chalk drawing formed the basis of *all* the human, animal, and demonic faces portrayed in the book.

- The faces in the enlarged image line up perfectly with indiscernible shadow images in the chalk drawing in the British Museum.

Consequently, the author questions whether three key elements of the book presented as fiction could, in fact, be true:

- Could the faces of the humans, animals, and demons that are clearly visible in the author's enlarged image of the chalk drawing have existed at one time in the drawing in the British Museum, given that the images in the reproduction line up with dim images in that drawing?

- Could the faces currently exist in the lost painting of *Christ on the Cross*?

- Could Vittoria Colonna have erased those images and faces from the chalk drawing?

There are also other details in the book that are factual:

- There is a Jesuit book, *The Secret Instructions of the Society of Jesus*.

- Bernard Stämpfle did help Adolf Hitler write *Mein Kampf,* and he mysteriously died.

- Wlodimir Ledochowski was the Superior General of the Jesuits during the time described.

- John LaFarge did write the encyclical *Humani Generis Unitas*, which was only recently released.

Though the story line surrounding these historical facts in the book is fictional, the author believes that Adolf Hitler was actually possessed by the demon Samael, the Angel of Death and the Venom of God now loose and increasing in power as the world is drawn into the End Times. And the author asserts that this horrific demon, pictured in his digital enlargement of the chalk study, has possessed or inspired all of the world leaders who have been described as such in the book.

The author believes that as events unfold preceding the End Times described by Christ in Matthew 24, the secular, modern world is giving too little credence to the increasing involvement of the supernatural in world events, consistent with the ultimate supreme supernatural event of all: the Second Coming of Jesus Christ. In the author's opinion, the demon Samael's goal has been, and will remain, the elimination of both the Jewish and Ishmael lines of Abraham, which continues to be played out in the Middle East, the location of Christ's Second Coming. Samael's attempts to reach this goal will *never* be stopped by humans.

Only with the return of Jesus Christ will Samael be stopped. And with His return, Samael and Samael's demonic horde of followers will be consigned to the Abyss forever by Jesus Christ, and only Jesus Christ, as He clearly stated in the New Testament.

Further to this Author's Note, there is a true story surrounding the writing of this book—a story that could reinforce the answer as "yes" to the questions outlined above.

The Story Surrounding the Writing of *Michelangelo's Last Painting*

I HAVE ALWAYS ENJOYED fine art and history books with spiritual underpinnings. As a result, I always wanted to write a work of historical fiction with these features.

I wanted to write about a visionary painting of evil, with Christ on the cross in the forefront by a famous artist. The story's "hook" would be that the painting was lost.

In thinking about how to write the book, I concluded right at the beginning that I needed a visionary artist to paint this fictional painting, and I knew that one of the most visionary painters of religious subjects of all time was Michelangelo, creator of the image of the final triumph of good over evil in the *Last Judgment* in the Sistine Chapel.

So to get a basis for the fictional painting I would create, I researched Michelangelo on the Internet.

In my research, I came across his beautiful chalk drawing of *Christ on the Cross*. Needless to say, I was very pleased with my discovery.

Further research showed that the chalk drawing of *Christ on the Cross* was done by Michelangelo for Vittoria Colonna, a Renaissance noblewoman, as a study for a painting by the same name, to be done by him, subject to her approval.

To my truly great surprise, I learned that the painting done by Michelangelo from the chalk drawing was lost, as noted by the British Museum, which holds the chalk drawing in its collection. Not only did the seemingly blank background behind *Christ on the Cross* form an ideal setting for my fictional portrayal of evil, but the fact that it was lost also provided the ideal "hook." For my purposes, the painting would be lost by being painted over by a different artist.

I was now ready to add a vision of evil to this drawing by Michelangelo. I began the process by saving a copy of the *Christ on the Cross* drawing onto my computer from the Internet.

Once it was on my computer, I enlarged the drawing, simply in order to see it more clearly. However, to my considerable surprise, instead of seeing the blank background that I had expected, I saw grotesque faces of animals, humans, and demons.

What immediately caught my eye was the number of human and animal faces that I actually *recognized*—in particular, incredible likenesses of Hitler, Osama Bin Laden, Mahmoud Ahmadinejad, and the animals of Revelation from scripture. The representation of these faces was nothing short of astonishing. Also unsettling were other faces that I didn't recognize, in particular those coming out of the lion's mouth and the vampiric face (which became Elijah Nabi in the book).

The vision of evil that I had in mind to include in my book was Nazism, thus seeing Hitler was an incredible coincidence. I was amazed to find out, through additional research, that the demon whose hideous face appears in the enlarged drawing on my computer, I believe is Samael. This was the specific demon that I had *already* chosen months earlier—from a book on demons that described Samael's annual calls for the liquidation of the Jews—to be part of the evil Nazi vision in my book. I had already intended to link Samael to the real-life evildoings of a number of the world leaders whose faces I now saw in the enlarged drawing on my computer screen.

I realized that I literally had my visionary painting of evil on the computer before me! All the faces of the animals, humans, and demons in the single enlarged image of the drawing of *Christ on the Cross* on my computer became the faces I depicted in Michelangelo's works in this book.

Fascinated by what I had seen in the enlarged drawing, I went back a second time to the same website to save another copy of the image of the drawing. However, when enlarging the second image on my computer, none of the faces were clear; they were blurred.

I have never again been able to obtain a clear image of the faces—either from the website I originally downloaded it from, or any other website hosting the image—as I did the first time.

What happened next further added to the mystery. I went personally with my companion to the British Museum in London, on two separate occasions, to look at the actual *Christ on the Cross* drawing done by Michelangelo for Vittoria Colonna.

In the drawing in the museum, both of us could definitely see very faint images of the faces of the same animals, humans, and demons seen in the image on my computer. They lined up perfectly with the images on my computer.

So, I wondered, what was the significance of all these twists and turns? Was the story in my book still fiction—or could the part that related to the painting potentially be possible? My investigation continued from two perspectives, the first utilizing computer technology, and the second drawing upon historical writings and research in the British Museum.

I turned to computer technology to answer the question: could images that were in the chalk study for *Christ on the Cross* and were erased by Vittoria Colonna appear again centuries later in the image of the drawing in my computer?

The answer would seem to be yes. Just as computer sleuths can go to deleted computer files and recreate what was deleted from an electronic shadow image that never goes away, so it seems that images of erasures made centuries ago in a drawing can be recreated by computers. That is because some form of image always remains of what had been erased; this is certainly evident from viewing the drawing in the British Museum. Furthermore, forensic digital technology has recently revealed drawings under paintings by Raphael and Michelangelo.

As I enlarged the erased images on my screen, there were infinite configurations of individual pixels that I could have zoomed in on. With the right specific configuration of pixels, those erased images could come back to life in their entirety, as they would seem to have done on my computer. The fact that the phenomenon was not replicable suggests that the pixels had to line up in a very specific way. The chances of that happening a second time appear to be quite low.

In regard to the aforementioned, please see Notes to the Story Surrounding the Writing of *Michelangelo's Last Painting* immediately following this section.

Looking for the answer to this mystery from the perspective of historical writing and research, I shifted my focus to extracts from a technical report by the British Museum, which centers on a revealing letter written by Vittoria Colonna to Michelangelo about the *Christ on the Cross* chalk drawing. The letter is in the British Museum.

When viewed in person at the British Museum, the background around the Christ figure on the cross looks to have been rubbed out, though there are still very faint images of background figures or faces present, which line up exactly with the images in the enlarged drawing saved to my computer.

The technical report seems to confirm that:

> Close inspection of the drawing reveals the labor expended on it: there are numerous *pentimenti* in the contours of Christ's body, especially visible in the area of the [right] hip. The rejected contours were rubbed out so as to not interfere with the definitive composition.

A *pentimento*, from the Latin *paenitēre*, is defined as "an underlying image in a painting, as an earlier painting, part of a painting, or original draft, that shows through, usually when the top layer of paint has become transparent with age."

In her letter to Michelangelo, Vittoria describes "looking at the drawing through a magnifying glass." What did Vittoria see through the magnifying glass besides Christ on the cross? Did she see these *pentimenti*, which she might have rejected and erased, thus creating the "rejected contours" referenced in the technical report? Or were the "rejected contours" just that, figures drawn by Michelangelo or a studio assistant, which, upon reflection, he or Michelangelo no longer wanted?

In the same letter, Vittoria questions Michelangelo: "If it is by another hand, never mind. If it is from yours I would certainly want to keep it." ("*Se questo è di altri, patientia; se è vostro, io in ogni modo nel vorrei.*")

What was Vittoria referring to, and what would elicit a comment like that? Was she referring to the images of the faces or the contours before they were rubbed out?

Vittoria's question was addressed in the following comments by a researcher in the British Museum's technical report: "Dussler [an art historian] draws attention to the fact that even in Colonna's letter cited above the question of authorship of the drawing was an issue." This comment seems to call into question the authenticity of the British Museum's *Christ on the Cross*, or possibly aspects of it, as suggested by Vittoria's letter.

In the same technical report, the following statement is made: "On the basis of this evidence, de Tolnay (1960 and 1978) discerns two hands in the execution of the drawing, Michelangelo's for the figure of Christ, a studio assistant's in the angels and background."

The same technical report cites two other experts: "For Gere and Turner (1979), de Tolnay's distinction is 'over subtle,' and they uphold the ascription of the whole composition to Michelangelo."

Another expert in the report agrees with Gere and Turner but says that the "true original chalk study of *Christ on the Cross* by Michelangelo, like the painting of *Christ on the Cross*, is lost."

However, the British Museum states that the chalk drawing is the original.

What are we to make of all this? What is fact and what is fiction?

I personally believe that there is enough evidence to conjecture that there could be startling visions of evil in the chalk drawing done by Michelangelo and that Vittoria, upon seeing these grotesque faces, questioned Michelangelo as to whether they were done by his hand, and erased them or rejected them, as described in this book.

I believe that the visions of evil in the enlarged image on my computer are those erased by either Vittoria or Michelangelo himself, but brought back for all to see through modern computer technology.

Furthermore, I expect that these images will soon become part of a formal exposition of the images of *Michelangelo's Last Painting*, for all to see.

Notes to the Story Surrounding the Writing of *Michelangelo's Last Painting*

I DISCUSSED MY DISCOVERY of the faces referenced in the preceding *Story Surrounding the Writing of Michelangelo's Last Painting* with Mr. Leslie Wilson, a friend and longtime business associate. He is a patent and intellectual rights attorney in Chicago. His experience includes computer science work and nuclear engineering. Wilson recounts the discussion as follows:

Andy had called about some discovery he had made. He was obviously highly curious, yet cautious in wanting to make sure that the information was protected. He stopped by the office and we brought up a copy of a computer file that he had saved. I recognized the drawing as being by one of the Old Masters, although at the time I didn't know any specifics. Andy explained that it was Christ on the Cross by Michelangelo and its provenance. He then directed my attention away from the central figure of Christ on the cross and towards the surrounding spaces. There, in a swirling fog, were a number of faces, human, animal and demonic. Some were clearly visible while others required more imagination. Andy pointed out a number of details based on his more extensive viewing of the image.

Andy asked if I had any thoughts about how such images could appear. I ventured the hypothesis that it could be a combination of material originally in the drawing and processing of the drawing through digitization, subtracting and adding information to the image. The existing drawing would include remnants of any original material that was faintly sketched in or was erased out of the final drawing. An analog photograph of the drawing was taken, then digitized. The digital file was transferred over the Internet, displayed on Andy's computer monitor, and stored in his computer file. The *unique* combination of photography, digitization, and display made the remnants visible again, so that all that remained was for a person with good pattern recognition skill set to see the images. That is where Andy's skill set came in along with my ability to see the figures.

About the Author

ANDREW BOEMI has collected fine art and studied art history, world history, and scripture for much of his adult life. He was introduced to masterpiece paintings by art history courses at Georgetown University from which he graduated.

Boemi has combined this background in the aforementioned disciplines with his business experience, which includes co-founding one of the first institutional-backed international farmland funds, initiating one of the most successful larger leveraged buyouts in US corporate history, and serving on public companies' boards of directors.

For his first book, Boemi has explored a new theory of the cause of one of the darkest periods in human history. A period which continues into today—and into the future.

Boemi lives in Chicago, Illinois.

Acknowledgments

NICCOLO MACHIAVELLI, was an Italian historian and philosopher in Florence during the Renaissance. He wrote his masterpiece, *The Prince* which, among the many wise thoughts, had one that certainly applies here.

> *"Surround yourself with people who are smarter than you, who will work with you and for you and who will make you look good."*

In this case those people are the following lovely ladies, Amy Collins of New Shelves; Bethany Brown of the Cadence Group; Vanessa Mickan; and Ronda Rawlins and Michele DeFilippo from 1106 Design. They have worked so efficiently and creatively with Dodd Merrill Press to make this book possible.

And to Roberta Rubin and her wonderful Book Stall book store in Winnetka, IL through which many a world famous authors have passed through. Roberta is a truly remarkable literary woman to the many people throughout the nation who know her. This first time author has been especially blessed in knowing her and receiving her support and guidance over the years.

CPSIA information can be obtained at www.ICGtesting.com
Printed in the USA
LVOW131803090113

315048LV00008B/714/P

9 780988 322912